Always Grace

TIM LaHAYE
AND GREGORY S. DINALLO

KENSINGTON BOOKS
http://www.kensingtonbooks.com

KENSINGTON BOOKS are published by

Kensington Publishing Corp.
850 Third Avenue
New York, NY 10022

All Kensington titles, imprints, and distributed lines are available at special quantity discounts for bulk purchases for sales promotion, premiums, fund-raising, educational, or institutional use.

Special book excerpts or customized printings can also be created to fit specific needs. For details write or phone the office of the Kensington Special Sales Manager: Attn. Special Sales Department. Kensington Publishing Corp., 850 Third Avenue, New York, NY 10022. Phone: 1-800-221-2647.

Kensington and the K logo Reg. U.S. Pat. & TM Off.

ISBN-13: 978-0-7582-3888-7
ISBN-10: 0-7582-3888-6

First Kensington Books Trade Paperback Printing: March 2008
First Kensington Books Mass-Market Printing: April 2009
10 9 8 7 6 5 4 3 2 1

Printed in the United States of America

THE KEYS TO MY HEART

Grace sighed, her eyes brimming with tears, "I can't believe that I won't . . . won't be seeing . . ." She couldn't finish it and buried her head in the curve of his neck, then looked up into his eyes and kissed him. "I'll wait a lifetime for you."

"And I for you, Grace," Cooper said, his eyes glistening with emotion.

"I love you so much," Grace said, tears rolling down her cheeks. "Please take good care of yourself and—" She was interrupted by the clanging bell of an approaching streetcar. "Go now. Please, you must."

Cooper hesitated, then swiftly pulled the valise and trunk from the back of the pickup while Grace flagged the trolley. After loading them aboard, he stood in the doorway, blowing her kisses as it pulled away. His antics brought a smile to Grace's face, but she was paralyzed with sadness as the trolley followed the curve of the tracks onto Beacon Street. She remained there long after it was out of sight, wondering if she'd ever see him again.

BOOK YOUR PLACE ON OUR WEBSITE AND MAKE THE READING CONNECTION!

We've created a customized website just for our very special readers, where you can get the inside scoop on everything that's going on with Zebra, Pinnacle and Kensington books.

When you come online, you'll have the exciting opportunity to:

- View covers of upcoming books
- Read sample chapters
- Learn about our future publishing schedule (listed by publication month *and author*)
- Find out when your favorite authors will be visiting a city near you
- Search for and order backlist books from our online catalog
- Check out author bios and background information
- Send e-mail to your favorite authors
- Meet the Kensington staff online
- Join us in weekly chats with authors, readers and other guests
- Get writing guidelines
- AND MUCH MORE!

Visit our website at
http://www.kensingtonbooks.com

Come Spring

Preface

∽

Boston, Massachusetts
February 1918

Europe had been at war for more than three years. British and French forces had fought the Germans to a standstill. More than three million men had already lost their lives. On April 6, 1917, two days before Easter, the United States declared war on Germany; but it would be almost a year before the American doughboys, one million strong, joined the fight.

At the time America was preparing to send her sons to war, the city of Boston had been an intellectually and culturally enriched city of fine universities, art galleries, and salons for almost three hundred years. The cradle of American Independence was also a churning metropolis of tough ethnic neighborhoods and warring political factions. Tickets to the Boston Symphony were as sought after as seats at Fenway Park. Babe Ruth was pitching for the Red Sox. They had won two of the last three World Series. Prohibition would not become law for at least a year. Women would not win the right to vote for more than two years.

Chapter One

⌒

A bone-chilling wind swept across the platforms of Boston's North Station as a locomotive thundered into view pulling a long line of coaches. Most of the passengers on the crowded train were standing at the windows straining to glimpse the city that would become their new home. Despite the cold, many of them wore clothing suited to more temperate climates. One of them, a young woman, framed by a window that had been opened, wore a tattered scarf that fluttered about her face, and cradled a swaddled infant in her arms as if protecting it from the crush of people behind her.

Within the tableau of faces were moving portraits of childlike innocence and worldly experience, of trembling fear and boundless hope, of weary acceptance and simmering rebellion. But it was the face of the young woman with the infant that had caught Cooper's eye as the train ground to a stop. Her chin raised in triumph, her eyes aglow with the knowledge that her yearning to be free was about to be realized, her heart thumping in anticipation of a long sought-after new beginning.

Cooper knew what would happen next, and waited patiently with his camera as she made her way to the door with her suitcase and child. As he anticipated, she stepped onto the platform and into the billowing cloud of steam that was coming from the train's wheel housings. Shafts of sunlight, streaming through the vapor that swirled around her, gave the scene a providential glow, intensifying its emotional impact. And in a mere sixtieth of a second, with a decisive click of his shutter, Dylan Cooper had captured this moment for all eternity.

That was weeks ago. And Cooper had taken countless photographs at the train station in the interim; photographs of the poor, the tired and the hungry who—as had Cooper years earlier—survived a harrowing sea voyage, endured the indignities of immigration processing, and made their way to America's towns and cities. Yet the image of the intrepid young woman on the train—the Madonna and child as Cooper thought of them—had stayed with him; and it was the first negative he developed and printed when he returned to his room on Dorchester Street in South Boston.

The stout Irish woman who ran the rooming house had shown Cooper a large room in the front when he inquired about vacancies. "Two dollars a week. You keep your own house. And you keep to yourself if I make myself clear?"

Cooper nodded as he looked the place over, drawing thoughtfully on his pipe, which was as much a part of him as his camera. "You wouldn't happen to have one with an electric service, now, would you?"

"Indeed, I would. But it's fifty cents more and it's in the back. Electric service," she sniffed, as she padded down the hall, leading Cooper to a room half the size of the first. "I can't imagine what the likes of you would be doin' with that."

The room was disappointingly small but Cooper was pleased to discover that along with its single electric outlet it also had a large closet. And since moving in, he had spent most of his time in the latter, printing photographs with the bare bulb and pull-chain he had rigged on the ceiling, and hunching over the trays of chemicals he used to develop them. He worked round the clock, leaving the closet only when he could no longer stay awake, or—because the strips of leather he had tacked around the door to keep traces of light out, also kept the smell of bromides in—until he could no longer tolerate the choking fumes. And it was here, in this makeshift darkroom, where Dylan Cooper was making the new beginning that had brought him to America.

A confident fellow with a bit of a swagger, Cooper had a mane of unruly salt-and-pepper curls that defied any attempt to control them—much like their owner. He had no doubt he would one day achieve the artistic acclaim that would afford him proper living quarters and more importantly a professionally equipped darkroom with running water and a sink to wash his prints, not to mention a gas-fired heater with a rotating drum to dry them.

For the time being, having spent his last penny on his prized Graflex view camera, he washed them in the tub in the bathroom down the hall—which did little to endear him to those with whom he shared it—and dried them the way local housewives dried their wash: instead of socks, shirts, and underwear, dozens of luminous eight-by-ten-inch prints hung from the clotheslines crisscrossing his room.

Cooper was convinced these were the best pictures he had ever taken. He had no doubt they would be hailed as works of art. He had become obsessed with getting each print just right with a full range of gray tones set off by velvety rich blacks and pure sparkling whites. When the last print had been made, dried, and adjudged perfect, Cooper carefully placed it in a box with others of equal quality; then he took his mackinaw that hung from a nail on the back of the door and left the rooming house, carrying the box under his arm.

A light snow was falling as he hurried to the trolley stop, trailing a stream of pipe smoke behind him. The streetcars that ran along Massachusetts Avenue linked the working-

class neighborhoods of Dorchester and Roxbury to the Back
Bay area that paralleled the Charles River. Here, the captains
of industry lived in limestone mansions close to their offices
in the North End where the investment banks and account-
ing firms that supported their business ventures were located
as were the clothiers, antique dealers, and art galleries that
catered to their appetite for opulence.

The Van Dusen Gallery, the one that Cooper hoped would
exhibit his work, occupied a grand space on the corner of
Beacon and Exeter Streets. He walked the few blocks from
the trolley stop, his heart pounding from anticipation rather
than exertion as he approached the entrance.

Two display easels stood in the window. One held a sign,
which in an elegant flowing script proclaimed: *New Impressionist Works*. The other held a large, ornately framed painting entitled: *Poplars on the Banks of the Epte*. It was signed
Claude Monet, 1891. A small red tag affixed to the frame indicated it had been sold.

Cooper was about to open the door and step into the
vestibule when he noticed a brass plaque next to it that
warned: By Appointment Only. The possibility had never
occurred to him, and Cooper stood there for a long moment
not knowing exactly what to do.

The ornate wrought iron door had a window through
which Cooper could see the interior beyond. Raw silk drapery framed the windows. Persian rugs formed an archipelago of subdued color on the parquet floors. Plush sofas
allowed clients to commune with a given work prior to acquiring it. A fireplace radiated inviting warmth. Purposely
understated to avoid competing with the works of art on display, the sophisticated decor made the brass plaque outside
all the more intimidating.

Cooper stepped back and took a deep breath. He had
come all the way across town—not to mention across the Atlantic—and was loath to waste the trolley fare. He had come
too far to give up so easily, to turn tail and run merely for

lack of an appointment. If that was the extent of his gumption, he'd still be in Dumbarton working in the textile mills as his father had before him. He had no doubt the new beginning he sought was on the other side of that door and, after taking a moment to gather his courage, he strode through it purposefully.

Chapter Two

Peter Van Dusen, the gallery's owner, was a highly respected purveyor of fine European painting and sculpture. A natty fellow with a well-groomed beard, he was at his desk in the rear of the gallery tending to paperwork when the bell affixed to the front door rang. It wasn't the gentle tinkling that usually announced a client's arrival but a harsh clanging that intensified when the door closed with a jarring slam. Van Dusen flinched at the sound and glared over the top of his spectacles at the man who had charged through the vestibule and was coming straight toward him.

Though the gallery had several rooms, Cooper took no notice whatsoever of the Impressionist masterpieces displayed on their walls, or of the attractive young woman who stood in front of a painting in the splay-footed stance of the dancers it depicted, affixing a red tag to the frame to signify it had been sold.

"Well, it's obvious you're not here to browse," Van Dusen sneered, sweeping his eyes over the wild-haired fellow who stood before him in a threadbare mackinaw dotted with melting snow.

"No, it's not in my nature, sir," Cooper replied, deflecting

Van Dusen's salvo. "I've brought you my work. My best work; and if you would—"

"Evidently you failed to notice, or more likely failed to *heed*, my sign," Van Dusen interrupted. "It clearly states: By appointment only. Even my clients do me the courtesy. Don't they, Grace?"

"They certainly do, Mr. Van Dusen," the young woman replied dutifully, stealing a glance at the brash fellow who had dared to arrive unannounced. Tall and willowy with hair the color of amber that was gathered at her neck and swayed behind her, Grace MacVicar looked as if she might have stepped out of a Dégas and carried herself in a way that did justice to her name.

Van Dusen slipped a timepiece from his vest and glanced at it. "Speaking of clients, we're expecting one shortly. Show the . . . the *gentleman* out, Grace."

"A client?" Cooper said, paying no attention to the young woman who was trying to guide him toward the entrance. "It wouldn't just happen to be one who's interested in collecting photographs, now, would it?"

"Photographs?" Van Dusen echoed with a derisive cackle. He had assumed Cooper's box contained water colors or pastels, or perhaps a few small scale oils that had become popular. "Photographs? No, sir, I daresay it wouldn't."

"Well, I've a feelin' they might soon as they see mine." Cooper placed the box of prints on the desk and went about opening it.

"I'm not at all amused by your arrogance, sir," Van Dusen said, getting to his feet with an angry huff. He intended to take this crass interloper by the arm and show him the door himself, but the print Cooper had slipped onto the desk caught Van Dusen's eye. He paused mid-stride as if he'd heard a gunshot; then all in one motion, he picked it up and placed it on an easel off to one side of his desk, stepping back to study it. It was the picture of the young mother getting off the train. He did this with another print and another, sighing with emotion at the poetic images: a child's innocent face, eyes filled with hope; a teetering pile of worn suitcases, their contents threatening to burst from within; a farmer's scythe bundled in a flower-patterned bedcover; an elderly man clutching a fishing pole and a crucifix. Van Dusen did this with the growing fervor of a man who, long deprived of his favorite delicacy, had come upon an entire box and couldn't consume them fast enough. "They are extraordinary," he said in an amazed whisper. "Truly extraordinary, Mister . . . ?"

"The name's Cooper," Cooper replied, feeling vindicated as his smile broadened. "*Dylan* Cooper, though Dylan be more than enough."

"Well, Cooper, your work has rare emotional resonance and an astonishing insight into the penumbra of the soul," Van Dusen went on. "The balance of radiant and softened sunlight, the fully envisioned scheme of tonality. They give it a . . . a spirituality that I've never seen in photographs."

"Thank you," Cooper said, genuinely humbled by Van Dusen's praise. "Does that mean you like them well enough to exhibit them?"

Van Dusen turned from the photograph on the easel and settled in his chair, shifting his weight several times as if making a decision. "Yes it does. Believe me, I'm tempted, more than tempted."

"Tempted," Cooper grunted, sensing Van Dusen was burdened. "With all due respect, when I was growing up being tempted meant you were thinking about doin' something you knew you shouldn't be doin'."

Van Dusen broke into a reflective smile. "That is precisely my dilemma."

"If I may?" Grace said in a deferential tone. "I think Mr. Cooper's pictures are all you say and more." Equally captivated, she had moved closer and closer as Van Dusen had placed them on the easel. "In my experience, some temptations are more than worth the risk they require."

"Well, young lady, *my* experience has taught me that this

one definitely *isn't*," Van Dusen said, his voice taking on a slight edge. "And neither your personal preference nor mine has anything to do with it." He turned back to Cooper and leaned across the desk as if about to share a confidence. "You see, I'm required to be more disciplined than my outspoken assistant. As much as I like your work, Cooper, I must remind myself that *I* am the seller, not the buyer; and knowing my clients as I do, I don't think they're ready to accept photographs as investment grade art and collect them the way they do paintings and sculpture."

"Maybe they are and maybe they aren't," Cooper protested. "There's really only one way to find out, isn't there?"

Grace nodded in emphatic agreement. "Your outspoken assistant thinks Mr. Cooper makes a valid point, sir. Why not exhibit his work and let your clients decide for themselves?"

The emotion in her voice enriched the lyrical burr of the Highlands Cooper thought he'd detected when she had first spoken, making him smile. "Aye, why not?"

"Because it would be like a shopkeeper stocking his shelves with goods he knows no one is going to buy. I'd be out of business in a month, and"—Van Dusen paused and sent a withering look in Grace's direction—"so would you, I might add." He stepped to the easel, looked longingly at the photograph, then removed it and handed it back to Cooper with the others. "I'm sorry. I hope you understand," he said with a finality that caused Cooper's posture to slacken. "Good luck. You're an extraordinarily talented fellow, Dylan. It was a pleasure seeing your work."

The gallery door creaked open activating the bell, which gave off its gentle tinkle. Van Dusen got to his feet, straightening his waistcoat and hurried toward the vestibule. He greeted his fashionably dressed client effusively and directed her to a room where a number of Cezannes were displayed.

Cooper wasted no time collecting his prints. As soon as he had returned them to the box, he replaced the lid and headed straight for the door, acknowledging Grace with a terse nod as he strode past her.

"Mr. Cooper?" she called out, hurrying after him. Cooper's long strides had taken him to the door by the time she caught up. "Mr. Cooper, I want you to know seeing your work was a pleasure for me, too."

"I daresay you made that quite clear to Mr. Van Dusen," Cooper said, managing an appreciative smile.

Grace responded with one of her own that could have melted the snow falling outside the window. "It's easy to tell the truth. Besides, we Highlanders have to stick together."

"Aye, I knew I heard it in your voice."

"And I in yours. Dumbarton?"

Cooper nodded.

"As am I. I'm really sorry this didn't work out."

"Not half as sorry as I, believe me," Cooper replied, unable to conceal his bitterness. It was a crushing disappointment and even the sympathies of a lovely young woman couldn't ease the pain of it. "Well, thanks for sticking up for my pictures."

Cooper left the gallery, trudging south in the general direction of Dorchester. The snow had begun to accumulate, and he'd have preferred to take the streetcar, but decided to walk and save the fare. It was a long journey on foot but he had another money-saving reason for making it, not to mention the time it would give him to think about Miss Grace MacVicar from Dumbarton in the Scottish Highlands.

Chapter Three

The weather had turned bitterly cold, and the storms that swept down across New England from Canada had sheathed the city in a shimmering coat of ice.

One morning, about a week before Cooper's visit to the gallery, an elderly resident of the rooming house was found frozen to death in his bed. He'd run out of coal—which working-class Bostonites burned in cast-iron stoves—and didn't have money for more. Cooper, who had already run out of the former, knew the latter would soon be next, and was determined to avoid the poor fellow's fate. Perhaps more importantly, he was also determined to keep the chemicals he used to process his photographs from freezing.

Upon leaving the Van Dusen Gallery, Cooper avoided the main thoroughfares in favor of side streets and back alleys in which he scavenged for anything that would burn. By the time he reached the rooming house, he had a hefty bundle of broken branches, discarded pieces of lumber and the odd fence picket balanced on his shoulder. It was secured at its girth by the leather belt that usually held up his trousers.

Weeks passed. The cold snap prevailed. Soon, Cooper had burned everything he'd gathered as well as the wooden shipping crate that had contained his Graflex, reams of prints that hadn't met his standards, and had since taken to burning newspapers he rolled into logs, along with anything else he could find that would combust. Despite his efforts, he awakened one morning to find his photo processing chemicals frozen in their trays as he had feared. He was beside himself, and on the verge of burning the prints he'd brought to Van Dusen as much for spite as for warmth when someone rapped loudly on his door.

"Mr. Cooper?" the landlady called out in her hoarse brogue. "Mr. Cooper, you in there?"

Cooper was behind in the rent and assumed she was there to collect. He was pleasantly surprised to see Grace MacVicar standing next to her when he opened the door. She was shivering and clutching at the collar of her coat, which seemed unable to keep her warm.

"I explained to 'er we don't fancy gentlemen entertaining ladies in their rooms," the landlady barked. "But she's a pushy one, she is."

"Mr. Cooper is not entertaining me," Grace protested, bristling with indignation. "Nor I him. As I told you, I'm here to discuss a business matter."

"Oh, I'll just bet you are," the landlady cracked with as much sarcasm as she could muster. She stepped forward as Grace entered the room, preventing Cooper from closing the door. "It's no wonder you're in arrears," she hissed with a condemning scowl.

Cooper matched it with one of his own and slowly closed the door, forcing her back into the hallway.

Grace was standing amidst the clotheslines, from which a few prints were still hanging. She was staring with discomfort at the cramped space, her eyes watering at the stinging fumes coming from the makeshift darkroom. Most of Cooper's clothes hung from nails he had driven into the walls. The remainder spilled from an old dresser whose drawers refused to close. A few discarded prints he hadn't yet burned were strewn on the floor. Grace stepped to the cast-iron stove to warm her hands but it was cold. "Oh, dear," she said, clearly troubled by Cooper's living conditions. "Now I know what they mean by starving artists."

"It's *freezing* artists this time of year," Cooper joked, concealing his embarrassment and getting a smile out of her. "Now what kind of business might you be here to discuss, Miss MacVicar?"

"Mr. Van Dusen's business," Grace replied, barely able to contain herself. She opened her purse and presented Cooper with an envelope on which *Dylan Cooper, Photographer* had been written in elegant script.

Cooper tore it open and found an equally well-scripted note on Van Dusen's stationery, which asked if he would come to the gallery at his earliest convenience and bring along his prints. It was signed: *With utmost sincerity and admiration, Peter Van Dusen.*

Cooper's heart was pounding in his chest. "Does this mean what I think it means?" he asked, afraid to commit to it.

"It certainly does, Mr. Cooper."

"He's decided to exhibit my pictures?"

Grace responded with an emphatic nod.

"I can't imagine why?" Cooper prompted with a suspicious smile that suggested she was responsible.

"Oh, no, Mr. Cooper. I had nothing to do with it, if that's what your thinking."

"Well, Mr. Van Dusen's not the type to change his mind on a whim. There's got to be a reason for it."

"Of course there is," Grace said. "Dozens of them." She recognized the box that Cooper had brought to the gallery atop a dresser and fetched it, deftly making her way between the clotheslines en route. "They're in this box."

"Oh, I've no doubt he's taken with my work," Cooper said, charmed by her unflagging spirit. "What I can't fathom is why it's investment grade art now when just weeks ago it wasn't. The man's a businessman first and foremost. I can't imagine it doesn't have something to do with *business*." He spat out the last word, emphasizing his distaste for it.

"Well, I'm afraid you'll have to ask Mr. Van Dusen about that," Grace said, supressing a smile that would have made Cooper suspect she knew more than she was telling if he'd seen it. "Shall we go?"

Cooper didn't want to appear eager and briefly considered having her tell Van Dusen he'd come by in a few days, but his circumstances made such posturing impractical. He slipped into his mackinaw, took the box of photographs from Grace, and led the way to the trolley stop.

Like all the streetcars that crossed the heart of Boston, the Massachusetts Avenue trolley locked onto a steel cable that ran beneath the street to move forward, and released it to stop. Consequently, it lurched toward its destination in an unnerving series of fits and starts, its bell clanging loudly at every stop, which seemed to be at just about every corner. By the time it reached the Back Bay, Cooper and Grace had spent more than an hour being jostled in the unheated car. They went straight to the fireplace when they reached the gallery. Its walls were bare. Since Cooper's last visit, the Impressionist masterpieces had been crated and shipped to the wealthy collectors who had purchased them.

Van Dusen took custody of Cooper's box and began laying the prints out across a table that ran beneath the window. "Astonishing . . ." he gushed, pausing at each one before setting it down. "Simply astonishing . . . even better than I remembered." He whirled to his desk, the tails of his coat flying about as he settled in his chair, and began turning the pages of his calendar. "Opening night is . . ."

"Two weeks Monday," Grace said before he found it.

Cooper's head snapped around from the fireplace in reaction. "The opening's in two weeks?"

"Not much time to install a show, is it?" Van Dusen prompted anxiously.

"I think Mr. Cooper and I can manage."

"Speak for yourself, lass," Cooper said. "It could take longer than that just to lay out the show properly, not to mention—" He paused suddenly at something that dawned on him. "Two weeks . . ." he repeated to himself, thinking aloud.

Grace nodded.

So did Cooper, in a way that suggested he had just figured something out. *Now we're getting to work on the crust of the bread,* he thought. As he'd told Grace at the rooming house, he sensed that there was more to Van Dusen's change of heart than an appreciation of his photographs, sensed that there had to be some business angle to it, and now he sensed just what that angle was. "Correct me if I'm wrong, Mr. Van Dusen, but I've been around long enough to know that galleries book their exhibitions months if not years in advance, don't they?"

"You're wrong," Van Dusen fired back. "Each gallery has its scheduling habits. Of course there is always the odd situation that—"

"*Very* odd in this case," Cooper interrupted, now convinced by Van Dusen's hair-trigger reaction. "Something's going on here, Mr. Van Dusen, and if you and I are going to do business, you'll need to put your cards on the table first."

"I thought what was going on here was plainly obvious," Van Dusen said, shifting in his chair. "After some reflection, I decided you were right. There *is* only one way to test the market for photographs as fine art, and your work has the best chance I've seen of success. Those are my cards, Mr. Cooper, and they've been on the table ever since you came barging into my gallery . . . without an appointment, I might add."

"Aye, but they're still not all face up, yet, are they?" Cooper went on, raising the ante. "You see, when you turn them *all* over, when they're *all* staring you square in the eye, it starts lookin' more and more like I'm the one who's doing you the favor not the other way round. That's the truth of it. Isn't it?"

Van Dusen squirmed in discomfort. His eyes darted to

Grace with an accusing stare. "I thought I made it clear you weren't to mention our . . . situation."

Grace held his look and nodded smartly. "*Very* clear, sir. And I didn't."

"You're certain."

"Whatever your . . . *situation*," Cooper said, about to lose his temper, "she didn't breathe a word of it to me, despite my prompting. Now out with it."

Van Dusen glared at him over his spectacles, then his expression softened, and he nodded in concession. "All right Cooper, you've more than earned the truth. I hope you can accept it."

"There's only one way to find out, isn't there?" Cooper said pointedly.

"The truth is—" Van Dusen paused. He got to his feet and came around the desk to be face to face with Cooper. "The truth is, one of the artists I represent is a temperamental fellow who, quite unfortunately and unnecessarily, doubts his talent. So much so, that at the last minute he decided his current work wasn't up to his standards and insisted I reschedule his show."

"In other words, you'd much prefer to be opening an exhibiton of his work in two weeks than mine."

"You asked for the truth," Van Dusen said, coolly.

Cooper's jaw tightened, his eyes hardened to angry pinpoints. "As a matter of fact, if it wasn't for him, for this temperamental fellow, you wouldn't be giving me this show at all, would you? *That's* the truth. Isn't it?!"

Grace knew what the answer would be and winced in anticipation of Cooper's reaction.

Van Dusen nodded with apprehension. "I'm afraid so. You see, Cooper, the only thing worse than a gallery full of artwork that might not sell, is a gallery without any artwork to sell at all."

Cooper was stung by the sheer crassness of Van Dusen's reply. He stood there for a long moment, absorbing the impact, then looked over at Grace. Her eyes were glistening with emotion, her face an alluring image of empathy and concern. Despite the unnerving circumstances, he couldn't help thinking it was an image he'd have given anything to capture with his camera. Instead, it was Cooper who'd been captured, taken prisoner by her eyes, which were pleading with him to accept the truth—the truth he'd demanded. It wasn't long before the fight went out of him. He broke into a smile. "Then I guess this is my lucky day, isn't it?"

"I wasn't sure you'd see it that way," Van Dusen said with a relieved sigh. "But I'm quite pleased you did. Now while we're at it, you wouldn't happen to have any other questions, would you, Mr. Cooper?"

"Aye, as a matter of fact I do . . ."

Van Dusen rolled his eyes and looked over at Grace who was now laughing to herself, clearly taken by Cooper's incorrigible behavior.

"Why is the opening to be on a work day?" Cooper asked, clearly puzzled by it. "Why not a weekend when people have time to . . . to browse, so to speak?"

"Perhaps, the people *you* know," Van Dusen replied, filling with self-importance. "But the people *I* know . . . well, they're all either skiing in Vermont or sailing off the Cape on the weekend."

"He's right, Mr. Cooper," Grace said, stepping in to make sure they didn't go at it again. "Openings are always on Monday night. The theaters are dark, the week's social whirl has yet to start, and the buyers, not to mention the critics and reviewers are all back in town with nothing to do."

"Exactly," Van Dusen said. "Simply put, if you had a choice between spending the evening in a gallery looking at photographs, or at the theater with a vivacious young woman on your arm, which would it be?"

"I'd be looking at photographs," Cooper replied, deadpan; then glancing over at Grace, he quickly added, "With a *lovely* young woman on my arm."

Van Dusen chuckled heartily. "You won't be the first to ask or the first to be turned down."

Cooper questioned Grace with a puzzled look.

"I usually don't attend openings, Mr. Cooper," she explained, demurely. "I prefer to spend my evenings at home, but I just might make an exception in your case."

"I've a good feelin' about this," Cooper said, heartened by her response and all that had happened.

"So do I," Grace said, scooping a fistful of red sold tags from Van Dusen's desk. "Photography's time has come. This show is going to sell out."

"Well, I'm *tempted* to agree," Van Dusen chimed in with a mischievous twinkle at his choice of words. "The difference is . . . I've learned from bitter experience not to trust it."

Chapter Four

❧

"We've a lot of work to do and little time to do it," Van Dusen said when the excitement had worn off and the full impact of their deadline hit home. He cocked his head in thought, then glanced to Cooper. "We'll need a second set of prints to lay out the show. I assume you have test prints, discards that weren't sharp enough, or lacked the proper tonal range . . ."

"Aye, more than I care to admit," Cooper replied, lighting his pipe as he continued. "Sometimes it takes ten just to get one that's right. I've been burning 'em for warmth, but I always keep one of each as a record."

"Good," Van Dusen said, gesturing to the prints he had placed on the table. "Because these, the originals so to speak, will be at the framers with you."

Cooper looked puzzled. "With me? At the framers? And what am I going to be doing there?"

"What you and only you can do, Mr. Cooper . . ." Van Dusen replied, with an enigmatic pause. ". . . making certain that each and every one of these magnificent photographs is properly framed."

"Nonsense," Cooper scoffed. "It's the picture that matters, not the frame; and since they're all eight-by-tens, couldn't we just order enough mattes and frames of a certain size and style and be done with it?"

"We could. But it would be a mistake. A very *costly* one," Van Dusen replied in crisp bursts that rang with authority. "We're presenting photographs as fine art, Cooper—as *investment grade* art—which mandates we emphasize their uniqueness. If I'm going to advise my clients to collect them as they would paintings, each print must be framed as if it were a painting. The tone and texture of the matte, the amount of breathing space between image and frame, not to mention the style and finish of the frame itself must all be selected with an eye to the subject matter and mood of a given picture. *And*—I hasten to add—it's not open for discussion."

"No need for any," Cooper said, raising a brow in tribute as he exhaled a stream of pipe smoke. He was impressed by Van Dusen's shrewd analysis of the market, and pleased at his commitment to photography as fine art. He wasn't pleased to learn that the framer's workshop was in Quincy about an hour's train ride from his rooming house in the opposite direction from where the gallery was located.

While Cooper spent his days in Quincy working with the framers, Grace spent them in the gallery working with the set of discarded prints he had provided. With Van Dusen's guidance, she tacked them up and moved them about from wall to wall, grouping them by subject and mood, in complement and contrast. Each was hung and rehung until she and Van Dusen were satisfied that each picture on its own, as well as in relation to the others, made a striking and compelling presentation.

When he wasn't consulting with Grace, Van Dusen focused on getting out invitations to clients, critics and reviewers, and placing advertisements in newspapers and society journals. Both heralded an exhibition of works by a new talent he had discovered—an exhibition which he had titled: *In Search of New Beginnings. The Photographs of Dylan Cooper.*

Almost two weeks had passed by the time Cooper finished his work with the framers; weeks during which he hadn't seen Grace. He arrived at the gallery as anxious to see her as he was to see his pictures displayed on its walls.

She looked even more beautiful than he remembered. Her hair was pulled back from her face that glowed with the vitality and strength of character that so attracted him. "You've done a fine job, lass," he said on seeing the groupings she'd made. Then he cocked his head with uncertainty and pulled the tacks from the corners of a print that had caught his eye, exchanging it with another. "Though I might be able to improve on it a little here and there."

"Might you, Mr. Cooper?" Grace said, pretending she was shocked. "I never thought a gentleman of your reserve could be so opinionated."

"Nor I," Van Dusen said, unable to keep a straight face as Cooper and Grace erupted with laughter.

The next morning, when the framed prints were delivered, the three of them went about replacing each of the discards that had been used to lay out the show with its beautifully framed mate. And soon, the walls that had, just weeks before, displayed Renoirs, Dégas, Monets, and Cezannes, now displayed—as the placard in the gallery's window proclaimed—The Photographs of Dylan Cooper.

As soon as they had finished hanging the framed prints, Van Dusen collected the set of discards and threw them into the fireplace.

"Wait," Cooper protested. "There's no need to be destroying those."

"Of course there is," Van Dusen replied, as the flames consumed them. "This may be an exhibition of photographs, but as of tonight, they're all one of a kind works of art; and I don't want any copies about." He paused, with that mischievous twinkle Cooper had seen before and added, "Of course, you can always print more if need be."

"Aye," Cooper said, unmollified. "I was planning on using those to heat my room."

Van Dusen emitted an amused cackle. "Have faith, Cooper. If all goes well tonight, you'll never have to worry about that again. Go home, have a bath, and be back here by five-thirty in your Sunday best."

Before walking to the trolley stop, Cooper stood outside the gallery staring at the placard that displayed his name, and at the sparkling photograph on the easel next to it—the picture of the young mother getting off the train. Now officially titled, Madonna and Child, the print had been matted with pale gray linen and set in a frame that had a burnished silver finish that gave it a befitting Renaissance grandeur.

It is only a matter of time now, Cooper thought. Perhaps days, a few weeks at most before his talent would be recognized and he'd be hailed as the fine artist he was, his works included in important private collections and displayed in major museums.

Grace had noticed him slip out the door and had been watching him from the vestibule. "You still can't believe it, can you, Mr. Cooper?" she prompted as she came outside to join him.

"Aye, a dream come true," Cooper said, drawing thoughtfully on his pipe.

"I'd give you a penny for them if I had one to spare," Grace prompted.

"I wouldn't take it if you had," Cooper said with an amused chuckle. "It's not fair for the person in your thoughts to be paying for them."

"I see," Grace mused curiously. "And just what were you thinking about the person in your thoughts?"

"Oh, just that perhaps it's time she considered calling me by my Christian name."

"Fine, Mr. Cooper, I'll see to it she does just that."

Cooper laughed good-naturedly. "Why am I gettin' the feeling I'll be a dodderin' old man before I hear the name, Dylan, come from your lips?"

"I've no idea. As a matter of fact the next opportunity I have to call you, Dylan, Dylan, I'll be sure and do so."

A smile that left no doubt of his fondness for her broke across Cooper's face. "You've got a lovely way about you, Grace."

"Most people from Dumbarton do," she said, leaving no doubt she was returning the compliment.

"Then, in the spirit of us Highlanders sticking together, shall I take that to mean you'll consider coming to the opening tonight?"

"You mean even though I prefer to spend my evenings at home?"

Cooper nodded with resignation. "Aye, even though . . ."

"Okay, I shall. That's a promise."

"I'm afraid I'm not sure what it is you're promising, Grace. To consider it? Or to be there?"

Grace looked up at him, waiting until his eyes had found hers; then in a wistful tone that intensified the moment, she said, "I'll be there, Dylan. I promise."

Chapter Five

The night of the opening turned out to be the first in weeks that the temperature had crept above freezing. The sky had the clarity of crystal and an umbrella of stars shone upon the city of Boston.

Likewise, the Van Dusen Gallery glowed like a jewel in the darkness. Shafts of light from its windows spilled across the cobblestones as a line of horseless carriages queued on Exeter Street. There was nary a Model-T in sight as one hand-crafted motorcoach after another pulled up to the gallery, depositing their well-dressed and well-heeled passengers at its entrance. As Van Dusen had hoped, the more clement weather had prompted the upper crust of Boston's social register to turn out en masse. Those who had money. Those who had lineage. Those who had power. And those who had all three.

As the guests entered the vestibule, valets in formal attire helped them from their greatcoats and floor-sweeping furs, then directed them inside where uniformed waiters, balancing trays, slithered deftly through the crowded rooms dispensing flutes of champagne, along with canapés and hors d'oeuvres.

Van Dusen worked each room like a patriarch at a family reunion. He lived for opening nights, for those moments when he presented an artist's works to those whom he knew would not only appreciate them, but could also afford to *continue* appreciating them on the walls of their homes, offices, and clubs. As he circulated among his esteemed clientele, they toasted him and the new talent he had discovered with congratulations and praise that went beyond the superlative.

Van Dusen basked in the accolades, but was more interested in the snippets of conversation he overheard in passing, in what the animated cliques of clients, critics, and reviewers were saying to each other when they didn't know he was listening. And soon, having heard phrases that extolled Cooper's "unique artistic expression," his "images of emotional intensity," and his "stunning insight into the human condition," emanating from every room in the gallery, Van Dusen knew that their enthusiasm for Cooper's work was indeed genuine.

Cooper heard the accolades as well and was visibly delighted, but he'd have preferred a tumbler of Laphroaig or a tankard of Guinness to the flute of Veuve Cliquot he held between thumb and forefinger. Try as he might, he mingled awkwardly at best, feeling out of place in his corduroys, plaid shirt, and tweed sports coat. Despite his discomfort, the collectors and haughty society matrons found Cooper's bohemian style charming and passed him on from one group to another, showing him off as if he were a newly acquired bauble, which made him feel all the more uncomfortable.

"I'm curious about the wellspring of your creative energy and insight, Mr. Cooper," one of the women who'd been fawning over him asked.

"Have you a muse?" another chimed in, eyeing him as she had the caviar she'd been devouring. "Or are you in search of one?"

"Aye, I'm always in search of amusement," Cooper replied, eliciting a chorus of laughter.

"Please tell us all about the source of your inspiration," a third prompted. "Is it external? Or does it all come from somewhere deep inside you?"

"I'm afraid all that ever comes from deep inside me are clouds of pipe smoke and the occasional belch."

The group of women thought it was hilarious and erupted with more laughter. Cooper used the distraction to disengage. The one person he wanted to see at the opening wasn't there. Every chance he got, he scanned the crowded rooms of the gallery in search of her, his eyes darting anxiously to the door in the vestibule with each tinkle of its bell.

Suddenly, he glimpsed her standing amid a group of people who were off in a corner, and began working his way toward them. He was reaching out to touch her arm when she sensed his presence and turned, revealing that she wasn't Grace MacVicar at all but a woman of similar height and hair color who swept her eyes over his attire and said, "Something tells me you're Mr. Cooper, aren't you?"

"Aye, guilty as charged, ma'am," Cooper replied.

"Well, Mr. Cooper, where *do* you get such artistic inspiration and insight?"

"I'm afraid it comes from somewhere deep inside me, ma'am," Cooper replied, trying not to roll his eyes, which had finally, beyond doubt, located the one person they had spent the evening searching for.

Radiant in a black dress of the simplest fashion Grace seemed to float just above the floor as she moved across it with a group of gentlemen who encircled her.

Cooper fought to keep her in sight, catching a glimpse of her here, a glimpse there among the crisscrossing waiters and swirling crowd that suddenly closed in around her, blocking his view. He quickened his pace, weaving between the knots of people that separated them when several of the group around Grace stepped aside to pursue a waiter with a tray of champagne flutes, revealing the Scottish goddess in their midst.

Cooper's heart, which had been fluttering like a school-boy's, sank like the *Lusitania* at the sight of her—at the sight of Grace MacVicar on the arm of a handsome, well-dressed fellow in his early thirties. Tall with the strapping build of an athlete, he was guiding Grace through the crowd in Cooper's direction with a degree of ease and familiarity that suggested they were more than casual acquaintances.

Chapter Six

Cooper was crestfallen. He needed all the time it took for Grace and her escort to reach him to marshall his courage and stand his ground to greet her. "Miss MacVicar," he said, forcing a smile. "I'm so pleased you could come."

"As am I, Mr. Cooper," Grace replied. She spoke in a formal tone and averted her eyes, which wasn't at all like her. "I'd like to introduce you to someone," she said, turning to the young man who had her arm. "Mr. Cooper, may I present . . ."

Before Grace could finish, the young fellow took hold of Cooper's hand and, shaking it vigorously, said, "Colin . . . Colin MacVicar. A pleasure to meet you, sir."

MacVicar? Colin MacVicar?! *How could I have been such a fool?!* Cooper thought, as it dawned on him that Colin was neither a suitor, nor her betrothed as he had feared on first seeing them together, but her husband!

His mind was racing fast as if, having fallen from a cliff, his entire life was passing before him in a matter of seconds; and he wasted no time chastising himself for coveting a young woman who was married. In truth he wanted nothing more than to crawl into a peat bog and never be seen again. For the life of him, he couldn't fathom how he could have failed to sense it! Or how she could have failed to mention it! Of course, when he added up the hours they'd spent in each other's company, he quickly realized it had hardly been the better part of a day. Other than each knowing the other was from Dumbarton, they hardly knew anything about each other at all. But hadn't Van Dusen referred to her as *Miss* MacVicar? Wasn't her ring finger bare of adornment, marital or otherwise? In the blink of an eye, his mind had raced through every permutation and possibility, and was racing on to the next when Grace, who had seen the panic in his eyes, said, "Colin is my brother, Mr. Cooper. I don't believe I've had the opportunity to mention him."

Cooper concealed his relief, managing not to blurt out, Thanks be to God! which were the words that came immediately to mind. "The pleasure's all mine," he said with a thin smile. "Believe me."

"On the contrary, sir, it's mine," Colin said with evident sincerity. "I'm quite enjoying your work. Especially those that suggest biblical themes."

"Aye, some of the greatest stories ever told in the Bible: famine, pestilence, destruction, death . . . The scripture is filled with themes that bring powerful images to mind."

Colin nodded and forced a smile. "I was thinking less of the Apocalypse and more of those like the one in the window. I believe it's titled Madonna and Child, isn't it?"

Cooper nodded emphatically. "Aye, it's a fine picture." He was desperately in search of a way to jettison Colin and have Grace to himself for a few moments when he spotted Van Dusen nearby, and sensed he had found it. "Mr. Van Dusen?" Cooper called out. "Mr. Van Dusen, this gentleman has expressed a strong interest in the Madonna."

"Oh, an excellent choice, sir," Van Dusen said, warming up his sales pitch as Cooper knew he would. "I may be wrong but I'm fairly certain it isn't yet spoken for. Why don't we step aside where we can discuss its acquisition?" Before Colin could protest or explain, Van Dusen was leading the way toward his desk in the rear of the gallery.

"Your brother!" Cooper hissed in an incredulous whisper as he took Grace aside. "I've a feeling *he's* the one who prefers you spend your evenings at home."

"He's my *eldest* brother, Dylan," Grace explained. "He worries about me. It's a long story."

"I'm all ears, lass."

"This is neither the time, nor the place. Suffice it to say, when I mentioned I was coming tonight, he insisted on coming along as my chaperone."

Cooper grunted and cocked his head in the direction of a group of young men who were preening nearby. "From the looks of these art lovers, you'll probably need one before the night's over."

"I can take care of myself, I assure you," Grace said, starting to laugh.

"Oh, I've no doubt of it, lass, it seems it's Doubting Colin who does."

"Shush," Grace said, putting a finger to her lips, which helped keep her from laughing even harder. She noticed Colin had extricated himself from Van Dusen and was making his way through the crowd in their direction. "He's coming this way."

"Ah, there you are," Colin said as he approached.

"How did you and Mr. Van Dusen get on?" Cooper prompted with as casual an air as he could muster.

"Uncomfortably at best," Colin replied. "Somehow he mistook my *interest* in your work for a wish to acquire it. I'm afraid we should be going, Grace."

"Oh, Colin, no. Not yet. It's much too early."

"Yes, I know, but I'm afraid we really must."

"If you don't mind me asking, Colin, just what is it that

you're so afraid of?" Cooper teased, an edge creeping into his voice.

"Of missing the streetcar, Mr. Cooper," Colin replied, matching his tone. "Our line stops running in less than an hour."

"Then we'll leave in *half* an hour," Grace said with finality. "I'm sure we'll have little trouble managing the stop in time." It was clear she intended to spend every one of those thirty minutes with Cooper. As she proceeded to move about the gallery on his arm, he seemed to overcome his awkwardness and enjoy the ongoing attention and accolades with a degree of comfort that had eluded him prior to her arrival.

The next morning, Grace was up at the crack of dawn, and left the apartment in East Cambridge she shared with her brother earlier than usual. She used the extra time to buy copies of all the newspapers at the stand opposite the trolley stop. Once on the streetcar, she tore through their pages searching for the reviews of Cooper's show, and read them all during the ride to the gallery.

Several janitors were dealing with the evening's aftermath—collecting the empty champagne flutes, half-eaten hors d'oeuvres, discarded napkins, and engraved invitations the guests had left strewn about—when Grace arrived. She found Cooper and Van Dusen slouched in chairs on opposite sides of Van Dusen's desk, drinking cups of black coffee. Both men were wearing the clothing they had worn the previous evening and appeared disheveled and subdued. It seemed to Grace as if they had spent the night there, which they had; though the amber-stained tumblers and empty bottle of malt whiskey on the desk suggested it wasn't coffee they had been drinking. *Boys will be boys,* she thought, realizing their current state was the result of their celebrating well into the wee hours of the morning.

The thwack of the newspapers Grace dropped on the desk pulled them from their stupor. "The reviews are all we'd hoped for and more," she said, bristling with excitement. "'Cooper's work soars to new artistic heights,'" she went on reading aloud from them. "'An eye for the human condition as sharp as an eagle in search of prey . . . Images of astonishing power that one won't soon forget.' And, believe it or not, someone from *Camera Work* was there!"

"Camera Work?" Cooper echoed, his head snapping around at the mention of the New York-based, Alfred Stieglitz-edited quarterly—the country's leading journal of avant-garde art and criticism. "How, pray tell, do you know that?"

Grace held up one of the reviews. "Because it says so right here," she replied, giving full rein to her enthusiasm. "It seems the art critic from the *Globe* is their Boston correspondent. It says *Camera Work* is planning to reprint his review and do a profile of 'the ever so talented photographer Mr. Dylan Cooper' . . . which means New York collectors will soon be making a pilgrimage to Boston—if there are any photographs left for them to collect!" She scooped a bundle of red sold tags from Van Dusen's desk and held them aloft in triumph, then began sorting through the papers on it in search of something.

"You're wasting your time, Grace," Van Dusen said, knowing what she was looking for. "It's not there."

"Well, would you mind telling me how I'm going to tag the ones that are spoken for without a sales list?"

"There is no sales list, Grace," Van Dusen replied.

"Does that mean you've misplaced it? Or that you've decided to keep which ones are spoken for and by whom in your head?"

Van Dusen stroked his beard, then glanced to Cooper and prompted him with a nod.

"I'm afraid none of my pictures are spoken for, Grace," Cooper explained, lowering his eyes as if shamed by it. "Not even one."

Grace stiffened, her head cocked at an angle that reflected her incredulity. The previous evening, she and Colin had been among the earliest to leave the gallery, hurrying off just as the opening was hitting its stride; and having heard nothing but praise for Cooper's work, and having just finished reading the reviews, she had every reason to believe it had been a resounding success. "Not even one . . ." she repeated, realizing that they'd been up the entire night commiserating, not celebrating, as she had thought.

"I'm afraid not, Grace," Van Dusen said with a look that left no doubt of it.

"Oh, dear," Grace sighed, her eyes glistening with emotion at the knowledge that Cooper was undoubtedly heartbroken. "But things are bound to change when they see these, aren't they?" she prompted, brandishing some of the reviews. "And then there's *Camera Work*, too!"

Van Dusen shook his head no. "I don't think they'll make one iota of difference, Grace."

"Why not? Why are you being so pessimistic?"

"Because all the major collectors have already made their decision; and no matter how complimentary those reviews, and any to come, may be, they haven't a chance of changing it."

"But everyone who was here last night loved Dylan's pictures, each and every one of them," she protested with characteristic tenacity.

"Indeed they did," Van Dusen replied. "As a matter of fact, I'd go so far as to say many were even *tempted* to buy them . . . and I've no doubt they would have, had they been paintings. The problem isn't with Dylan's pictures, Grace, it's with photography."

Cooper nodded with resignation. "I said there was only one way to find out if collectors would accept photographs as fine art. Well, the answer is no. Mr. Van Dusen was right from the start."

And Van Dusen *was* right. Weeks passed. The pictures

hung unspoken for on the gallery walls. And with each passing day, it became clear that, though Cooper was roundly toasted as an exceptional talent, the accolades hadn't turned into sales and never would. As Van Dusen had initially feared, collectors weren't ready to accept photographs as investment grade art.

Chapter Seven

"It's been weeks, Dylan. Where have you been?" Grace's voice rang with a mixture of anger and relief as Cooper entered the gallery and strode toward her in his lumbering gait. "I came by your room. I left messages with your landlady . . ."

"Aye," Cooper said, his eyes sweeping across the gallery's walls. Grace and Van Dusen were in the process of taking down his photographs, and a few of the walls were bare. "The one about the show closing was waiting for me when I got back this morning. So, I thought I'd better come by and collect my work."

"Back from where?" Grace wondered.

"Nowhere," Cooper grunted sullenly. "Camping."

"In this cold?" she said, chastising him like a misbehaving child.

Cooper responded with a disheartened shrug and took a moment to light his pipe. "I was in need of some solitude and soul-searching."

Grace sighed, her eyes softening with empathy. "You mustn't lose faith in yourself, Dylan. You mustn't make the mistake of doubting your talent. *I* certainly haven't."

"Nor have I," Van Dusen added. "I've no doubt they'll all be collector's items one day."

Cooper exhaled a stream of pipe smoke and smiled thinly. "You're just saying all this to lift my spirits from the gutter, aren't you?"

"Go to church if you want your spirits lifted," Van Dusen retorted. "I meant what I said about your pictures, and I'm prepared to prove it."

"Prove it, eh?" Cooper challenged. "And how do you propose to do that? By buying them all yourself?"

"No, by storing them here until my clients do, and providing you with a stipend in the meantime."

Cooper recoiled as if offended. "A stipend? Am I to understand you're offering me money?"

Van Dusen nodded smartly. "It won't keep you in champagne and caviar; but frugal fellow that you are, I've no doubt it will keep you afloat."

Cooper's face reddened with embarrassment. The idea of finding himself the subject of such an offer, let alone in front of Grace, was a devastating blow to his pride. "I prefer to sink or swim on my own, Mr. Van Dusen. Truth be told, I've no need of assistance; and if the state of my finances was dire, which I assure you it isn't, I still couldn't be taking your money."

"You wouldn't be *taking* it, Cooper," Van Dusen explained, about to lose his patience. "It would be a loan against future sales. I've done it with promising artists before, and I've never been sorry."

Cooper's eyes widened in reaction.

"That's right," Van Dusen said, seeing it. "You're not the first artist in Boston to find himself behind in his rent."

"Where, pray tell, did you get that idea?"

Van Dusen squirmed in discomfort and exchanged an apprehensive glance with Grace.

"From me," she said in a forthright tone. "Your landlady kept asking me if I knew where you were. When I asked why she wanted to know . . ." Grace let it trail off, suggesting the rest was obvious. "There's no shame in accepting help, Dylan. It won't leave some indelible stain on your soul, you know."

"I'm afraid it's already been blackened beyond redemption, lass," Cooper joked, trying to save face. "It's generous of you, Mr. Van Dusen, but as I said I've always managed on my own, and I've no intention of changin' now. None whatsoever."

"I don't know why you're being so stubborn, but suit yourself," Van Dusen conceded. He was concerned Cooper wasn't up to taking advice, but decided to speak his mind regardless. "Don't take this the wrong way, but under the circumstances, you might be wise to consider commercial photography for a while."

"Commercial work?" Cooper bristled, perceiving it as an insult as Van Dusen had feared.

"I'm your friend, not your enemy, Cooper," Van Dusen counseled evenly. "It won't cost anything to hear me out."

Cooper responded with an indulgent nod.

"I was chatting with one of my clients," Van Dusen went on. "His name's Latour, Georges Latour. You might recall him from the opening? A rather flamboyant chap. French accent. Somewhat full of himself."

"They were all full of something, I recall that," Cooper cracked. "But if I had the pleasure of meeting Mr. Latour, I'm afraid it escapes me."

"Well, he was there, and as it happens he's a—"

"Aye, for all the good it did me."

"If you'll do me the courtesy of listening, he might do you some good *now*," Van Dusen snapped in a tone that silenced Cooper. "As I was saying, he's a merchant, an extremely successful one. His emporium on Marlborough Street sells expensive and fashionable European haute couture for women."

"Quite fashionable, indeed," Grace said, her eyes brightening at the mention of it. "Georges Latour . . . Every woman in Boston wishes she could shop there."

"It just so happens," Van Dusen went on, "that he's looking for someone to photograph his Spring collection. The pictures will be used in newspaper advertisements, which he's planning to—"

Cooper nearly bit through his pipe stem. "Fashion photography?" he erupted, stung by an insult which, as far as he was concerned, exceeded that of the stipend.

"The job would pay well," Van Dusen pressed on, ignoring the outburst. "And since he was quite taken with your work, I'm certain he would—"

"I'm certain of it too!" Cooper roared. "But there's not enough money on God's good earth to tempt Dylan Cooper to take on an assignment in . . . in . . ." He paused and, as if spitting out something distasteful, growled, "Advertising!"

"Well, the decision's yours, Cooper," Van Dusen said, managing to keep his composure. "Think it over and let me know."

"Oh, I need no such assurance," Cooper said, his eyes hardening to angry pinpoints. "When it comes to my pictures, the decision has always been mine! And always will be mine!"

"There's no need to get upset. It was just a figure of speech and I—"

"Furthermore," Cooper went on, "there's no need to think it over because the decision's already been made. I said no. I meant no. And, no, it is! Have I made myself clear?!" He jammed his pipe hard into the corner of his mouth, then turned on a heel and strode swiftly toward the entrance.

"Dylan?" Grace called out, hurrying after him. "Dylan, wait!" Before she could catch up, Cooper was through the vestibule and charging out the door. It shut with a startling slam that stopped her in her tracks and set the bell to clanging. She stood there trying to regain her composure, the bell ringing as loudly as if a fire truck was racing past outside.

Cooper made the long journey back to his rooming house on foot only to find the door to his room had been padlocked. He slammed it against the hasp in anger, then went to the landlady's apartment and knocked on the door.

"Mr. Cooper . . . I thought you might be dropping by," she said, clearly pleased with herself. "I'm afraid you've had your last grace period. You'll have to pay what you owe or vacate the premises."

Cooper glared at her for a moment, then accepted the inevitable and nodded. "It's to be the latter, I'm afraid. If you'll be good enough to unlock the door, I'll get my things."

"Oh, you're a shrewd one, aren't you?" she said, her voice dripping with suspicion. "But I'm no fool, Mr. Cooper. Once you 'ave your belongings, I'd never set eyes on you again, let alone the money I'm owed."

"You don't understand, my camera is in there. And I can't—"

"Is it now?" she said with a sly smile. "Fetch a pretty penny it would, I imagine. Might even fetch enough to cover what you're in arrears."

"Perhaps, it would," Cooper conceded, knowing it would fetch more, much more. "But the truth of the matter is, I can't earn a living without it; and if I can't earn a living, I'll *never* be able to pay you."

"Well, if you ask me," she said, laughing at what she was about to say. "The *real* truth of the matter is, you weren't earning one with it, either!"

Cooper took a deep breath, fighting the urge to retaliate. "Please, you have my word on it."

"It's not your word I'm after, Mr. Cooper. It's your rent. Soon as I 'ave it, you'll 'ave your camera and the rest of your belongings. In the meantime, it's out in the cold with you."

Cooper glared at her, seething, his jaw clenched with anger.

"Of course, if by some miracle you come up with your arrears, *plus* a week in advance, I'd be 'appy to let you stay on."

Miracle?! It's a miracle I haven't wrung your neck! Cooper thought, resisting the impulse to do just that. "I've no belief in them. It's either luck or the lack of it."

"So true, Mr. Cooper. As they say, even a blind squirrel finds an acorn every now and then. You'll just have to get your nails dirty, now, won't you?"

Cooper's eyes flared at the insult, then softened at a sobering thought that seemed to take the steam out of him. Deep down he knew that he'd already found his acorn—*without* getting his nails dirty in the process. On the contrary, Van Dusen had actually handed it to him, but he'd given in to his pride and rejected it. He let out a long breath then smiled thinly at the landlady and said, "Aye, and even a blind beggar knows when someone's dropped a coin in his cup—unless he's deaf and dumb as well."

The landlady chuckled with glee. "Oh, that's a good one, Mr. Cooper, I'll have to remember it."

"Truth be told, lately I've been all three," Cooper said, thinking aloud as he turned and hurried down the hallway. "I'll soon be back for my belongings."

"I 'ope so, Mr. Cooper," the landlady called out after him. "But I've been running this rooming house since the summer of ninety-two, and if you come walking in here with that money, it'd be a miracle to me!"

Chapter Eight

"Bienvenue, Monsieur Cooper!" Georges Latour called out in his French accent, pronouncing it Coupaire. He sauntered down the staircase, which swept in a graceful arc from the balcony of his opulent emporium to the lobby, and shook Cooper's hand. "I'm so sorry we did not have an introduction at the Gallery Van Dusen. Now, I have the chance to say I find your work to be just superb, par excellence."

But not "excellence" enough to buy it, Cooper thought with an ironic smile. After his confrontation with his landlady, he returned to the gallery, agreed to the assignment and took an advance against it from Van Dusen, which he used to pay his rent and, much more importantly, reclaim his camera. "Aye, I'm pleased you enjoyed it. All the critics who review fine art seemed to agree. You're in good company."

"Ah, I know what you're thinking," Latour said, scolding him with a finger. "I can see it in the eyes. But just because a man appreciates something does not mean he succumbs to the temptation to possess it for his own. It's like a beautiful woman who passes you on the street. You have had such experiences, no?"

Cooper couldn't help but smile at the analogy and nodded. "Aye, more times than I can count."

"*Mais oui.* As Madame Latour often reminds me, '*Regarde, oui. Touche, non.*'"

Cooper nodded. "If there was a Madame Cooper, I'm sure she'd say the same."

"*Alors,* I'm so glad you found time in your busy schedule to come by. Monsieur Van Dusen cautioned me about getting my hopes up, but *voila*! Here we are!" Latour summoned two well-groomed and finely attired gentlemen, who had been keeping a discreet distance, and introduced them to Cooper as John Ogilvy and Edgar Altman, advertising and sales directors, respectively. After an exchange of pleasantries, Latour led the way up the sweeping staircase, across the polished marble floors, and through the "salles d'exposition," as he called them, where avant-garde paintings and sculptures acquired from the Van Dusen gallery were prominently displayed along with various ensembles from his collection, and where the distant strains of classical music could be heard.

En route, Cooper's head filled with the musky aroma of perfume. Was the air in the building being purposely scented? Or was Georges Latour himself trailing it in his wake? Cooper had just concluded it was the latter when Latour threw open a set of ornate doors revealing an elegantly appointed showroom beyond which equally elegantly appointed women sat on plush sofas, previewing the Latour Spring Collection. A Bach flute concerto filled the air. The music came from a Victrola atop a table that also held a large vase of freshly cut and beautifully arranged flowers. A white-gloved attendant, standing next to it, gave the Victrola an occasional crank, keeping it up to speed.

"My wealthiest and most loyal clientele," Latour whispered in an aside. "The crème de la crème of the Social Register."

The collection featured dresses with loosely draped bodices, flowing floor length skirts and wide-brimmed bonnets bedecked with flowers. As was the custom at couture houses, the ensembles were being modeled by a steady parade of mannequins.

"You see?" Latour prompted with a rhetorical flourish, addressing his clientele. "No more the waist-strangling corset, no more the bustle *sur la derrière*, no more the rustle of the crinoline. Gone! All gone! Women are free, liberated! *This* is how ladies of the Social Register want to look while attending church services and the Easter Parade! *Très magnifique? Non?*"

While Latour played to his adoring audience, advertising director Ogilvy, leaned to Cooper and said, "Mr. Latour means this is how they *will* want to look . . . as soon as we convince them of it."

"Aye, the power of suggestion knows no bounds."

"Exactly," Ogilvy said, smartly. "And once high society women are seen about town in these ensembles, *every* woman will want to dress as fashionably."

"But they couldn't afford to, until now," Altman explained. "Why has this changed? Because we at Georges Latour have just developed a line of similar clothing priced to fit their pocketbooks."

"And empty them as well," Cooper quipped.

"Exactement!" Latour exclaimed, rejoining them. "These advertisements—*your pictures, Coupaire*—will have *such* power of suggestion that every housewife in Boston will be at the door of Georges Latour to buy her Easter bonnet and more."

"All because of my pictures . . ." Cooper mused, emitting a stream of pipe smoke.

"But of course! As a smart gentleman Chinois once observed, each one of them will be worth a thousand words. But time is short, so, if you will leave the address of your studio with one of my assistants, the selected ensembles will be delivered within the week."

Cooper's jaw slackened. *Studio?! What studio?!* he

thought, his mind racing in search of a way to avoid revealing he didn't have one. "We might just be putting the cart before the horse here," he cautioned, stalling as the pieces of a solution began falling into place.

Latour's brows knitted into a puzzled frown. "And why is this cart standing before its horse?"

"Because we're deciding where I'll be taking these pictures before deciding what we want them to express, what the power of suggestion should be suggesting, so to speak," Cooper replied. Then, planting the face-saving idea that had dawned on him, he casually prompted, "For example, shouldn't pictures advertising the *Spring* Collection have the feeling of *springtime*, of the out of doors, of nature?"

"Absolument," Latour exclaimed, conquered by the power of suggestion as Cooper fervently hoped. "The budding trees, the fields of flowers, the sunlight . . ."

"Aye, but there's little chance of finding *them* in my studio. No, these pictures must be taken in an outdoor setting with natural light if they're to have what you're after, if they're to fulfill the promise of the Georges Latour Spring Collection."

Latour's eyes came to life, then clouded. *"Extérieur . . . avec lumière au naturelle,"* he mused, on the horns of a dilemma. "But it is still winter. Where does one go at this time of year for trees and flowers and such?" He questioned Ogilvy and Altman with a look and received baffled shrugs in return. "You have something to propose, Coupaire?"

Cooper drew thoughtfully on his pipe as if entertaining a profound vision and nodded. "Aye, I've been givin' it a fair bit of thought, and what keeps coming to mind is a softly focused image . . . of an elegantly dressed woman with a white parasol . . . strolling through the Botanical Gardens."

"Mon Dieu!" Latour exclaimed. "Of course, the glass-roofed pavilions, the natural light, the trees, the flowers, the sea of Easter lilies! Madame Latour herself is a member and generous contributor. A stroke of genius, Coupaire!" Altman

and Ogilvy were already nodding in emphatic sales and advertising approval when Latour glanced to them and prompted, *"Excellent! Non?"*

Cooper stifled a sigh of relief and was basking in the accolades when Latour cocked his head in thought, and said, "One last thing . . . the mannequin. As you have seen, we have many young ladies who would be happy to model for you; and as you might imagine, I have my favorites among them; but you are an artist, sir, and I have wisdom to know that an artist and his model have, as we say *en Français, le rapport spécial*. I'm sure you have a special young woman with whom you always work in these situations. *Non?"*

Once again faced with being found out, Cooper thought fast, and without the slightest hesitation, replied, "Aye, I've just the lass who's perfect for it."

Chapter Nine

◇

"Oh, no, Dylan, no, I couldn't," Grace said, her voice a mixture of embarrassment and intrigue. She and Cooper were in the North End, strolling through one of the glass-domed pavilions that were part of the Botanical Gardens. It was like being in an enchanted forest where vast beds of flowers and budding trees basked in the soft light that came through the glazed latticework above. "I had a feeling there was more to this than a Sunday morning stroll."

"Aye, guilty as charged," Cooper said, his burr thickening with charm. "But why not, lass? You clearly possess the necessary qualities." He picked a lily and offered it to her. "You're easily as lovely as this flower, and carry yourself in ways that go well beyond your name. There's no doubt you're perfectly suited to these pictures and this place."

Grace blushed as she took the flower and inhaled its fragrance. "As I'm afraid you can clearly see, I'm more than flattered. But a photographer's model? My brother would never allow it."

"Him again? Colin? Doubting Colin?" Cooper exclaimed, coaxing a smile out of her. "You don't seem to be the kind to cower, lass."

Grace's smile faded. Her eyes narrowed with defiance. "You know very well I'm not, Dylan Cooper."

"Aye, I know very well it's a big favor I'm asking, too, but I've no one else to turn to, Grace. Certainly not anyone with qualities such as yours."

"Mr. Latour must have dozens of models who are more than qualified. Why not employ one of them?"

"Because, despite his aversion to photography as investment grade art, Mr. Latour deigned to pronounce me an artist and, as such, assumed I have a model with whom I have a special rapport. It would've been unwise to contradict him then, and would be unwise now."

"I want to help you, Dylan, you know I do," Grace said, her voice rife with conflict. "But you saw how Colin was at the opening. This would be a much bigger problem. I wouldn't even be here if he weren't at church this morning. Please try to understand."

"A little help would go a long way, Grace. The opening might not have been the place or the time to explain, but it seems we have both now."

Grace nodded and led the way to a bench near a pond dotted with water lilies and clusters of bullrushes. "When you decided photography would be your life's work, what was your family's reaction?"

"Well . . ." Cooper replied, thumbing tobacco into his pipe, "they were a wee bit upset when I sold my sister's bicycle to buy my first camera."

Grace giggled like an adoring schoolgirl.

"They're just simple hardworking folks who aren't in touch with the arts," Cooper went on. "But they saw I was consumed with it and let me go my way. I guess they sensed I was put on this earth to take pictures."

"You're very fortunate," Grace said, trying not to sound envious. "My parents are simple and hardworking people, too, but, unlike yours, they have an extremely provincial view of life."

"You mean, provincial as in strict Scottish Presbyterians who believe a daughter should know her place and carry out her parents' wishes?"

"Precisely. You can imagine how they reacted when their daughter turned out to be a fiercely independent free spirit with a bent for the performing arts."

"The *performing* arts," Cooper echoed, surprised. "I thought it would be painting, sculpture, photography . . ."

"I'm taken with them all, Dylan; but I work at the gallery out of necessity, not choice. The dance has my heart. I'm classically trained."

"A ballerina," Cooper said with an amused chuckle, "which explains why you walk like a duck, doesn't it?"

Grace nodded, laughing along with him. "You know of Isadora Duncan?"

"Of course. She's famous the world over."

"Well, she was my inspiration as a child. I wanted to be just like her and dance the world over, too. So I began taking lessons in school."

"Aye, and your parents didn't think it was a proper way for a young lady to spend her time, and they set out to crush your ambition."

Grace nodded sadly. "I'm afraid so."

"Well, don't look so gloomy, Grace," Cooper said with a jaunty cackle. "They didn't do a very good job of it, now did they?"

"No, thanks be to God. As it turned out, I was accepted by the Royal Ballet School in Edinburgh and eventually became a member of a company that performed throughout the United Kingdom. Then at the end of one season, the director announced we'd be touring America next. That's when my parents turned over the burden of protecting my virtue to Colin. He's been my chaperone ever since."

"Now we're getting to work on the crust of the bread aren't we?" Cooper said, his eyes twinkling with understanding and delight at her rebellious nature.

"I told you it was a long story."

"So . . ." Cooper said with a thoughtful draw on his pipe, ". . . If ballet is what brought you to America, why aren't you dancing?"

"Because at the end of the tour, the booking agent stole the proceeds, and Colin and I found ourselves stranded in Boston with no way to get home."

"And your big strapping brother just let this crook get away with it without a word?"

"On the contrary, Colin confronted him; but he laughed and said a woman as pretty as I shouldn't have any trouble earning enough for two steamer tickets. You can just imagine Colin's reaction to that!"

"I daresay, I'd have bloodied the man's nose at that point," Cooper said, his fists clenched and raised like a pugilist's.

Grace nodded emphatically. "Oh, Colin did more than that! Fortunately, after all his shenanigans, the agent couldn't very well go to the police; but after Colin pounded him, neither could we, and that was the end of the money. It's been more than a year. We've been saving every spare penny for steamer tickets, but there aren't many left over at the end of the month. I barely earn enough at the gallery to make ends meet."

"I should think there'd be a place for you at the city's ballet company."

"As did I, but the few openings are given to girls from its student corps, just as we do at home. As for dancing jobs that *are* available, well, they're not the kind even a fiercely independent, free-spirited lass would consider."

"And what of Colin? He seems able-bodied enough."

"Oh, indeed, he's quite fit. Like our father and his before him, Colin went to work in the mines; but there's no coal to be mined in all of Massachusetts, let alone Boston. He took the train to Pennsylvania once, but it's just like back home there, the companies aren't hiring, they're letting people go instead."

"Aye, the lack of work is what brought so many of us here in the first place, isn't it?"

"Yes, that and now this awful war . . ."

Cooper nodded gravely. "It's a horrible situation at best. So many young men dying. Kipling's son killed, and Gladstone's grandson, too. The sons of America will soon join them, I'm afraid."

"Yes, but it's been nearly a year since Congress declared war," Grace observed. "Just the other day, I read the Europeans are asking, 'Where are the Americans?' "

"Aye, the President claims a million doughboys'll be there by summer," Cooper replied, relighting his pipe as they left the bench and strolled beneath a canopy of budding trees. "So, Grace, with things being so bad at home, why are you in such a rush to get back there?"

"Oh, I'm not sure I'm in such a rush now, Dylan," Grace replied flirtatiously. "Life seems to have taken a turn for the better as of late."

"Good, because I'm getting the feeling I'd miss you more than a little if you were to go back."

Grace smiled and lowered her eyes demurely, then cocked her head with a question. "And what about Dylan Cooper, Photographer? Was it the bad times at home that brought him to America? Or was it a sense of adventure? A burning drive to take pictures of the new world?"

"A bit of each, I imagine; but it's simpler than that," Cooper replied, emitting a stream of pipe smoke. "It was just time for a new beginning."

"Well, it will soon be that time of year, won't it? Springtime, I mean."

"Aye, but the truth of it is I much prefer autumn and winter. Something about the clarity of the light . . ."

"You know, I'm not a terribly religious person, but I always get a special feeling around Easter . . . the whole idea of it . . . especially the resurrection. I look forward to that feeling of things coming back to life. It's like having a fresh, new begining every year."

"I'm afraid it went in one ear and out the other with me,"

Cooper replied. "I do recall being marched into church with my classmates on Good Friday, once; and the minister saying, 'Forgive us Jesus for crucifying thee.' Well, I said to myself this fellow's brain must have more mold than a month old haggis, because I'd nothing to do with that."

"Nor I," Grace said with a chuckle. "But Colin—now he bought it hook, line and sinker. Five minutes with him and he'll have you covinced you were the one who drove home the nails."

"He'd have little success with me."

Grace found his swagger utterly endearing and smiled like a student with a crush on a young professor. "So have you found it yet?"

"Have I found what yet?"

"The new beginning you came here for?"

Cooper stopped walking and captured her eyes with his. "Oh, lately, I've a feeling I'm getting closer."

"Good," Grace said, a smile dimpling her cheeks. "Because I think I'd miss you more than a little, too."

Cooper knew she had purposely repeated his words and smiled in acknowledgement. "So, Miss Grace MacVicar from Dumbarton in the Scottish Highlands," he said, rolling his r's like thunder, "am I to take that to mean I have a mannequin for my pictures?"

Grace's eyes brightened then clouded, reflecting her conflict. "I meant it when I said I'd do anything to help you, Dylan, but I'm concerned the pleasure would be more than ruined by the pain that would be sure to follow."

"Colin."

Grace nodded. "I doubt he'd agree to it."

"Have we Doubting Grace, now, too?" Cooper teased gently. "Doubting Grace to go along with Doubting Colin? No. *He's* the one with the doubts, lass. And since I'm the one who's responsible for them, it seems it's up to me to remove them."

Chapter Ten

❦

"Pose for fashion photographs?" Colin exclaimed, his eyes flared in condemnation of what Cooper had just proposed. He had returned from church services to the house in which he and his sister shared an apartment and found Cooper and Grace sitting on the porch. The rundown structure was located in the low-rent district of East Cambridge where the ethnic workers who serviced the local universities lived. "It's totally out of the question," Colin went on. "It wouldn't be proper for a young lady of Grace's virtue to be involved in such . . . such tawdry activities." He rapped the railing with the newspaper he was carrying and charged inside.

Grace emitted an exasperated sigh and hurried after him. "Colin? Colin, I'm tired of being treated like a child."

"Then stop acting like one," Colin retorted as they entered the apartment, Cooper right behind them. "You're my younger sister and, as such, you should know your place and accept my decision." He settled in a chair and went about reading his paper as if dismissing them. The overstuffed chair was tattered and worn as were the other sparse furnishings that had come with the apartment. The uncomfortable silence was broken by the rustling of the newspaper as Colin turned the page.

"Colin? *Colin?!*" Grace said in a tone Cooper hadn't heard before. "You've no cause to be rude."

Colin lowered the paper and eyed her sullenly.

"Furthermore, I'll have none of your carping about my place, Colin. My place, which you and I know all too well, is earning enough to keep us off the dole and get us back home."

"I'll still not condone such tawdry activities."

"What activities might you be referring to, Colin?" Cooper asked, calmly, lighting his pipe. "Apparently, working in a gallery where avante-garde paintings are sold—some of them paintings of unclothed women, no less—isn't one of them."

"Grace's job is a necessary evil, which I've come to tolerate," Colin replied with an impatient snap of his newspaper. "Furthermore, Mr. Van Dusen's clients are some of Boston's most upstanding citizens. Their manners and mores are impeccable and beyond reproach."

"Aye, the very same citizens who'll be buying and wearing the clothes Grace will be modeling," Cooper concluded, smartly. "So what might you be suggesting about this that's improper, Colin?"

Colin set the paper aside and got to his feet. "You know exactly what I mean, Mr. Cooper. Throughout history artists' models have been thought of as morally corrupt women with tarnished reputations and, in my opinion, deservedly so."

"Your sister would no more partake of an activity that would corrupt her morals or tarnish her reputation than would the Blessed Virgin Mary herself."

"Yes, well, evidently you're not familiar with Grace's zeal to cavort half-naked on the stage," Colin said, his voice tinged with sanctimony.

Cooper looked aghast, incredulous. "You can't be referring to the ballet?"

"Indeed, I am. You'll not see her doing that here, I promise you, let alone pose for pictures. As those of us who work in the mines know all too well, the coal tar goes on a lot easier than it washes off. I assured my family Grace would remain . . . unsoiled . . . during our time in America and I intend to do just that."

"Of course you do, and you do it well," Cooper said, sensing the way to Colin's heart was through his ego. "You're her chaperone, Colin, and that's what a chaperone does, isn't it?"

"Well," Colin said, sounding pleasantly surprised. "I'm glad you understand."

"Aye, but do *you?*" Cooper challenged, springing the trap he'd set. "You see, Colin, human nature being what it is, some folks are eager to believe the worst of even the finest among us. So society, in its wisdom, invented the chaperone. *Not* to prohibit innocent behavior but to witness it. To testify to what *actually* happened rather than what the gossip mongers want us to believe happened. Isn't that so, Colin?"

Colin glared at him, then nodded grudgingly.

"Then do your job, Colin," Cooper exhorted. "And Grace will do hers; and I will do mine; and we'll all profit from it, and handsomely I might add."

Colin's eyes narrowed in calculation, then darted back to Cooper's. "You're suggesting it would pay well?"

Cooper allowed himself a thin smile, and nodded, emitting a stream of pipe smoke. "Aye, but I won't mislead you. If it's steamer tickets you're thinking of, it wouldn't be enough for even one; but you'd be closer to having them than you are now."

"I needn't remind you, Colin," Grace chimed in, picking up on Cooper's strategy, "as things are, we've made little headway, if any."

Colin's lips tightened, loath to admit it, then he nodded in concession. "All right, under one condition . . ."

Grace fired an anxious glance to Cooper.

"When you've finished your work and the rotogravures are made, the negatives and prints are to be destroyed."

"Destroyed?!" Cooper exclaimed. "As conditions go that's not one I'm prone to agree to, Colin."

"Then I'm forced to withdraw my approval," Colin said with finality. "I'll not have pictures of my sister posing in clothing she would never wear, let alone afford, in the hands of people who shouldn't have them."

"I don't like what you're insinuating," Cooper said, on the verge of losing his temper.

Grace groaned with impatience. "What's the difference, Colin? They'll be in all the papers anyway."

"Yes, for a day, perhaps two, after which they will be discarded and this . . . this sinful interlude will have never happened."

"Sinful interlude?!" Grace erupted, losing her composure. "I'll have none of your sanctimonious posturing, Colin! Your needless opposition has only made me more of a mind to do this despite it!"

"You'd defy me though I forbade it?"

"Yes, I'm going to do this for Mr. Cooper and for us. So, you'll either be there as chaperone, or you won't. Truth be told, I'd much prefer the latter."

Colin let out an exasperated breath and glared at her. "Then I shall be there. But the negatives and prints must be destroyed, Mr. Cooper. Agreed?"

Cooper bristled at his arrogance and was on the verge of bolting when he caught sight of Grace whose eyes were pleading with him to do otherwise. He stuck his pipe hard into the corner of his mouth, then calmed himself, and grunted in the affirmative.

Chapter Eleven

Rays of filtered light were streaming through the glass-domed pavilions of the Botanical Gardens just as they were on the morning Cooper and Grace had first strolled beneath them. But now, despite the late winter chill outside—which caused the moist air in the pavilions to coat each pane with luminous condensation—the trees were exploding with foliage and the flower beds, which radiated in ever widening arcs beneath the soaring vaults of steel and glass, were fully blossoming.

Though Cooper had chafed mightily at the idea of accepting a commercial assignment, once committed, he brought all his creative powers and obsessive attention to detail to the task. After positioning Grace against a background of wisteria that cascaded from an arched trellis filtering the light, he crouched beneath the blackout cloth of his view camera, sharpening focus, adjusting perspective, and framing the composition until he had everything exactly how he wanted it—everything except its alluring mannequin.

Despite her years of training and performing on the world's stages, there was something about the camera and Cooper crouching behind it like a hunter stalking his prey that made Grace uncharacteristically self-conscious. Furthermore, every time she seemed about to overcome it, Colin, who was sitting on a nearby bench writing a letter, would look up with a disapproving gaze, and she would stiffen in disturbing contrast to the setting's serene mood and the flowing lines of the elegant couture ensemble she was modeling.

"Will you dance for me, Grace?" Cooper asked brightly, popping up like a jack-in-the-box from beneath the blackout cloth.

"Dance for you?" Grace echoed, laughing at his antics, as he intended.

"Aye. Place your trust in me, Grace, and dance," Cooper replied, waving his arms comically as if he were dancing. "It will bring out the best in you."

"Am I to dance without music?" Grace wondered, unable to contain her laughter. "Or will you and Colin whistle a happy tune for me?"

"Oh, I suppose we could," Cooper replied with a good-natured grin. "But since I was never recruited for the choir, and Colin doesn't appear to have a happy tune in his repertoire right now, I've a better idea."

Cooper stepped to an iron-wheeled cart that he was using to move his camera gear about the grounds. It was one of several the Gardens' landscaping staff used to transport equipment and botanical specimens. A number of wooden boxes were stacked neatly on its bed. They contained sheet film, lenses, filters, tripods, and film holders. One box, with light-tight hand holes, was used to load film into the latter. Another, a well-crafted case of varnished mahogany with polished brass fittings was the box Cooper was after.

Cooper set it next to his camera and raised the lid, revealing it was a Victrola, the one from Latour's emporium. Cooper had anticipated the possibility of Grace's stage fright—or Colin fright as he thought of it—and had wisely borrowed it.

After affixing the speaker horn, he slipped a record from one of the sleeves within the Victrola's base and placed it on the turntable, then gave the crank handle to Colin.

"And what am I supposed to do with this?" Colin asked, sounding offended.

"Get it up to speed, Colin, and keep it there," Cooper replied sharply. "And if you can't manage it, I'll find me an organ grinder's monkey who can."

Colin rolled his eyes and literally prayed for patience as he inserted the handle into the mechanism and began cranking. When the turntable was up to speed, he lowered the needle onto the record, and the lyrical strains of Vivaldi's *Four Seasons* began wafting through the beautifully landscaped pavilion.

Soon, as Cooper had expected—and eagerly awaited, for he had never seen her dance—Grace became infused with a ballerina's aura and lost in the music. His eyes crinkled with delight as she began executing rhythmic phrases of movement, seguing from petit temps lié to grand, and into a series of port de bras, then into a series of arabesques, maintaining a flowing line from toe point to fingertip. Each phrase of choreography would lead naturally to a pose that Grace would hold until she heard the click of the shutter, then she would lyrically pirouette out of it and into the next, giving each a sense of flowing movement.

Colin looked up from his letter and watched with a painful scowl throughout; but, once, after Grace had performed an especially lovely pas jeté, Cooper thought he detected a thin smile of delight flickering across her brother's tight-lipped countenance.

Cooper kept it to himself and continued taking photographs. As soon as he finished, Grace hurried to an office in a nearby administrative building, which served as a dressing room, to change into the next ensemble. She had spent the previous week at Latour's emporium being attended to by a draper and a seamstress who fitted and tailored each ensemble to her willowy figure; and they had come along to help her change from one to the next and assure each was properly accessorized. As soon as Grace was out of earshot, Cooper glanced to Colin and prompted, "Something tells me you're enjoying this a wee bit more than you thought."

"I've no idea what you're talking about, Mr. Cooper," Colin replied, stiffly.

Cooper sighed with frustration as he folded the tripod and shouldered the camera to move it to a new position. "Be honest with yourself, Colin. Grace is not only a most beautiful and immensely talented creature, but she's your sister as well. I caught you smiling before when she was dancing. Wasn't it because deep in your heart you take a special pride in her?"

"Deep in my heart, Mr. Cooper, I find it very hard to take pride in someone who engages in an activity of which I disapprove. That doesn't mean I'm blind to my sister's beauty and talent."

"Aye, there's hope for you yet, Colin," Cooper said with a mischievous twinkle as he set the camera down opposite the pond and secured the tripod. "I knew you were too intelligent to be equating it with the *sin* of pride—which I must admit I've been all too guilty of as of late." He ducked beneath the blackout cloth and began framing the scene on the camera's glass.

"I find neither your conceit nor rude behavior at all flattering, Mr. Cooper," Colin said, his tone sharpening. "I don't care if you think I'm intelligent or not, which I *am*; or if you think I'm a church-going prude, which I am *not*. Am I a God-fearing man? Yes. And my faith is important to me. Of *that* I am very proud."

Cooper reappeared from beneath the blackout cloth and nodded emphatically. "And you have every right to be. I just sensed you weren't as offended by this *tawdry* activity as you'd expected."

"Make fun of me all you like, Mr. Cooper. But be warned.

I love my sister very much; and I would do anything, *anything*, to ensure her safety and virtue. As for this tawdry activity, the sooner we return home the better, which as you very well know is the reason—and the only reason—I agreed to it in the first place."

"Aye, but Grace is a grown woman, Colin. Has it ever occurred to you that perhaps she's able to decide what's best for her on her own?"

"As grown as she may be, Mr. Cooper, Grace is still blissfully naive, prone to take risks, and much too willing to think the best of people. All of which, along with her goodness, makes her easy prey for the predators of this world, of which there are many."

"Aye, I thought we'd found some common ground," Cooper said with a disappointed shake of his head. "But *I* find those traits to be strengths and *you* find them weaknesses. Besides, she's not as vulnerable as you think she is; though, I daresay, with each passing day, I find myself becoming more and more deeply motivated to protect her."

"I need no help from the likes of you, Mr. Cooper."

"I wasn't offering to help, Colin, but to relieve you of the burden."

"I'm more than happy to shoulder it," Colin replied, dismayed at the sight of Grace entering the pavilion. She was wearing the next ensemble to be photographed; it featured a low, loosely draped bodice. "Besides, you've already done enough damage."

"For example?" Cooper said, sounding amused.

"That disgraceful dress Grace is wearing."

"Oh, I was thinking more of danger than disgrace, Colin, such as those predators you seemed so worried about. I can't think of any you could protect her from that I couldn't."

Colin locked his eyes onto Cooper's and said, "I can, Mr. Cooper. I can protect her from *you*."

Chapter Twelve

When the last ensemble had been photographed, Cooper retreated to his makeshift darkroom. He worked round the clock for days to develop the negatives and produce the set of prints that would be used in the newspaper advertisements; and despite their commercial end, he was bursting with pride when he and Grace, whom he insisted accompany him, delivered them.

Georges Latour, along with Altman and Ogilvy, gathered anxiously around a long table in the emporium's main salon. Cooper began laying the prints out across the expanse of polished marble; and as eager as Latour was to see them, he seemed equally intrigued by Grace's presence and couldn't take his eyes from her. "I can see why you would have *'le rapport à spécial'* with this young lady, Coupaire. If it were not for Madame Latour, I could have one myself."

"I'm more than flattered, Mr. Latour," Grace said with a winsome smile. "But, as I'm sure Madame Latour would agree, more than one *'rapport à spécial'* is one *'rapport'* too many."

"*Mon Dieu*, a sense of humor, too!" Latour exclaimed as he began circling the table, his eyes widening with delight at

Cooper's pictures. *"Très magnifique, Coupaire!"* he exclaimed. *"Très, très magnifique!"*

Grace fired an excited glance at Cooper who was having little success suppressing a smile.

"They are everything I expected and more," Latour went on, the collector in him responding to their artistic excellence. "The dramatic compositions, the theatrical poses and sense of movement, the haunting diffusion of natural light—" He paused, prompting his colleagues with a look. *"Par excellence . . . Non?"*

Ogilvy and Altman exchanged anxious glances, neither wanting to be the first to say whatever had caused their foreboding silence.

"Are they not everything I say?!" Latour prompted again, unnerved by it. *"N'est pas?!"*

"Indeed they are, sir," Ogilvy finally replied. "Their artistic merit is undeniable and impressive. However, I'm concerned they will prove to be an advertising and commercial disaster."

"As am I," Altman chimed in smartly.

Latour's jaw slackened as if he'd been punched.

So did Cooper's. He shot an anxious glance to Grace who looked equally unsettled.

"Artistique?! Où commercial?!" Latour said, throwing up his hands in frustration. "The question in the mind is: Will they, or will they not, motivate women to buy this line of clothing?"

"They will not," Altman said with unequivocal finality. "They won't generate satisfactory sales volume."

"Pourquoi?!" Latour demanded, his eyes flaring.

Altman glanced to Grace and forced a smile. "Because, with all due respect to the young lady, the mannequin is too exotic looking, too—too European."

Latour's brows twitched with confusion. *"Trop exotique?* But she is the epitome of our carriage trade clientele, and more. *N'est pas?"*

"She certainly is," Ogilvy replied. "The epitome. But

these advertisements are intended to attract a different class of buyer; and those buyers are, well, less sophisticated, and more—more, for lack of a better term, full-figured women."

Altman was nodding emphatically, if grimly. "They won't be able to put themselves in the picture, so to speak, or, therefore, into the clothes."

"Furthermore, and with all due respect to the gentleman," Ogilvy said with a nod to Cooper, "these pictures are too painterly, much too . . . too museum-like. To put it bluntly, they just aren't commercial enough."

"Not commercial enough . . ." Cooper said under his breath, chewing on his pipe stem to maintain his composure.

"Yes," Ogilvy replied. "Perhaps, if I show you an example of what I have in mind?" Without waiting for a reply the suave, advertising director hurried off to one of the offices that ringed the salon. Cooper seethed, pacing like a caged animal until Ogilvy returned with a folder. He untied the ribbon and opened the flaps with a reverence that, had the folder contained Michelangelo sketches or pages from the DaVinci Codex, might have been appropriate. Cooper gave the prints a cursory inspection and scowled. "Stiffly posed, harsh lighting, pedestrian work at best."

"Exactly," Ogilvy replied. "That's exactly what we're looking for."

Latour grimaced with apprehension. "Do you think you could do something like that, Coupaire?"

"Not in a month of Sundays," Cooper replied without a flicker of hesitation. "You want to know what I really think, Mr. Latour?"

"*Mais oui,* Coupaire. I have nothing but respect for your opinion as well your talent."

"I think you hired the wrong photographer." With that Cooper swiftly gathered his prints and slipped them into the box; then, without a word, he strode out of the salon and headed down the grand staircase before Grace could stop him.

Chapter Thirteen

Cooper took the trolley back to South Boston, and headed straight for the Bonawe Furnace, a tavern just down the street from his rooming house. Named after a once legendary iron smelter in western Scotland, it served a hearty plowman's lunch, and smelled of stale beer and men who earned a living with their hands—men who gathered daily in a raucous crowd at the bar for a sandwich and midday draft.

Cooper sat alone at a table, staring into a half-empty tankard of ale that stood next to the box of rejected pictures. He'd been there about an hour when he sensed a presence and squinted through the haze to see Grace's willowy figure silhouetted against the bottle glass windows. "What brings you here, lass?" His voice had equal amounts of surprise, embarrassment, and concern. "This is no place for a lady."

"Yes, your landlady said as much," Grace replied, raising her voice above the din as she settled next to him. "I was concerned you'd be in the doldrums, Dylan. Not that you don't have a right after what happened."

"It was sweet of you to come all this way, Grace," Cooper said, touched by her gesture. "But a good wallow in them is just and proper punishment for compromising my principles, I suppose. And you, lass?"

"Well, it seems I'm no longer welcome at Monsieur Latour's emporium."

"Aye, guilt by association," Cooper concluded, feeling responsible.

"More like reckless abandon," Grace corrected with a mischievous grin. "That's what my mother would say. After you left I couldn't help but tell Latour and his minions I thought they were making a terrible mistake. He became quite unhinged and scolded me in French for what he called my *'insolence à très franche,'* which I imagine, thanks be to God, means I'll be spared further discomfort of his *'rapport à spécial'* innuendos."

Cooper chuckled heartily, envisioning the moment. "I'm sorry, I didn't mean to leave you standing there, but I'd have bloodied some noses if I hadn't." He drained the remaining ale from the tankard, then cocked his head curiously. "I thought you'd be at the gallery the rest of the day."

"As did I, but when I told Mr. Van Dusen what happened, the dear man gave me the afternoon off."

"Aye, makes two of us," Cooper said with a sarcastic cackle just as several garrulous men standing nearby burst into laughter at a joke that had just been told. One of them lost his balance and staggered backwards spilling beer across the table where Grace and Cooper were sitting. Cooper caught hold of the crude fellow just as he was about to go sprawling across Grace's lap, and helped him to his feet. "This *is* no place for a lady," Cooper said, tossing some change on the table. He tucked the box of pictures under his arm, then guided Grace through the crowd and out the door onto East Broadway, a cobbled street that ran arrow straight to the waterfront.

A brisk wind that carried a hint of spring and the fresh scent of brine was coming off the water. An armada of fishing boats returning to port extended to the horizon in a sweeping arc. Cooper and Grace walked arm in arm along the rows of slips where the vessels were docking with the day's catch.

"Lest you think I came all this way just to see if you were in the doldrums," Grace said coyly. "I've another reason as well."

Cooper gestured to some bushels of shellfish that were spilling over onto the dock. "You wouldn't have come in search of cockles and mussels alive, alive-o, now, would you?"

"Not a bad idea now that you mention it; but I came for those," Grace replied, pointing to the box of photographs he was carrying. "Latour and his fools may not want them but I do."

"And I'd like nothing better than for you to have them, Grace," Cooper said, sounding as if there was a reason she couldn't. "But what of Colin?"

Grace looked puzzled. "Colin?"

Cooper nodded. "I did promise him I'd destroy all the prints and negatives, now, didn't I?"

"Yes, I know," Grace said with a frustrated sigh. "But they're pictures of *me*, Dylan; and I want them."

"I gave my word, Grace, and I'm in the habit of keeping it."

"Yes, and an admirable habit it is, but Colin's request was terribly unreasonable; I see no reason why you should feel bound by it."

Cooper thought it over and nodded. "At best, they will be meager pay for all your hard work."

Grace studied him out of the corner of her eye. "You've no hope of being paid for yours, have you?"

Cooper shook his head no, his brow furrowing with concern. "What is it, lass? Are you in difficulty?"

"No. No, I'm fine," Grace replied, averting her eyes. "I was just wondering."

"Aye," Cooper said with understanding. "Colin will be wondering, too. Won't he?"

Grace nodded imperceptibly.

"Well, make my apologies and tell him I'll soon be back to avoiding the landlady and begging for grace periods," Cooper said, feeling lower than he had in months. "Not to mention I've no idea how I'll ever repay the advance I accepted from Mr. Van Dusen."

"He'll sell some of your pictures one day, Dylan. I know he will," Grace said, imploring him to believe it. "You can't lose faith in yourself."

"How could I with the likes of you around?" Cooper said, coaxing a smile out of her.

Grace stepped to the railing that ran along the water's edge and looked out across the harbor, her chin raised into the wind, her hair blowing in amber waves behind her, her long dress billowing like the mainsails of the ships at sea. The scene had an aesthetic and emotional power that raised Cooper's pores. He stood awestruck, feasting on it for a long moment; then, stepping closer, he put an arm around Grace's waist and tilted his head close to hers. "Can you stay with me for a while tonight, Grace?"

Grace turned to face him, her eyes filled with conflict. "Oh, Dylan, I want to," she replied, clearly torn by it. "But you know Colin will be worried. Not to mention he's expecting supper and I've yet to do my marketing."

"Aye," Cooper said forlornly. "Doubting Colin strikes again."

"Please try to understand," Grace pleaded, crushed by the disappointment in his voice. "I want to stay with you, Dylan; and truth be told I . . . I . . ." She paused, deciding whether or not she would continue. "I know I shouldn't be so forward as to say this. Lord knows it's not at all my place, but I want to stay with you forever, Dylan; and if you're of the same mind, given time, I've no doubt I shall."

"Aye, I've plenty of time, Grace, if you're saying what I think you're saying."

"Yes, I am," Grace replied in a tender whisper. "You know, my mother used to say good things come to those who wait."

The sound of a ship's bells rode the wind as Cooper gently embraced her, holding her eyes with his. "I'd wait a lifetime for you, Grace."

"And I for you," she said softly, her eyes glistening with emotion as she caressed his face with the tips of her fingers and kissed him.

Chapter Fourteen

Dusk had fallen by the time Grace took the trolley back to Cambridge and returned to her apartment. Colin was sitting at the dining table by the window writing a letter when she came through the door with the box of Cooper's photographs and a bag that contained some cockles she'd bought while walking the waterfront with him. There was something judgmental about the way Colin held himself, she thought, as she set her things on the opposite end of the table. Since that was the rule rather than the exception, she didn't pay it any mind until she noticed the mason jar on the table next to him. It was her piggy bank. She kept it in a kitchen cupboard and, every week when she got paid, she put some money into it that Colin used at the end of the month to pay the rent. "Grace?" he called out as she slipped out of her coat and hung it in the closet. "Grace, we're short a week's rent money."

Grace nodded with apprehension. "Yes, I know. I've been meaning to talk to you about it."

"There's no time like the present, is there?" he said drumming his fingers on the tabletop.

"It's quite simple," she replied. "I didn't get paid for the week I took off from the gallery."

"I wouldn't expect Mr. Van Dusen to pay you when you weren't working," Colin said, suddenly the voice of reason. "But what of the money for your . . . your modeling work? Cooper said it would pay well."

"Yes," Grace replied, wincing at what she was about to say. "I'm afraid I didn't get paid for that, either."

Colin folded his letter as if concealing its contents from her, then set it aside and got to his feet. "Cooper didn't pay you?" he asked, sensing his low opinion of him was about to be confirmed.

"No, you see, he *couldn't* pay me, because when he delivered the prints to Mr. Latour—"

"I knew it!" Colin exclaimed, interrupting. "He's cut from the same cloth as that crooked booking agent." He charged toward the door, rolling up his sleeves. "And he deserves the same fate!"

Grace hurried after him and caught hold of his arm as he opened the door. "No, no, wait! Listen, you don't understand. Dylan couldn't pay me because they rejected his pictures and refused to pay him."

Colin had pulled free, and was halfway out the door when Grace's words struck him. He took a moment to settle, then closed it and turned to face her. "They rejected them?" he asked, his eyes brightening. "You mean, they'll not appear in the newspapers?"

Grace nodded solemnly.

"Thanks be to God!" Colin exclaimed. "My prayers have been answered." He was enjoying the moment to the fullest when his eyes narrowed at the sight of the box on the table. "What is that, Grace?"

Grace knew all too well he meant the box of photographs, but picked up the paper bag next to it, instead. "Fresh cockles," she replied, hoping beyond hope to change the subject. "I'm going to make us a nice dinner." She took the bag and started for the kitchen without waiting for a reply.

"Not *that* Grace, *that*," Colin said, blocking her way and pointing to the box. "What is *that?*"

"A box, Colin. Just a box."

"What is *in* the box, Grace?"

"Pictures," Grace conceded, grudgingly. "The pictures Dylan took of me."

"The fashion pictures . . ."

Grace nodded.

"He gave me his word he'd destroy them."

"Yes and he intended to keep it, but I insisted otherwise."

"Why?"

"Because I wanted them."

"You wanted them?!" Colin said, raising his voice. "Well, the landlord wants the rent, Grace. I thought you were at work. Where did you find time to go all the way across town, today?"

"Mr. Van Dusen gave me the day off."

"You shirked your professional responsibilities to spend time with that shiftless photographer?"

"You sound like a jealous suitor, Colin. You're always reminding me you're my brother, perhaps it's time I reminded *you.*"

"I need no reminding, Grace. I promised Father I'd get you home safe and sound; and despite your lack of cooperation, I'll find a way to keep that promise."

"Has it ever occurred to you that I may not be going home with you, Colin?"

Colin recoiled as if slapped. "And why not?"

Grace responded with a sideways glance and a thin smile, then walked into the kitchen, carrying the bag of cockles.

Colin saw the answer in her expression and pursued her. "To take up with *him?!*" Colin demanded, beside himself. "No, no not *him!* You'll get hurt if that's what you're suggesting. I forbid it."

"I'll be fine," Grace said, taking a pot from the cupboard. "I can take care of myself."

"I know his type, Grace," Colin warned in the most foreboding tone he could manage. "He's a loner. What they call a rugged individualist. The kind of man who can't commit to a . . . a normal, stable lifestyle let alone the state of matrimony."

Grace set the pot in the sink and began filling it with water. "Matrimony?" she echoed calmly. "I didn't say anything about matrimony."

Colin emitted a relieved sigh. "Good, because there's someone at church, a gentleman who I've been meaning to introduce you to. He comes from a fine family and is a man of substance *and* means."

"I'm sure he is, Colin, and it's very thoughtful of you. But it's Mr. Cooper who has my heart."

"You're in love with him?!" Colin exclaimed, aghast at the thought. "In love with a shiftless artist?! With a man who by your own admission has no means?!"

"Such are the ways of the heart, Colin. And there's nothing you can say that will change how I feel."

"This is not acceptable, Grace," Colin protested, raising his voice. "He's too old. Too set in his ways. The man's at least forty if he's a day."

"Forty-two, actually," Grace replied undaunted. "And I'm sorry if it upsets you to hear it, but I've fallen in love with him."

Colin groaned with exasperation. "And he with you?"

"Suffice it to say, he's given me every indication of it, yes." She shut off the water, set the pot on the stove, then struck a match and lit the burner.

"Then I demand you ask Mr. Cooper if he has any intention of making an honest woman of you. If you won't, I promise you, I will."

"I *am* an honest woman, Colin," Grace protested, bristling with indignation. "And if you want some supper I suggest you refrain from implying otherwise."

"Does that mean he *hasn't* taken advantage of you?"

"No one can take advantage of me, Colin," Grace replied evenly. "And I'd have thought you of all people would know that by now."

"You still haven't answered my question, Grace."

"And I don't intend to," she said with the gentle elusiveness that he had always found frustrating. It was as if she enjoyed keeping him off balance and guessing. "It's not *my* honesty you should be questioning but your own," Grace went on, baiting him.

"Mine? What am I not being honest about?"

"About the fact that your obsession with the state of matrimony is a selfish one."

"Selfish?"

"Father would be furious if he thought you'd left me in Boston to fend for myself, wouldn't he?!"

"What's that got to do with it?"

"Be honest, Colin," she said, setting the hook she'd cast for him. "You want nothing more than to go home; and once I'm Cooper's wife, or anyone's wife for that matter, then— and only then—can you go."

"That's . . . that's . . . not fair . . ." Colin sputtered, stung by the truth, his hands splayed in futile objection.

Grace took the bag of cockles and dropped them into his outstreched palms. "These go in the water as soon as it starts to simmer. In the meantime, you can slice the carrots and those stalks of celery. As I said, I can care for myself. It's time you started doing the same." She strode into the parlor, took the box of photographs from the small dining table by the window and carried it to her bedroom.

She closed the door and looked about for a moment in search of a place to conceal it; then she bent to the dresser, opened one of the drawers, and slipped the box of photographs beneath some clothing. When she straightened, she caught sight of her reflection in the mirror above the dresser that revealed a profound sadness in her eyes. Colin was her brother. She loved him as he did her and she took no pleasure in hurting him; but the thought of Cooper and the feelings they'd shared that afternoon, feelings that she knew they would continue sharing for the rest of their lives, lifted her spirits and helped assuage her guilt. Maybe, she thought, just maybe, *better* things come to those who don't wait too long.

Chapter Fifteen

❧

Easter Sunday, March 31, 1918, dawned bright and balmy along the New England coast, and the first rays of light were creeping above the rooftops as Cooper shouldered his camera and left the rooming house.

South Boston's teeming neighborhoods were always quiet at this hour on Sunday. The clatter of hooves, the rumble of internal combustion engines, the harsh cacophony of men working on the docks were all stilled. Instead, it was the smell of creosote and brine that greeted Cooper as he walked along the waterfront to the spot where he and Grace had stopped a week before. He set down his camera and looked out across the harbor, reflecting on the time they had spent there. Shafts of light were streaming between the few boats that had put to sea and, like the fingers of an outstretched hand, seemed to be offering them up to the heavens.

As the boats moved across the rising sun, Cooper quickly positioned his camera on the wood decking, then bent to the ground glass and framed his picture. Suddenly, as if someone had thrown an electric switch, the backlighting illuminated their sails like paper lanterns against the nearly black water. He was about to fire the shutter when two seagulls, which had been soaring high above, peeled off in tandem and descended toward the water. Cooper sensed what would happen and waited, firing just as the two gulls came gliding through the frame. It was a providential moment, he thought, one that captured the special feelings he and Grace had shared when they were there, and now he had captured it for her.

After packing up his camera gear, he rewarded himself with a cup of bracing black coffee and a fresh pipeful of tobacco, then bought a newspaper and sat atop the seawall reading it.

The headline proclaimed: AMERICAN CASUALTIES MOUNT. The front-page story reported that despite three years of fierce fighting on the Western Front, neither side had been able to advance. British and French forces had been bogged down in the trenches on one side of no-man's-land. The Germans had been bogged down in trenches on the other. More than three million men had been killed in this standoff. Though the United States had declared war on Germany exactly one year ago, American troops had only just begun arriving in France, albeit in huge numbers, three hundred thousand in the month of March alone. The American Expeditionary Forces, under General Pershing, were now fighting alongside the French and British to break the stalemate. More and more doughboys were among the casualties. It seemed they were being killed and wounded faster than they could be replaced, and many more recruits were needed.

The story continued inside the paper, and when Cooper turned the page, he found himself staring at a recruiting poster that depicted Uncle Sam in his star-spangled jacket and striped pants. His eyes were fixed in a fierce gaze, and his forefinger was pointing directly at the reader in intimidating confirmation of the message that—in extremely large type across the top of the poster—exclaimed: UNCLE SAM WANTS YOU! And all other able-bodied men to sign up for military duty.

Cooper took a deep, thoughtful draw on his pipe and exhaled slowly. The wind took the smoke in a thin stream that stretched along the waterfront. He folded the newspaper and slipped it into his gadget bag, then shouldered the camera and headed back toward his rooming house where his dark-room awaited.

The city's neighborhoods had begun to come alive. Many of the residents, dressed in their Easter Sunday finery, were responding to the beckoning peal of church bells that were heralding the risen Christ.

The bells of the First Presbyterian Community Church on Auburn Street in East Cambridge were among them. It was a short walk from the apartment Grace and Colin shared, and they could feel the sound of its carillon resonating through the walls of the old house.

Colin had dressed in his Sunday best for church. He was straightening his tie when Grace emerged from her bed-room. She was wearing a floor length dress tied with a loose sash at the waist. The pale green silk was printed with a pat-tern of delicate spring flowers.

"Happy Easter, Grace," Colin said cheerily. "What a lovely dress. Does it mean you've decided to join me at church?"

"No, it means while I was at the salon being fitted, Mr. Latour offered me my pick of the ensembles, and I chose this one."

"Oh," Colin said, wishing he hadn't said it.

"Besides, it's too lovely a day to be indoors. I'm meeting Dylan at the Common."

"At what time?"

"About noon. Why?"

"Well, the Easter service is at ten. That would still give you plenty of time. And considering your circumstances, it's a perfect opportunity to pray for divine guidance."

"If you're referring to my feelings for Dylan, *I* believe it was divine guidance that brought us together."

"But it's Easter, Grace," Colin said, imploring her. "You've always had a special place for it. Remember when we were children we'd go to church together and buy scones afterwards on the way home?"

"We're not children anymore, Colin. Please try to remember that." Grace turned away from him and walked to the window that overlooked the street.

"Grace, please? Can't we put this contention behind us? I know we've had some difficult moments as of late, but you know I'm always well-intentioned."

"Yes," she sighed, sounding contrite as she turned to face him. "Truth be told, I suppose I do."

"Good, because I was thinking, since it's Easter, perhaps *we* could have a new beginning. Come to church with me, Grace? Please? I've a feeling it would give us the strength to put our differences aside." He paused and in an earnest tone, added, "And if *my* truth were to be told, nothing would make me happier."

Grace was both surprised and moved by his unabashed sincerity. She took a moment to sort out her feelings, then nodded, and in a commanding voice, said, "Under one condition—there'll be no matchmaking with any of your fellow church members from fine families with substance and means. Agreed?"

"Agreed," Colin echoed grudgingly.

"Raise your right hand," Grace commanded smartly. "Do you, Colin MacVicar, swear here and now before Almighty God to abide by this agreement, cross your heart and hope to die, with the Lord as your witness?"

Grace had recited the oath they had sworn as children, verbatim; and Colin couldn't help but picture his little sister, hands on hips, pigtails bristling, face scrunched in a pout, swearing him to do, or not do, whatever it was she wanted. The memory touched him deeply and brought a wistful smile to his face.

The flicker of joy was a welcome respite from the usual flash of anger. Grace couldn't recall when she had last seen anything remotely like it from Colin; and she was suddenly glad she had agreed to accompany him.

The First Presbyterian Community Church was crafted of stone blocks and hand-hewn timbers that had survived hundreds of harsh New England winters and a raging fire set by Redcoats during the Revolution. Beams of light shone through its stained glass windows that depicted biblical themes and scripture. Exhuberant sprays of lilies encircled the altar and the crucifix adjacent to the crow's nest pulpit. Pastor John Forsyth stood beneath its sounding board, which would project his voice to the most distant pew. His black robe displayed insignia that, to those familiar with the symbols of academia, meant he held a doctorate from the Yale Divinity School.

"Well, I see you all look stunning in your Easter attire on this most significant of Christian holidays," Pastor Forsyth began in his mellifluous baritone. "The new beginning we celebrate each year at Easter brings to mind the three women who came to Christ's tomb to find the angel who had rolled away the stone waiting for them. On seeing their profound sadness, he greeted them with the words, 'He is not here, He is risen as He said!'" Pastor Forsyth paused, his voice resonating in the hushed silence, then he repeated the angel's greeting, emphasizing each word. "And that's the real message of Easter. And when we add to that Jesus's promise, 'because I live, you too shall live,' we understand that His resurrection guarantees our own.

"Indeed, it is Christ's resurrection that makes Easter the most important of Christian holidays. For without it there would be no Christianity, no salvation and no eternal life. Most importantly, the resurrection of Jesus answers the question, Who really is Jesus Christ? In case you're wondering, He is the person who died for the sins of the whole world.

"As I look at you beautiful people today, it is hard to think of you as sinners. But as we know, the Bible says '. . . all have sinned and come short of the glory of God.' That is why Jesus sacrificed Himself on the cross and rose again three days later, so that we might have forgiveness of our sins and eternal life.

"You know, the resurrection came as no surprise to Jesus. He knew the prophets had clearly predicted it, and He went them one better. Yes, He, Himself, predicted nine times that He would rise again 'the third day.'

"As we gather here nineteen hundred years later, it's important to note that He did not rise the fourth day, or the sixth day, but the *third* day exactly as He predicted! After the resurrection, Jesus showed Himself alive to His disciples and followers for a period of forty days. Why? Because seeing the empty tomb did not turn them into believers—*seeing Christ risen did*! I'm sure you all recall Thomas, the doubting disciple, who would not believe unless he could put his fingers into the nail wounds on His hands; and then, on seeing the risen Christ, fell at His feet and worshiped Him.

"What I find incredible is that all of Christianity is built upon the resurrection of its founder. His is the only tomb in the world that is famous because it is empty. There are many tombs in this world that contain the bones of famous people. But His tomb is famous for what it does *not* contain. This is further evidence that He really did rise from the dead.

"But, you know, the Bible doesn't expect us to become believers because it says so, or even because of tradition. The prophet Isaiah said, 'Come now let us reason together, saith the Lord, though your sins be as scarlet, they shall be as white as snow.' In other words, faith is not like a viral infection that strikes some people and not others. It is the result of reason based squarely on the Scripture. Yes, we need to find *reasons* for believing. Here are just a few.

"The body of Jesus was never found. If it existed, surely his enemies would have used it to discredit the disciples who were preaching that he rose from the dead.

"History shows that before the resurrection of Jesus, the

disciples were so timid and afraid they forsook him and fled. After they met the resurrected Christ, they were so infused by the fire of the Holy Spirit, they all became powerful evangelists.

"Their efforts to spread the word of Christ were so successful, their enemies sentenced them to death. Even as they were being executed by stoning, beheading, and crucifixion, every one of them still said Jesus rose from the dead. Would they have *all* died for a lie? Perhaps six, perhaps ten, but twelve out of twelve?!

"We owe much to those twelve men who died for the cause of Christianity; and today, we owe much to the many young men of America who have given their lives for the cause of freedom. Exactly one year ago, when this great country of ours officially entered the war in Europe, I asked you to pray for their safety. On *this* Easter Sunday, I'm asking you to pray for their souls."

Pastor Forsyth paused and bowed his head in prayer as did the congregation; then he resumed, "The simple fact that you are all here today and that you identify yourselves as Christian is evidence that you believe in Christ's resurrection. You may have been baptized as a baby, gone through confirmation, even been married in the church. But have you ever made your faith personal by inviting Christ to come into your heart to cleanse your sins and save your soul? Like doubting Thomas of old, are you willing to say to Him, You are 'my Lord and my God, this day I give my life to you'?

"Since we're commemorating our Savior's sacrifice for our sins, I'm asking you to publicly acknowledge your personal faith in Christ and His resurrection by standing in testimony of that faith." Pastor Forsyth made an uplifting gesture with his arms, bringing many members of the congregation to their feet.

Colin was among them. He had been powerfully moved by the sermon, recognizing that the pastor had been speaking about someone like *him*. Indeed, *he* had been born into a

Christian family, baptized and confirmed, but had never had a personal experience of receiving Christ. Colin touched his sister's hand and smiled sweetly. "Come with me, Grace. Let's join those who are taking the Lord into their hearts."

"He *is* in my heart, Colin," Grace whispered in reply. "I've no need to make a show of it."

"I think it would be a fitting commencement to *our* new beginning to do this together, don't you?"

"Coming here with you was commencement enough, Colin," Grace replied softly.

"Please, I'm going to commit my heart to Christ, Grace, and it would make me happy if you did the same."

"I want you to be happy, Colin," Grace replied, glancing at her watch. "But my heart is committed to Dylan Cooper. And though I found the sermon eloquent and thought provoking, its duration has made me late."

Colin sighed with resignation, then walked toward the altar with other members of the congregation who had responded to Pastor Forsyth's call. For several moments, Colin knelt before the crucifix, his head bowed in prayer as the pastor asked God's blessing be bestowed upon those who had come forward. When Colin returned to the pew, Grace was gone.

Chapter Sixteen

Boston Common was a public park in the heart of downtown encircled by the wealthy enclaves of Beacon Hill and Back Bay, and the government and financial districts. The massive parcel of land was a pastoral landscape of rolling meadows, stands of lush trees, and vast plains of shrubs traversed by carriage drives and pedestrian walks. It adjoined the Botanical Gardens, which were set around a meandering lake, on the opposite side of Charles Street.

Every Easter, it seemed as if all the residents of the city made their way to the Common after church services and the Easter Parade; and it was crowded with couples strolling arm in arm, gentlemen in their Easter finery, ladies in their ensembles and bonnets; young mothers pushing prams, children playing catch, and entire families picnicking on the broad lawns.

Cooper was sitting on a bench at the west end of the lake when Grace came walking toward him aglow in her Georges Latour dress that blended with the blossoming springtime landscape.

"Happy Easter, Dylan," she called out.

"Happy Easter, lass," Cooper echoed as he got up from

the bench and embraced her. Then, taking a step back, he swept his eyes over her appreciatively. "Look at you . . ." he exclaimed, starting to laugh at what he was about to say, "You're as pretty as a picture I once took."

Grace laughed along with him. "Yes, it's at home in my dresser with all the others."

"You can add this one to your collection," Cooper said, getting her undivided attention. He unfolded the newspaper and removed a print of the photograph he had taken that morning of the waterfront at sunrise. He had returned to his rooming house in plenty of time to process and print the negative prior to taking the trolley across town to the Common.

"Oh, it's lovely," Grace said, clearly moved by it.

"See?" Cooper prompted, indicating the seagulls. "Two lovebirds soaring in the clouds. Just like us."

"You mean one's a boy gull and one's a girl?"

"Aye, that they are."

"I can't imagine how you can tell?"

"Well, I'm sure we can agree that, like you, this one is obviously the younger and more beautiful of the two, and is therefore the girl."

"Obviously . . ."

"By the process of elimination," Cooper went on, "the other weather-beaten one with the scarred beak and the ruffled feathers, like me, must be the boy."

"Beauty and the beast, is that it?" Grace teased.

"Perhaps we can be a bit more charitable than that. How about beauty and the chap with the finely chiseled—"

"Beauty and the old warhorse?" she interrupted, bursting into laughter.

Cooper laughed along with her, then his expression darkened. "There won't be many of them around after this war, I'm afraid. Have you seen the paper?" He held it up displaying the headline.

Grace winced at its message. "No, but the pastor spoke of

it this morning," she replied sadly. "It was a very moving sermon."

"You attended an Easter service?" Cooper said momentarily surprised. "Ah, Colin, I suppose."

"Yes, he really wanted me to accompany him. I just couldn't say no. Actually, I'm glad I went."

Cooper nodded, offered her his arm and they began walking along the edge of the lake. She in her Georges Latour ensemble, he in his tweed jacket, plaid shirt, and worn corduroys, somehow in perfect compliment and contrast. They had gone a distance around the curving bank when they stopped to watch some children sailing toy boats. Cooper lit his pipe and tossed the flaming match into the water, then glanced over at Grace. "So, is he going to sign up?" he prompted, broaching the subject, obliquely.

"Colin? For the military?"

Cooper exhaled a stream of smoke and nodded.

"I don't know. He's never said anything about—" She paused as the real reason Cooper had asked suddenly dawned on her. "Oh dear, Dylan, please tell me you haven't."

"I haven't."

"Oh," she sighed, relieved. "Thanks be to God."

"But I feel a strong obligation," Cooper confided. "I've not one country to serve, Grace, but two."

Grace's posture slackened. "But why? Just when we're starting to see a life together . . ."

Cooper's eyes softened with empathy. "I know, lass. It's been weighing on me all morning."

"It's just not fair."

"Aye, not a'tall," Cooper said, visibly distraught. "The trouble is the Germans have not only taken Belgium and invaded France, but, according to the paper, they have far grander designs."

"Yes, everyone's saying Great Britain will be next. Despite the Channel, Calais is still closer to London than Paris. Isn't it?"

"Aye, I'm afraid so. They have to be stopped. If everyone turns a deaf ear, they'll overrun the whole of Europe. Look!" He tapped the newspaper headline with the stem of his pipe. "Young Americans are giving their lives for *us*, Grace. They're dying to protect your family and mine. How could I fail to sign up?"

Grace lunged into his arms, hugging him tightly. "Oh, I know you're right," she said in an anxious whisper. "I'm afraid your sense of duty only makes me love you more." She tightened her grasp, then leaned away slightly and looked up into his eyes. "I don't want to be a lone seagull, Dylan. I've been one for too long."

"As have I," Cooper said softly, embracing her.

They spent the remainder of the afternoon together in the Common, holding hands and embracing more than they spoke, for there was little left to be said other than the heart-felt expressions of affection and emotion they shared; and there was a haunting sadness in their eyes when they parted.

"I'll wait a lifetime for you, Dylan," Grace said, kissing him for what might be the last time.

"And I for you," Cooper said, softly, when their lips reluctantly parted.

Chapter Seventeen

⌢

Early the next morning, Cooper went to the Army Induction Center in the Federal Building on Congress Street. He joined the line of enlistees that already extended out the door, down the steps, and across the pavement to the corner and beyond. Some of the faces were filled with the eager innocence of boys still in their teens, others were etched with the weary concern of men well past middle age.

Several hours later, Cooper found himself in a massive assembly hall. Long tables ran in parallel rows across the cavernous space where hundreds of men sat filling out registration forms.

In the box labeled Occupation, Cooper wrote: *Photographer*. Though he assigned no special significance to it, the officer who reviewed his paperwork took note of it. Seated behind one of the many processing desks that ringed the hall, he wore a crisply pressed uniform with captain's bars on the epaulets and a field of campaign ribbons and medals carefully arranged above the left breast pocket. "Take a seat," he said as he looked up from the forms Cooper had filled out. "So, you're a professional photographer, Mr. Cooper?"

"I'm an artist," Cooper replied, sitting upright in the chair. "I don't take commercial assignments."

"But you're professionally trained. It says here you attended the University of Glasgow."

"Aye, the School of Technical Arts, they called it," Cooper said with a disdainful scowl.

"But you didn't graduate . . ."

"I ran out of funds, I'm afraid."

The Captain smiled knowingly. "I'd have given anything to have had someone like you in my unit when I was over there."

Cooper looked puzzled. "What could *I* have done that any of the others couldn't?"

"Field intelligence," the Captain replied smartly. "I used to play cards with an officer who was heading up an Air Force squadron at the time. Bright fellow. Always thinking. Well, he had this idea to take pictures of enemy troop emplacements."

Cooper's eyes widened with intrigue. "You mean, he wanted to take a camera up in a plane and take pictures of the ground."

"Exactly. *I* thought it quite clever, too," the Captain said, seeing Cooper's reaction. "He called it aerial reconaissance. Sixty-three of my men would still be alive if you, or someone like you, had been there."

Cooper's jaw dropped. "Sixty-three?" he repeated in an incredulous whisper.

The Captain nodded grimly. "We were trying to evacuate some wounded from a ravine and got caught in a crossfire. We had no way of knowing there were enemy machine-gun positions above us on both sides. It was like shooting fish in a barrel. A bloodbath. Just one aerial picture would've . . ." He let the sentence fade off with a grimace, then slipped Cooper's paperwork into a file folder and printed his name on it. "Get in that line for your physical," he said, gesturing to it with the folder. "The doc'll have this by the time you reach him."

Cooper nodded tight-lipped and got to his feet. He was about to leave when the Captain pushed back in his chair and did the same. Cooper recoiled slightly, his eyes widening in shock at what the desk had, up to this moment, concealed: The Captain was standing on one leg. The other had been amputated above the knee and the lower half of his pants was pinned up against his thigh. Cooper was momentarily paralyzed, neither able to speak nor move. The Captain fetched a pair of crutches that was leaning in the corner behind his desk and set them under his arms, then noticed Cooper standing there slack jawed. "Get in that line," the Captain commanded.

The officer's sharp tone pulled Cooper out of it and sent him hurrying across the hall. From the end of the long queue, Cooper watched as the Captain secured his file folder in the Y of one of his crutches, then made his way on them to a nearby office. The door was open and another officer came from behind his desk to join the Captain who opened Cooper's folder and began gesturing to its contents, animatedly, as he spoke.

In the military, the joke was that truck drivers ended up as clerks, clerks ended up as pilots, and pilots ended up as truck drivers. At least for the moment, it seemed to Cooper that a photographer might just end up as a photographer with a chance to save lives rather than take them; and the possibility propelled him through the remainder of the induction process with a clear sense of purpose and resolve.

Chapter Eighteen

Grace spent the day at the gallery, trying to lose herself in work, but she couldn't stop thinking about Cooper. Would she see him again before he went off to war? Would she ever see him again at all? Try as she might, she couldn't keep her mind on the paintings she was cataloguing, and when Van Dusen discovered an error, she apologized and confided in him. Despite his efforts throughout the day to lift her spirits, she was still out of sorts when she returned home that evening.

After dinner, Grace settled with the evening paper beneath the glow of a flickering gaslight; and like a moth to a flame, read every word of every story that had anything to do with the war in Europe, which further unsettled her.

"You're awfully quiet, Grace," Colin prompted. He signed a letter he had been writing, then slipped it into an envelope and addressed it.

"I should think you'd be pleased," Grace said from behind the newspaper.

"So would the family," Colin teased. "I sent them your love. I hope you don't mind?"

"Not at all. Though I should think they've more than enough of it with all the letters you send."

Colin forced a smile, then crossed to the closet and slipped the envelope into a pocket in his coat. "You know, whenever you get like this it's because you're unhappy about something." He hooked a finger in the fold of the newspaper, peering over the top of it at her. "And though I don't approve of your seeing Cooper, I must admit it's made you quite the opposite. So I can only conclude you've had some sort of a spat."

"Well, your conclusion is incorrect," Grace retorted with a dismissive snap of the newspaper.

"Very well, but knowing you as I do, I'm quite certain it has something to do with him."

"What if it does?" Grace said, remaining hidden behind the newspaper. "It's still no business of yours."

"I'm your brother Grace. If he's done something that's made you unhappy, well, I think—"

"He enlisted today," Grace interrupted sharply. She lowered the newspaper and glared at him.

"Really? Enlisted?" Colin echoed, brightening; then laughing at what he was about to say next, added, "Oh, I wouldn't be concerned if I were you, Grace. They're looking for men, not *old* men."

"That's not funny, Colin," Grace protested. "As a matter of fact it's horrid and . . . and uncharitable. I don't see *you* enlisting."

"*I'm* not faced with the looming prospect of making a lifetime commitment to a young lady, now, am I?"

Grace tossed the paper aside and leapt from the chair. "How dare you suggest Dylan would enlist merely to avoid the . . . the 'state of matrimony' as you call it."

"No need to get so upset, Grace," Colin counseled coolly. "As you might imagine, I'm glad to be rid of him, whatever his reasons."

Grace's face reddened with anger. "I've put no pressure

on Dylan. None whatsoever, and you know it. Being together is all that matters to me."

"Please," Colin said, rolling his eyes. "No need to remind
me. These things have a way of working out for the best.
You'll see."

"He's a good man, a courageous man," Grace went on in
passionate defense of Cooper. "I'm going to miss him terribly."

"You have your opinion of him and I have mine," Colin
said in his haughty way, which further incensed her. "If you
ask me, I think the war appeals more to his sense of adventure than his sense of patriotism."

"You can't bring yourself to admit he's well-motivated,
can you, Colin?"

Colin folded his arms and shook his head with dismay.
"You know, Grace, it's very disappointing that we still
haven't found a way to air our differences without you getting so worked up over them."

"*You're* the one who gets worked up, Colin," Grace retorted, jabbing a finger at him. "I've grown weary of your incessant antagonism. This new beginning, which you pined
for, is turning out to be terribly one-sided."

"I care about what's best for you, Grace, and—" Several
sharp raps on the door interrupted him, indeed startled him
since he was standing next to it. Colin undid the latch, then
opened the door and groaned at the sight of Cooper standing
in the hallway. "I told you he was a bad penny, Grace."

Grace nearly knocked Colin over as she dashed across the
room. "Dylan?" she exclaimed, looking as confused as she
did excited as he stepped inside and closed the door. "I was
afraid you'd be sent off for training immediately. How long
have we before you're to report?"

A funny smile broke across Cooper's face. "We've a lifetime, Grace."

"A lifetime? I don't understand."

"They turned me down."

Colin sighed like a deflating balloon.

Grace lunged into Cooper's arms bursting with joy. "I'll put up some water for tea," she said, calling back over her shoulder as she headed into the kitchen. "I don't know whether to cheer or cry."

"So what was it," Colin asked, rhetorically. "Poor vision, flat feet or . . . your artistic bent?"

Cooper glared at him, angered by the innuendo. "Be advised, Colin, it was my artistic bent that caused them to consider me at all!"

"I see. So then what was it that ultimately did you in?"

Cooper seethed, loath to reveal the reason. "My age," he finally replied, unable to conceal his chagrin and disappointment. "The limit is thirty for general conscripts and, in my case, forty for technical specialists."

"Did you hear that, Grace?" Colin prompted, trumpeting his Pyrrhic victory. "I told you."

"You certainly did, Colin!" Grace said, her voice ringing with unbridled enthusiasm and an equal measure of sarcasm. "Things do have a way of working out, don't they?"

And in the weeks that followed, they did. Grace spent her days at the gallery and Cooper went camping. Not because he was in need of solitude and soul-searching as he had been earlier, but because he needed to throw himself into his work.

Venturing off alone on a photographic expedition, he took the train that ran along the coast to the fishing village of Gloucester about thirty miles north of Boston. Camera and tripod balancing on one shoulder, gadget bag and survival gear hanging from the other, Cooper spent weeks exploring and photographing the area. He hiked vast distances one day and, coming upon something of visual intrigue, stayed put the next. But it was the village of Newbury, nestled in a cove just south of the New Hampshire line, that inspired him beyond anything he had seen. Taken by its dense wilderness, rugged coastline, small town charm and hearty people, all of which powerfully reminded him of home, he remained there taking pictures until he ran out of film.

Cooper returned to Boston immediately and spent the next week in his makeshift darkroom processing and printing the negatives. When finished, he took the trolley across town to the Van Dusen gallery and surprised Grace.

"I've no appointment I'm afraid," Cooper said with a grin, handing her a box of prints.

"I'll have to clear it with Mr. Van Dusen," she said, playing along, before erupting with delight at the sight of him. Cooper enfolded her in his arms, holding her tightly, his head swimming with the scent of her perfume. When he finally released her, she took a moment to catch her breath and straighten her clothing. Then she opened the box and began sorting through the prints. Her eyes were soon sparkling with delight at what they beheld. "Oh, Dylan, they're breathtaking. Just breathtaking. They have something special, extra special."

"Aye, I've had the same feeling for weeks."

"And these . . ." Grace paused and sorted through the prints again, this time culling out the ones of Newbury. "These remind me so much of home."

"I knew they would, lass," Cooper said, his eyes aglow at sharing it with her. "I had the same reaction. Newbury. Just up the coast a ways."

"You must take me there one day. Will you?"

"Of course, lass."

"Promise?"

Cooper responded with an emphatic nod. "We'll need to get some proper transportation first. It took me a week to get there and a week back with a lot of camping out along the way."

"Oh, I can't wait for Mr. Van Dusen to see these!" Grace exclaimed, spacing out the prints on the long table. She selected one—a picture of a wave smashing against a rock formation filling the air with sparkling droplets of water—and set it on the easel, then hurried off to fetch Van Dusen from a back room where paintings were stored in racks that went from floor to ceiling.

"Good to see you, Cooper," Van Dusen said with an enthusiastic handshake. "Grace seems to think you've outdone yourself." He stepped to the table and swept his eyes over the photographs, his head nodding, tilting, bobbing in agreement at each and every one. "Indeed, up to your standard and beyond," Van Dusen said, his voice breaking with emotion at the sight of the print on the easel. "Oh, yes, breathtaking to be sure. Your time will come, Cooper. I've no doubt of it."

Cooper's brows arched with uncertainty. "Aye, but I'm getting the feeling that as far as the Van Dusen gallery is concerned, it hasn't come yet, has it?"

"I'm afraid not," Van Dusen replied with a sigh. "The war has had an enormously depressive effect on the art market. My clientele are more risk averse than ever. They aren't buying much of anything. I suspect the only thing they're investing in these days is gold."

"Well, they won't go to waste," Cooper said sarcastically. "I'll put them away and burn them next winter for warmth."

Van Dusen's head tilted as if struck by a thought. "I wouldn't do that if I were you."

"And why not?"

"Because someone who might be interested in them, perhaps in all of them, just came to mind," Van Dusen replied with growing excitement.

"All of them?" Cooper echoed, astounded.

Van Dusen nodded, then turned to a bookcase and began searching for something.

"One or two would be sufficient," Cooper went on. "But dozens? I'd be a fool to believe it, and they'd be fools to do it."

"Fools or not, they've been around since the late eighties, if I recall correctly," Van Dusen replied, looking through the publications on the shelf. "Here we are . . ." He pulled a thick pamphlet from between some books and handed it to Cooper. It had a bright yellow border and large typography that proclaimed: The National Geographic Society. "You familiar with them?"

"Nope, can't say that I am," Cooper replied, as he thumbed through it and the pages of black and white photographs it contained.

"Well, it came recently," Van Dusen explained. "It seems they're soliciting material: scholarly writings, photographs. The Society also funds geographic explorations. They subscribed a substantial sum to Admiral Peary's expeditions to the North Pole."

"This is high quality work," Cooper said, clearly impressed by the pictures in the pamphlet. "Very high quality work. All of it."

Van Dusen nodded and took the pamphlet from Cooper. "And as I recall, they reward it with high quality pay." He turned to the inside of the front cover, scanning it until he found what he was after, then read aloud, "'Organized for the increase and diffusion of geographic knowledge. Articles and photographs are desired. For material which the Society can use . . . *generous remuneration is made*.'"

"For material which the Society can *use*," Cooper admonished. "With my luck, they won't be remunerating me for my pictures, they'll just be returning them."

"Perhaps," Grace chimed in. "But as a soon to be famous photographer once said . . . 'There's only one way to find out,' isn't there?"

"You're just all sugar and spice and everything nice, aren't you, lass?" Cooper teased in response to her using his own argument against him.

"I wouldn't count on everything nice," Grace retorted with a mischievous grin.

"I suppose I could settle for two out of three," Cooper said, matching it. "But I'm afraid you're both forgetting that soon to be famous photographer found out something he didn't want to find out."

Despite his skepticism, with Grace's assistance, Cooper selected and packaged several dozen prints between sheets of cardboard in an envelope that she addressed to the National Geographic Society, Hubbard Memorial Hall, Washington, D.C. As the pamphlet instructed, Cooper included a similar self-addressed, stamped envelope in which rejected material would be returned. He also included a sheet of paper on which he wrote: *Might you be able to use any of these?* And signed his name.

"I've got a good feeling about this," Van Dusen said as they sealed the envelope.

"So do I," Grace said. "Dylan's time has come."

"Well," Cooper said with a wily smile, "I'm *tempted* to agree. But I've learned from bitter experience not to trust it."

Chapter Nineteen

❦

"Mr. Cooper? Mr. Cooper?" the landlady called out. Cooper had just returned to the rooming house after a sandwich and midday draft at the Bonawe Furnace when she came running down the corridor after him. "I have something for you, Mr. Cooper. Came this morning," she went on, waving an envelope at him, which she seemed intent on retaining. "I can't imagine why some *society*, in Washington, D.C. no less, would be sending post to the likes of you?"

Weeks had passed since Cooper had mailed his photographs to The National Geographic Society. One look at the envelope, which the landlady finally relinquished, set his heart to pounding. He had no doubt it was the self-addressed, stamped envelope he had included at the Society's request; but it was as thin as if it were empty; and obviously hadn't been used to return the prints he had sent them.

Instead, it contained a one page letter on the Society's beautifully engraved stationery. Its well-crafted paragraphs of praise, encouragement, and interest in acquiring more of Cooper's work left no doubt that Van Dusen was right! The National Geographic Society had bought every one of Cooper's photographs; and, as the enclosed check confirmed, it meant every word of its offer, because the amount more than qualified as "generous remuneration."

Cooper had never had enough money, let alone *extra* money, and therefore never needed a safe place to keep it; but having suddenly acquired both, he opened a savings account at South Boston Savings and Loan on Dorchester Street. The next thing he did was pay back Van Dusen the advance he had taken against the Latour assignment.

After so many years of struggling to make ends meet, Cooper wanted to enjoy the sense of security his windfall provided, not squander it; but there was something he had always wanted. It would be useful in his work and would require he expend but a small percentage of his funds. He considered having Grace come along to advise him on the purchase, but decided to surprise her instead, and made it on his own.

The next day was Saturday. Cooper and Grace had been spending weekends together and this one would be the same—with one exception. He paid the landlady for the use of the rooming house phone and placed a call to the gallery. When Grace answered, Cooper suggested that rather than meeting at her apartment—as was their habit before going off into the city—they meet at the trolley stop down the street instead. To Grace's bemusement and intrigue, he humorously refused to divulge the reason.

Grace was there at the appointed hour, expecting Cooper to get off the trolley or come sauntering around the corner at any moment; but a half hour later, there still wasn't any sign of him. She was about to leave when the incessant honking of a horn got her attention. She turned in the direction of the sound and saw a gray pickup truck barrelling down the street toward her.

Cooper was behind the wheel, depressing the horn with one hand and waving out the window with the other.

The truck ground to a stop beside Grace with a chilling screech of its mechanical brakes. It had a two-passenger cab and an enclosed cargo bed in which Cooper's camera, tripod, and boxes of gear were secured. The fenders were dinged and the running boards were worn, but it had a sturdy look to it and the engine seeemed to be running with surprising smoothness.

"What's this?" Grace asked with astonishment.

"A proper mode of transportation," Cooper replied with a jaunty air. He reached across the seat and unlatched the passenger door, letting it swing open. "Climb aboard, lass. We're going for a ride!"

"Newbury?" Grace prompted with hope and excitement in her voice.

"Aye, Newbury it is." He put the truck in gear and drove off. "Sorry to be so tardy, but the engine refused to turn over. I suppose it's going to take me awhile to get the hang of cranking it."

"I'm sure you'll get the 'hang' of it," Grace said with a laugh, mimicking him as he made the turn onto Main Street, which ran arrow straight to the Longfellow Bridge, depositing them in the North End. Cooper negotiated the knot of interconnecting roads taking Route 1, the Boston Post Road, the main coastal highway that ran north from New York through Connecticut and Massachusetts to the New Hampshire line and beyond.

Still, it took over two hours to cover the forty miles to Newbury. Finally, the quaint, small town architecture and shop-lined streets that fanned out from its snug harbor where a small armada of vessels bobbed at anchor, came into view.

Grace could hardly contain her excitement at the sight of it, which raised her pores. "Oh, it is so much like home, Dylan! I can hardly believe it!"

"Nor I," Cooper said, equally enthused. "I've a feeling that I could spend the rest of my days here."

He and Grace spent the day exploring the town and surrounding area. They drove past the shops on Sycamore Street where a youngster, named Joe Clements, was sweeping the sidewalk in front of his father's printing shop; and had an impromptu lunch—of bread, cheese and wine—on a rock jetty that swept out into the placid waters of Newbury Cove. Far below, sixth-grader Alicia Johnson, her fists locked around the oars of a bobbing dinghy, was being taught to row by her father.

It was mid-afternoon when Cooper pulled into the one-pump gas station where a sign proclaimed: GAS 8¢ GA, and asked the proprietor, an older fellow in a pair of grease-smudged coveralls, to fill the tank.

"Look at that," Grace said, pointing to another sign, this one in the station's window, which advertised: Cottage For Sale $1,200.

Cooper shrugged. "What of it?"

"I think we should inquire about it."

"Why?"

"I don't know. Just a feeling, I guess. Aren't you the one who said you could spend the rest of your days here?"

"Aye, but not by spending my last penny to do it," Cooper replied. "I came here intending to buy a few gallons of gasoline, Grace, not a cottage."

"I know, but sometimes things happen for a reason, Dylan," she said with a playful wiggle of her brows. "It seems almost providential if you ask me."

"You're starting to sound like Colin, if you ask *me*," Cooper joked. "It will be the most expensive fill up this fellow's ever had."

"Why don't you find out where it is?"

Cooper grimaced.

"*I'll* ask him, all right?" Grace got out of the cab without waiting for an answer and approached the old fellow who was filling the tank.

"It's just a short drive up the coast," he replied to Grace's query. "Up on a hill, view of the harbor, property's real nice, too." He went on to explain he had put the cottage up for sale because his children had grown and were long gone and he and his wife had recently moved into town. "Got the keys right here." He slipped them from a pocket in his coveralls and handed them to Grace, then sketched a map and jotted a few directions on a slip of paper she took from her handbag. "It needs some work, but you'll see it's worth the price. Of course, if a nice young couple really wanted it . . ." He let it trail off with its implication, then pulled the nozzle from the fill pipe and hung it on the pump. "Twelve and a half gallons," he said to Cooper, stepping to the driver's side window, "makes it exactly a dollar. No charge for directions," he added jovially.

Cooper's brow furrowed with confusion. He swung a look to Grace who had gotten back into the cab and was settling next to him. "Directions to where?"

"To a new beginning," Grace replied, displaying the slip of paper and the keys to the cottage, which were dangling inches from Cooper's nose on the ring she held between thumb and forefinger.

Chapter Twenty

A short time later, Cooper was guiding the pickup through the twisting turns of the two-lane blacktop that snaked along the coastline. Waves were smashing against the craggy rocks, sending up sprays of water that spattered across the windshield.

"There should be a dirt road coming up on the right," Grace said, navigating from the map.

Cooper found it and made the turn. The unpaved road climbed a steep hill, then flattened out across a plateau at the summit; and there, beneath a stand of trees that were bending in the wind, stood a weathered cottage. Rambling was the adjective that best described its architectural style. Indeed, it appeared as if it had grown this way and that, a room at time with little regard for what had gone before, producing a meandering floor plan and mismatched rooflines.

Grace thought it seemed perfectly suited to Cooper's bohemian style and serendipitous character. "It's wonderful," she exclaimed as they left the pickup truck and walked the grounds. "It's so much like you, Dylan."

"It's also twelve hundred dollars," Cooper protested, though he was already eyeing the double-width garage. He thought it would make a perfect darkroom. "That's a lot of money, Grace. Almost six times what I paid for my truck."

"I've a feeling the price might be open to negotiation," Grace said, recalling what the old fellow had implied.

"Perhaps, but there still wouldn't be much left from what the Society paid for my pictures."

"Didn't their letter say they were interested in purchasing more of them?"

"Aye, but I don't know if I'd be wise to trust it, lass. Truth be told I want to, but . . ."

"Then trust it, Dylan," Grace said in her spirited way. "Take a chance."

Cooper winced with uncertainty. "I don't know, I'm finally feeling a bit secure—just a *wee* bit mind you. But it's no time to be feeling my oats and turning into a spendthrift. Though Lord knows it's tempting . . ."

"Some temptations are worth the risk, remember?" Grace prompted with as much spunk as she could muster. "I'll take it with you. We could be happy here, Dylan. I know we could."

"Aye, it does feel a whole lot like home doesn't it?" Cooper said, sweeping his eyes over the vista.

Grace nodded emphatically. "It gives me a feeling of comfort and sense of belonging," she said, her eyes brightening with an idea. "Maybe you should take some pictures of the place? We could show them to Mr. Van Dusen and see what he thinks."

"That's a fine idea, lass," Cooper said, wasting no time unloading his gear from the back of the pickup.

While he went about photographing the cottage and grounds, Grace went inside. The kitchen had serviceable appliances along with ample closets and cupboards. There was a large stone fireplace in the parlor, and an atrium where the disparate wings of the cottage intersected. It was capped by a skylight beneath which Grace imagined a botanical garden of potted plants would thrive. She continued to tour the other rooms, thinking about how they might be furnished, and entertaining thoughts of curtains, throw rugs, and other homey touches.

A short time later, Cooper had the camera trained on the front of the cottage. He was on the verge of firing the shutter when the screen door swung open and Grace emerged from within. Cooper paused, waiting until she was right where he wanted her in the composition, then fired it.

"Oh, I hope I didn't spoil your picture."

"Nope, I only fire the shutter when I want to."

"I suppose I should know that by now, shouldn't I?" Grace said, laughing at herself. She walked to a corner of the cottage and gestured to the windows that overlooked the sea. "It seems this room gets the morning sun," she said with a coy smile. "It would make a perfect nursery."

"Nursery?" Cooper echoed, a broad grin breaking across his face. "I think we'd best own the place before we start filling it with little ones, don't you?"

"Does that mean you've decided to purchase it?"

An impish smile broke across Cooper's face. "I'm so inclined, aye. But I thought we were going to get Mr. Van Dusen's opinion first." He tilted his head with uncertainty and lit his pipe. "Come to think of it, we might be wise to consider what Colin might have to say about it, too."

"Colin?" Grace echoed with a puzzled expression. "I don't see the value of his opinion in this matter."

"I'm afraid I didn't make myself clear, Grace," Cooper said, drawing on his pipe. "I meant, what would he be thinking if you and I left Boston and moved up here together?"

"You know very well he'd pronounce me a wanton woman living in sin, and forbid it with his customary histrionics."

Cooper nodded, emitting a stream of pipe smoke. "It's a matter of some concern, isn't it?"

Grace's lips tightened with defiance. "Not to me. I just want to be with you, Dylan. *Here* with you, together for the rest of our lives."

"Aye, as do I," Cooper said, a grin tugging at a corner of his mouth at what he was about to say. "Of course, there is one thing we could do that would forever end Colin's histrionics, isn't there?"

Grace cocked her head, eyeing him with suspicion. "Might you be saying what I think you're saying?"

Cooper smiled enigmatically and guided her to a weathered bench that had been positioned on the bluff to take full advantage of the view. The late afternoon golden light made the cottage appear to glow from within, and the breeze coming off the water filled the air with the salty scent of brine. When Grace was comfortably seated, Cooper took her hand in his and dropped to one knee. "I'm saying, I want you to marry me, Grace."

Grace seemed stunned by his proposal, but it was actually a disturbing thought that had silenced her. "Why?" she finally responded. "Because it would make Colin happy? I can't think of a worse reason, I'm afraid."

"No, to make *me* happy, Grace," Cooper replied with utmost sincerity. "You have my heart, lass, and always will," he went on, pressing her palm to his chest. "Every beat that's left in it is yours and yours alone. And I want you . . . and the little ones that'll be in that nursery one day . . . to have my name." He paused, an uncertain look crinkling his eyes. "I thought you wanted the same."

Grace's eyes filled with remorse. "I'm sorry, I didn't mean to sound so harsh. I guess I'm just tired of always worrying about what Colin will think, or what Colin will say, or what—"

"Shush lass," Cooper said, putting a finger to her lips, silencing her. "No need for any of that. A simple yes or no answer will suffice."

Grace nodded, her eyes glistening with emotion. "Yes . . . I'll marry you. Truth be told, I'd have agreed to it the morning you first walked into the gallery."

Chapter Twenty-One

Several months had passed. Summer warmth had come to New England, bathing its endless miles of coastline in golden sunshine and making its vast forests lush with verdant foliage and vegetation.

After seeing the photographs of the cottage, Van Dusen conferred with a real estate broker he knew well and trusted. The broker agreed that the cottage would be an excellent investment and encouraged Cooper to purchase it. As Grace had surmised, the price was more than negotiable, and when all was said and done, Cooper had paid the proprietor of Newbury's one-pump gas station the unnerving sum of one thousand dollars for it.

Despite his initial anxiety, buying the cottage turned out to be a providential event that had a positive effect on everyone connected to it, and suddenly life was good. The National Geographic Society had been making regular purchases of Cooper's photographs, providing him with steady income. Grace and Colin had made their new beginning, which was really a resumption of the more playful, less contentious brother-sister relationship of their childhood. Colin had come to accept Cooper as the man who would be his sister's husband

and was pleased they were making plans to marry and settle down in the cottage.

Cooper had wasted no time moving out of the rooming house in South Boston and into the cottage. He immediately went about tackling the long list of badly needed repairs, and, most importantly, turning the garage into a darkroom. He blacked out the windows, built storage racks and work surfaces, and ran in electrical and plumbing lines, then installed a sink, and a cast-iron stove to keep him and the chemicals he used to process photographs from freezing in winter.

Occasionally on weekends, Cooper would drive down to Boston in his pickup to shop for furnishings with Grace; but, most often, she and Colin would take the train to Newbury, giving Grace the opportunity to nest and bring a woman's touch to the cottage's many rooms; and give Colin the opportunity to help Cooper with the repairs. With the cause of their friction removed, they had come to like each other, bonding over the manly endeavors of carpentry, painting, plumbing, roofing, and brush clearing. As soon as Grace had the kitchen up and running, they cleared out an area in a grove of trees where they set up a table and chairs. The three of them often ate in the leafy shade, cooled by the breezes that came off the sea.

As part of their commitment to their new community, Grace and Cooper decided to be married in the Newbury Presbyterian Church—a white clapboard structure with a soaring steeple that stood on the town square. Colin had been attending Sunday services when in Newbury and was put in charge of making the wedding arrangements with Pastor Martin who would perform the ceremony. A date had been set. Grace was sending out invitations; Cooper was shopping for a ring.

One sweltering Saturday, as he did every day after lunch, Cooper headed down to the row of mailboxes at the end of the dirt road to collect the newpaper and post. There was rarely any of the latter, and today was no exception. He removed the newspaper, immediately unfolding it to read the headline and scan the front page stories as he walked back to the cottage. A letter-sized manila envelope dropped to the ground. Evidently the postman had folded the newspaper around it before slipping them into the box. Cooper picked up the envelope and froze at the return address in the upper left corner that in bold, black type proclaimed: United States Government, Department of the Army. Heart pounding and hands shaking at what it might portend, he tore open the envelope and, as he feared, found it contained a Notice to Report. His heart sank at the sight of it. He stood in the rutted drive staring at the notice for a long moment, then trudged back up the hill to the cottage.

Grace and Colin were still at the table in the shady grove when Cooper returned. The lunch dishes had been cleared and Grace was at one end arranging a bunch of wildflowers from the garden in a vase. Colin sat at the other end, writing a letter. Shocked by Cooper's news, he lifted his pen in mid-sentence and angrily crumpled the sheet of stationery in his fist.

"I thought you were too . . . too old," Grace said, her lips trembling as she spoke.

"Aye, I *was*," Cooper replied, trying to collect himself. "But no longer. According to this, the age has been raised to forty-five for technical specialists."

"When do you have to report?" Grace asked anxiously.

"It says sixty days . . ."

"Thanks be to God the wedding's but a month away." Grace continued arranging the flowers in the vase as if this occupation might restrain the flood of emotion that was welling up inside her.

"Sixty days from the date of this notice," Cooper said grimly. "Which was . . . the eighteenth of May."

"Eighteenth of May?" Grace exclaimed. She flinched at the snip of the shears, having cut a stem without intending to. "That's . . . that's almost two months ago."

"Aye," Cooper replied, making the calculation. "It seems I've three days before I'm to report."

Grace sighed with confusion and set the shears aside. "How could that be?"

Cooper showed her the envelope and pointed to the address. "The notice was sent to the rooming house, lass. That's where I was living when I registered, and that's the address I put on the forms. Since I'd been turned down, it never occurred to me to give them the new one. I'm afraid all the weeks spent returning and forwarding it has left me little time to report"—he pointed to a paragraph in the notice—"with my camera equipment, I might add."

Grace looked puzzled. "Your camera equipment?"

"Aye, it seems I'm in the Army Aeronautical Service, assigned to an aerial reconnaissance unit."

"Oh," Grace said, taking a moment to collect her thoughts. "What shall we do about the wedding?"

"I'm afraid it will have to be postponed," Cooper replied. "I don't see that we have any choice."

Colin, who up until now seemed to be in shock, straightened in his chair. "Not necessarily," he said sharply, getting their attention.

"What do you mean by that?" Cooper asked.

"Quite simply, there's no need to postpone the wedding if you don't report," Colin explained, pleased with his cleverness. "The notice was posted and delivered to the wrong address. Why not just make believe you never got it?"

"I couldn't do that," Cooper stated with finality. "It wouldn't be right. As much as I want to marry Grace and have a life here with her, I just couldn't."

"Why not?" Colin challenged, getting to his feet. "If you really mean that, why go running off to war if you don't have to?" He answered the question before Cooper had a chance. "Unless of course you've come down with a case of cold feet and this is a convenient excuse to avoid it."

"You know better than that," Cooper said, an edge creeping into his voice. "I registered for a reason, Colin; and it hasn't changed." He slapped the newspaper on the table in front of him. The headline read: 10,000 DOUGHBOYS DEAD. "Furthermore, it's against the law not to report. And since I'm not yet naturalized, if found out, I'll not only be prosecuted, I'll be deported. Now, *you* may have a burning desire to go home to Scotland, Colin, but *I* don't. My home is here, now."

"Yes, it's no secret I want to go home," Colin said in an embittered voice. "After all the time I've spent looking after Grace, I've every right to resume my life."

"Now we're getting to work on the crust of the bread, Colin, aren't we?" Cooper said, assembling the pieces in his mind. "You see, Grace, postponing the wedding isn't Colin's problem. No, his problem is me going off to war. Because, if I do, married or no, *he's* duty bound to stay here with you."

"Oh dear, you're right," Grace said, shifting her eyes to Colin. "You couldn't leave me here alone and go home, could you?"

"You know very well I couldn't, Grace," Colin replied, stung by the irony and Cooper's insight.

"Aye," Cooper said, his eyes narrowing with suspicion. "And I've a feeling his plans to do so are, perhaps, further along than we thought."

"Further along?" Grace prompted, looking puzzled.

"I'd bet a dollar to a dime that he finally has enough saved for a steamer ticket," Cooper replied with a wily grin. "Haven't you, Colin?"

"Finally," Colin replied evenly. "Enough for one. And, yes, I've been planning to purchase it sometime after the wedding."

"Maybe it's time to think of someone other than yourself, Colin," Grace said, bristling with indignation. "Do you think I want Dylan to go off to war? Lord knows I don't know how I'll sleep nights when he's gone . . . worrying if I'll ever see him again . . . if he's been hurt or . . . or God forbid, killed. I'm going to be beside myself every minute of every day, and all you can worry about is going home? How can you be so selfish?"

Colin swallowed hard, stung by her words, and took a moment to collect himself. "Has it ever occurred to you, Grace, that I might have a *reason* for going home? A *special* reason much the same as the one *you* have for deciding not to?"

Grace flinched at the implication and exchanged a look with Cooper. "What special reason, Colin?"

"It's quite simple," Colin replied. "You see, when I accepted responsibility for your well-being, I gave up something—" He paused and, correcting himself, said, "some*one*. Yes, Grace, I left someone behind who I care for just as deeply as you care for Cooper."

Grace's eyes welled, sending tears streaming down her cheeks. "Oh, Colin, I'd no idea," she sighed, overcome with empathy. "The letters you write, they're . . . they're not all to the family are they?"

"Not all of them, no," Colin replied, feeling vindicated. He opened his fist and glanced to the crumpled letter in his palm. "I can't very well post one to her that says I'll soon be home, now, can I?"

"No, I suppose not," Grace replied through her tears. "Why didn't you say something?"

"Because as you can see, talking about it only makes it more painful," Colin replied, biting his lip as the anger welled up inside him. "What good would it have done?! Would it have changed anything?!" he challenged, raising his voice. "No, of course not! Call me selfish, if you must; but it's not fair that I'm forced to remain here while *he's* off satisfying his sense of adventure!"

Cooper's eyes flared at the insult. "Sense of adventure?!" he echoed, his burr thickening with anger.

"What is it then? Love for the homeland you've forsaken?!" Colin prompted with a sarcastic sneer. "Then again, patriotism *is* the the last refuge of a scoundrel, isn't it?!"

Struck by a surge of adrenaline, Cooper lunged across the table, grabbing a fistful of Colin's shirt. Grace recoiled in horror with a frightened yelp. The two men's reddened faces were inches apart. "I'm going because I would have to live with myself, afterwards, if I didn't!" Cooper shouted, spattering Colin with spittle. "And so would Grace!"

Colin tried to pull free, then took a wild swing at Cooper who slipped the punch and tightened his grasp, tearing Colin's shirt. The rip of fabric fueled Colin's anger and sent him diving across the table at Cooper. His momentum knocked over the vase of flowers and sent the two men tumbling to the ground. They went rolling across the grass between the trees, pummeling each other and grappling for the advantage.

Cooper came out on top, pinning Colin's arms with his knees. "And while I'm at it!" Cooper went on, seething as Colin struggled beneath him to get free. "I'll give you another reason! A man who had half his leg blown off told me one picture would have saved it! And the lives of sixty-three of his men! Sixty-three, Colin! If I might save even one, how could I not report?!" He took hold of Colin's collar and, shaking him with anger, shouted, "How?! How?! How?!"

"Dylan! Dylan, stop it! Stop! What are you doing?!" Grace shouted, bear-hugging him from behind in an effort to pull him off Colin. To her dismay her actions had the unintended consequence of allowing Colin to free his arms and begin throwing punches at Cooper. "Stop! Stop it! Both of you! You're acting like children!"

The two men flailed at each other as if deaf to her pleas, but Cooper finally responded and rolled off Colin onto the ground. Slowly, the two men got to their feet and stood a distance apart gasping for breath and glaring at each other. Cooper tugged his pipe from a shirt pocket and jammed it hard into the corner of his mouth, venting his anger on the stem.

While the two men settled and brushed off their clothes, Grace quickly gathered the scattered flowers, put them in the vase, and set it down hard on the table like a judge rapping a gavel to restore order. "Now—both of you—sit down like gentlemen," she commanded in crisp phrases. "I'll have no more of this adolescent behavior." Though shaken by what she had witnessed, Grace took a seat at one end of the table and, like a stern headmistress about to dispense punishment, waited until Colin and Cooper, in slow and grudging compliance with her order, had taken seats on opposite sides of it. "Colin, you were insulting and rude," Grace said in a condemning tone. "To be charitable, I can only conclude your anger poorly affected your judgement."

Colin's lips tightened into a thin line. "Yes," he said, flushed with embarrassment. "It seems to have bested me."

Grace shifted her glare to Cooper who was still chewing on his pipe stem. "And *you*—you responded to an insult with fisticuffs. You're clearly guilty of the same offense, only more so."

"Aye, my anger seems to have bested me as well," Cooper said, equally contrite.

"Good," Grace said as if she had just gotten toddlers to agree to share a toy. "I'll not have the two men in my life fighting like sworn enemies. Doubly so under the circumstances. You both have many good qualities and I thought you'd come to appreciate them . . ." She emitted an exasperated sigh. ". . . or so it seemed."

Colin nodded in agreement and glanced at Cooper. "If I'm

to be honest with myself, I must admit I find your strength of conscience and sense of duty more than admirable. But—"

"Aye," Cooper interupted. "I'm able to say the same."

"But it's not fair," Colin resumed, "that I'm paying the price for you to be true to them."

"Aye, I can't argue with that," Cooper said with evident sincerity. "It's *not* fair—to you, or to any of us for that matter. And I'm truly sorry for whatever pain it may cause; but it's not my doing, Colin. Blame the United States Army. Blame the Kaiser. Blame the chaps who killed the Archduke or sank the *Lusitania*, if it will make you feel better. But, truth be told, I don't see that I've a choice but to report. "

Colin's eyes softened with understanding. He cocked his head in thought, then glanced over at Grace. "What I'm about to say will have no effect whatsoever on my situation, Grace; but, in my heart, I still feel strongly that you should be husband and wife before Cooper leaves."

"How?" Grace protested. "There isn't enough time."

"Not for the wedding you've planned, but there's plenty of time for a handfast ceremony," Colin said, referring to an ancient Scottish ritual that was binding on any couple who locked hands and pledged their troth, no witnesses or minister necessary.

"No," Grace said without the slightest hesitation. "It's what's in your heart that matters, not a 'secret handshake' and some hastily spoken words. Dylan and I are already bound to each other, Colin—bound for life in our hearts and souls, of that I've no doubt."

"Aye, that we are," Cooper said, his tone implying more would follow. "But while I'm off doing *my* duty, Grace, Colin will be here doing *his*, won't he?"

Grace nodded and raised her brows curiously.

"Which means," Cooper went on, "I'll have the peace of mind that comes from knowing he's looking after you and caring for the cottage. In all fairness, shouldn't he have the peace of mind that comes from knowing—with the absolute certainty that an exchange of vows would provide—that one day, he'll be free of the responsibility he has so earnestly shouldered?"

Colin stared at Cooper for a long moment, then emitted a relieved sigh and nodded. "Well-said, Cooper. Your forthrightness is much appreciated."

Grace's face was filled with remorse. "*Very* much appreciated," she whispered, wiping tears from her eyes that came to life with a thought. "Tomorrow is Sunday, isn't it? Well, instead of settling for a handfast, why don't we attend the morning service and then ask Pastor Martin to marry us?!"

Cooper leaned back in his chair, lighting his pipe as he considered it. "Why not?"

"Yes," Colin chimed in. "And there's no reason why you can't have the wedding ceremony and celebration you've been planning as soon as Cooper comes back."

The next day, after the Sunday service, they approached Pastor Martin who immediately agreed to their request. "It won't be the first nuptial I've performed ahead of schedule because of the war," the youthful minister replied.

During the short and simple ceremony that followed, Colin gave the bride away; then he and the pastor's wife served as witnesses while Grace and Dylan exchanged vows and Pastor Martin pronounced them husband and wife to have and to hold from this day forward until death do they part.

After the ceremony, the three of them headed off to the Lobster Trap, a rustic, dockside tavern in the heart of Newbury Harbor, where they celebrated quietly with the catch of the day and tankards of ale. That afternoon, Colin took the train back to Boston, leaving Grace and Cooper to honeymoon in the cottage. They had until the next morning to be together, at which time they would both return to Boston, Cooper to the induction center, Grace to the gallery. After dropping Colin at the station, they drove to the seashore and spent the remainder of the afternoon walking the sandy beaches and frolicking in the shallow surf, then as the sun dropped behind the trees, they returned to the cottage.

And that evening—on their wedding night, the night before Cooper left for duty—as the intoxicating aroma of the sea permeated the air, and moonlight streamed through the lace curtains of their bedroom windows, they became lovers. It was the tender and considerate lovemaking of people who cared deeply for each other. Once their soaring passion had been unleashed, their intimate caresses served as further testimony to the lifelong commitment they had made in their hearts and in the presence of God; and crested in satiating fulfillment as the joys of their physical union became a moving spiritual one as well.

The next morning, Cooper and Grace loaded his valise and a small trunk that contained his camera gear into the pickup truck, and drove back to Boston in saddened silence. He parked on the street in front of the gallery and gave her the keys so she and Colin could have use of his truck while he was gone.

"The keys to my heart, Mrs. Cooper," he said, trying to sound lighthearted though he was emotionally overwhelmed by the thought of leaving her.

Grace sighed, her eyes brimming with tears, "I can't believe that I won't . . . won't be seeing . . ." She couldn't finish it and buried her head in the curve of his neck, then looked up into his eyes and kissed him. "I'll wait a lifetime for you, Dylan."

"And I for you, Grace," Cooper said, his eyes glistening with emotion.

"I love you so much," Grace said, tears rolling down her cheeks. "Please take good care of yourself and—" She was interrupted by the clanging bell of an approaching streetcar. "Go. Go now. Please, you must."

Cooper hesitated, then swiftly pulled the valise and trunk from the back of the pickup while Grace flagged the trolley.

After loading them aboard, he stood in the doorway, blowing her kisses as it pulled away. His antics brought a smile to Grace's face, but she was paralyzed with sadness as the trolley followed the curve of the tracks onto Beacon Street. She remained there long after it was out of sight, wondering if she'd ever see him again.

Chapter Twenty-Two

The trolley took Cooper to the Federal Building on Congress Street. He hauled his suitcase and trunk into the Induction Center and spent the day being processed. That evening, he and dozens of the other inductees were trucked a short distance to Boston's South Station and put aboard a troop train. Twenty hours later, after stops in New York and Philadelphia to pick up more inductees, it arrived in Harrisburg, Pennsylvania, where a convoy of trucks transported them to Carlisle Military Barracks to undergo basic training.

During the twelve weeks Cooper spent there, he wrote to Grace at every opportunity, regaling her with humorous stories of how, as the "old man" of his unit, he'd been made to dig trenches, crawl through mud, and taught to field strip and fire a rifle—all the while existing on food that not even a haggis-fated hog would consider edible. Fortunately, mail was delivered to stateside military bases regularly, and it was Grace's letters and pictures of her that he'd brought with him that got him through the daily grind. On a more curious note, he wrote that he had never laid eyes on a combat aircraft and had received no instruction on taking reconnaissance pictures while flying in one.

When basic training ended, Cooper was sporting corporal's stripes on his sleeve and a Signal Corps patch on his shoulder due to his specialist status. He shipped out of Philadelphia Harbor on a troopship with thousands of other doughboys. The weather in the North Atlantic was as miserable as the conditions aboard the overcrowded vessel. Cooper wrote to Grace, joking that the military's unappetizing food was, at long last, of no consequence, because nearly everyone aboard was seasick, and the mere smell of it sent them dashing to the railing. Indeed, the steerage-class accomodations of his immigrant voyage to America seemed like a posh, first-class cruise in comparison.

After weeks at sea, Cooper disembarked in Le Havre, France, gaunt, pale, and in need of rest and relaxation. Instead, he found himself on yet another troop train. It chugged noisily through the French countryside until it reached an air base near Châtillon-sur-Seine, sixty miles southeast of Paris, where Cooper was assigned to the Army Aeronautical Service barracks. Hungry and exhausted, he dragged his valise and trunk of camera gear to his bunk, and was about to fall face down on the bare mattress when a voice called out, "Hey there, you must be Corporal Cooper."

Cooper turned to see three uniformed men—jodphurs, leggings, wool blouses, and corporal's stripes, like his own—approaching. "Aye, that I am," he replied wearily.

"Welcome to the First Aerial Reconnaissance Squadron," Kenyon said, extending a hand.

"The first and *only*," Arkoff joked.

"You're just in time for the briefing," Wallace said. "Follow us."

En route, Cooper learned that, like him, they were all newly assigned to the Aerial Reconnaissance Squadron. Kenyon was an adventure-seeking photojournalist; Wallace did weddings and bar mitzvahs; and Arkoff had worked at a movie studio taking publicity shots of silent film stars. They entered a hangar where the four pilots with whom they'd be flying, and Colonel Jenkins, the Squadron Commander, had assembled. Jenkins paired them off, then outlined the general scope of their mission. "There'll be a two week training period," he concluded. "After which you'll be upgraded to mission status."

"Training?" Kenyon echoed. "Sir, we're not puppies who need to be housebroke. I signed up to go flying and shoot Huns with my camera. My editor is waiting with bated breath for—"

"At ease, Corporal," Jenkins interrupted smartly. "It's not your editor's life that's going to be on the line up there, it's yours and your pilot's. Therefore, you'll train in the air with him first. Teamwork is everything in this business. That's why, despite the regulations that prohibit officers and enlisted men from sharing living quarters, I ordered that you all be billeted in the same barracks. *Teamwork.*"

Cooper was teamed with Captain Tyler Mottram, a Georgia farmboy who flew crop dusters in civilian life. A welcome departure from the military's habit of turning pilots into truck drivers and clerks into pilots, Cooper thought.

Captain Mottram took Cooper to a maintenance bay where two mechanics were working on his biplane. One was patching bullet holes in its wings. The other was removing its wooden airscrew, which had been splintered by gunfire. The Breuget-Bristol Type 14-A2 had been designed by the French, manufactured by the British, and flown and serviced by Americans. Its top speed exceeded 125 mph. It carried forty gallons of fuel, which could keep it aloft for approximately two and one half hours.

"For reasons y'all will soon come to know," Mottram said, "we call this aeroplane the Tin Whistle."

"Aye," Cooper grunted, thinking the rickety craft resembled the models children made from kits. Painted canvas, glued and nailed to a painfully thin aluminum airframe, formed its fuselage and sheathed its wings. The upper wing was connected to the lower with struts braced by what looked like bailing wire. The aircraft had two cockpits—pilot up front and gunner behind where the machine gun was mounted. "With all due respect, sir, am I expected to get in there with my camera?"

"Y'all catch on right quick, Cooper," Mottram drawled with a broad grin, pronouncing it Coopah.

"Aye, sir, but who's goin' to catch the camera?" Cooper retorted, matching Mottram's grin. "Just keeping hold of it, let alone while trying to focus or change film holders, would confound a four-armed acrobat."

"Yep, y'all might have a dickens of a time of it, Corporal," Mottram conceded. "When it comes to combat, it seems we're always flying upside down."

Cooper's brows were arched. "Aye, I'm afraid it'll be over the side before I get to fire the shutter."

"Well, long as y'all don't go over with it," Mottram joked with a cackle. "'Cause if you do, there won't be anyone left to operate the machine gun."

Cooper's jaw slackened.

"It's easier than fallin' out of your bunk at reveille," Mottram said, seeing his reaction. "Y'all just aim and fire. The bullets do the rest. The trick is to avoid shooting me or the aircraft."

As soon as his Tin Whistle was airworthy, Mottram took Cooper flying—without his camera—to familiarize him with its weapons systems and the sensations of flight and to get used to the piercing whistle it emitted in a dive, hence its nickname. He gradually increased the severity of the maneuvers and decreased their interval until Cooper could function despite the feeling that his weight had suddenly doubled, pinning him to his seat and pressing his goggles tight against his face; and could endure the violent repetitions of snaps, rolls and dives that were critical to combat flying without becoming light-headed or sick to his stomach.

During the training period, Cooper spent his spare time thinking up ways to secure the camera in the air. Observing that the military police patrolled the air base on horseback, he got an idea and headed over to the barn where the horses were billetted and the saddlery was located. Sergeant Halstead, the master saddlemaker, sparked to Cooper's challenge. By the end of the training period, they had fashioned a harness of straps and buckles that fit over Cooper's shoulders and around his torso, and attached to the camera with snap latches. The harness would support its weight, prevent it from falling over the side, and keep his hands free to operate it.

"That's a work of genius, Dylan," Wallace said when Cooper returned to the barracks with the harness. "Boy oh boy, imagine what you could do with one of these at a wedding!" Kenyon and Arkoff were equally impressed and the three of them wasted no time heading for the saddlery.

Cooper wrote to Grace telling her how much his colleagues admired his resourcefulness and how much he enjoyed their camaraderie. He went on about the thrill of flying, and being tutored by Captain Mottram; though truth be told, he'd much prefer to be at home with her working on the cottage and taking pictures of whatever happened to catch his eye. He concluded by reassuring her he was safe, and that despite being away for over four months, he had yet to see any combat. He didn't mention that the Air Mission Manifest had just been posted or that the Mottram-Cooper team was on it. Nor that they'd be taking aerial reconnaissance photographs of the rail yards at Metz, a highly fortified enemy distribution depot in German territory about thirty miles beyond the Franco-Prussian border.

The first spark of morning light was burning on the horizon when the ground crew pulled the chocks from the biplane's tires. Captain Mottram responded with a thumbs up, then walled the throttle and the Breguet-Bristol began rolling down the runway, gathering speed. He eased back on the joystick and the plane rose from the tarmac and climbed into the morning haze. Cooper checked his camera gear, then swiveled about in his cockpit, scanning the horizon for enemy aircraft as the Captain put the Tin Whistle into a sweeping turn and set a course for Germany.

Chapter Twenty-Three

Aerial reconnaissance missions were scheduled in early morning or late afternoon because the low angle of the sun created brilliant highlights and long, dark shadows. The contrast made troops, tanks, artillery and ground fortifications stand out against the terrain, producing sharply defined and highly informative photographs. The altitude from which they were taken was determined by the cloud cover and haze over the target, and the need to avoid detection by enemy spotters who would launch Fokker interceptors, jeopardizing the mission, not to mention the lives of the pilot and photographer. This need for stealth dictated a low altitude approach followed by a corkscrew climb over the target during which photographs would be taken from various altitudes and angles.

Captain Mottram had the biplane over Metz and on approach to target in just over forty minutes. In the distance, rails of polished steel reflected the fiery sunlight, sharply defining the sinuous pattern of the rail yards. Cooper was thinking each rail looked like it had just emerged from a blast furnace when Mottram dipped a wing, putting the plane over on its side. His camera secured by its harness,

Cooper set it on the rim of his cockpit, centered the rail yards in the frame, fine-tuned the focus, inserted the film holder, pulled the slide and fired the shutter, signaling Mottram with a slap on his flying helmet when it was done.

While Mottram put the aircraft into a sweeping climb, Cooper went through the steps again: frame, focus, holder, slide, shutter. He had removed the film holder and was readying another when a German Fokker dove out of the sun.

Machine-gun bullets were whizzing around Cooper and Mottram like a swarm of attacking bees, punching holes in the aircraft's canvas fuselage and wings, and pinging loudly off the aluminum airframe. Mottram used a snap roll to put the plane into a dive, a maneuver that, if not for its harness, would have thrown the camera from the plane; and, if not for his seat belt, tossed Cooper after it. Instinctively, he set the camera in his lap, whirled in his seat, grasped the machine gun and began firing at the pursuing Fokker.

Cooper found the pulse-pounding dogfight exciting and terrifying at the same time. To Captain Mottram's delight, Cooper's relentless return fire forced the German pilot to disengage. The Fokker peeled off toward the horizon, a long trail of smoke spiraling from its engine housing.

In the following months, Cooper went on many such missions. Some were without incident; others were as hair-raising as the first; and a few were even more so. One afternoon he was sitting in his bunk writing a letter to Grace when Colonel Jenkins entered the barracks. "Gather round, gentlemen," he said in a voice that belied his casual demeanor. "One of our code-breakers has decrypted a top secret German radio signal, alerting us to a major offensive at Reims."

"Sounds like the tide's turning in our direction, sir," Arkoff said, effusively.

"Maybe," Jenkins grunted. "But Operations thinks it might be a trick. A way to get us to redeploy our troops on the Western Front, exposing the real target to attack. We need to know if German troops are massing in the areas around Reims, or not. Thousands of lives are at stake. Now, I'm not going to sugarcoat it. This is a dangerous mission. Some people are calling it a suicide mission. So, we've decided to ask for volunteers. I need one pilot and one—"

Captain Mottram stepped forward before he could finish. "I'm your man, Colonel."

"Very well, Captain. We have a pilot. Now we—"

Cooper raised his hand and was about to verbally volunteer as the photographer.

"I'll fly with him," Kenyon blurted, beating Cooper to it.

"Hold on there," Cooper said, his burr thickening. "If Captain Mottram's the pilot, then *I'm* the photographer. We're a team, sir, and a fine one at that. I see no reason to be changing, now."

"Captain?" Jenkins prompted turning to Mottram.

"Kenyon is a fine man, suh," Mottram replied in his Georgia drawl. "But Coopah's right. The nature of the mission makes teamwork paramount; and thanks to his performance under fire, I'm still alive to say it."

"Then Mottram-Cooper it is," Colonel Jenkins said without hesitation. "Good luck, gentlemen. Briefing's at nineteen hundred. Takeoff at zero six hundred tomorrow."

Jenkins turned on a heel and strode off. He had barely left the barracks when a flash of lightning followed by rolling claps of thunder rattled the windows, heralding the onset of a storm. Within minutes, the air base was being lashed by forty mile an hour winds and blinding sheets of rain.

That's when it dawned on Cooper and the others that Wallace and his pilot, who had taken off several hours earlier on one of the late afternoon missions, hadn't returned. It was more than possible that the pilot had put his aircraft down safely on a roadway or in a farmer's field to wait out the storm. But their hopes were dashed when another pilot, who had managed to make it back despite the weather, reported seeing Wallace's aircraft go down in a flaming crash.

The violent weather grounded every aircraft on the base,

forcing the mission to be postponed. For weeks, floodwaters raged throughout France, drowning soldiers in their trenches on both sides of no-man's-land. The incessant rain, the ankle-deep mud, and the death of his colleague took their toll on Cooper's spirit. Lonely and depressed, he was lying in his bunk, staring at a picture of Grace when someone shouted, "Mail call!"

A crush of men gathered around the squadron clerk in anxious silence. He opened a sack of envelopes and packages, and began calling out names. He had gone through more than a dozen before he shouted, "Cooper!" and handed him an envelope.

Unlike stateside military mail, delivery in war-torn Europe was unreliable and erratic. Many letters were lost. Those that weren't often took months to get there as the Newbury postmark on Cooper's confirmed; but he didn't need to see it or the return address to know who had sent it, because the penmanship was clearly Grace's; and his spirits soared as he hurried back to his bunk and tore it open.

"My goodness, Coopah," Mottram said. "Do I detect the scent of a woman permeating these barracks?"

"Smell's like the perfume of a ballet dancer that I . . . ah . . . that I took some pictures of, once," Arkoff teased.

Cooper forced a smile and kept reading in silence.

Mottram noticed his face had paled and the letter was shaking in his hands. "Coopah, y'all look like you've just seen your pappy's ghost."

Cooper failed to respond, despite the provocation, and stared at Grace's letter, appearing to be in shock.

"Five'll get you ten it's a Dear John," Kenyon said.

"Maybe it's a love poem," Mottram ventured with a lascivious cackle. "I promised y'all my heart to the core, but now that y'all gone off to war, I've become a little ol' whore."

The men erupted with raucous laughter.

Though clearly shaken by whatever news the letter contained, Cooper couldn't help but laugh with them. ". . . And soon a baby will be crawling on the floor!" he rhymed, good-naturedly, finishing the poem.

Suddenly, they sensed Cooper was doing more than partaking in the bawdy barracks banter, and questioned him with looks. "Coopah?" Mottram prompted, knowingly.

"Yes, yes, she's pregnant!" Cooper exclaimed in reply. "Grace is pregnant. I'm going to be a daddy!"

"Assuming you *are* the daddy," Kenyon joked with a sarcastic chuckle. "Congratulations, Dylan! Now all you need to do is get home alive."

Cooper nodded resolutely. "Aye, that I do."

"There's still the matter of that little suicide mission I volunteered us for," Mottram prompted, catching Kenyon's eye.

"I'll take your place, Cooper," Kenyon offered, picking up on Mottram's signal. "I volunteered before you did, anyway. Remember?"

"Aye," Cooper said, genuinely touched by the gesture. "I don't know what to say."

"Say yes, you Scottish fool," Arkoff prompted.

"I'm tempted," Cooper conceded. "But I'm afraid, it's my mission. I'm going on it. And there's no discussing it. Teamwork, Captain, remember?"

The mission was rescheduled as soon as the skies over the Western Front had cleared. That night, Mottram and Cooper, Kenyon and Arkoff and their pilots, along with some members of the ground crew, and Halstead, the saddlemaker, were in a local cafe toasting Cooper's upcoming fatherhood with tankards of ale. At one point, they all bunched together with jaunty smiles, their tankards raised, while someone took a picture.

"To the men of the First, and only, Aerial Recon Squadron!" Arkoff shouted as the shutter fired.

Unseen by Cooper amidst the jocularity, a look passed between Mottram and Kenyon suggesting they were up to something. "Another round!" Mottram exclaimed, making certain Cooper's tankard had been refilled. Over the next several hours, Mottram and Kenyon alternated as refillers of Cooper's tankard more times than they dared count. "Take-off is at zero six hundred, Coopah," Mottram finally announced. "I'm goin' to get me some sack time. Y'all better do the same."

Early the next morning, Cooper awoke with a start and a nasty headache. It took him a few moments to realize that the barracks were strangely silent at a time when he expected everyone involved in the early morning mission to be rising. That's when he realized Mottram's bunk was empty and neatly made. So was Kenyon's. As were those of the ground crew. Cooper donned his flight gear, grabbed his camera and harness, and dashed to the flight line. He arrived just as Mottram's Tin Whistle was lifting off the runway. Kenyon, nestled in the rear cockpit, spotted Cooper and snapped off a jaunty salute. Cooper was still groggy from his rude awakening and stood on the tarmac watching as the plane vanished into the haze.

"Looks like you overslept, Corporal," a member of the ground crew prompted.

"Overslept?" Cooper protested. "It's zero five ten. The Captain said takeoff was at zero six hundred."

"*Five* hundred, Corporal," the crewman corrected, with a knowing smile. "Amazing isn't it? How even an officer can make a mistake, every now and then."

"This one was made accidentally on purpose, wasn't it?" Cooper prompted.

The crewman nodded. "Way I heard it, they want to make sure that baby of yours gets to know his daddy."

Cooper nodded in humble appreciation, then checked the clipboard where the Air Mission Manifest was posted. "Looks like my name's still on the AMM."

"Well, the SC doesn't like last minute changes to mission crews," he explained, referring to the Squadron Commander.

"Too much paperwork, I guess. So Captain Mottram decided we'd be smart to just leave it."

Barring complications, a gas tank with two and one half hours of fuel made it easy to calculate the maximum time a flight, to target and back, could take. Cooper decided to remain on the flight line until Mottram and Kenyon returned. At which time he would generously applaud their bravery and selfless friendship, then angrily denounce their duplicitous conspiracy. They should have been back by mid-morning at the latest—but they weren't. At noon, Cooper had every reason to fear the worst. As dusk fell, it was clear they wouldn't ever be returning.

Cooper headed back to the barracks and fell into his bunk distraught at the tragic turn of events and reflecting on the life he'd had in Boston with Grace and the new beginning they'd made in Newbury. Now, he felt strangely detached, as if he'd fallen asleep in a place of peace, love and sanity, only to awaken in a hellish nightmare of whistling aircraft, blazing machine guns and senseless, flaming death—a death that, if not for this bizarre twist, would have been his own. He turned to thoughts of Grace and of the upcoming birth of their child to raise his spirits and buttress his belief that he would return home safely.

Several weeks later, Cooper had been paired with a new pilot and was awaiting his next mission assignment when Germany sued for peace and word spread that the war to end all wars was, at last, over.

Chapter Twenty-Four

The armistice was signed on November 11, 1918.

The American Expeditionary Force had done its job. Many military units were swiftly decommissioned and countless thousands of doughboys were being discharged and sent home.

Cooper was excited by the thought of celebrating Christmas with Grace in Newbury and at being with her for the birth of their baby. In mid-November he got a letter in which Grace joked that her tummy was starting to resemble a keg of ale—his *favorite* ale of course—and that the doctor had calculated the blessed event would be sometime in March.

The letter had taken well over a month to reach him and Cooper was lying in his bunk, imagining what she must look like now, when Colonel Jenkins called a meeting of the squadron. The men assumed he would be issuing their discharge orders. Instead he informed them that they had an important role to play in the immediate postwar period; and to Cooper's dismay, he and the rest of his squadron were soon back in the air, flying compliance verification missions. Their assignment was to provide photographic evidence that German troops were withdrawing from French territory and returning to their homeland. Though the threat of being shot down by enemy aircraft had been removed, the winter weather and the ever-present danger of flight made every mission a risky one.

There were no missions scheduled for Christmas day, and Cooper would have given anything to have been celebrating it with Grace in the snow-blanketed cottage in Newbury. Instead, he spent it with the members of his squadron in their barracks on the air base in Châtillon-sur-Seine, bemoaning their miserable luck, and the even more upsetting fact that there had been no Christmas mail call.

As the squadron clerk, in danger of being lashed to a spinning airscrew in retaliation, explained: the postwar decommissioning of units in every branch of the military and the discharging and mustering out of personnel had made logistics into a disorganized nightmare. As a result, mail delivery had become even more unreliable, and often non-existent. Cooper had been anxiously awaiting a Christmas letter from Grace. Now he realized he might not be getting any of her letters at all, nor might she be getting any of his.

Cooper was finally discharged in early March. He had been away almost ten months; and at about the time Grace was due to have the baby, he was on a troopship somewhere in the stormy North Atlantic. The vessel, taking him and thousands of other doughboys home, berthed temporarily in St. John's, Newfoundland, to take on fuel and supplies. While there, he sent a telegram to Grace with the date of its arrival in Boston Harbor.

He had every reason to expect Grace and his newborn child would be there when it docked. To his disappointment they weren't among the waving throngs when he came down the gangplank. He took the train to Newbury, but they weren't at the station when he got off the train, either. So, he took a taxi to the cottage, only to find it was empty. There was no sign of Grace or of a cooing baby. Neither was there a cradle, diapers, nor any other evidence of a newborn; and little evidence of Grace being in residence either. Furthermore, his pickup truck was nowhere to be seen.

Cooper was baffled and beside himself until he heard the sound of a vehicle coming up the dirt road toward the cottage. He ran to the door, his heart thumping joyously and swung it open just as his truck rolled to a stop. Colin was its only passenger. He got out with a bag of groceries, then froze at the sight of Cooper standing in the doorway and stared at him for a long moment. He saw the question in Cooper's eyes and answered it before he could ask. "Grace is gone, I'm afraid."

Cooper looked puzzled. "What do you mean gone?"

Colin winced. "Gone home to Scotland."

"To Scotland? Why?" Cooper wondered, looking as if confronted by puzzle pieces that didn't fit; then, despite its seemingly thin logic, he grasped at the only reason he could imagine that made any sense, and concluded, "Because she wanted the family to see the baby. Of course, that's it, isn't it?" He could tell from Colin's reaction that there was more to it, and went back inside the cottage. The bottles of liquor were still on the sideboard where they were when he'd left. He poured himself a shot of brandy and was about to pour another for Colin, who had followed him inside, when he was struck by a disturbing thought, and set the bottle down. "Why didn't you go with her, Colin? A woman traveling alone with a baby. It was your job to protect her, wasn't it?"

Colin set the grocery bag on the table and nodded emphatically. "Indeed, and God knows I wanted to; but as you recall we had only enough saved for one ticket, and try as we might, we weren't able to add to it once you'd gone."

"You mean, the money you were planning to use for *your* ticket," Cooper said, admiringly, recalling how much returning to Scotland meant to Colin.

Colin nodded humbly, then opened a desk drawer and removed a slip of pale yellow paper. It was a telegram. "I gave

Grace the money after this came," he went on, handing it to Cooper.

It was from the Department of the Army, dated December 2, 1918, and read: We regret to inform you that Corporal Dylan Cooper was killed in action on October 29, 1918. He served his country with honor and bravery. The President wishes to extend his heartfelt sympathy and condolences for your loss.

"Oh, dear Lord," Cooper gasped, reflecting on the Air Mission Manifest that hadn't been revised. "But I wrote to Grace throughout the winter. The post was troublesome; but she didn't get *any* of my letters?"

Colin shook his head no. "She left a week before Christmas. A few arrived well after the New Year. You can imagine my surprise when I saw the dates on the postmarks. I got the cable you sent from Newfoundland but thought it best we talk about this here."

Cooper nodded solemnly and folded the telegram in half. "Yes, of course, reading this must've been so devastating for Grace. Even with you here, it's easy to understand why she felt it best to go back home to have the baby."

Colin sighed and took a deep breath. "Yes, it was a terribly crushing blow; but it was made all the more devastating because it came . . ." Colin swallowed hard and bit a lip to hold back tears. "I'm sorry, I've been trying to find a way to say this, Cooper. It came a few weeks after she . . . after she *lost* the baby."

The color drained from Cooper's face. He felt hollow, as if he'd been gutted by the fusillades of machine-gun fire he had somehow escaped. Stunned to silence, he turned to the window, staring blankly at the distant sea, a watershed of tears running down his cheeks.

"It was an all too early labor," Colin went on softly. "The doctor did everything possible. The baby lived for just a few hours . . ."

"Oh dear, Grace . . ." Cooper groaned in a mournful sigh.

"She sent you a letter, but from what you said about the post . . ."

Cooper nodded imperceptibly. It seemed as if an eternity had passed by the time he muttered, "It was months behind at best."

Colin put a comforting hand on his shoulder. "Rest assured your tiny son is with the Lord in Heaven," he said, trying in vain to brighten the gloom.

"And Grace?" Cooper whispered, his voice breaking with emotion.

Colin shook his head sadly. "She was hoping and praying you'd come home. As devastated as she was, she was certain that once you were here with her, she'd somehow find the strength to cope with the loss. But when the telegram from the Army came . . . Well, it was just more than she could bear. She became deeply depressed, wouldn't touch her food, or go into town to do her marketing. She would just sit by the window staring out at the sea for hours and hours. The doctor thought perhaps if she went home . . ." Colin let it trail off and splayed his hands in a helpless gesture.

Cooper fought to keep his emotions under control and took a few moments to recover from the devastating news; then he drained the glass of brandy, and met Colin's gaze with eyes that were filled with tears and remorse. "You're a good brother, Colin, and a fine man; and for those times that I judged you harshly or spoke of you uncharitably I sincerely apologize." He shook his head with dismay at this, the *most* tragic war casualty of all. "If I'd taken your advice, if I'd been here as you wanted, none of this would've happened."

Colin's lips tightened into a thin line. "The good Lord works in mysterious ways," he offered, trying to soften Cooper's pain.

"The *good* Lord?" Cooper prompted with a weary sigh. "I'm afraid this is one of His mysteries I can neither fathom, nor accept."

There was no doubt in Cooper's mind what he would do

next. Grace was his wife, and he was more in love with her now than he had ever been, if that were possible. They could still spend the rest of their lives together, raise a family, and live happily ever after, he thought. Though he hadn't been able to be there for her then, he could be there for her now, and vowed to do so. Indeed, he had often said he would wait a lifetime for her and, now, he promised himself he would spend a lifetime searching for her if need be.

He sent a telegram to Grace at her parents' address to let her know that contrary to what she'd been told, he had survived the war, and would soon be with her. Then, he withdrew all the funds that remained in their account, added his mustering out pay from the Army, and bought two steamer tickets to Scotland. He gave one to Colin, kept the other for himself, and set off to find her.

The Best
Christmas Gift

Chapter Twenty-Five

Twenty years had passed.

The roaring twenties had ended with a devastating crash that buried the thirties in its wreckage; but, for Cooper, this morning dawned like any other; and the air inside the rambling cottage was alive with the chemical scent that always started his day. The fumes permeated his cupboards and clothing, and overpowered the bracing rush of brine that rode the wind to the foothills.

Cooper sat on the edge of the bed and inhaled the acrid bouquet. Neither the aroma of black coffee, nor that of fine whiskey could compete with it for his affection. He slipped his suspenders up over his shoulders, then trudged to the window and listened intently. Not for the sound of birds or surf or wind rustling the autumnal wilderness, but for the clatter of an internal combustion engine.

He always heard the truck before he could see it, snaking along the shoreline, then up a secondary road to the row of mailboxes that leaned this way and that on their angled posts. Every morning for a week, Cooper had gone out to meet it; and every morning the mud-spattered truck with RFD on the side continued past. The day Cooper decided to forego the trek, it chugged up the hill, announcing its arrival with a horn that had the honk of an angry grouse.

Cooper hurried from the cottage, his breath coming in gray puffs that hung in the frosty air, and pushed through the gate, its hinges creaking louder than his own. Underwear the color of oatmeal filled the neck of his Pendleton; and his corduroy trousers whisked with each stride, the frayed cuffs skimming brown high-top shoes that hadn't seen polish since the day they left the factory. The years had deepened the lines in his face and turned his salt-and-pepper curls into a sea of raging whitecaps. "How are you, Ben?"

"Fine, Mister Cooper. Just fine."

"Does that racket you're makin' mean you finally have my parcel?"

Ben shrugged, feigning uncertainty. "Well, when I didn't see you out here waiting, I figured maybe I'd just keep on going, but I had a change of heart."

"Real thoughtful of you, Ben."

The mailman grinned, then leaned into the back of the truck and fetched a package. It measured about ten-by-twelve-by-four inches, and was wrapped in brown paper secured with sturdy twine. "This the one?"

Cooper's wintry eyes sparkled at the sight of the postmark that identified it as *the* package. "Aye. Rochester, New York. That's my parcel. Puts me back in business. Well, I best be—"

"Good place to be these days," Ben interrupted.

Cooper nodded in tight-lipped agreement. "Not the best of times. Well, I best be—"

"Nope," Ben interrupted again. "You hear, they let half the people down at the mill go yesterday? Paper's full of stories. Got an extra here somewhere." Ben twisted in his seat to find it, and turned back to the window. "Here we go, Mr. Coo—" He paused when he saw Cooper was gone, then shrugged and drove off along the road that wound through the valley. Its idyllic beauty belied the fact that, despite President Roosevelt's

New Deal, much of rural America was still struggling to recover from the Depression.

Cooper set the package on the kitchen table, and snipped the twine, then began tearing at the wrapping like a starving man who'd just received a sack of groceries. The lettering on the shiny yellow box said: Eastman Kodak Company Orthochromatic Sheet Film. An anxious tingle rose in the pit of his stomach as he carried it into the crimson blackness of his darkroom where the stinging odor of chemicals reached full intensity. He used a thumbnail to break the seal, then removed the black envelope, and opened the flap. His fingers found the edges of the celluloid sheets, and went about loading the film holders that he used with his camera.

A short time later, he emerged from the cottage, looking somewhat like a door-to-door salesman burdened with his wares. A cracked leather bag stuffed with equipment hung from one shoulder, and his prized eight-by-ten Graflex affixed to its wooden tripod balanced on the other. Decades of service had given the finely crafted instrument the look of a burnished antique. Cooper pulled the door closed behind him, then paused and craned his neck skyward.

The sun burned softly behind clouds that the wind had sculpted into long lyrical wisps. Cooper studied them for a moment, then smiled approvingly and strode down the leaf-covered drive beneath bare, iron-gray trees that perfectly suited the hint of snow he sensed in the air.

Chapter Twenty-Six

The village of Newbury had been built by people who were acutely sensitive to scale and proportion and paid careful attention to detail; but, of late, despite the warmth of crackling fires that sent graceful plumes curling from chimneys, and the snow flurries that made rooftops sparkle, its prim dwellings appeared tattered, and the people who lived in them seemed to have lost their sense of vitality and well-being.

Joe Clements drove down Main Street, as he did every morning, troubled by the Out Of Business signs that papered many of the storefronts. A lean man in his early thirties with chiseled features and neatly parted hair, Joe had lived in Newbury all his life and believed there was no better place to raise a family and run a business. He parked outside a shop where a sign proclaimed Clements & Son Printers, and smiled at the racket of the presses and linotypes that made the pavement vibrate beneath his feet—a racket he'd grown to love as a child. It served as a subtle reminder of how he had worked at his father's knee, sweeping floors, making deliveries, and learning the fine points of typography, the properties of papers and inks, and the need to treat employees and clients alike with fairness and respect.

Joe greeted his workers as he made his way between the clanking machines to his office, a small space separated from the work area by a mahogany and textured glass partition that muted the noise. Proofs of jobs that Clements & Son had run over the years—calendars, catalogues, business forms, posters, and everything in between—hung on the walls. In front of the window stood a stalwart oak desk piled with papers and a chair with tired leather cushions studded with brass tacks.

"Mornin', Mr. Clements," Lucas Bartlett said as Joe entered. An energetic fellow in his early twenties, he stood next to a potbellied stove warming his hands.

"Lucas," Joe said, hanging his mackinaw and scarf behind the door. "I hope this means you're finished."

Bartlett nodded and broke into a complacent grin, then handed him a thick manila envelope. It contained several dozen black-and-white photographs of hand tools and farming equipment.

Joe spread them out across the desk. "Good work, Lucas," he finally said. "Sharp, plenty of contrast. They'll make beautiful halftones."

"Yeah, I know. Mr. Mitchell was really tickled."

"Speaking of Ed," Joe said, surprised to see a balding paunchy fellow coming toward the office. "Ed, didn't expect you by today."

Mitchell brushed the snow from his coat as he entered, then pulled off a glove and shook Joe's hand. "Neither did I, I'm afraid."

"I was just telling Lucas, I think he did an excellent job on these."

Bartlett's chest filled with pride threatening to pop the buttons on his shirt. "They're the makings of the best Christmas catalogue Mitchell Hardware'll ever have, if I do say so myself."

Ed Mitchell nodded halfheartedly. "I thought so too. Unfortunately, the bank didn't agree."

The color began draining from Joe's face.

"They just turned down my loan," Mitchell went on. "I'm afraid I'm going to have to cancel the order."

"Cancel?" Joe gasped.

Mitchell's lips tightened into a thin line as he nodded. "I'm sorry. I've no choice, Joe. My business just went under."

"But we're running the job right now," Joe protested. "The halftones are all that's left."

Mitchell shrugged in frustration. "Care to tell me what I'm going to do with ten thousand mail order catalogues? I mean, you can print 'em if you want; but I'll never be able to pay you for 'em."

"What about the stock, inks, and plates? I mean, they're already bought and paid for, Ed. You're going to have to cover those expenses."

"I would if I could, Joe, but I'm bankrupt. Broke. There's nothing left."

Bartlett groaned and glanced to his photographs. "Nothing?"

"Nothing," Mitchell echoed. "I'm sorry. Believe me, I really am." He backed away a few steps, then turned, and hurried from the office.

Bartlett emitted a forlorn sigh. "Only work I had."

"You and me both," Joe said. He was staring at the photographs in disbelief when he sensed the silence and realized the racket in the shop had abated. He exchanged looks with Bartlett, then went to the doorway.

All the machinery was shut down.

His employees stood next to the suddenly stilled behemoths, staring at Joe with hopeless eyes. Foreman Gundersen; linotype operators Murphy and O'Hara; pressmen Benedetti, Lecont and Hendricks; and Porter, the kid who handled the paper cutter. They were all standing there, spirits broken, heads hanging, eyes taut with apprehension.

Joe swallowed hard, forced a smile, and went out onto the floor to reassure them.

Chapter Twenty-Seven

Cooper always thought the white clapboard bungalow that stood back from the beach beneath a stand of wind-shaped pines had a quiet dignity and seemed at peace with nature; and he'd always wanted to photograph it; but the angle of light, or patterns of shadow, or his mood, was never quite right. Not until this morning. Not until a brief flurry of powder-fine snow had given the scene a breathtaking crystalline sparkle.

The spiked legs of his tripod were set securely in the sand; and Cooper crouched behind the Graflex, the blackout cloth draped over his head, listening to the ebb and flow of the surf as he composed the picture. He extended the bellows, enhancing the trees with their swooping branches that embraced the bungalow as if protecting it, fine-tuned the focus, then threw off the cloth, and inserted one of the film holders. He was about to fire the shutter when a young woman emerged from the bungalow, pulling on a coat. It struck him that something about her presence complemented the scene. So, he waited until she was just where he wanted her, then thumbed the cable release.

"Hello there," she called out as she approached. "I hope I didn't spoil your picture?"

"Nope," Cooper grunted. "I only fire that shutter when I want to."

"Well, good," she said brightly. "I've often seen you passing by and decided it was time to say hello. I'm Alicia. Alicia Clements."

"Cooper. Dylan Cooper. Dylan's more than enough."

Alicia smiled, then glanced curiously to the Graflex. "I've never seen a camera like that before. Not up close anyway." She squinted at it, and pointed to the lens. "What are the little numbers for?"

"They're called 'F' stops," he replied, grasping the serrated lens ring. The harsh daylight emphasized the coarseness of his hands and called attention to his fingernails which were cracked and totally blackened. "See that iris openin' and closin' in there?" he prompted as he clicked through the stops.

Alicia leaned closer to the lens and saw the overlapping steel blades stepping down in precise increments from a wide open position to a pinpoint.

"Just like the human eye," Cooper went on, clicking through them again. "It controls how much light gets to the film, among other things."

Alicia responded with a pensive nod, then crouched to the ground glass, and pulled the cloth over her head. "Hey?" she called out, her voice ringing with surprise. "Everything's upside down in here?"

"It'll take me till tomorrow to explain that to you," Cooper replied with an amused grin.

Alicia reappeared from beneath the cloth. "That's okay. I've got plenty of time."

Cooper glanced to the sky. "Well, I'm afraid I don't. Take my word for it. It all comes out right side up when it's done." Another anxious glance to the sky heightened his sense of urgency. "Just about where I want it. But not for long."

"What do you mean?"

"The light. I'm either sitting around waitin' for it, or I'm chasin' after it." He gestured to her bulging tummy and, letting his burr thicken with charm, added, "Rather like having a baby, I imagine."

Alicia chuckled, clearly taken by him. A wholesome woman of simple beauty, she was in her seventh month and her skin had taken on a lush radiance.

"Sorry to be hurrying off like this." Cooper bent to the camera, gathered the legs of the tripod and tilted it onto his shoulder. "This time of year, I'm always on the lookout for a special Christmas picture."

"Oh, I hope you find it," Alicia said, pulling her coat around her against the cold.

"I always do," Cooper said with a mysterious twinkle. "And I've been doing it every year for as long as I can remember." He smiled and started off down the beach, bent beneath the weight of the equipment that sent each step deep into the sand.

Chapter Twenty-Eight

The Clements's bungalow was heated by a cast-iron furnace in the basement along with a stone fireplace in the parlor. The latter was tastefully furnished with a floral patterned sofa, several wicker easy chairs on opposite sides of a coffee table, a wall of bookcases, and a rolltop desk where Joe sat poring over bills and invoices that were getting the best of him.

"Time for a break," Alicia announced, bringing him a cup of coffee. "I just made it."

"Thanks," Joe said glumly, reviewing the bills. "We had a coal delivery this week?"

Alicia nodded. "Everyone's saying it's going to be a long winter. Best to make sure the bin is full."

"We still have to pay for it." He sipped his coffee, then went to a window. A crescent moon hung in the darkness, dappling the sea with silver-blue light.

Alicia drifted after him and ran her palm across his back. "It'll be okay, darling. It will."

"It's hard to believe, after what happened today."

"You're not being fair to yourself, Joe. This isn't the first order you've had cancelled."

"True, but what's going on in the rest of the country is

going on in Newbury too. These are bad times. No time to be starting a family."

Alicia forced a comical frown; then cradled her tummy. "I hope he didn't hear you. He'll come into this world thinking he isn't wanted."

"Hey, no jokes, okay?" Joe fetched a sheet of paper from the desk and held it up to her. "One new order—one—unconfirmed. If I lose it, I'm out of business."

Alicia's jaw slackened. "I didn't realize it was that bad. I mean, it's the—"

"Well, it is!" Joe snapped, wishing he could take it back the instant he'd said it. "I'm sorry. I don't mean to take it out on you; but I'll have to close up at the end of the month and . . . and let everyone go."

"Oh, Joseph, no," Alicia groaned. "I'd no idea. I mean, it's the first time you mentioned it."

"Wasn't any sense worrying you." He dropped into the desk chair and took a long swallow of coffee.

"When will you hear about that order?"

"Tomorrow. I'm taking the train down to Boston."

Alicia wrapped her arms around him. "You'll get it, Joe. I know you will."

Joe stared at his coffee for a moment; then, still far from convinced that she was right, he leaned against the gentle swell of her stomach and looked up at her. "I love you," he whispered.

"I love you too," she said, kissing his forehead. "Don't worry, it'll all work out."

Joe nodded morosely.

"It will," Alicia said. "Did you notice the poinsettias in the yard have already started to bud?"

"No, what's that have to do with this?"

"The holidays, Joe. Things seem to have a way of working out at this time of year." Alicia said it with as much conviction as she could muster; but it was clear the business was in serious difficulty and she was deeply concerned.

Chapter Twenty-Nine

The next morning, after dropping Joe at the train station, Alicia drove to the Town Square and parked their roadster in front of a house where a neatly lettered shingle proclaimed: Edward F. Cheever, M.D.

Doctor Cheever had been caring for the people of Newbury for more than thirty years, and had brought many of them into the world, Alicia among them. After a routine examination, he peered over his rimless spectacles, declared that mommy and baby were doing fine, and sent Alicia on her way.

The doctor's stately fieldstone house was just across the square from the Newbury Community Church. It was sheathed in white-painted clapboard and topped by a steeple that soared into the autumn foliage above; and as Alicia went to her car, her attention was drawn to the spirited singing that was coming from within.

"God rest ye merry gentlemen,
Let nothing you dismay . . .
Remember Christ our Savior,
Was born on Christmas day . . ."

To save us all from Satan's power,
When we were gone astray . . .
O tidings of comfort and joy,
Comfort and joy.
O tidings of comfort and joy!

Alicia paused in reflection. She had been a member of the choir as a teenager and a regular at weekly services with her parents who gave generously of their time and what little money they could spare; but after their passing Alicia's commitment to her church waned.

Now, humming the carol to herself, she hurried past the roadster and across the square to the church.

The pastor was clapping his hands to silence the choir as Alicia entered. "You're rushing the tempo. Slow down, savor the words, extend the phrases fully," he instructed before sweeping his hands in a graceful arc and the church filled with soaring voices.

Alicia slipped into one of the pews near the back and knelt in prayer. She prayed that her baby would be born healthy as Dr. Cheever said, then said a special prayer that Joe's business meeting would go well. She became so caught up in her hopes, fears and thoughts that she didn't realize choir practice had ended until she felt a hand on her shoulder.

"Alicia?" the pastor said, pleased to see her.

"Oh, Pastor Martin," Alicia exclaimed in surprise. "The choir . . . it sounds just . . . just wonderful."

"Well, we still miss your cheerful soprano," he said, sounding as if he meant it. The slight fellow with sparkling eyes and gray-flecked hair had been the pastor here for nearly three decades. "We miss you at Sunday services too."

Alicia nodded in contrition. "Well, between keeping house and helping out with the business and now the baby coming, the days just seem to get filled."

Pastor Martin absolved her with a smile. "Speaking of the business, how's Joe doing these days?"

"Working harder than ever. He'll soon have another mouth to feed," Alicia replied, forcing a laugh; then her eyes clouded and she added, "Business has been terrible, Pastor Martin. He's . . . he's been talking about closing the shop."

"Oh, I'm sorry to hear that," Pastor Martin said. "But I can't say I'm surprised. So many of our parishioners are struggling to get by. I remind them that God has a plan for each of us; and these tough times are undoubtedly part of it. A test perhaps."

Alicia nodded, then her eyes filled. "Will you say a prayer that Joe gets this order he's after?"

"Of course, I will. Why don't you both come by one day. I can't save Joe's business, but I might be able to raise his spirits."

"I'm sure you could, but you know Joe . . . he isn't much of a churchgoer."

The Pastor's eyes narrowed. "The last time was the day I married you, if I'm not mistaken."

Alicia nodded and glanced to her tummy. "And the next will be for the christening, I imagine."

"Well, don't you be a stranger," Pastor Martin said. "And don't give up on Joe. We'll soon be celebrating the birth of Jesus. God sent Him to redeem us all, Alicia. I don't recall anything in the Bible excluding men from Newbury who aren't churchgoers."

Chapter Thirty

Just down the beach from the Clements's bungalow, a massive rock formation cut through the tidal pools in a sweeping arc that extended into the sea. For millennia, the windward face had been pounded smooth by angry surf, while the leeward, gently lapped by harbor waters, had remained craggy and untouched. Cooper was drawn to the contrast and photographed it often: at dawn, at dusk, at the height of thunderstorms, and raging blizzards; and, today, in wintry fog, his Graflex aimed at a dock where a weathered rowboat which had been pulled out for the winter, lay upside down on the salt-stained decking. He racked the bellows back and forth, bringing the vessel's craggy hull into sharp focus, then made his exposure. The snap of the shutter segued to a voice.

"Hello up there?"

Cooper turned and looked down to see Alicia bundled against the cold, waving a mittened hand. She had just returned home from the doctor's and her impromptu church visit and spotted the old fellow as she got out of her car.

"Well, hello," Cooper said, pleasantly surprised, as he clambered off the rocks and joined her. "Sorry, I couldn't chat longer yesterday. You sure seemed to be full of questions."

Alicia nodded emphatically. "I still am."

Cooper had sensed this inevitability and broke into a knowing smile. "Answer 'em as best I can."

"Okay. Will you tell me what makes you haul that heavy camera around day after day?"

"Well," Cooper mused, "I could say since the Depression there isn't much else to do anyway. But it's simpler than that. It's what I do. Dylan Cooper was put on this earth to take pictures."

"You certainly sound sure of that."

"Aye. I'm positive."

"Since when? I mean, when did you know?"

Cooper's eyes took on a mischievous glint. "I guess when I sold my sister's bicycle to buy my first camera. Caught a nasty caning for that one, I did. My bottom stung for a week."

Alicia chuckled heartily.

Cooper laughed along with her, then glanced to his equipment. "Time for me to be going, if I'm ever going to get to work on these negatives."

Alicia's eyes widened with curiosity.

"I'm afraid, there's no time for questions about that, now," Cooper added before she could ask.

"Okay. No questions," Alicia said, undaunted. "Suppose I just tag along and watch?"

"Nothing to see. It's all done in darkness."

"Really? That sounds fascinating."

"It's a small space. There's only room for one."

"But you've taken pictures of my bungalow and my boat," Alicia pleaded. "I just want to see what happens next. I think it's only fair, don't you?"

"*Your* boat?" Cooper asked, changing the subject.

Alicia nodded proudly. The dinghy had been built in the

classic New England style with brass oarlocks and a hull of lapstrake planking that formed a graceful curve at the prow. "It was my father's," she replied. "He was a lobsterman. Worked these waters for nearly fifty years. He taught me to row when I was nine. Same boat as a matter of fact. We're old friends."

"Ah, they're the best kind, aren't they?"

"And what does that mean?" she asked, a hint of indignation creeping into her voice.

"It means they're dependable, loyal. You can count on them, and they can count on you." Cooper's burr thickened with charm. "Of course, they all start out as new ones, don't they?"

"They certainly do," Alicia replied, pleased by the gesture. "You live nearby?"

"Up the hill a ways," he replied.

"We can take my car if you like, it'll be faster."

Cooper thought it over for a moment, then nodded. He gathered his equipment, and a short time later they were settled in the roadster, winding up the road that led from the coast to his cottage. Alicia parked next to Cooper's battered truck.

He headed straight for the darkroom. The mild odor of gas and oil that had once permeated the garage had long ago been replaced by the heady blend of bromides, sulfites, and hydroquinone. "Sit over there, and don't be underfoot," Cooper growled as if to a child. He wasted no time developing his negatives; and now, while they were drying, he fetched the one he'd taken of the bungalow yesterday and stepped to the small table where he made his prints.

Alicia perched on the stool to which she'd been assigned, watching as he cleaned the negative with a soft brush. When satisfied it was free of dust, he placed it atop an eight-by-ten sheet of Royal Velox—the photographic paper he had come to favor because of its rich luster and fine gradation quality—and covered it with a piece of glass which kept the surfaces in contact; then he grasped a length of beaded chain hanging from a light fixture directly above the table. "Ready?"

Alicia nodded.

Cooper pulled on the chain.

The switch emitted a loud click, the bare bulb came to life, and Cooper began counting.

Alicia squinted at the blinding glare and looked about curiously. They'd been working in red-tinged blackness from the start, and this was her first look at the darkroom. The walls, ceiling and floor were painted black. A long table along one wall held three enameled trays filled with chemicals that had the clarity of water. Above the table, yellow boxes of printing papers were stacked neatly on shelves. Below, brown bottles of chemicals with matching yellow labels and graduated measuring beakers stood in wooden racks. The sound of trickling water came from a sink at the far end where a number of negatives were still washing. Alicia was thinking: stark, efficient, organized, not a speck of dust anywhere when the light switch clicked and the room was suddenly plunged back into darkness.

Cooper removed the sheet of glass, separated the negative and print, and slipped the latter into the tray of developer.

Alicia's curiosity got the best of her. She left the stool and crept up next to him, watching as the chemical did its work. The wind-shaped trees that framed the bungalow were the first images to emerge. "You sure I didn't spoil it?"

"No, of course not," Cooper replied as her figure appeared in the foreground of the photograph. "There you are. Aye, it's a fine picture." He was gently rocking the tray, coaxing every nuance of tone and texture from the print when the muffled ring of a telephone came from somewhere in the cottage. Cooper ignored it, letting it ring and ring. "They'll call back if it's important," he said, continuing to rock the tray until the blacks had attained the richness of velvet, and the whites the crystalline sparkle of the snow that dusted the trees. Then he offered a pair of wooden tongs to Alicia. "Now, by the corner; and careful, that stuff blackens everything it touches, especially fingernails."

Alicia glanced with apprehension from his hands to hers, then gingerly transferred the print to the stop bath, an acid which neutralized the developer on contact and arrested the process.

"That's it," Cooper said, encouraging her. He rocked the tray to ensure the print was submerged, and left it there for a few moments. "Okay, now into the last one. It has to stay in there for a while."

"Why?"

"It's a special chemical that fixes the image in the paper. Makes it permanent."

"Photographers have to know a lot about chemistry, don't they?"

Cooper shook his head no. "Not really. I don't have half the knowledge my father did."

"Oh, then I imagine he was either a pharmacist or chemistry professor, wasn't he?"

"Neither, I'm afraid. Not that he wasn't keen enough, mind you; but no, he was apprenticed to the mills as a boy. Learned his craft and worked his way up. A dyemaster, he was. All the wools had to pass his inspection. He could pick out the slightest imperfection in color or tone; had the most incredible eye." Cooper paused in reflection, then covered the tray that held the finished print and opened the door. "Now, what do you say to some tea and biscuits?"

"They have to smell better than these chemicals."

"I've never been able to make up my mind about that," Cooper said without a hint of levity as he showed Alicia into the parlor. "Make yourself comfortable. I'll just be a few minutes."

In marked contrast to the darkroom, it was dusty and cluttered. The windows were rain-spattered, the curtains tattered and yellowed with age, the upholstery threadbare, and the floors unwaxed. Books were stuffed into rickety cases and piled on every surface; various photogenic objects—rusted machinery, twisted pieces of driftwood, sun-bleached bones, dried flowers—were scattered about, along with unopened mail, newspapers, copies of the *National Geographic* magazine, and potted plants that begged to be watered.

Alicia frowned at their droopy leaves and rock-hard soil. She was about to follow Cooper into the kitchen to fetch some water and give them a lifesaving drink when the photographs that literally papered the walls caught her eye: pictures of Newbury with its snug harbor and fishing boats. Of its houses, farms and shops. Its sawmills and canneries. Its snowcapped mountains and lush forests. Its pastoral landscapes and raging sea. And its townsfolk. Pictures of tradesmen, field hands, fishermen, blacksmiths, and bankers; of schoolteachers and loggers; of rugged faces, weathered hands, and weary eyes. Each black-and-white print had a powerful vision and sparkling luminosity that made it all the more moving, all the more breathtaking; and it dawned on Alicia that though the people and places had been part of her life for more than twenty-five years, she'd never really seen them before; never been aware of their inherent beauty and poetic themes.

She was lost in her thoughts when she came upon several whose subject matter wasn't at all familiar. Taken from the air, they were displayed above the fireplace where an aviator's scuffed helmet and pitted goggles hung from a nail. A snapshot of uniformed flyers, posing in front of an open cockpit biplane, hung next to them. Alicia was studying it when Cooper returned with a tray that, along with biscuits, teapot, and china, held a bottle of whiskey.

"This is you, isn't it?" Alicia prompted, pointing to one of the men in the snapshot.

"Aye," Cooper grunted. He placed the tray on an upside down packing crate that served as a table. "The funny looking frightened one in the middle."

Alicia emitted a fetching chuckle. "Frightened? I've always thought of flyers as fearless and handsome."

"Oh, that they were," Cooper replied, basking in the compliment. "But I wasn't a flyer, you see. I was assigned to an aerial reconnaissance unit. We'd go up, over enemy territory, and I'd hang over the side with my camera and take pictures of the ground."

Alicia hugged herself and shivered at the thought. "Oh, I'd be frightened too."

"Aye, I was glad when the war was over and I could get back home; back to . . . to—" Cooper almost said, to my wife, but paused, deciding whether or not he'd share it with her. "—back to taking pictures of whatever happens to catch my eye." He sipped his tea in reflection, then seemed to stiffen with anger. "Something about being told what to photograph has never sat right with me. Cost me a job once."

"You mean you were fired?" Alicia prompted.

Cooper's eyes flared as if he'd been insulted. "I quit," he snapped. Then sensing he'd startled her, he gently explained, "It was years ago. I was exhibiting at one of those fancy Beacon Hill galleries at the time. The reviews were . . ."

"In Boston?" Alicia asked, sounding impressed.

Cooper nodded. "The Van Dusen. One of the best. The reviews were quite favorable, as I recall. I had visions of fame and fortune, of my work being acquired by museums and private collectors . . ."

"So what happened?" Alicia asked, hearing the disappointment in his voice.

"Nothing. Didn't sell a picture. Not even one. It seems the carriage trade didn't think photographs were investment grade art." Cooper chortled at what he was about to say, then added, "I was broke, in debt, and being evicted from my rooming house."

"That's where the job comes in, doesn't it?" Alicia prompted.

Cooper nodded smartly. "Aye. I took on an assignment—a commercial assignment—fashion photography. I even convinced a young lady I was sweet on to model for me."

Alicia's brows arched with intrigue. "I see."

"Aye, and commercial work or no, the pictures were magnificent," Cooper went on, caught up in the memory. "I was bursting with pride when I delivered them to the client. You know what he did?"

"I can't imagine," Alicia replied, apprehensively.

"He rejected them. That's what! The fool claimed that they were too artistic; that—that the model was too exotic. He actually had the gall to show me someone else's pictures—uninspired, pedestrian trash—as an example of what he wanted." Then in a burr thicker than the molasses he sometimes spooned into his tea, Cooper boomed, "And you know why?! Because he thought they'd sell more bonnets! Well, that's when I headed for the door. All he was interested in was making money! Unprincipled son of a—agghhh!" Cooper groaned with disgust. "Enough of that nonsense."

Alicia was taken by his intensity, and could only nod in response. They settled into overstuffed chairs that faced each other across the packing crate. Cooper poured two cups of tea. "Lemon?"

"Please," Alicia replied, smiling at what she was about to say. "But not too bitter."

"Oh, clever aren't you?" Cooper bristled, stung by her insight. "But oh, no. No, that I'm not. Not bitter a'tall." He squeezed some lemon into Alicia's tea, then poured some whiskey into his own. "As it turns out, Mr. Van Dusen was a very supportive fellow. Suggested I send my pictures to the National Geographic Society. They ended up buying every one of 'em; and I ended up buying this cottage. Best part is, they've been buying 'em on and off, ever since."

"Well," Alicia said with a sip of her tea, "things have a way of working out, don't they?" She set the cup down, and went about spreading marmalade on a biscuit.

Cooper's face brightened as he watched her. "You know, I'm really enjoying this. I mean, it isn't often I have a young visitor to spar with."

"I'm rather enjoying it too. It's the first time I've ever made friends with—" She paused, realizing she was about to say something she shouldn't. "Well, I mean, I've never known—"

Cooper laughed and interrupted. "An old man?"

Alicia reddened with embarrassment. "I'm sorry. I didn't mean to—Well, I guess that is what I was going to say."

"Well, I guess I am old to someone of your tender years. But maybe we can be a little more charitable than that. How about . . ." Cooper paused and searched for an appropriate description. "Someone who's managed a fair amount of livin', and is showin' a bit of wear?"

Alicia considered it and smiled. "I think I could accept that." She took a sip of tea, then glanced at her watch. "Oh my," she exclaimed. "I seem to have lost track of time." She jumped to her feet, made her apologies, and headed for the door, pulling on her coat.

"I'll bring the picture by tomorrow," Cooper called out as she got into the roadster.

"Why don't you come for dinner?"

Cooper wrestled with it briefly. "Why not?"

"Good," Alicia exclaimed. "Six-thirty." She drove off with a wave, then glanced back over her shoulder and shouted, "Your plants need watering!"

Cooper stood at the gate and waved back. Alicia's sudden departure had left him with misty eyes and a vast emptiness that brought on an alarming surge of emotion. It wasn't that he was smitten, which of course he was, but that the feelings she stirred had been dormant for so long; feelings that, though crushed by life's vicissitudes, had steadfastly refused to die; and, now, as the bittersweet memories surfaced, Grace's lithe figure pirouetted in the bubbling surf; and her contagious laugh echoed off the hills; and then, for the briefest of moments, her fragrance filled his head, replacing the stinging scent of chemicals.

It had been twenty years since Cooper had left his bride to go off to war; but, it wasn't the memory of their poignant farewell that had so powerfully touched him, but of his painful homecoming almost a year later; and, now, as if it were yesterday, he recalled how he had returned to their cottage in Newbury, expecting to find his beloved Grace and their newly born child waiting for him, only to learn of the tragic events that had caused Grace to return to Scotland.

Cooper's anguish at the heartbreaking news had been tempered by time, but never forgotten; nor, despite his immediate return to Scotland and the months he'd spent in a frustrating and finally futile search for Grace, nor despite the many letters he had written her over the years without receiving a single reply had he ever forsaken his vow to find her. Indeed, for two decades now, his heart had kept the hope alive; but she had long ago slipped away, and he'd since lived alone with the emptiness.

Chapter Thirty-One

The sun always set directly behind Newbury's train station at this time of year. It framed the steep roof against a pewter sky, and made the tracks shimmer like polished silver. The afternoon local from Boston had already come and gone; and the few passengers who'd gotten off had long ago headed home. All except one.

In fedora and woollen overcoat, Joe Clements stood inside the unheated station, keeping one eye on the parking area, the other on a newspaper. The headline read: Economic Recovery Expected To Be Slow. The story stated that despite the Public Works Programs funded by Congress, it would be years before small businesses and rural communities were expected to benefit. Joe sighed and glanced at his watch with impatience. His eyes were drifting to another story about the massing of German troops along the western border of Poland when he heard a vehicle approaching. The station's old window panes distorted the scene beyond, but it was undoubtedly their roadster.

"Sorry I'm late, darling," Alicia said as Joe got in next to her.

"I've only been waiting a few minutes," he said coolly, kissing her cheek.

"Good," Alicia chirped, oblivious to his mood. "It's a long story. I'll tell you on the way."

Minutes later, they were racing along the beach road toward the bungalow. Alicia talked above the roar of the motor, punctuating her bubbly chatter with shift changes and bursts of acceleration: "Of course, he wasn't very keen on the idea—and it took a little coaxing—but I finally talked him into letting me come along."

"Uh-huh," Joe muttered distantly.

"He's really an amazing old fellow."

"I'll bet."

"His name's Cooper. Dylan Cooper. We printed a photograph of the bungalow. I just lost track of time."

"I said I only waited a few minutes, Alicia," Joe said indulgently. "It's okay."

"Then we had biscuits and tea and just talked and talked . . . and . . ."

"Better turn on your lights."

"What?"

"Your lights."

"Lights? Oh, lights." Alicia flipped the switch, then shifted down a gear, and guided the car into a sharp turn. The headlights swept across the road and flickered between the bare trees, painting the darkness a soft yellow. "Wait till you see it," she resumed without missing a beat. "The picture, I mean. It's really beautiful. He said he would—"

"I'm sure it's very nice."

"Oh, it is. He said he'd bring it by tomorrow. So I asked him to dinner. I hope that's okay?"

"Well, I suppose. I mean—"

"Good. I know you're going to—"

"Alicia?" Joe interrupted gently.

"I know, you're going to like him," she charged on undaunted. "He's—"

"Alicia?!" Joe said, his tone sharpening. "Alicia, I wish you'd listen."

"Oh, sure. What is it?"

"You just drove past the house."

"Oh my goodness!" She hit the brakes, made a U-turn, and headed back toward the bungalow. "I just got so wrapped up in my story that I—"

"Really?" Joe snapped. "I hadn't noticed."

"Pardon me?!" Alicia exclaimed, stung by his tone. She pulled the car into the drive behind the bungalow. It had barely come to a stop when Joe opened the door to get out. "Not so fast, Clements," she said, stopping him. "Now, what was that all about?"

"Well, to be brutally frank, Alicia, you haven't stopped talking since I got in the car; and right now, I need a listener."

Alicia nodded in apology. "Your meeting . . . you want to tell me about your meeting, don't you? You know," she raced on before Joe could utter a word, "I stopped in at church after Dr. Cheever's this morning and I—"

"Church?" Joe's tone had a disapproving timbre. "What's church got to do with this?"

"Well, I said a prayer that your meeting would go well and you'd get that order."

"So much for the power of prayer," Joe snapped.

"I guess that means you . . . you . . ." The words caught in her throat and she took a deep breath before continuing. ". . . You didn't get it?"

"No, Alicia, I didn't."

"I'm sorry. I guess I just didn't want to hear it."

"Neither did I, believe me," Joe retorted.

Alicia's shoulders sagged. She'd been hoping beyond hope that he would reply to the contrary; and the disappointment and sense of failure in his eyes nearly moved her to tears. She reached out and touched his face. They sat there in silence, hugging each other, then went inside.

Alicia took a few moments to pull herself together, then washed her face with cold water and went about preparing dinner. She was setting the table when she noticed Joe at the desk, staring at the pile of bills. "How about taking in a movie, tonight?" she suggested, trying to cheer him.

Joe lit a cigarette in silence.

"Joe?"

"We can't afford it."

"I know, but *Animal Crackers* is playing, and—"

"The Marx Brothers?" Joe interrupted, his mood brightening somewhat.

"Uh-huh. I think we should go."

"We'll see," he mumbled as he exhaled, filling the space between them with smoke.

Like its church and train station, Newbury's movie theater had an inviting charm; and for ninety minutes, Joe, Alicia, and a capacity crowd of townsfolk sat in red velvet seats and doubled over with laughter at the madcap antics; at Groucho's African lecture—"One morning I shot an elephant in my pajamas. How he got into my pajamas I'll never know!" And at the side-splitting humor of Harpo's bridge game; and when the image faded, and the house lights came up, the audience headed for the exits, buzzing with renewed vitality.

"Well," Alicia said brightly as they huddled against the cold and crossed the street to the roadster. "You seem to be feeling a little better."

"I am. It was a good idea. Thanks."

Joe had just gotten her settled in the car when the newsstand on the corner caught his eye. "Be right back." He closed the door and hurried off, joining the crowd that surged around the kiosk.

The dealer was doing a brisk business in newspapers and magazines: *Liberty*, *Colliers*, *Life*, *The Saturday Evening Post* were the bestsellers among the latter. The front page stories ranged from the World's Fair in New York to the advent of war in Europe. The slight fellow chatted amiably with customers, most of whom he greeted by name, while his ink-smudged fingers made change with amazing speed and dexterity, darting in and out of the pockets of his apron that bulged with pennies, nickels, dimes, and quarters respectively.

Joe spotted a copy of *Life* and quickly plucked it from the rack, then paid for it and sauntered back toward the car where Alicia sat watching the action, quietly entertaining an idea that had occurred to her.

Chapter Thirty-Two

He'd already showered, shaved, and dressed for work, but Joe Clements was anything but ready to face this day. He sat in the breakfast nook that overlooked the beach, stirring his coffee, and thumbing through the magazine he'd purchased the night before; though, at the moment, he had little interest in it.

Alicia was the one who found it intriguing. Hands wrapped around her cup to warm them, she watched as page after page of pictures went by; then glanced out the frosty window, reflecting on the idea she'd had last night. A wind had come up, rattling the shutters, and whipping the sea into a frenzy that sent waves crashing over the tiny dock.

"Well," Joe said in a morose tone, "I guess, I can't put it off any longer, can I?"

"Put off what?" Alicia wondered, still lost in her thoughts.

"The people in the shop. Today's the day."

"Today? So soon?"

"Good as any other day. It's only right to give them fair warning."

"Oh no," Alicia sighed, turning up the collar of her robe against the chill. "I'm sorry."

"I mean, some of them have been there since before I was born. A few actually began with Dad. He gave them Christmas bonuses this time of year. I'll be giving them pink slips. I was up half the night worrying about it."

"I know," she said softly, taking his hand in hers.

"And I still haven't figured out how to break it to them." He leaned back, staring at the ceiling in search of the answer.

"Well . . ." Alicia mused, her eyes drifting back to the window while she decided if she'd continue. "Maybe . . . Maybe you won't have to, Joe."

"I won't?" he wondered, mystified. "What do you mean? You going to do it for me?"

"No. I have an idea. I'm not sure about it, but with God's help, it might work."

"God?" Joe echoed with a sarcastic snicker. "Since when did you two become such pals?"

"Since you and I used to steal glances at each other at Sunday school," Alicia replied with a smile. "Under the circumstances, it seemed like a good time to get back in touch with Him."

"So what did He have to say?"

"Well, according to Pastor Martin, we should accept these difficult times as part of His plan. You remember the lesson about God having a plan for everyone? That it's up to each of us to trust in Him to reveal it to us?"

"Yeah, well, when it comes to Clements & Son Printers, it seems God's plan is to put a lot of decent people out of work."

"Joe, I know you're upset that you didn't get that order," Alicia resumed, undaunted, "but maybe it isn't part of the Plan. I can't be sure, but maybe, just maybe, this idea I have is. It wouldn't cost anything to hear me out."

"I'm sorry. Go ahead."

Alicia reached across the table and picked up the copy of *Life* magazine. "How many of these do you think that newsdealer sold last night?"

"Dozens. He couldn't make change fast enough."

Alicia nodded emphatically. "Right. And neither could the ticket seller at the movies. I'll bet half the people in that theater were out of work. And the other half facing financial difficulty of some kind."

"No question about it."

"But they were still there, weren't they?"

"Sure were," Joe conceded, curiously. He pulled a cigarette from the pack with his lips and lit it. "What does that have to do with the business?"

"My point is that people are spending the little money they have on things that will help them forget the misery in their lives; things that will take them to another place, a better time. Think about it." She put the copy of *Life* back in front of him. "This magazine didn't exist a few years ago. It was born in bad times, Joe, but it survived; it's doing well. And from the look of things, it's not the only one. I guess what I'm saying is, the printing business isn't dead. What's dead is business printing."

Joe nodded thoughtfully, struck by her incisive observation. "I can't argue with that; but we're a small shop with limited capacity, miles from where that kind of material is published. No one's going to give us an order to print a national magazine. Our work has always come from local sources."

"Exactly," Alicia exclaimed with a broad grin. "And I've got one for you."

"You do?"

"Dylan Cooper, my photographer friend. I did tell you he's coming to dinner, didn't I?"

Joe nodded, then his brow furrowed with confusion. "But how does he fit into this?"

"Well, while he's here, I think you should talk to him about publishing a book; a book of—"

Joe looked incredulous. "A book?"

"Uh-huh. A book of his pictures. His Christmas pictures. He said he takes a special one every year."

Joe stared at her dumbfounded. "Alicia, I'm not a publisher. I don't know the first thing about it. Not to mention that—"

"That's okay," she interrupted, gesturing to her bulging tummy. "I've never been a mother before either. What makes you think you can't learn?"

"That's different. Something like this could take the last of our savings."

"Well, as I recall, you do have the paper and inks left over from Ed Mitchell's job, don't you?"

"True. Still, we could end up with thousands of copies of that book in the shop and nothing in the bank. Besides, why do you think anyone would buy it?"

"Because I've seen Dylan's pictures, Joe. They're good, really good. He's been photographing this area for thirty years." She got to her feet, her voice rising with enthusiasm and a sense of awe, and resumed: "The mountains cloaked in mist; fishing boats at sunrise; winding lanes carpeted with leaves; Main Street with horses and buggies; the harbor blanketed in snow. Other places, better times, Joe. I'm convinced people around here would buy a book like that. And there are thousands of them . . ." She let it trail off, then found Joe's eyes with hers, and added, "And Christmas is just a few months away."

Joe leaned back in the chair, sorting it out. He'd always been taken by her resourcefulness and spunk. They were teenagers when he first experienced it. She was working after school in the local bakery at the time. The stern Dutch proprietor had a rule that only broken cookies be given to customers as samples; and one day, when Joe stopped by to flirt with Alicia and help himself to some free samples, the jar was empty. She discreetly smashed several of his favorites with her fist and slipped them beneath the lid. "It's not empty now," she said with a mischievous giggle. That was the moment he fell in love with her; and ever since, when he was beaten, she was undaunted; when he lost his way, she somehow found it; and when he ran out of ideas, she always managed to come up with one.

Now, Joe looked at her with a mixture of wary interest, and renewed hope. "You're really serious, aren't you?"

"Yes, I am," Alicia replied in her spirited way. "I have a good feeling about Dylan—about this idea. I think he'd be very receptive to it."

Chapter Thirty-Three

"Nope. Not interested," Cooper said with finality.

Joe forced a smile. "Well, I guess I got my answer, didn't I?"

"Aye. That you did."

"Well, it's not the one I was hoping for, I'm afraid. Perhaps, if I explained it more clearly . . ."

"Nope," Cooper grunted, unmoved. He drew on his pipe, emitting a stream of smoke that rose in graceful twists to the bungalow's peaked ceiling. "Christmas pictures or no, a book's just not in the cards for me."

"I don't see why not," Joe said, glancing to Alicia in search of support.

She was standing to one side of the crackling fire hanging Cooper's poetic photograph of the bungalow. He had set the print in a simple black frame that didn't compete with it for attention; and Alicia wasted no time fetching a hammer and nail from a drawer in the kitchen and finding just the right spot for it.

She was so intent on what she was doing that she seemed not to have noticed Joe's plaintive glance, though she had. Indeed, instead of acknowledging him, she was tilting the picture frame this way and that, making certain it was straight, and using the time to work out her strategy. "Well?" she finally prompted, stepping aside so they could see it.

"Perfect," Joe said.

Cooper's eyes narrowed. "A little lower on the left, Alicia."

Alicia smiled and made the adjustment. "You were right, Dylan. It's a *fine* picture," she said in her brightest voice. "Isn't it, Joe?"

"Oh, yes," Joe replied preoccupied. "Certainly is."

Alicia crossed the room and settled on the sofa opposite Cooper. "I guess I owe you an apology," she said in a matter-of-fact tone.

Cooper's brows went up as she anticipated. "Do you, now?"

"Uh-huh. You see, this was all my doing," she replied, further embellishing the mystery.

"And what might it be that was your doing?"

"The book. I mean, I'm the one who suggested to Joe that he talk to you about it."

Cooper toyed with his pipe stem. "Really, I'd no idea," he said with a wily smile. "Now, why would you do such a thing?"

"Because I thought you'd be interested in having a book of your Christmas pictures published; and if we did it in time for the holidays, I have a feeling it would be very—"

"Well, I'm not," Cooper interrupted, his burr taking on an abrasive edge. "And if *that's* the reason you invited me to dinner, then we'd best forget that, too." He jammed his pipe hard into the corner of his mouth, pulled himself from the chair, and lumbered across the room, scooping his well-worn mackinaw from the coat rack that stood near the door.

"Dylan?" Alicia called out. "Dylan, wait!"

Cooper paused and looked back at her, then tugged the pipe from between his teeth and fired his parting shot. "Like I said, old friends are the best kind."

Alicia flinched, stung by his words and the cocky thrust

of his jaw which he used to remind her that she knew all too well what he meant; but instead of taking offense, Alicia saw beyond the insult and the anger, and there was compassion not retaliation, in her eyes.

Cooper saw the emotion in them and, flushed with remorse, was not at all pleased with what he'd just done. "I suppose if I was really honest with myself, I'd have to admit it is something I've thought about on occasion."

Alicia broke into a knowing smile.

Cooper took a moment to regain his composure. "I guess, if I'm going to do something about it, I shouldn't wait too long, should I?"

"Oh, Dylan, don't say that," Alicia replied, guiding him to his chair. "You're—"

"I'm sixty-two, that's what I am," Cooper bellowed, unwilling to take his seat. "And when you get that far into the tunnel, you start seeing the other end pretty clear." He fidgeted self-consciously, then as if confiding in them, said, "You know, I take most of my pictures in my mind first, or at least I think I do, and lately I—" His voice broke and he faltered briefly. "Lately, I keep seeing this one picture, and I'm in it—me, and . . . and—" He paused, then dismissed it with a wave of his hand. "Well, that one won't be in the book, will it?"

The question hung there unanswered, the silence filled by the crackling that came from the fireplace.

Alicia caught Joe's eye and prompted him with a nod.

"So, Mr. Cooper," he began.

"Dylan."

"Dylan," Joe repeated. "Am I to take that to mean you've changed your mind?"

"No," Cooper replied, his tone sharpening. "It means I've decided to speak it." He looked Joe square in the eye, taking his measure of him. "If we're going to do this, Joe, I want to do it right. What do you know about publishing books?"

Joe held the old fellow's gaze for a moment. There was

only one answer. "Not a thing." He glanced to Alicia, then added, "But I'm willing to work day and night to learn."

Cooper tamped his pipe. "Well, you won't be the first fellow to do something who didn't know a thing about it when he started. I like people who are forthright, Joe. I think you and I are going to get along."

"So do I."

"Good. Now, would you mind telling me why you want to do this book?"

"Of course not. To make money. Right now, nothing's more important to me than keeping my business from going under."

Cooper's eyes hardened momentarily, then they took on a mischievous gleam and shifted to Alicia. "He sounds like a publisher already, if you ask me."

Alicia erupted with laughter.

Joe smiled good-naturedly and waited as Cooper took his seat. "All kidding aside, Dylan," he said as the painted wicker shifted and creaked. "I think we should get this issue settled right now."

"So do I. Besides, I've a feeling dinner'll be far more enjoyable if we do. Proceed."

"You want something and I want something, right?"

"Good a way as any of putting it."

"The way I see it, there's nothing wrong with making money from your book as long as it's the book you want. My employees are honest, hard working people with families who are counting on me to save their jobs. You know, not everyone is blessed with your talent, or the courage to live the way you do."

Cooper nodded in agreement. "I'm a lucky man, Joe. Very lucky," he said, smiling in reflection before his eyes narrowed with a question. "Have you thought about *how* you're going to pay them? I've enough to get by, but I don't have any funds to be advancing for that sort of thing. All I've got are my pictures."

Joe responded with a confident smile. "If Alicia is right, they're all we'll need."

Cooper settled back in the chair basking in the compliment. "Well, they say that everything has its time. I guess that's true, isn't it?"

"What do you mean, Dylan?" Alicia prompted.

"Oh, I've been meaning to take a picture of this bungalow for years; but I could never quite get around to it—not until the other day that is—and I've always wondered, why?" He struck a match on his pants and brought it to his pipe. "Now, I know."

"You've found this year's Christmas picture, haven't you?" Alicia prompted with a knowing smile.

"Aye," Cooper replied with a poignant sigh. "And perhaps much more."

Chapter Thirty-Four

The men who worked at Clements & Son were stunned by Joe's proposal. They stood around one of the layout tables in the middle of the shop, their eyes, along with their hopes, pinned on a man of ample girth wrapped in an ink-smeared printer's apron.

"In other words, Joe," Olaf Gundersen challenged in a voice that rang with disbelief and the graceful lilt of his Scandinavian ancestors, "You're asking us to work for no wages, aren't you?"

"No. No, Gundy, I'm not. What I said was—"

"Well, it bloody well sure sounds that way to me!" one of the linotype operators interrupted.

"To me too!" another bellowed, eliciting a chorus of angry rejoinders from the group.

"Hey! Hey, pipe down, now!" Gundersen scolded. An old-world craftsman in his sixties, he was the acknowledged master here as well as father figure, general adviser, and foreman. "Let the man speak."

Joe thanked him with a nod and resumed. "I said that if we do a good job, if the book is a success and sells, we'll all get paid and our families'll have the kind of Christmas we want for them. If it doesn't, well . . ." He let it trail off and splayed his hands. "Then we're all back to where we are right now."

The men nodded in grudging agreement.

"So," Gundersen said, "there's still a chance we could do a lot of work without making a dime in the end. Right?"

"I'm afraid so," Joe replied. "It's risky. No doubt about it. I'm taking a chance, and I'm asking you to do the same."

Another disgruntled murmur rose from the group.

Cooper was standing in a distant corner of the shop with a portfolio tucked under his arm, and an ambivalent scowl on his face. On one hand, he'd known all along it was too good to be true, and was fighting an impulse to storm out of there. On the other, he was champing at the bit to come forward and let the pictures speak for themselves.

Joe caught his eye and signaled him to be patient, then fixed his gaze on his employees. "I understand how you all feel; but if you think it through, you'll realize you have everything to gain and nothing to lose. Unless—" A cacophony of protests erupted. Joe waited until the group settled down, then played his trump card. "I was about to say, unless you have other jobs lined up already. Is that the case?"

The fight went out of them, as Joe knew it would, and left a gloomy silence in its place. Most of the men just shrugged. A few shook their heads no. Others exchanged uncertain looks.

"Then that's your choice," Joe concluded. "Take a chance here, or take a chance out there."

Cooper raised a brow, clearly impressed by Joe's timing and canny reasoning.

Gundersen nodded and took the men aside. They huddled in animated discussion for a few moments until a consensus was reached, then drifted back toward Joe. "All right, Joseph," Gundersen challenged like a feisty schoolmaster. "You said you figure this book will be successful because people are going to buy it, that right?"

"That's right, Gundy."

"That means you're looking a bunch of your customers in the eye, right now," the rotund foreman concluded, gesturing to the workers behind him. "We figure the best way to make our decision is to have a look at those pictures."

"I was planning to show them to you," Joe replied, his voice ringing with confidence. He was about to wave Cooper over, but Cooper was already making his way between the huge machines. He charged into the middle of the group, placed the portfolio on the table and removed a neat stack of his Christmas pictures. He was still spacing them out when Joe's employees surged forward to examine them, buzzing with excitement.

Chapter Thirty-Five

~~~~~~~~~~

The photoengravers on Dorchester Street in East Boston had spent the week cutting plates from a sampling of Cooper's pictures; and Clements & Son's finest press, a Mergenthaler rotary gravure with automatic and single-sheet feed, had spent it being cleaned, oiled, and recalibrated to microscopic tolerances.

Now, Gundersen set the first plate into the bed and locked it in position. The apprentices usually adjusted the inking rollers and fine-tuned the platen, but the old master insisted on doing it himself this time. When satisfied all was in order, he double-checked the paper feeder, and thumbed the green bakelite start button that was labeled in German. The press hissed to life, and quickly settled into its five-beat syncopation, spewing out proofs.

Joe slipped one from the stack and carried it to a layout table where Cooper was waiting with the original—a stunning print of a young woman cradling an infant that he'd taken at the Boston North Station decades ago. The one that had come to be called Madonna and Child. "Not bad for a test run," Joe announced proudly, placing them side by side.

"No, not bad at all," Gundersen chimed in after shutting down the press.

They both searched Cooper's face for a reaction.

"Dylan?" Joe finally prompted.

Cooper had remained impassive. Now he scowled. "Not bad, Joe, *terrible*."

"Terrible?" Joe gasped.

"That's a hundred-twenty line screen," Gundersen protested.

"Gundy's right. It sure couldn't be any sharper."

"Aye, it's plenty sharp," Cooper conceded. "The trouble is, it's flat. No sparkle. See?" He stabbed a gnarled finger at the offending proof, then flicked it across the table toward Joe. "The blacks are weak. They don't have enough depth. No, it's just not good enough. It has to be darker, richer."

Joe's troubled eyes shifted back to his foreman. "Gundy?" he pleaded.

Gundersen hooked his thumbs behind the yoke of his apron and shook his head no. "Darker? You know as well as I, it's impossible without losing definition."

"Why?" Cooper challenged. He'd always been as uncompromising with others as he was with himself, and decided this was no time to change.

"Because the process has limitations," Joe replied, his voice taking on a bit of an edge. "If we force the plate to hold any more ink, the detail will block up, and the whites will start going gray." He looked to his foreman for confirmation, but Gundersen was deep in thought, and didn't notice.

"Well, we have to do something, Joe," Cooper exhorted, unwilling to accept it. "Because we sure aren't publishing them like this."

Joe's shoulders sagged in defeat. "Then I guess we aren't publishing them at all."

Cooper sighed with frustration.

"Excuse me, gentlemen," Gundersen said in an assertive tone. "I may have been a bit hasty before."

"Oh?" Joe prompted.

"Well, for what it's worth, it occurred to me we might try running these like a two-color job."

"Two-color job?" Joe echoed, mystified. "I'm not sure I follow you, Gundy."

"Well, you're absolutely right when you say we can't put any more ink on the plate," Gundersen replied trying to be diplomatic. "But there's nothing that says we can't put more ink on the page."

Joe tilted his head in thought. "Yes, yes, that just might do it."

Cooper's eyes were darting back and forth between them. "Would you mind explaining what you two are going on about?"

"Instead of using two plates and two colors," Joe replied with growing enthusiasm. "We run the same plate and same color ink, twice, on the same page."

"Black on black," Cooper grunted, his face taking on a skeptical glower.

"The registration's got to be perfect, Gundy," Joe warned. "Think you can hold it?"

"Only one way to find out." Gundersen stepped to his press. Joe and the others gathered around him. Cooper folded his arms across his chest, and watched from a distance as Gundersen transferred the first run proofs to the paper-feed mechanism; then arranged them precisely, and started the press.

Joe took the first double-printed proof from the press and brightened. "It's better, Gundy; a lot better."

He handed it to Cooper. "Get your original, Dylan."

Cooper studied it briefly. "No need to, Joe. Look, it has life. It breathes." His book was suddenly a step closer to becoming a reality; and his heart pounded as he shook Gundersen's hand. "You're quite a genius, Gundy. Thanks."

Gundersen smiled with pride.

"Well," Joe said with relief, as he and Cooper walked to

his office. "You can't ask for higher quality reproduction than that."

"Aye," Cooper replied with a preoccupied nod as they came through the door.

Joe sensed his distance. "Something wrong, Dylan?"

"No, not really," he replied evasively.

"Suit yourself; but your brow's got more furrows than a corn field. Has to be a reason for it."

"Well, it just dawned on me that Christmas is awful close, and, well . . ."

"True. We're going to be on a tight schedule. But I don't see any problem."

"I'm afraid I do, Joseph," Cooper said, fidgeting with his tobacco pouch. "I don't mean to rain on our parade, Joe; but I'm not sure I can make the rest of the prints in time."

Joe kicked back in his desk chair jauntily. "We'll just have to get you some help."

Cooper stiffened. "Help?" he echoed, displeased. "Oh, I don't know about that. I've always worked alone. Besides, I can't think of anyone who'd be—"

"I can," Joe interrupted, undaunted. "His name's Bartlett. Lucas Bartlett. He's young and talented, and has experience with halftone reproduction too."

"A photographer?"

"Uh-huh. I have some of his work right here. It wouldn't hurt to take a look. I think it's pretty good."

Cooper frowned. "I'll be the judge of that."

"Fair enough." Joe crossed to a filing cabinet and removed a manila envelope. It contained the shots of hand tools and farming equipment Bartlett had taken for Ed Mitchell's defunct hardware catalogue.

Cooper sorted through a few prints, then tossed the remainder onto Joe's desk. "Commercial work," he grunted, dismissing them.

"Well, sure. He's young and just starting out. A man has to earn a living."

"Indeed so, but I'm afraid it's just not my kind of photography, Joe."

"I'm well aware of that. Maybe, he's just never been exposed to it. This could be a chance for you to pass on your—"

"Legacy?" Cooper interrupted with a penetrating stare. "You weren't going to say that now, were you?"

Joe nodded with apprehension.

Cooper made no effort to soften the blow and scowled. "My pictures are my legacy, Joe."

"True, but all the great artists had apprentices—Michelangelo, da Vinci, Rembrandt—and I thought, maybe in the spirit of the season you might share some of your knowledge and experience with—"

"Enough, Joseph, enough," Cooper muttered with the pained expression of an adolescent being forced to do his chores. "You've more than made your point." He took several of Bartlett's prints from the desk and scrutinized them. "Well, technically they're quite sound. I imagine he'll do."

Chapter Thirty-Six

Autumn's color had long faded and fallen, and the air in Cooper's darkroom had taken on a wintry chill. He and Bartlett had been literally living amid its soft red glow and pungent fumes. Prints were tacked on the walls, piled on every surface, and hung from drying racks. Test strips littered the floor. Empty cups and dishes with half eaten meals were scattered about in testimony to their single-mindedness.

Bartlett was standing at the long table bathed in crimson light. His hands, raw from constant contact with the chemicals, were gently rocking a print submerged in a tray of fixer.

Nearby, Cooper hunched over the printing table cleaning every last speck of dust from yet another eight-by-ten negative before sandwiching it beneath the cover glass with a sheet of photographic paper. When ready, he grasped the chain that hung from the bare bulb overhead, and squinted at Bartlett. "That one sufficiently fixed?"

Bartlett angled his watch to catch the red light. "Nope. Still about thirty seconds to go." The darkness concealed his smug expression, but not his tone, when he added, "There's a better way to do this, you know."

"Oh, is there now?" Cooper challenged, bristling at the remark.

"Sure is. For what it's worth, you wouldn't be waiting to make that exposure, if we had a proper contact printer. It'd contain the light and you wouldn't have to worry about it fogging this—"

"Listen here, young man," Cooper interrupted, his burr rolling like angry thunder. "I've been doing it this way—my way—for fifty years; and I'm not about to be changing, now. Furthermore, speaking of worth—and it'd be a far sight from a king's ransom, mind you—your opinion would be best kept to yourself unless solicited." He scowled at the trays of chemicals on the table. "Besides, if you were tending to your business instead of mine, you'd have noticed we're low on developer, and already be mixing a fresh batch."

Bartlett scowled and began removing bottles of chemicals from the rack beneath the table. "Ought to be using ready-made, anyway," he said under his breath.

"Don't mumble, lad," Cooper prodded. "If you have something to say, say it."

Bartlett glanced at his watch. "I said you can make your exposure now."

Cooper grunted, and pulled the chain. The darkroom filled with blinding white light. He counted to ten and pulled it again, then removed the print from beneath the negative and glass, and slipped it into the tray of developer, hovering over it expectantly.

Several hours and countless prints later, cool rays of early morning light were streaming through the parlor windows as Cooper led the way from the darkroom, carrying a thick stack of prints.

"It's freezing in here," Bartlett said, his breath coming in little puffs between the words.

"That it is. I trust you can make a fire without burning the place to the ground?"

Bartlett nodded, shivering.

"Then get on with it, lad," Cooper bellowed in a feisty tone. "Or are you too tired?"

The young man stiffened with defiance. "Sounds to me like maybe the pot's calling the kettle black."

Cooper snorted with disdain, doing his best to conceal his shortness of breath. The years spent in fume-filled darkrooms had taken their toll, and Dr. Cheever had diagnosed him as consumptive.

They'd both been up all night, and neither would give the other the satisfaction of knowing he was exhausted; nor would Bartlett acknowledge that he was amazed by his elder's stamina. Bleary-eyed, he went to the woodbox and began tossing pieces of kindling and split logs into the fireplace.

Cooper began spacing the prints out in neat rows on the floor beneath the windows. They were all made from the same negative—a magnificent picture of the Newbury Community Church after a heavy snowfall—but they weren't the same at all. Indeed, there were differences of tone, contrast, and sharpness. Some that would be obvious to anyone, others that only Cooper could see. He knelt on the floor evaluating them, culling out those that were unacceptable until only two prints remained; then with the popping and creaking of aching joints, he struggled to his feet, and glanced to his assistant. "Come over 'ere, lad."

Bartlett had already put a match to the newspaper he'd stuffed beneath the andirons, and hungry flames were licking at the logs and soot-coated bricks that lined the fireplace. He rubbed his hands together, spreading the warmth, then joined Cooper at the window.

"You have a preference?" Cooper prompted, holding the prints side by side in the daylight.

"I may be wrong," Bartlett said with a facetious grin, "but I have a vague feeling you're soliciting my opinion?"

Cooper broke into a self-satisfied smile and nodded. "For what it's worth."

Bartlett studied the prints, his head tilting this way and that. "This one," Bartlett said decisively, indicating the one on the left.

"Really?" Cooper said in his intimidating way. "Did you play eenie meenie minie moe? Or do you actually have a reason?"

"I've a reason."

"Let's hear it then."

"Okay. I picked that one because it has a little more snap than the other."

"Snap, eh?"

Bartlett nodded, sensing he was in trouble.

"Aye, that it does; but you see, lad, that much contrast doesn't suit the nature of the picture, now does it?" Cooper punctuated the remark with a crisp nod; and without waiting for a reply, tossed the print Bartlett had selected to the floor with the other discards. "Better gather those up."

Bartlett knew Cooper was right but was loath to admit it. He waited until his back was turned, then took a half-hearted swipe at the prints with his foot, and went about collecting them.

Cooper bent to the packing crate that he used as a coffee table, and placed the chosen print in a box with others that had survived the culling-out process. A smile of weary satisfaction spread across his face as he closed the lid.

"What do you want to do with these?" Bartlett asked, scooping up the last of the discards.

"Give them here, lad." Cooper snatched the prints from Bartlett, crossed to the fireplace, and without hesitation, tossed them into the roaring blaze.

Bartlett winced. Despite the subtle differences, he thought that each print had artistic merit if taken on its own, and was shocked by Cooper's indifference.

Cooper broke into a knowing smile as the prints curled and burst into flame. "Good work, Lucas," he said, his face aglow in the flickering light. "That's a fine fire."

Chapter Thirty-Seven

Cooper's truck turned into Sycamore Street, sending leaves swirling across the pavement, and parked in front of the printing shop. He got out and hurried inside with the box of photographs, greeting the workmen as he made his way between the noisy equipment to Joe's office.

Prints of his Christmas pictures covered the walls now. A layout table, where Alicia sat blocking out the pages for the book, ran the length of the glass partition. Joe was directly opposite her at his desk, the phone pressed to his ear. He seemed tethered to it of late, taking orders from the many buyers, shopkeepers, and book distributors to whom he'd sent samples of Cooper's photographs.

"That's right, Mr. Hastings," he said smartly. "We'll guarantee delivery in time—I know it's tight, but the book's worth waiting for, and you know it—Fine. We won't let you down—Do our best, Mr. Hastings. With luck, we might even get them to you sooner—Sure, I have that information right here." He swiveled to a bookcase, fetched a binder, and began flipping through the pages, nodding to Cooper who trudged into the office.

Alicia looked up from her work and brightened as he handed her the box. "Well, good morning."

"You said it. That's the last of 'em."

Alicia removed the prints, and began shuffling through them with growing anticipation. "They're beautiful, Dylan. Beautiful," she exclaimed, her eyes widening with delight. "Every one of them."

Cooper beamed, and settled his weary body into a chair. "Thank you. I was up the entire weekend printing them."

"The entire weekend?" she echoed puzzled. "What about Lucas? I thought he was helping?"

Cooper grinned wryly and waggled a hand. "Well, as we say in Scotland, 'More than one cook to a haggis, is one cook to a haggis too many.'"

Alicia laughed and returned her attention to the photographs. She was nearing the last few when she paused at a landscape. The rhythmic composition of rolling countryside, dark winter sky, and road lined by bare, perfectly aligned trees was breathtaking; but it was the young woman in the foreground that caught Alicia's eye. Bathed in delicate crosslight that made her dress appear to be illuminated from within, she had a tranquil beauty about her and held herself with the balanced poise of a dancer.

Alicia held the print up to Cooper. "That's the road that goes by your cottage, isn't it?"

"Uh-huh. Years ago. Before they paved it."

"And what about her? Who's she?"

"Oh, just a girl."

"The one you were sweet on?" Alicia prompted coyly.

Cooper emitted a nervous chuckle. "No, she just happened to be walking by one day, and I just happened to be there with my camera, that's all."

"Like the morning you were photographing our bungalow and I came out to say hello?"

"Rather like that."

"Just another Christmas picture, hmmm?"

"I didn't say that," Cooper chided. "And if it will spare me further interrogation, the fact of the matter is, it's not re-

ally a Christmas picture—I've included it because it's—
it's—a picture of—" He noticed Joe had just hung up the
phone and promptly changed the subject. "Joe? Joe, I think
that grin you're wearing means we ought to be listening to
what you've got to say."

Joe smiled, letting the suspense build as he pushed back
from the desk and joined them. "We just got another order.
Hastings and Brown, they're one of the biggest wholesalers
in Boston."

"Good work, lad!" Cooper bellowed, getting to his feet to
shake Joe's hand.

Alicia let out a whoop, wrapped one arm around Joe, the
other around Cooper, and pulled them as close as her pregnant tummy would allow.

Chapter Thirty-Eight

Several weeks had passed, and on this chilly autumn morning in Newbury, a large forest green van was parked amidst the colorful leaves outside the printing shop. Fanciful gold lettering on the side proclaimed Agostini's Bindery.

Inside, where the presses were going full tilt, a wiry man with Mediterranean features and a flowing mustache stood in animated conversation with Gundersen.

Joe was at his desk reassuring another prospective buyer that they could deliver Cooper's book in time when Gundersen stuck his head into the office. "Joe? Joe, see you for a minute?"

"Sure," Joe replied, concerned by his foreman's tone. "You have a problem?"

"In a manner of speaking," Gundersen replied unhappily. "Actually, Mr. Agostini does."

Joe was leading the way from the office when Mr. Agostini came charging toward them. "Look, Mister Clements," he said, raising his voice over the racket. "We can do anything; anything within reason; but, as I've explained to your foreman—"

"Of course you can," Joe interrupted. "That's why we came to you."

"Ah, yes, well," Agostini sputtered, momentarily confounded. "I was about to say, you want quality binding, and you want it fast, and you want it cheap. Now, something has to give."

"Well, Mr. Agostini," Joe said, sounding perplexed. "I'm running out of time—and I have a tight budget, which leaves—" he paused for effect and splayed his hands before concluding "—dare I say, quality?"

Agostini's moustache twitched as if electrified.

"Of course," Joe went on before Agostini could interject. "I'd be very disappointed if you were forced to lower your standards, and produce a—"

Agostini flared at the insult. "Hold on right there, Mr. Clements. Forty-five years I build this business. Forty-five years I work hard and make a reputation. Forty-five years I sweat and—" Agostini paused suddenly, realizing that Joe had shrewdly cornered him, and nodded in resignation. "Okay, when do I get the rest of the pages?"

"Gundy?" Joe prompted, his brow arched with apprehension.

"End of the month," Gundersen replied.

Agostini groaned in dismay. "Tomorrow is already too late. I do my best. Remember, I make no promises."

Joe smiled, feeling a bit more confident. "I'll remember, Mr. Agostini." They shook hands, and Agostini hurried off between the thundering presses.

Indeed, in the weeks that followed, the shop vibrated day and night with their catchy syncopation, augmented by the crisp whisk of the paper cutter, the supportive chatter among the workers, and the growing sense that something special was happening here. Soon, everyone had become imbued with the Christmas spirit. Alicia hung a large wreath with a bright red bow and clusters of pine cones and berries in the front window, and spent the day decorating the shop with sprigs of holly and magnificent poinsettias from her garden.

Then, all of a sudden, the last plate was locked in the Mergenthaler's bed, the last of the photographs printed, the last pages trimmed and sent to the bindery, the last orders filled, and the last truck loaded. Gundersen and the workers joined Joe, Alicia, and Cooper on the loading dock to see it off. They cheered and waved as the truck pulled away, leaving them with a euphoric sense of satisfaction.

"You know, I never dreamed we'd get so many orders," Alicia said brightly.

"We wouldn't have gotten any if it wasn't for you," Joe said, gazing at her with affection and pride.

"I've a feeling this is going to be the best Christmas we've ever had!" Gundersen exclaimed.

"Let's not get overconfident," Joe cautioned.

"That usually means trouble," Gundersen prompted.

"I wouldn't say trouble, Gundy, but there's still the possibility that people won't buy the book."

"So?" one of the workers challenged. "That's not our problem, is it?"

"I'm afraid so," Joe replied, squirming like a worm on a hook. "You see, books are bought by retailers on consignment. That means every one they don't sell can be sent back to the publisher. That's how the business works."

"Hold on there," another piped up. "We've never had anything sent back before."

"Because we've never been the publisher before."

"And they get their bloody money back?" a third asked, his voice ringing with disbelief.

Joe responded with a sheepish nod.

"You should have said something when you first came to us, Joe," Gundersen protested.

"I would have, Gundy, believe me. But I've been learning as I go. I didn't know at the time. Would it have mattered?"

The workers exchanged looks then, realizing they'd still

have had little choice, began shrugging and shaking their heads no. "I suppose not," Gundersen finally said. "Nothing we can do now, anyway."

"Well, there is one thing," Alicia said, her voice taking on a reverent timbre as she glanced at Joe. "We can all start praying that people buy them."

Joe frowned. "Pray? I'm not sure that would do any good."

"Pray all you like, lass," Cooper chimed in, "but take my word for it, people will be buying them, regardless."

"You sound awfully sure of that, Dylan," Alicia observed. "Have you a special reason why?"

"My Christmas pictures," the old fellow replied proudly. "Or have you all forgotten they're what sold you on doing this in the first place?"

Chapter Thirty-Nine

The apprehensive silence that descended on the printing shop turned everyone's attention outward, to the other stores and shops that lined Newbury's bare-treed streets. And soon, despite hard times and the pressures to make ends meet, the village came alive with the sparkle of Christmas decorations, the scent of ginger and rum-laced fruit from the bakery, and the energetic cacophony of holiday activity: The cheery salutations of street corner Santas; the clatter of vehicles hurrying home with freshly cut evergreens lashed to their roofs; the squeals and laughter of children; the spirited voices of carolers; and the heartening ring of cash registers.

Alicia spent the time writing Christmas cards and shopping for simple gifts; and Joe spent it pacing in his office, worrying that they couldn't afford them; but just as the weeks of tension and suspense were threatening to overwhelm him, the pin-drop quiet that had fallen over the shop was suddenly broken. Not by the rumble of trucks returning cartons of unsold books as they had all feared, but by the ringing phone in Joe's office, and by the anxious voices of sales clerks, buyers, and distributors who had sold their last book and were calling to order more copies. One call was especially encouraging and sent Joe hurrying into the shop to announce, "Hastings and Brown just doubled their order!"

He returned to his desk and was happily tallying sales figures when it dawned on him that this was like the first pump of oil out of a new well. He spent the next several hours looking for a way to keep it coming. The idea that finally struck him was far too ambitious to undertake on his own, so he called Arthur Hastings back and asked if he'd come to Newbury to discuss it. He decided not to mention it to anyone—not even to Alicia—until he was certain he had the canny businessman's support.

In the meantime, the flood of orders continued, setting off a wave of activity and excitement that kept the presses going, and finally crested with the promise of snow and the peal of church bells. They reverberated throughout every home and touched every heart, and had special meaning for those gathered at Clements & Son on Sycamore Street.

Christmas was barely a week away and all of Joe's employees, their wives and children, along with Alicia, Cooper, Bartlett, and Mr. Agostini, had come together to celebrate the book's success.

The atmosphere in the gaily decorated shop, where clusters of red candles flickered, was one of satisfaction and quiet reflection at first; then, thanks to the plates of homemade Christmas cookies and a kettle of steaming mulled wine, it became more jovial and alive—especially when Gundersen came bursting in dressed up as Santa Claus and began passing out candy canes to the children who, one by one, sat on his knee, telling Santa what they wanted for Christmas.

Alicia fetched a box camera and began taking pictures of them, and Joe, like his father before him, began passing out thick pay envelopes and Christmas bonuses to their parents.

When they'd finished, Alicia produced a beautifully wrapped package and handed it to Cooper. "Merry Christmas, Dylan!"

"And what might that be?" Cooper wondered, eyes widening with intrigue as everyone gathered around him.

"Open it and find out," Alicia prompted.

"Yes—come on—open it," a chorus of anxious voices shouted, joining in.

Cooper tore at the wrapping and removed a copy of his book that had been bound in leather. The cover was inscribed in gold leaf which proclaimed: *The Christmas Pictures*, Photographs by Dylan Cooper. The old fellow's eyes glistened with emotion. "Well, I . . . I don't know what to say. Thank you. Thank you all for everything." He ran his fingers over the binding, impressed with the craftsmanship. "It's a fine job."

"Mr. Agostini did it for us," Joe explained. "It's just about the only copy we didn't sell."

"Well, that calls for a toast," Cooper growled with a wink to the proud bookbinder as he raised his mug of wine. "Merry Christmas everyone!"

"Merry Christmas, Dylan!" everyone shouted in response. They were all remarking there hadn't been a better one in years when Joe fetched Alicia's camera and aimed it at Cooper.

The old fellow held up a hand in protest. Others did the posing, not he. "Oh, Joe, no. None of that, now. Come on, Joseph. Joseph."

"Oh, let him, Dylan," Alicia pleaded. "I'd like to have one. Please?"

Cooper stood there, awkwardly, not sure what to do with his hands. Finally, he jammed one into a pocket and made the other into a fist that he set against a hip. "All right," he growled, satisfied with his defiant pose. "Let's be done with it."

"Come on, a big smile now," Alicia said brightly.

Cooper's jaw tightened further, then, an instant before the shutter clicked, he relented and allowed an impish grin to break across his face.

Alicia smiled with amusement. Pure, unabridged Dylan

Cooper, she thought as Joe embraced her, their eyes glistening with joy, and the knowledge that next Christmas there'd be another member of the family to share their happiness. "As Pastor Martin would say, all is going according to Plan, isn't it, darling?"

"Yeah, I guess so," Joe replied as everyone broke into song.

"God rest ye merry gentlemen,
Let nothing you dismay . . .
Remember Christ our Savior
Was born on Christmas day . . ."

Alicia and Joe joined in the spirited singing that brought the party to a rousing conclusion. Later, after everyone had left, the two of them embraced, savoring their good fortune, then went about cleaning up the shop. Alicia was humming the carol and reflecting on its lyrics as she cleared the work tables when something occurred to her. "You know, I think sometimes we forget the true meaning of Christmas."

"Maybe. But not today," Joe said with evident pride. "I've never seen so many happy faces."

"Yes, it was very special," Alicia said, deciding on a subtle approach to an idea she'd been entertaining. "Tomorrow is the Sunday before Christmas, isn't it?"

"Uh-huh, I believe so. Why?"

"Well, I may be wrong," she replied, pretending she couldn't remember, "but I vaguely recall that if Christmas doesn't fall on a Sunday, that's when the children put on the annual Christmas play, isn't it?"

"Yeah, I guess," Joe replied, sweeping bits of party debris into a corner. "The only thing I remember about the Christmas play is that I was always a shepherd, never a wise man."

"Well, there's hope for you yet."

Joe responded with a good-natured chuckle. "Of course, you were always the Blessed Virgin."

"Not anymore," Alicia said with an alluring giggle, before blithely adding, "By the way, Pastor Martin said it's at evening services this year. I think we should go."

Joe stopped his broom in midstroke and looked over at her. "You mean to church?"

"Yes, Joe, to church," Alicia replied, unable to suppress a little smile at his reaction. "We have a lot to be thankful for, and . . ."

"True," Joe groaned, sensing the inevitable. "I can't argue with that, but—"

". . . and it'd be the perfect opportunity to ask God's blessing on the blessed event, too."

"Yes, I guess it would . . ."

"Does that mean you're coming with us?" Alicia prompted, brightly, cradling her tummy.

Joe smiled in capitulation. "Sure, why not, if it'll make you happy."

Alicia's eyes widened with delight. "Happy? Oh, Joe, it would be the best Christmas present ever."

Chapter Forty

The next evening, the Town Square was crowded with vehicles and alive with people streaming toward the Newbury Community Church from every street and corner. Aglow with light and bedecked with colorful Christmas decor, the white-steepled structure resonated with the soaring voices of the choir as Joe and Alicia joined the other members of the congregation who filled every pew to capacity.

A large crèche that served as the setting for the Christmas play stood on one side of the altar. Two school children dressed as Mary and Joseph knelt at the hay-filled manger where a figure of the infant Jesus lay. As church bells rang, a procession of children in homemade costumes came down the aisle to the altar and encircled the crèche.

As the choir reached its final crescendo, Pastor Martin, resplendent in the white alb and red sash he wore for holiday services, stepped to the pulpit. "In these troubled times, with Europe once again beset by war, it is especially fitting that I welcome you to our annual Christmas play that celebrates the birth of our Lord Jesus Christ, the Prince of Peace." He paused and gestured to the nativity scene. "It takes place on the night when the wise men, having journeyed from the East, arrived at the stable in Bethlehem to worship the new-born Messiah."

Pastor Martin paused again as three children, dressed as wise men, came forward carrying gifts. They knelt at the manger, heads bowed in tribute to the Christ child.

"Though there is no specific number in the scriptures," Pastor Martin resumed, "we assume there were three 'magi' because the Bible mentions three different gifts that were offered to the Lord.

"The second chapter of Matthew tells us these wise men had been guided by His star." The pastor's eyes drifted to a shimmering tinfoil star suspended above the crèche. "No doubt they were aware of Numbers, Chapter 24, verse 17, which records that . . . ." He paused and nodded in the direction of the children.

". . . 'A Star shall come out of Jacob, and a scepter shall rise out of Israel'," a girl of eight recited, barely able to contain her excitement.

"What exactly was this star that guided them to Bethelem?" Pastor Martin resumed. "Some believe it was a natural phenomenon caused by the simultaneous aligning of Mars, Jupiter, and Saturn. Others believe it was a supernatural phenomenon similar to the 'pillar of fire' witnessed by many in the Old Testament.

"Though we aren't certain which phenomena the wise men observed, many biblical scholars believe they were descended from a group of astronomers in the sixth century BC who were taught by the prophet Daniel how to recognize the birth of Christ.

"In Matthew, Chapter 2, verses 9 and 10, we're told that . . ." Pastor Martin let it tail off and nodded to the children again.

". . . that . . . that the Star the wise men had seen 'went before them and stood over . . . stood over where the young Child was'," one of the children responded, beset by a mild case of stage fright. "'When they saw the star, they rejoiced with exceedingly great joy'."

"And why were the wise men so filled with joy?" Pastor Martin asked with a rhetorical pause. "Because they knew that the hundreds of prophecies concerning the coming Messiah were finally coming true!" he concluded, his voice rising with fervor. "As the angel announced to the shepherds in the field . . ."

". . . 'For there is born to you this day in the City of David a Savior who is Christ the Lord'," a girl wearing an angel costume with floppy wings said.

"And as an angel speaking to Joseph said of his wife Mary . . ." Pastor Martin went on with another pause.

". . . 'She will bring forth a son, and you shall call His name Jesus,'" another of the children replied, his voice cracking with adolescent charm. "'For He will save His people from their sins.'"

"To save His people," Pastor Martin repeated. "That was His whole reason for coming, wasn't it? To give His life in atonement for the sins of the world. That's the true meaning of Christmas."

Joe couldn't help but recall Alicia's comment the day before about the true meaning of Christmas being forgotten; though, he didn't think Alicia had Pastor Martin's meaning in mind. On the contrary, far from seeing them as sinners in need of redemption, Joe was certain that, like him, Alicia thought of them as decent people who cared deeply for their fellow man, and had done well on behalf of those who were dependent on them.

"And because of Christ's death on the cross," Pastor Martin went on, "you can have forgiveness of sins here tonight by accepting the sacrifice He made on your behalf, and by inviting Him into your heart. If any of you would like to have your sins forgiven by the Lord and receive the gift of eternal life, please come forward," the Pastor concluded, signaling the choir with a wave of his hand.

As the church once again filled with soaring voices, more than a dozen members of the congregation stood and slipped from their pews. The town's mayor, Dr. Cheever, and Olaf Gundersen, the foreman in Joe's shop, were among those who walked down the aisle and knelt at the manger that held the Christ child.

Alicia stole an anxious glance at Joe, hoping he would join them; but Joe remained seated in the pew, unmoved by the pastor's invitation.

A short time later, they were driving home along the coast road when Joe sensed Alicia wasn't sitting close to him as she usually did, but far across the seat, her gaze fixed out the side window. "Alicia?"

"Uh-huh?"

"Are you okay?"

"I'm fine."

"You're sure? Nothing starting to happen with the baby or anything?"

"Nope, too early."

"Good. By the way, just in case you're wondering," Joe said with a hint of sarcasm, "I asked because you haven't said a word since we left the church. Now I'm getting the silent treatment. What's going on?"

Alicia pursed her lips, making a decision. "Well, I guess I'm a little disappointed you didn't respond to Pastor Martin's invitation to come forward and—"

"Stop right there, young lady," Joe commanded, guiding the roadster through a curve. "You said my coming along this evening would be the best Christmas gift ever, didn't you?"

"Yes, I did, but—"

"But what? You just said it to make sure I—"

"No. No, it's just that I was hoping you'd—"

"You know how you sound, Alicia? Like a child who gets a new bicycle for Christmas and complains it doesn't have a bell on the handlebar."

Alicia sighed in contrition. "You're right. I'm sorry. It's just that, despite our good fortune, these are still uncertain times; and I thought, maybe as . . . as Pastor Martin said . . . inviting Christ into your heart might help you cope with them."

"You're right," Joe said in a tone that belied his words. "The business barely survived; and I have serious concerns about the future. But I didn't ask for God's help—then—or now. I went to church tonight because I thought it would make you happy, remember?"

"Oh, Joseph, of course I do; and it did; but I want *you* to be happy, too. I hate to see you worrying about your workers . . . about making ends meet . . . about—"

"I *am* happy," Joe protested. He swung the roadster into the driveway and parked behind the bungalow, then turned to Alicia. "You want to know what's really going to make me happy?"

Alicia nodded, expecting it had something to do with her, and brightened in anticipation.

". . . If this meeting I'm having with Mr. Hastings tomorrow goes well."

Alicia looked surprised. "Mr. Hastings? You didn't say anything about a meeting."

Joe winced, wishing he hadn't said it. "I didn't want to get your hopes up. No questions, okay? I don't want to hear another word about it."

Alicia nodded, then smiled at what she was about to say. "I'll pray in silence, I promise."

Chapter Forty-One

A light snow was dusting the rugged landscape as the train from Boston wound through the foothills and thundered into Newbury Station, clouds of steam hissing from its wheel-housings.

Arthur Hastings, an angular man in a heavy winter coat, stepped from the coach, carrying an impressive briefcase, and strode to the taxi stand.

Clements & Son was shut down for the holidays, but Joe had been waiting in his office for over an hour when Hastings arrived. "Mr. Hastings," he said brightly, getting to his feet to greet him.

"Arthur, please," Hastings said extending a hand. "This has turned out to be quite a holiday season, hasn't it?"

"Thanks to all those books you ordered. More than anyone else, according to my records."

"I'm not surprised. The response from my outlets has been nothing short of amazing," Hastings said, the planes of his face animating along with his tone. "Needless to say, I'm more than curious about this idea you mentioned. What kind of book do you have in mind?"

"Not a book, Arthur," Joe replied, his voice rising in excitement. "A *series* of books. Each one will feature something special about the New England area: the people, the industries, the landscape, the sea coast, the rivers and streams, and so on."

Hastings's eyes widened with interest. "Good idea, Joe. Very good, but . . ." He let it tail off, then nodded toward the shop. ". . . it doesn't look to me like you're set up to handle it."

"Nothing that buying a couple of presses and putting on some more people wouldn't cure."

Hastings broke into a knowing smile. "That's where I come in, isn't it?"

"Exactly. Things have been looking up as of late, but I'm still in no position to finance the operation. I was hoping you'd see the potential and—"

"I'd have to be a fool not to," Hastings enthused. "I'm sure we can work out a financial arrangement that would be satisfactory to both of us."

"I've no doubt of it, Arthur."

"Good. There is one condition, though," Hastings said with a suspenseful pause. "Cooper has to take the pictures. He has a reverence for this area, Joe. An intimacy with it that gives his pictures a certain—" he paused, searching for a word that eluded him—"a certain nostalgic quality. That's what sold his Christmas pictures, and that's what'll sell these."

"I couldn't agree more."

"But you haven't approached Cooper with the idea yet, have you?"

"No, I wanted to talk to you first. Why?"

"Well, I've heard rumors he's an independent old bird who won't take on a commercial assignment."

"They're not rumors," Joe said with an affectionate chuckle.

"Not surprising. Of all my European suppliers, the Scotsmen, despite their canny knack for business, are the most stubborn and set in their ways."

"Dylan can be stubborn; but if you're his friend, if he trusts you . . . Well, that's another matter."

Hastings nodded sagely, then stood and shook Joe's hand. "I'll be waiting to hear from you. Merry Christmas."

"Merry Christmas to you, Arthur."

The meeting left Joe's heart pounding with hope and apprehension. He leaned back in his chair and stared out the window at the falling snow, thinking about how and when he'd broach the subject with Cooper.

Chapter Forty-Two

The storm continued throughout the day and most of the next; and as Christmas Eve descended upon Newbury, the bungalow nestled amidst drifts of wind-driven snow. It dotted every thicket and coated every tree, and crunched beneath the tires of Cooper's truck that cut graceful tracks in the thick blanket on the shoreline road.

Inside the cab, Cooper and Joe sat side by side singing England's Carol at the top of their lungs to the rhythmic slap of the wipers; and when they reached the bungalow, their exuberant voices brought Alicia to the door just in time to see them hoisting a Christmas tree from the truck's bed. The magnificent spruce filled the parlor with its rich aroma and, when secured in its stand, came to within a foot of the peaked ceiling.

After dinner, Alicia went to the fireplace and hung three stockings from the mantel with thumb tacks. She crossed her arms above her bulging tummy, and smiled at the tiny stocking on the end before joining Joe and Dylan who were trimming the tree with lights, ornaments and shimmering tinsel.

"That's the nicest tree we've ever had, isn't it?" Alicia enthused.

"It certainly is," Joe replied, stepping back to admire it. He had just placed an illuminated star atop the tree, and the mirrored facets sent shafts of light dancing across the ceiling.

Cooper looked almost misty-eyed. "Can't remember the last time I had one," he whispered; then struck by a thought, he exclaimed, "Oh, I almost forgot!" He hurried outside to his truck and, moments later, returned with a faded Christmas box that he had tied with new ribbon. "Merry Christmas," he said, handing it to Alicia. "You might want to open it now."

Alicia settled on the floor next to the tree, then undid the bow with childlike enthusiasm and lifted the top. Within the folds of tissue, she found a small wooden stable, along with figures of Joseph, Mary, the Three Wise Men, a manger that held the Christ child, and an angel with a flowing sash that proclaimed: Gloria In Excelsis Deo. Sculpted of fired clay, they were all of exquisite proportion and detail. "Oh, Dylan, they're so beautiful," Alicia exclaimed as she continued unwrapping them. "Where did you get them?"

Cooper had settled in one of the wicker chairs with a brandy and his pipe, and was staring at the crackling Christmas Eve fire, lost in his thoughts.

"Dylan?"

"Oh, sorry," he said, coming out of it.

"I was wondering where you got these," Alicia prompted, handing one of the figures to Joe.

"From the bottom of a closet," Cooper replied with an impish grin.

Alicia looked skeptical. "A closet?"

"Aye, they were a gift. Christmas . . . nineteen-eighteen; but I was away at war, so they were set aside, or so I imagine. Years later, I was cleaning out some closets, and there was the box beneath a pile of junk with a lovely Christmas card affixed to it."

"Well, whoever gave them to you had a fine eye," Joe observed, appreciating the figure's graceful gesture.

"Aye, that she did . . ."

"She?" Alicia echoed with a knowing smile. "The girl in the photograph," she declared.

"Aye, the girl in the photograph," Cooper finally conceded with a poignant sigh. "Her name was Grace. Grace MacVicar." He rolled the r's, clearly savoring the sound of them.

"Something tells me she was from Scotland too," Alicia prompted.

"Aye. A dancer she was. Classically trained. Her ballet troupe performed the world over." He paused and drew thoughtfully on his pipe, deciding whether or not he'd share the rest with them. "She was my soul mate, and I hers. Right from the beginning it was as if our hearts beat as one. We'd been married for just three days when I went off to war. A few months later Grace wrote that she was pregnant. As you might imagine, I was overcome with joy and couldn't wait to get home to be with her and the baby." He set the pipe aside and took a long sip of brandy. ". . . but I didn't get there in time. The baby came early . . . too early. Didn't live for more than a couple of hours."

"Oh, Dylan, no," Alicia said, her voice ringing with empathy.

A veil of sadness clouded Cooper's eyes. "Such is life, I'm afraid. Things might've been different if I'd been with her . . ." He took a long swallow of brandy then shook his head at the tragic irony of what he was about to say. "As it turned out, Grace was still suffering from the loss when the Army sent a telegram sayin' I'd been killed in action."

"Oh, dear," Alicia groaned, her hand tightening around the figure from the creche she'd been holding. "What a horrible mistake."

"Aye, as horrible as they come; but not uncommon in the

chaos of war. After that, well, Grace just wasn't the same. By the time I got home, she'd already gone back to Scotland to be with her family." Cooper took another swallow of brandy, then another, draining the glass. "My tongue gets any looser, I'll start talking about the time I went home to find her."

"Did you?" Alicia wondered.

"No. No, Alicia, I didn't," Cooper replied with a wistful sigh. "You see, her family never approved of her life on the stage, and when she appeared on their doorstep, they agreed to help her only if she agreed to give it up."

"They were shamed by her dancing?" Alicia asked.

"Aye, they weren't much for the arts," Cooper replied with a sarcastic scowl. "Her father was a . . .a . . . well, I was about to say, a meanspirited fool, but since it's Christmas, let's just say he was a rather provincial chap, who looked me square in the eye and insisted that Grace's misfortune was fair and just punishment for her wantonness. I could hardly believe what I was hearing; and when I took exception to it, the man had the nerve to say that she'd have come to see the error of her ways and become the dutiful daughter had she not married me."

"He—he—he blamed you for what happened?" Alicia sputtered in disbelief.

"Aye, along with her brother who was entrusted with protecting her virtue," Cooper replied with an angry snort. "You'd think I was the devil himself. Her father not only accused me of destroying her, but vowed I'd never have an opportunity to do so again."

"But you were away at war, and—and Grace thought you'd been killed. How could he—"

Cooper nodded emphatically. "And he let her go on thinking it—to this day as far as I know."

"In other words," Joe concluded, "Grace's family wouldn't tell her you were alive; and wouldn't tell you—wouldn't tell her husband—where to find her?"

"Not only that, they did whatever they could to stop me. Even threatened her brother with disownment if he revealed her whereabouts or told her I'd survived the war." Cooper paused and looked off in reflection. "Not a bad fellow, Colin. He cared deeply for his sister, just didn't have her backbone. I looked for her anyway; traveled to more towns and villages . . . made inquiries at post offices, churches, and hospitals . . . all to no avail, of course. That's where I'm from too, by the way, Dumbarton. It's just outside of Glasgow. Rugged coastal terrain, hearty people."

"Sounds familiar," Joe observed.

"Aye, much like New England in many ways," Cooper replied with a reflective smile. "But maybe—maybe I'll get back to Scotland just once more. You never know . . ." He then came out of the reverie and pushed up from the chair, unsteadily. "Enough of that now. Where's my jacket?"

"Not so fast. We haven't opened our presents yet," Joe said, guiding him back to the chair. "There's a special one for you."

Cooper looked surprised. "For me? I already have my present, Joe."

"Well, it's for both of you," Joe explained with a wink to Alicia who looked as surprised as Cooper. "We're going to be publishing another book. Actually a whole series of them."

"Joe . . ." Alicia admonished, a hint of fatigue creeping into her voice. "Something tells me your meeting went well."

Joe nodded emphatically. "Couldn't have gone better. The best part is . . ." Joe let it trail off as he uncorked the bottle of brandy and refilled Cooper's glass. "Our favorite photographer here is part of it."

Cooper forced a smile. "Am I now?"

"That's right," Joe replied. "A big part."

"Well," Alicia said, getting to her feet. "I'm afraid mother and 'son' are going to have to wait until morning to see what else Santa brought them. Aren't we? Yes. Yes, we are," she cooed, cradling her tummy in her arms. "I'm really pooped. I think I'll head off to bed. Okay?"

Joe nodded. "Of course, you 'both' need your rest. Merry Christmas."

"Merry Christmas, darling. You too, Dylan."

"Aye," Cooper replied, with a halfhearted smile as Alicia kissed his cheek, and left.

Joe waited until he heard the bedroom door close then turned to Cooper. "You know, it's hard to believe we almost went under."

"Joe," Cooper said with apprehension. "Joe, I hope—"

"This is really going to put us over the top," Joe went on. "It'll keep us going for years."

Cooper responded with an indulgent nod. "I hope you haven't committed me to anything."

"Of course not," Joe admonished. "Now, let's see if I can bring a smile to that sad old face?"

"Doubt it," Cooper grunted.

"You remember that fellow Hastings?" Joe began.

Cooper struck a match and brought it to his pipe. "Named a famous battle after him, didn't they?" he replied, pretending he couldn't recall.

"He sold more of your books than anyone else, and you know it."

Dylan nodded and exhaled a stream of pipe smoke. "Aye, it seems to ring a bell now."

"Well, he's going to finance us."

Dylan took a long swallow of brandy. "Finance us . . ."

"Uh-huh. Of course, we want all the pictures to be just like your book. Your—"

"Joe," Cooper interrupted.

"—Your style, your way of seeing things," Joe pressed on. "We want you to—"

"Joe? Joe, listen to me for a minute, will you?" Cooper interrupted, his tone sharpening. "There aren't going to be any more books. Not even one."

Joe took a moment to gather his thoughts. Then, sounding apologetic and somewhat hurt, he said, "Well, to be honest, I thought you might say that. I know you don't like taking on assignments. But we're friends, and I thought that might count for something. I wouldn't suggest you get involved, if I didn't think you'd enjoy it."

"I don't doubt that for a minute, Joe."

"Then, why not hear me out?"

"Because I have my book, Joe. I've no interest in another."

"But you'd have all the artistic freedom you'd require. And you could—"

Cooper shook his head no, emphatically.

"Why?" Joe challenged, his voice taking on a slight edge. "I mean, what are you afraid of?"

Cooper's eyes widened. "I'm not afraid, Joe. I'm just not interested." He rapped his pipe loudly against the side of an ashtray.

"You're serious, aren't you?"

Cooper rapped the pipe several more times in reply, knocking some smoldering ashes from the bowl. "Just like always, no is no." He jammed the pipe stem hard into the corner of his mouth and got to his feet.

"Well, no may be no; but no doesn't make sense, Dylan. This could bring you recognition. Even fame."

Cooper's brow knitted with frustration. "They're of no interest to me, Joe. I have what I want." He looked about, then pointed to a copy of his book on the table. "And I have you and Alicia to thank for it." His voice broke with emotion and he paused before adding, "I'll be forever grateful, Joe, believe me."

"No, no, Dylan, I'm the one who's grateful. I just wish you'd let me show it. You've worked so hard all these years. How can you turn your back on the rewards?"

"But I haven't, Joseph. I've always been my own man, and that's been my reward."

"Look," Joe snapped, losing patience with Cooper's obstinacy. "A lot of people worked on your book; and for some of us, the rewards are just beginning. You can't say no, just like that. It isn't fair."

Cooper took a deep breath, trying to maintain his composure. "But I can, Joseph; and I have. Now, why don't you just calm down, and—"

"Calm down?!" Joe exploded, his voice rising in half-octaves as he continued. "This may not mean much to you, but it's a once in a lifetime opportunity for me. The best chance I've ever had at getting some financial security."

"Well, go right ahead and take it!" Cooper shouted matching his volume. "Just stop lecturing me like I'm standing in your way. Like I'm the one who's keeping you from—" Cooper paused, struck by the implication of his own words. "Ah, now we're getting to work on the crust of the bread, aren't we, Joe?"

Joe winced in discomfort.

"All this talk about fame and recognition," Cooper went on, his burr thickening, his eyes taking on a feisty sparkle. "You can't hide mold with marmalade, Joe. What you're really saying is, I'm the key to you getting the financing. That's it. Isn't it?"

"So what if it is?" Joe replied, angry at being caught. "You have any idea how much money we could—"

"I don't care about money!" Cooper retorted.

"Well, I do!"

"Fine. You've every right to make as much as you can. But you'll have to do it without Dylan Cooper!"

Joe's gut churned. He knew Cooper meant what he said, but he could neither fathom nor accept it. "You're just being a stubborn old fool, aren't you? I mean, why not hear me out before you—"

"You're absolutely right!" Cooper snapped, his chin quivering with anger. "I'm old and I'm stubborn, but I'm not a fool. I haven't taken on an assignment in over twenty years, and I'm not taking one on now!"

"No, you're not a fool, Dylan. You're an, an—an—" Joe paused, searching for something vicious. "An ungrateful fool!"

"Ungrateful, eh?! I wouldn't worry about making money if I were you. It's clear you've got all the makings of a successful businessman!" Cooper snarled and spit the word out like an expletive.

Every muscle in Joe's body stiffened. His hands tightened into white-knuckled fists. Cooper saw them and cocked his head in defiance. They stood there seething, eyes locked in mutual hatred and disdain, neither wanting to strike the first blow, nor be the one to weaken and back down.

The tense silence was shattered by the creak of a hinge. Alicia was standing in the doorway in absolute shock. "Joe? What happened? My God, I was just dozing off. I thought I was having a nightmare. I—"

"Stubborn old fool!"

"Joe—" Alicia admonished sharply. She reached out and took hold of Cooper's arm as he charged past her. "Dylan, please?"

Cooper thundered across the parlor without breaking stride, then paused in front of the Christmas tree, his eyes welling with remorse. "I'm sorry, Alicia." He hurried from the bungalow, slamming the door after him. Alicia jumped at the sharp report, then stood there in stunned silence.

"Stubborn fool!" Joe bellowed, shaking with rage. He swept the copy of Cooper's book from the table. It hit the floor with a loud thump and went sliding into a pot of poinsettias in the corner.

"What happened?" Alicia asked again. "I mean . . . it's . . . it's Christmas Eve. I . . . I just can't believe you . . . you and Dylan . . . fighting like enemies. Why?"

Joe shrugged sullenly and turned away.

"This is supposed to be a time of happiness and joy," she said, trembling with emotion. "Joe?"

Joe ignored her and stared out the window in silence for a moment. "You know that old saying, the best laid plans of mice and men? Well, you can add God to that list."

Cooper was coming down the steps from the porch when he felt his chest tighten, and began wheezing audibly. He leaned against the truck for a moment, his breath coming in thin gray puffs; then he struggled into the cab and drove off into the blinding snow that came at an angle from the sea.

Chapter Forty-Three

Several days had passed. Alicia was tidying up the kitchen after breakfast when Joe came through the door from the garage carrying some boxes.

"Where are you going with those?"

"Inside," he replied, evading the question.

Alicia hurried after him into the parlor. "Why? What are you doing?"

"I'm taking down the tree."

"The Christmas tree? It isn't even New Year's yet. We always leave it up until the sixth."

"Not this year," Joe said with finality, setting the boxes on the coffee table. "Look at it. The branches are drooping. The needles are all dry . . ."

"Well, it probably just needs some water."

"Too late for that now," Joe declared, removing one of the ornaments. "It's on its last legs. I'm getting rid of it."

Alicia stepped in front of the tree protectively. "You don't stand a chance and you know it."

"It's dangerous," Joe persisted, about to remove another ornament. "It could catch fire. It's outlived its usefulness and it's got to go."

Alicia stood her ground and locked her eyes with his, stopping him; then her expression softened and she broke into a knowing smile. "I wasn't sure what this was all about, at first, but I think I know now."

"You do?"

"Uh-huh," she replied smugly. "What could possibly have caused you to come charging in here this morning and declare that our Christmas tree has, and I quote, 'outlived its usefulness'?"

Joe shrugged. "I'm not sure I follow you."

"I'm not surprised."

"I hate when you do this, Alicia. Come on, what are you talking about?"

"Your disagreement with Dylan."

"Oh. What about it?"

"Peace on earth. Good will toward men, Joe. I think it's time you got back into the Christmas spirit, and got over it. You owe him an apology."

"You don't stand a chance and you know it," Joe retorted, purposely repeating her earlier response.

"Oh, Joe," Alicia sighed. "He's lived an entire lifetime according to his code. Do you really expect him to change now?"

"Yes, I do," Joe replied with an exasperated groan. "He's so . . . so . . . stubborn."

"Especially when he's right."

"When he's right?!" Joe erupted.

"He is, Joe. You're just too proud to admit it. Your father's sweat gave you this business; and Dylan's book saved it for you; but now you're going to have to—"

"Dylan's book?!" Joe interrupted angrily. "It's yours, and mine, and Gundy's, and Lucas's too. It's the least Dylan could do to show his appreciation!"

Alicia took a deep breath, reconsidering. "You're right to care about your employees, Joe," she conceded, softening her tone. "But you're wrong about Dylan; and if you're honest with yourself, you'll start the New Year off right and re-solve to make it the rest of the way on your own."

Joe held her look in angry silence, then his eyes flickered with a thought. "I just might do that," he said in a spiteful tone. He scooped up the boxes and charged back through the kitchen and into the garage.

Alicia fetched the ornament Joe had removed from the tree and hung it on a branch; then noticed that one of the fig-ures in the crèche had toppled. She stooped and righted it, and was repositioning the others around the manger just so, when she heard the roadster start up.

Joe drove straight to the printing shop, called Lucas Bartlett, and told him he had a job he might find interesting. A half hour later, the young photographer was in Joe's office listening to his proposal.

"That's very interesting," Bartlett said, mulling it over. The fire in the potbellied stove had long ago died, and they sat bundled in hats, coats and gloves. "A project like that could keep us all busy for years."

"That's the idea. You think you're up to it?"

"You bet I am," Bartlett replied with a cocky grin. "Still something I don't get, though. Why isn't Cooper taking the pictures?"

"Because he's a stubborn old fool. You know how set in his ways he can be."

Bartlett's eyes rolled. "I wouldn't work with him again if it was the last job on earth."

Joe smiled sagely. "Well, sometimes these things have a way of paying off in the end. I imagine you're more than fa-miliar with any special techniques he uses."

"Special techniques?" Bartlett echoed with a derisive sneer. "Archaic'd be more like it. Chemicals, paper, a bare light bulb. That's it, that's all he—" Bartlett paused as it dawned on him. "Oh, oh, I get it. You want me to copy his style . . ."

"I wouldn't blame you for being offended, Lucas," Joe

offered. "But I didn't think it'd be fair for me to make the decision for you."

The young photographer considered it for a moment, then cocked his head challengingly. "Whose name is going to be on the books? Cooper's or mine?"

"Yours, of course."

"Then there's nothing to be offended about," Bartlett said.

"Good. Put together some samples as fast as you can," Joe instructed, shaking Bartlett's hand. He waited until Bartlett had left the office then pulled off a glove and lifted the phone. His finger spun the dial, once, twice, then paused with uncertainty. He hung up, wrestling with what he was about to do. The silence reminded him of how close the shop had come to being silent forever, of how desperate he felt at the prospect of failure, of how his employees had come through for him and had every right to expect him to do the same for them.

Joe dialed again. Resolutely, this time. "Arthur? Joe Clements calling. I'm not in the habit of doing business over the holidays, but I've got some good news."

Arthur Hastings sat next to a window in the study of his elegantly furnished home. Beyond the frosty panes that framed a Christmas tree, the Charles River cut a graceful swath through Back Bay Boston. "You've talked to Cooper about the assignment," he declared, setting his newspaper aside.

"Yes. Yes, I did," Joe said, trying to keep any hint of disappointment from his voice. "To make a long story short, we're ready to go to work whenever you are."

"Good. Let's meet in my office, on Monday. Say about eleven?"

"Monday, at eleven it is."

"Looking forward to it," Hastings concluded brightly. "After all I've heard about Cooper, I'm quite anxious to meet him."

Chapter Forty-Four

Cooper's truck was parked in front of Dr. Cheever's stately house that was blanketed with snow. The front door opened, and the old fellow came onto the porch pulling on a sheepskin parka as he trudged to the pickup. Chronic consumption was the diagnosis. A ban on pipe-smoking and less time spent in his fume-filled darkroom, the remedy.

The engine coughed and sputtered, refusing to start, when Cooper turned the key. It sounded like the old truck's death rattle, he thought. He jammed his pipe into the corner of his mouth and gave the engine one last try. It finally kicked over, chugging erratically as he drove off. The weary truck was snaking along shoreline road when the engine started sputtering again. Cooper thumbed the lever on the steering column, advancing the spark, but the engine gasped and wheezed and finally died.

Cooper groaned in disgust and guided the truck onto the shoulder. He took a moment to gather his strength, then got out and hinged up the bonnet. All the ignition wires appeared fastened, but he fetched a wrench and began tightening them anyway. He was still at it when he heard a vehicle approaching and came out from under the bonnet in search of help. The sight of Joe's roadster sent him ducking back into the engine compartment with a scowl.

Joe's mind was on the dilemma Hastings had just unknowingly created for him, and he hadn't noticed the disabled vehicle from afar; but, as he neared and slowed to offer his assistance, his eyes widened in angry recognition. Serves the old fool right, Joe thought as he stepped on the gas.

Cooper spat on the ground as the roadster roared past, then got back into the truck. It took several attempts but the balky engine finally caught. Cooper let it idle, got out again, and closed the bonnet with an angry slam. Old friends may be the best kind, he thought, but this one was letting him down. He stood, hands on hips, glaring at the beat up old truck, then his eyes softened with empathy. "Guess we're both about ready for the scrap heap."

Chapter Forty-Five

Alicia was in the parlor hanging several prints of Cooper's Christmas pictures next to the one of the bungalow when the phone rang. She cleaned her hands on her apron and answered it. "Mr. Hastings, how are you? Just fine, thanks—No, he isn't. Have you tried the shop?—Oh, then he's probably on his way. I'll have him call you soon as he gets home—Oh, sure, good idea. I'd be happy to." She nodded as she jotted on a pad, then her jaw slackened and her eyes narrowed with concern at the content of Hastings's message. A short time later, she heard the roadster pulling into the drive.

Joe took the steps to the porch two at a time, and sauntered into the parlor where Alicia was waiting. "Hi," he said, sensing her mood. "What's up?"

"Arthur Hastings just called."

Joe's stomach fluttered with apprehension. "Hastings?" he echoed, doing his best to conceal it.

"Yes. He said he forgot he has an appointment on Monday morning and wants to meet at two instead. He said to call back if it was a problem."

Joe shrugged, trying to appear nonchalant. There was something about Alicia now, something condemning or judgmental in the way she held herself, that unsettled him. "No, two o'clock's all right."

Alicia studied him out of the corner of her eye. "You didn't say anything about a meeting."

"Well, you said to find a way to make it on my own, and that's what I'm doing."

"Yes, I'm afraid so."

"What do you mean by that?"

"Well, Mr. Hastings just happened to mention how pleased he was that you were able to convince Dylan to take on the assignment."

"Why wouldn't he be?" Joe challenged, in a bold lie. He held her look for a moment, then sent a threatening glance to the Christmas tree. "I still say it should go."

"And we say it shouldn't," Alicia retorted firmly.

"—And those along with it," Joe added, having noticed the Christmas pictures she'd hung.

"Sorry, majority rules," she declared, cradling her tummy. "You were just out-voted two to one."

On Monday morning, the Christmas tree and Cooper's pictures still graced the parlor; Alicia was still troubled; and Joe was on the train to Boston.

Hastings and Brown's offices were in an impressive limestone building on Hanover Street, a short walk from North Station. The smell of leather and cigars mixed with the scent of freshly cut pine from the Christmas tree in the reception area; and despite the uncertain economy, the place was alive with bustling employees and the clatter of adding machines, typewriters, and telephones.

Hastings looked puzzled as he shook Joe's hand. "Where's Cooper? I expected he'd be with you?"

"So did I," Joe replied unflinchingly. He knew Hastings would ask, and had spent the journey deciding how he'd respond. "I did my best to convince him to come along; but you know how he is."

Hastings shrugged in resignation. "I guess we'll have to chalk it up to artistic temperament, won't we?"

"I guess so," Joe said, forcing a smile. "I'll just have to continue acting as an intermediary."

"I don't see that we have a choice."

Joe nodded, relieved to be past it. "Let's talk about subject matter, Arthur."

"Fine. Where do you want to begin?"

"With people. The first volume should be about people. I want it to pay tribute to their spirit; to their determination to survive; to their belief that this is still the land of opportunity. I want to see it in their faces, in their eyes, in their hands"—He paused, then, in a voice that rang with emotion, concluded—"in their souls."

Hastings was moved by Joe's fervor and took a moment to reply. "That's an excellent choice, Joe. It's all up to Cooper now."

"It certainly is." Joe sensed that a chance to prepare him for the inevitable moment of truth was at hand, and casually added, "Up to a point, anyway."

Hastings's brows arched. "I'm not sure I follow you?"

"Well, it dawned on me that no matter who takes them, it still comes down to the pictures in the end."

Hastings cocked his head thoughtfully. "True. I can't argue with that."

Joe suppressed a sigh of relief and nodded.

Chapter Forty-Six

The roadster wound along the snow-packed road to Cooper's house, and parked next to the faded pickup.

Alicia hurried from the car, carrying a worn mackinaw. "Dylan?" she called out, knocking on the door. "Dylan, it's Alicia." She brightened at the sound of footsteps and the creak of hinges that followed.

"Oh, I was hoping you'd come to see me," Cooper exclaimed with delight as they lunged into each other's arms. "Come on in. I'll put up some water for tea."

"I'd love to, but dinner's on the stove. I can't stay." She held up the mackinaw. "You left this at our place. I just wanted to drop it off and say hello."

"Thank you. We've been together a long time. Now, I have something for you—so to speak."

Alicia turned up her collar against the cold and waited in the entry as Cooper hurried off and returned with a small teddy bear.

Alicia's eyes widened like a child's. "Oh, Dylan you didn't have to do that."

"Of course I did," Cooper enthused, pleased to be sharing a moment of happiness with her. "I'd planned on waiting until the blessed event, but thought it best to take advantage of the moment."

Alicia hugged the stuffed animal to her bosom, then, prompted by her conversation with Hastings and by Joe's troubling reaction, she added, "I can't wait to show it to Joe."

Cooper bristled at the name, but maintained his composure. "Well," he said in a formal tone that was uncharacteristic, "He's yours now, Alicia. You're free to do with him what you will."

Alicia's shoulders sagged in disappointment, not at Cooper's words, but at his detached tone which confirmed her suspicions. "I take it you and Joe—you haven't talked, have you?"

Dylan shook his head no emphatically. "Not since we—well—since I saw you last," he replied, shaken by the memory. "Why do you ask?"

Alicia shrugged, deciding against confiding in him until she'd given Joe a chance to explain. "Just wishful thinking, I guess."

"I'm afraid I can't make that wish come true."

"I know," Alicia whispered, her eyes glistening with emotion.

"Now, now, none of that," the old fellow scolded. "Promise me you'll come by again soon?"

Alicia wiped away a tear, and nodded.

Cooper was hugging her when Alicia kissed his cheek, then hurried to the car. He watched her drive off as he had the last time, remaining in the doorway long after she was gone. Once again, a surge of emotion set his mind racing through decades past; and once again, the memories were just as strong, the sense of loss just as painful, and the chance of ever seeing his beloved Grace again, just as hopeless.

Chapter Forty-Seven

Moonlight painted the bungalow with a bluish glow that spilled through the window into the kitchen where Alicia was clearing dishes. Joe was sitting at the table with a cup of coffee. The meeting with Hastings had improved his disposition, but he'd kept a smug silence about it.

"Joe," Alicia finally said, breaking it. "Joe, we have to talk about something. I was going to mention it before but I didn't want to spoil dinner."

"So you decided to spoil the rest of the evening instead . . ." he said, sounding facetious.

"I went to see Dylan this morning."

Joe's eyes sharpened to pinpoints. "You what?"

"You heard me. I went to see Dylan."

"That's a heck of a way to start the New Year." He got to his feet, glaring at her with anger and disbelief. "Whose side are you on anyway?"

"It's not about taking sides, Joe. It's about truthfulness. I didn't want to say anything until I was sure. Dylan isn't taking the pictures, is he?"

"I never said he was."

"Maybe, *you* didn't say it, but Mr. Hastings did," Alicia

retorted, on the verge of losing her temper. "If Dylan isn't taking them, who is?"

"Lucas," Joe replied.

"I see . . . But Mr. Hastings doesn't know that, does he?" she challenged, her eyes burning with condemnation. "It's not like you to be deceptive, Joe."

"I'm not being deceptive, Alicia. I'm being smart. I knew it'd be impossible to convince Hastings to use another photographer, so I decided to show him instead."

"Show him?"

"Yes. You know what they say: A picture's worth a thousand words? Well, once he sees the pictures, sees how good they are, he won't care who took them."

"Okay," she said crossing her arms. "Then what?"

"Then," Joe repeated, pausing before delivering the punch line, "then I'll tell Hastings the truth."

Alicia's face fell. Her posture slackened. She was stopped cold. "Oh."

"Right. Oh," Joe said, implying he'd been vindicated. "Hastings has to meet a payroll every week just like me. Given an equal alternative, he's not going to let a cantankerous old man stand in the way."

"I guess not," Alicia conceded, feeling she'd judged him rashly. "Looks like I owe you an apology."

Joe smirked.

"Don't gloat. It's not becoming."

"I'm waiting, Alicia."

"I apologize."

"Thank you." Joe punctuated it with a snap of his head, then pushed past her and left the kitchen.

Alicia gathered her thoughts, then found Joe at the rolltop desk in the parlor, sorting through papers. She fetched the teddy bear Cooper had given her from amongst the gifts under the Christmas tree, and set it on the desk in front of Joe. "Isn't he cute?"

"Sure is," Joe replied, his mood brightening. "Where'd he come from?"

"Dylan gave him to me," Alicia replied a little too brightly. "I thought you'd like to see it."

Joe's expression darkened. He grasped one of the teddy's floppy ears between thumb and forefinger, as if the stuffed animal was contaminated, and handed it back to her. "Okay. I've seen it." Joe swiveled around in the chair, and resumed sorting papers as if she wasn't there.

Chapter Forty-Eight

〜

The temperature had dropped into the teens, and the pot-bellied stove was creaking in protest as Bartlett covered the layout table in Joe's office with his sample photographs: proud faces and gnarled hands; blue-collar workers and hardscrabble farm families; bright-eyed children and blissful infants. "I think I've got the old guy's style down pretty good."

Joe nodded smartly in agreement. "I'd say so. I can't wait to show them to Hastings."

The next afternoon, despite a snowstorm that wrought havoc with the train schedule, Joe was in Boston spreading the photographs across the table in Hastings and Brown's conference room.

Hastings circled the table, studying each picture. "I don't know, Joe," he finally said with grave expression. "There's something missing."

Joe's stomach began tighting into a knot. "Missing? What do you mean?"

"Well, they have the technical polish I expected. But they fall short artistically. They're just not up to Cooper's standards. They're stiff and awkward. Like—like pictures of machines."

Joe looked stunned. "Machines? Gosh, Arthur, I—I thought they were pretty good."

"They are," Hastings said with an enigmatic pause. "Just not good enough. Cooper always said he wasn't interested in taking on assignments. Now we know why."

"I guess," Joe said, his mind racing to find a way to salvage the project. "I'm sure if I told him what you said, he could make some adjustments and—"

"You'd be wasting your time, Joe. Some people, no matter how talented, can't channel their creativity to someone else's vision. We were wrong to force him."

Joe emitted a forlorn sigh, realizing that neither pressing the lie nor telling the truth would affect Hastings's decision.

"You know," Hastings went on, holding one of the prints to the light. "If I didn't know better, I'd think someone was trying to copy Cooper's style."

Joe swallowed hard, then looked Hastings square in the eye. "You're right, Arthur. Someone was. You probably won't believe this, but I was planning to tell you. I just wanted you to see them first." Joe lowered his eyes and went about collecting the prints.

Hastings watched with growing empathy. Every business had its ups and downs. He'd experienced Joe's desperation more times than he cared to remember; and, despite the sleight of hand, he admired the young man's tenacity and willingness to take chances to keep his business from failing. "You know, I feel badly about this, Joe," he finally said.

Joe shrugged in resignation. "So do I."

Hastings looked off thoughtfully for a moment. "Come to think of it, there's a project in the offing. No guarantees, but I may be able to steer it your way."

Joe nodded weakly in acknowledgment.

"Nothing like this of course; but it's right up your alley: a catalogue . . . mail order stuff. I should have word in a few days."

"That'd be swell, Arthur," Joe said. He forced a smile, and placed the last photographs into the leather folio.

"By the way, I recall you mentioning a photographer you've used for this kind of work. What was his name again? Barton? Bennett?"

"Bartlett," Joe replied in a barely audible voice. "Lucas Bartlett."

"That's it. Think he might be available?"

"Yes," Joe muttered, stung by the irony. "I have a feeling he might."

A short while later on the train back to Newbury, Joe slouched in his seat, staring out the window at the wintry landscape racing past. Hypnotized by the fleeting images and the rhythmic clack of train wheels, he was thinking about how, after saving his company and keeping his employees from losing their jobs, he had somehow lost his way and broken his integrity to get the second book published.

He'd always been an honest man who prided himself on his word being his bond. Now he felt ashamed of his greed and uncharacteristic deceptiveness, and guilt-ridden over his falling out with Cooper, not to mention how he had quarreled with Alicia and scorned her goodness and sense of decency.

It was almost dusk when the train arrived in Newbury. Joe trudged through the snow to the roadster, carrying the portfolio, then slipped behind the wheel and lit a cigarette. That morning, he had driven himself to the station to keep Alicia off the treacherous roads. Now, as he drove the icy ribbon that paralleled the coast, the feelings of shame and guilt he'd felt on the train resurfaced with overwhelming force.

Like a wounded animal retreating to its lair, Joe wanted nothing more than to get home and take refuge in Alicia's reassuring embrace; but his heart was pounding like a pile driver, and his breath was coming in short tight puffs, and his brow was dotted with perspiration despite the cold, and he suddenly pulled off onto the shoulder, unable to cope with the unnerving torment. He dragged deeply on his cigarette, exhaling slowly as if expelling the demons that had taken hold of him, and sat there atop the bluff, staring down at the storm-tossed sea, his anxiety soaring with each metronomic sweep of the wipers across the windshield.

Chapter Forty-Nine

The same morning, the gusting winds that sent the snowstorm slashing across the harbor were threatening to blow Cooper off the ice-encrusted breakwater into the raging surf below. Gurgling torrents swirled about his scuffed hightops as he bent to his Graflex. In the distance, where the blizzard marched over snow-capped mountains, a shaft of light pierced the cloud cover, turning each flake of snow into a sparkling gemstone. Cooper made a half dozen exposures, capturing the visual tour de force in all its glory, then hurried back to his darkroom with his booty.

He spent the rest of the morning developing the negatives and was about to make his first print when the muffled ring of the phone came from the cottage. As always, he assumed it would stop after several rings, and whoever it was would call back if it were really important; but this time, the phone rang and rang. Cooper set his negative aside and went into the cottage to answer it. "Cooper."

"Dylan? Dylan, oh, thank God you're there," Alicia exclaimed, trying to catch her breath. "I'm—I'm—" she gasped, lurching back against the sofa.

"Lass? What is it, lass? Are you all right?"

"The baby," Alicia blurted in the throes of a contraction. "Doctor Cheever said it wouldn't be for a couple more weeks but—" She suddenly stiffened and gasped, cradling her tummy.

"The baby—the baby," Cooper's voice rose with excitement. "You're going to have the baby."

"Yes, yes, Joe isn't here and I've no way to get to the hospital. I called Dr. Cheever but there was no answer. Hurry, please?"

"Hold on, lass. I'm on my way."

The old fellow dashed from the cottage pulling on his mackinaw and climbed into the pickup. The engine refused to start, and he was beside himself by the time it finally kicked over. He slammed it in gear and headed down the hill, pushing the old vehicle to the limit, the worn tires slipping and sliding on the icy roads. Fifteen minutes later, he turned into the drive behind the Clements's bungalow. Cooper got out and left the engine running.

"Alicia?" he called out, his anxiety soaring as he burst into the parlor. "Alicia, are you all right?"

Alicia hadn't moved from the sofa. Teeth clenched against the onset of another contraction, she responded with an affirmative nod.

"Good," Cooper grunted. "Better gather your things, lass. Hurry. No telling how long it'll take us to get to hospital with these roads."

Alicia started to rise, then stiffened again. "No. No, Dylan, it's too late. We'll never make it."

"Never make it?" Cooper echoed with disbelief. "Am I to take that to mean that—"

"Yes," Alicia interrupted. "The baby's coming, now." She emitted a painful gasp, then another, arching back against the cushions. "Right now. Better help me into bed, then try Dr. Cheever again."

Cooper took her arm and guided her down the hall toward the bedroom, his mind racing through decades past to another such night; to another young woman, his beloved Grace, frightened and alone; to the child he never knew, the infant son he had come home from the war to learn was with the Lord in Heaven. Shaken by the memories, his eyes glistening with emotion, he helped Alicia into the bed, then hurried back to the parlor and dialed the phone.

Chapter Fifty

⌒

The Newbury Community Church was darkened at this hour except for the soft glow of a light above the altar. Pastor Martin came from a door in an alcove next to the altar and strode up the aisle, squinting to identify the figure hunched in the last pew. "Joe?" he wondered with uncertainty as he approached. "Joe Clements?"

Joe shifted anxiously and nodded.

"I thought I heard a car," the pastor explained, then in an attempt at levity, added, "I'll do anything to avoid facing paperwork. Even minister to a congregant."

Joe smiled thinly. "But you didn't expect it would be me. Did you, Pastor Martin?"

"No, I can't say I did; but it's good to see you, Joseph. I recall encouraging Alicia to bring you to Sunday services."

"This couldn't wait until Sunday, Pastor Martin."

"That sounds serious," the pastor said, slipping into the pew next to him. "How can I help you?"

Joe shrugged with pained uncertainty. "I'm not sure you can. I'm not sure anyone can. I'm not even sure why I'm here. Really. All I know is, we had a wonderful Christmas, and then everything started going wrong. I feel like my whole world's falling apart. This meeting I had today was the last straw." He shook his head and groaned in despair. "I just wanted to get home to Alicia; but all of a sudden I felt so . . . so . . . overwhelmed . . . that I had to pull over. I just couldn't go home like this. I . . . I guess, with the baby coming, I was afraid of upsetting her. I was trying to sort things out when I thought of something she said on the way home from the Christmas play and . . . and here I am."

"Well, I'm glad you are," Pastor Martin said softly. "Now let's talk about what's troubling you."

Joe splayed his hands in a helpless gesture. "I don't know, I'm . . . I'm just not myself . . . I feel confused and cornered." He shifted in the pew and folded his arms as if trying to contain himself, then unfolded them and began tugging at his shirt collar. "Truth is, I feel so guilty. My father taught me to be a man of integrity . . . to always tell the truth and keep my word."

Pastor Martin nodded with empathy. "Guilt is common to all human beings, Joe. God gave each of us a conscience, and when we violate it, we feel bad. I'm sure you can think of a good reason for your guilt."

"A half dozen of 'em," Joe blurted, launching into a litany of his offenses that poured out of him like water bursting from a dam. "I've been selfish and prideful and . . . and . . . yes, deceitful. I'm guilty of being greedy and unreasonable, too. Not to mention disrespectful to my wife and . . . and downright mean-spirited to the person most responsible for keeping my business from going under." The deluge ended only after his falling out with Cooper and his attempt to deceive Hastings had been spelled out in detail.

"Well," Pastor Martin sighed as if trying to catch his breath. "It sounds as if you've given the Seven Deadly Sins quite a run for their money . . ." He paused and smiled at what he was about to say. ". . . Though I don't recall any mention of gluttony or sloth."

"I'm sure it wasn't for lack of trying."

"Yes, I do recall, you're not the sort to do things half way, are you?"

Joe managed a smile but it was the truth of the pastor's remark, not its humor, that hit home. "No, now that you mention it, Pastor Martin, I'm not; and that's the worst part. I've always been able to . . . to handle things on my own. If I have a problem, I tackle it head on; and I keep at it till it's solved. I've never been in this situation before . . . never felt the need to ask for anyone's help . . . let alone God's." His shoulders sagged under the weight of his own observation, and he sighed, seeming totally dispirited. "I guess, I better add hypocritical to that list, too, shouldn't I?"

"Well, I think we've had quite enough mea culpas for one day," the pastor said, unmoved by Joe's self-pity; then his expression softened. "You know, many of us instinctively tend to draw closer to our Creator when beset by adversity. I think that's probably one of the reasons He allows it. The more we feel as if we're not in control of events, the more we're prone to acknowledge the existence of a God who is in control. With every day, the world is becoming a more chaotic place, a more . . . formidable adversary. It's not only difficult, but foolish to try to cope with it alone."

Joe responded with a sheepish nod. "That's exactly what Alicia's been trying to tell me, but I wouldn't listen to her. Instead, when things went wrong I tried to convince her—along with myself, of course—that I had a perfectly good reason for doing what I did; but . . . but . . . the end doesn't justify the means, does it?"

"No," Pastor Martin replied. "But of course we think it's much easier to dismiss an ethical lapse if it's born of a well-intentioned effort."

Joe nodded. "It sure is; but it's not working, Pastor Martin. Not working at all. As I said, I'm not myself. It's . . . it's as if I've become someone I don't recognize. Someone . . . someone who I . . . " He bit off the sentence as the source of his unbearable turmoil dawned on him; then his eyes hardened and, in a condemning tone, he concluded, ". . . someone who I don't like."

Pastor Martin nodded with the wisdom of his experience. "You're a decent soul at heart, Joe. It's not surprising that, try as you might to justify your behavior as being a benefit to others, your conscience isn't buying it. Instead of giving you peace with God, it's making you feel guilty before God. And peace of mind is something you want, especially during Christmas. That's really it, isn't it?"

Joe sighed with relief and nodded.

"Well, the mere fact that you're here is powerful evidence that you know what you have to do next."

Joe nodded, again, resolutely; and enumerated in reply: "Swallow my pride, confess my sins before God, apologize to the people I've hurt, and—most important of all—find a way to make things right with Cooper."

"Sounds like a sensible course of action," Pastor Martin said, his eyes brightening at the mention of Cooper's name. "Extraordinarily talented fellow. That was quite a lovely book you published, wasn't it?"

"You've seen it?"

"Of course, who hasn't? I've a copy in my office. Even bought several as Christmas gifts. Lovely picture of the church, by the way. Did you know he got married here?"

Joe looked surprised. "Cooper?"

Pastor Martin nodded. "Almost twenty years ago. I performed the ceremony."

Joe's eyes widened with intrigue. "So . . . so you knew his wife? You knew Grace?"

Pastor's Martin's eyes clouded with sadness. "A lovely young woman. Intelligent, spirited, much like Alicia in many ways. Theirs is a tragic story."

"Yes, I know," Joe said, his voice reduced to a contrite whisper. "I guess I should be counting my blessings, shouldn't I?"

"Indeed, and as I understand it, you've had your share of

late, not to mention another on the way. You know, in my experience, making peace with God is the first step to making peace with oneself and with those we're estranged from. We all tend to lose our way at some time or other . . ." Pastor Martin paused, then glanced to the cross that hung above the altar. "Always remember, Joe—He didn't die on that cross for people who are perfect, but for sinners like you and me. And there is no sin in the world that He cannot forgive if we ask Him. The shining example is the thief who was crucified alongside of Jesus. When he asked for forgiveness, Jesus promised him that '. . . on this day you will be with me in paradise.' By inviting Him into your heart and asking Him for forgiveness, He can, as the Bible says, 'make you white as snow'."

"Thanks, Pastor Martin. Thanks for everything," Joe said, extending a hand. "Oh, and Happy New Year."

"Yes, Happy New Year, Joe," Pastor Martin said, pleased he had helped Joe put things right. He patted him on the shoulder, then slipped out of the pew and melted into the shadows of the darkened church.

Joe sat there for a moment in quiet reflection, then fell to his knees, bowed his head in prayer, confessed his sins, and invited Christ into his life.

Chapter Fifty-One

⟨~⟩

Darkness had fallen by the time Joe arrived at the bungalow. The roadster's headlights swept across two vehicles parked in the drive. One was Cooper's pickup; the other, a black sedan that Joe recognized as Dr. Cheever's Packard. He bolted from the car and dashed inside, his heart pounding so hard he could hear it.

Joe burst into the parlor to find Dr. Cheever sitting on the sofa sipping a brandy, and Cooper in one of the wicker chairs, calmly smoking his pipe. The old fellow stiffened at the sight of him, glaring in condemnation. Joe was too upset to notice and exclaimed, "What happened? Is everything okay?"

"Yes, mother and son are doing just fine," Cheever replied getting to his feet to shake Joe's hand. "Congratulations."

"Mother and son?!" Joe echoed in amazement. "You're sure? You're positive?" he went on rapid fire. "They're both all right?"

Cheever responded with an emphatic nod.

"But—but I thought it wasn't going to be for a couple more weeks?"

"So did I," Cheever replied, his eyes smiling from behind

rimless glasses. "Evidently, your boy has a mind of his own. Would you like to see him?"

"Oh. Oh, yes," Joe replied, still stunned by the turn of events. "Of course I would."

Cooper remained behind as Cheever led the way into the bedroom. All the pillows were propped against the head-board, and Alicia was sitting up, nursing the baby. "Hi, darling," she whispered.

"Gosh, I'm—I'm so sorry," Joe sighed, riddled with guilt. "I'd have never gone, if I'd known . . ."

"Oh, Joe, how could you have known?" Alicia said, absolving him. "Dr. Cheever says he's a little trouper. Ten fingers, ten toes, an appetite like his father's . . . Want to hold him?"

Joe hesitated for a moment, then took the baby and cradled him in his arms, awkwardly; but the tiny, peaceful face peering from within the blanket seemed to soothe his uneasiness. "He's beautiful, darling," Joe whispered with the combined sense of excitement, pride and awe that touches every new parent. "I don't know how to thank you, Doc," he said, turning to Cheever. "But, I promise you, I'll find a way."

"Me?" Cheever wondered. "I was making a house call down in Rowley. It was all over by the time I got here. Don't thank me, thank Dylan. God knows what might have happened if it wasn't for him."

Joe let out a long breath and glanced at Alicia. No words were necessary. He had sorted it out with Pastor Martin and had made his peace with God, and his eyes said it all.

Alicia sensed the profound change in him and shifted her gaze to the door.

Joe knew exactly what she was thinking and nodded. "I'll be right back." He nestled the baby in Alicia's arms, and went into the parlor to make his peace with Cooper, but the old fellow was gone.

Joe heard the truck sputtering and refusing to start, and hurried to the door. Just as he opened it, the engine kicked over and Cooper slammed the truck in gear. Joe was on the verge of calling out and running after him, but despite his need to make amends, Joe suddenly sensed his apology should be something special, something that went beyond words, and remained in the doorway as the truck went down the drive.

The next morning, awakened early by the baby's hungry cry, Joe headed into the kitchen and made some breakfast. He was carrying a tray laden with toast, coffee, butter, and jam to the bedroom when he glanced into the parlor and was surprised to see Alicia standing in front of the Christmas tree with the baby.

"Alicia?" Joe said with concern. "Didn't Dr. Cheever say you were supposed to stay in bed?"

"He certainly did," she replied with a mischievous twinkle. "But I don't think he'd disapprove of me showing Joseph Clements Jr. his first Christmas tree."

"Oh," Joe said, a little chagrined; then in a self-deprecating tone, joked, "See? Aren't you glad I talked you out of taking it down?"

Alicia laughed and settled on the sofa with the baby. Joe sat next to her and began stirring his coffee, lost in his thoughts.

Alicia sensed what was troubling him, and took his hand in hers. "It didn't go very well with Mr. Hastings yesterday, did it?"

"No, I'm afraid not," Joe replied with a defeated sigh. "I guess I never appreciated just how special Dylan's talent is."

"How special he is, Joe."

Joe nodded in contrite agreement. "I was the one who was being stubborn and foolish."

"Not to mention greedy, selfish, and downright ornery," Alicia teased.

"I know. I'm sorry. I've said hurtful things and—"

"Shush," she whispered, putting a finger to his lips to silence him.

"Okay, but I thought you'd be pleased to know it was Pastor Martin who helped me sort things out."

"Pastor Martin?"

"See? I knew that'd get your attention. I stopped by to see him on the way home yesterday. That's why I was late."

"Oh, Joe . . ."

"You know, you were right. For the first time in my life, I have real peace with God."

Alicia's eyes glistened with emotion. "This is the best Christmas gift of all, Joe."

Joe smiled, savoring the moment, then glancing down to the baby, said, "I think we should call it a tie."

"So do I," Alicia replied in a way that suggested she was up to something. "Now, I don't mean to sound selfish or anything, but there is one more gift that I'm still praying for."

"I'm working on it," Joe said with an impish smile, knowing she was referring to his making peace with Cooper.

Alicia looked puzzled. "Working on it? Repeat after me: I'm sorry, Dylan. I was wrong. I apologize. I hope you'll forgive me. It's that simple, isn't it?"

"Yes, but I want to give him something too; something special to make sure he knows I really mean it. I want him to know how badly I feel and how much I value his friendship." Joe fetched the teddy bear from beneath the tree and tucked it next to his newborn son. He was thinking about what that gift might be when he noticed the Christmas pictures that Alicia had hung next to the one of the bungalow. One of them—the picture of Grace walking in the wintery landscape—held Joe's attention for a long moment, then his eyes came to life with the special idea he sought.

That afternoon when Alicia and the baby were napping, Joe made sure the bedroom door was closed, then went to his desk and called Hastings at his office in Boston. Joe told him he was working on a special project, a very special and personal one that involved Cooper, and asked for his help.

Chapter Fifty-Two

~~~~~

Almost a month of the new year had passed. The snow had stopped. The roads had been plowed. And the morning sun rose in a clear sky, but Newbury was still caught in winter's frigid grasp.

Though Joe had gotten over the impact of his fateful meeting with Hastings, he hadn't forgotten the mail order project Hastings had mentioned at its conclusion. To Joe's relief, neither had Hastings; and this morning the canny businessman had taken the train up from Boston to discuss it. The two men were in Joe's office going over the details when the mailman knocked on the half-open door.

"Morning, Ben," Joe said, brightening.

"Mr. Clements," Ben grunted, handing him a special delivery envelope. "Sorry to interrupt, but I need your John Hancock right here."

"My pleasure," Joe said, signing the receipt.

"By the way, I hear congratulations are in order."

Joe plucked a cigar from a box on his desk and handed it to Ben. "Thanks, everyone says he looks like his mother."

"Lucky boy," Ben joked, as he hurried off.

"Well," Hastings said, gesturing to the material he'd

spread across the layout table, "I'd say you've got plenty to keep you busy."

"Plenty," Joe replied. "By the way, you remember that special project we spoke about?"

"Yes, I understand my people came through with the information you were after."

"They sure did. Cabled it to my office weeks ago . . ." Joe held up the special delivery envelope. ". . . and the payoff's in here."

Later that afternoon, the sun was hanging above the horizon as Joe turned into the bungalow's snow covered drive. Alicia heard the car and came to the door to greet him. "Hi, darling! How did it go?"

"Well, we've got the job . . ."

"That's wonderful," she exclaimed, leading the way inside. "I want to hear all about it."

"Frankly, I've had my fill of business for today. It's time to get on to more important matters."

Alicia's brows arched with curiosity. "Really?"

"Uh-huh. I was about to suggest we take a ride over to Dylan's."

"Dylan's?" Alicia repeated, sounding as uncertain as she did pleased.

"Yes, I have a surprise for him."

Alicia's eyes narrowed with concern. "I hope it isn't like the last one?"

Joe smiled and slipped the special delivery envelope from his pocket. "No, it's in here."

"Well, come on. What is it?"

"A steamer ticket."

"A steamer ticket?" she exclaimed.

"Uh-huh. First class cabin, round trip to Scotland in the name of one D. Cooper."

"Oh, Joe! Let's go give it to him right now!"

"Try and stop me. There's more to it, by the way."

"There is?"

"Uh-huh. Let's get Joseph bundled up and I'll tell you on the way." A short time later, they were racing along the snow-blanketed coast, Joe at the wheel. Alicia sat next to him, cradling the baby. He turned onto the road that wound through the foothills, guiding the roadster along the un-plowed switchbacks to Cooper's place.

Alicia brightened at the sight of the battered truck parked outside. "Oh, good, he's here," she said, as Joe stopped next to it. They got out and hurried to the front door. Joe knocked, then knocked again. "Dylan? Dylan, you in there?" No reply, no footsteps, not a sound. "He's probably out taking pictures."

"I don't know," Alicia said, glancing at the darkening sky. "He's usually here at this hour."

Joe stepped to a window, rubbed off some frost with his glove, and peered inside. His eyes darted to Cooper's camera standing next to the fireplace. "Well, he may be out, but he's not taking pictures."

Alicia tried the door with her free hand. It creaked open, and she walked into the parlor. The frigid air was ripe with the scent of chemicals and an aroma of pipe smoke. "Dylan? Dylan, you here?" she called out, a hint of concern creeping into her voice.

"Where the heck is he?" Joe said, following her.

Alicia shrugged. A few tense seconds passed before it dawned on her. "Oh, I know," she said, relieved. "Wait here with daddy, okay?" She handed the baby to Joe and hurried off down the corridor.

The darkroom was closed. Alicia put an ear to the door; but heard neither rustling paper, nor sloshing chemicals, nor shuffling feet. She rapped on it lightly, hesitant to interrupt Cooper's work. "Dylan?" she called out. "Dylan, you in there?" Still no response. She knocked again, harder this time, then tried the knob. The door was locked from the in-side and wouldn't budge. Her anxiety soared. "Dylan?! Dylan, it's Alicia. Are you all right?!" Silence. She was beside herself, and about to fetch Joe when she heard the sound of the latch lifting. The door creaked open, inviting her into the darkness. She squinted until her eyes became accustomed to the dark and found Cooper slouched in a chair. "Dylan?" she said softly, making her way through the blackness. "Dylan, you all right?"

A long moment passed before the old fellow nodded. "Aye. I'm fine. I didn't mean to frighten you."

"Then why didn't you answer?" Alicia asked, glancing about. "What are you doing in here? It doesn't look like you're working."

"I'm not. I was watering the plants when I heard the car, and went to the window. When I saw you and—and—" The name caught in his throat, and he started over. "When I saw who was with you, I decided I wasn't up to having visitors."

"He knows he was wrong, Dylan."

"I recall mentioning that to him several times."

"He feels terrible. He—"

"That he should."

"Please? He wants to apologize."

"It's too late for that."

"It's never too late. He has something for you. Something special."

Cooper glowered defiantly and shook his head no. "My mind's made up on the matter."

Alicia's mind raced in search of a way to change the situation, and came up with an idea. "I thought we were friends?" she began, hoping the vulnerable timbre in her voice would reach him.

"Of course, we are," Cooper replied. "You and I, that is," he added, making the distinction.

"Old friends?" she prompted, shrewdly.

Cooper's head cocked with suspicion, then his eyes narrowed with understanding, and he nodded.

"Dependable, loyal, you can count on them and they can count on you?" she went on rapid fire, sensing she had him where she wanted him.

The old fellow nodded again. "Aye."

"Well, I'm counting on you, Dylan."

Cooper considered it for a long moment. He put his unlit pipe in the corner of his mouth, conceding the point, then followed Alicia to the parlor where Joe waited with the baby. She took him from his father's arms, and drifted aside, leaving the two men staring at each other in tense silence.

"I'm sorry, Dylan," Joe finally said. "I was wrong, and I'd like to make it up to you if I can." He took the envelope from his jacket and offered it to Cooper.

The old fellow stared at it suspiciously, then sensed Alicia's eyes, and snatched it from Joe's hand, stuffing it into a pocket. "Accepted," he growled.

"No. No, you have to open it," Alicia prompted.

Cooper stiffened with resistance.

"I'm counting on you, remember?"

Cooper groaned, then retrieved the envelope and tore it open. His eyes widened at the sight of the steamer ticket that moved him beyond words.

"Well," Alicia said, beaming. "Aren't you going to say something?"

"A ticket to Scotland?" Cooper responded in an amazed whisper.

Joe sighed with relief. "Well, after all you said about wanting to get back home again, I didn't think it'd be fair to keep Grace waiting forever."

Cooper's eyes flickered with delight. "Grace? My Grace?"

"Unless you know another woman named Grace?"

"Oh Joseph. I don't know what to say." Cooper was giving his enthusiasm full rein when his eyes suddenly clouded with concern.

"What is it?" Alicia asked.

"Well it just dawned on me that if I couldn't find Grace then, it'd be next to impossible now."

Alicia and Joe exchanged knowing smiles.

"And what does that mean?" Cooper prompted.

"Oh, just a feeling," Joe replied. "But if I were a betting man, I'd wager you'll have much better luck this time."

Cooper stared at him, afraid to commit his heart to it. "You've—you've found her?"

"Well, I had a hand in it," Joe replied with a modest smile. "Remember that fellow, Hastings?"

Cooper responded with a cautious nod.

"Turns out he has a number of European suppliers. One of them is a company in Glasgow. It seems they have a few government . . . connections. So, he sent them a cable, and they got in touch with someone in the Main Social Services Office in Edinburgh, and there she was."

"And there she was, where?" Cooper wondered, bristling with curiosity.

"In a town called Stirling. She's been teaching dance in a private school there for almost twenty years. She lives in the faculty residence hall."

Cooper's eyes widened with surprise. "No wonder I couldn't find her."

"To make a long story short, arrangements are being made for her to be there in Glasgow when the steamer docks. All you have to do is book passage and drop her a note with the arrival date."

Cooper was overcome with emotion. "So many years," he said, repeating it over and over. "Why, I'd probably walk right past her."

"Perhaps, but something tells me she'll have no trouble recognizing you."

"Oh, I don't know, Joseph. I'm afraid I've changed just a wee bit too."

"I still think she'll manage somehow." Joe took something from a pocket and handed it to him. It was a snapshot of Cooper Joe had taken at the Christmas party with the box camera. Its serrated edges seemed perfectly suited to Cooper's jut-jawed defiance. "We've already sent her one of these."

Cooper chuckled at what he was about to say. "Then I've little hope she'll show up."

"Dylan," Alicia gently admonished.

The baby gurgled and seemed to be reaching for Cooper's face with his fingers.

"See? Even little Joseph agrees."

"I think it's an excellent likeness," Joe said.

Cooper studied the snapshot, then looked up misty-eyed. "Aye," he conceded, his voice breaking with emotion. "It's a fine picture, Joe."

The Reunion

Chapter Fifty-Three

$\backsim$

By the Spring of 1940, the world had descended into political turmoil. The New York World's Fair had been forced to change its theme from "Building the World of Tomorrow" to "For Peace and Freedom." Albert Einstein had informed President Roosevelt of the development of an atomic bomb. And Europe was once again torn by war. Poland, Norway, Holland and Belgium had already fallen. Now the Nazi juggernaut was rolling across France and threatening to attack Great Britain. The United States had declared its neutrality the previous September, and more than two years would pass before the Japanese attack on Pearl Harbor would force America to join the fight.

War raged at sea as well. Despite Hitler's decree that passenger ships would not be attacked, the *Athenia* was torpedoed by a German U-boat off the Scottish coast. Many civilians lost their lives. Soon after, another passenger liner was fire-bombed by the Luftwaffe in the English Channel, running aground off the Isle of Wight.

Consequently, passenger ships were forced to travel in convoys escorted by British warships. Regularly scheduled sailings were disrupted, and each passenger ship's departure was determined by that of the convoy to which it was assigned.

These restricted schedules and the fact that many passenger liners had been pressed into service as troop transports made transatlantic bookings more and more difficult to secure; and despite having the ticket Joe and Alicia had given him in hand, Cooper was unable to arrange passage to Scotland until the first of June.

Chapter Fifty-Four

A warm breeze rose off the Cape and stirred the waters of Boston Harbor as the S.S. *Britannic*, the third in a succession of stately ocean liners to be so christened, prepared for departure. Deckhands were securing hawsers to two tugboats that would ease the flagship of the storied White Star Line from its berth. Porters were rolling hand trucks piled with luggage and supplies into the hold. Stewards were settling passengers in their cabins. An animated crowd was surging across the pier, up the boarding ramp, and onto the main deck where many passengers gathered with the friends and family members who had come to see them off.

Cooper was with a group of townsfolk from Newbury: Joe and Alicia Clements and their infant son, Joseph, were among them, as were the workers from Joe's shop who had printed Cooper's book of Christmas pictures, along with Dr. Cheever, the town's M.D., and Pastor Martin of the Newbury Community Church. Boston book distributor Arthur Hastings, who had used his business connections in Scotland to locate Grace, was also there.

"I wish we were all going with you, Dylan," Alicia teased

in her spirited way, though her voice had a wistful timbre that suggested she meant it.

"So do I," Joe chimed in. "But I hear they've taken to tossing stowaways overboard, these days."

"Aye," Cooper grunted with a hearty chuckle. "I'm afraid I'll be more than enough for Grace to handle."

"I'm sure she'll do fine," Pastor Martin said with a warm smile. Twenty years ago, just days before Cooper went off to war, he had performed the quickly arranged ceremony that made Dylan Cooper and Grace MacVicar husband and wife. Long saddened by their tragic story, the pastor was heartened by this providential turn of events. "The Lord in his infinite goodness has seen fit to reunite you. Trust in Him to make it come out right."

They were all nodding in agreement when the ship's bell began ringing, and the first mate called out, "All ashore that's going ashore!"

Moments later, after a round of heartfelt hugs and farewells, those who *were* going ashore hurried to disembark.

Cooper stood at the railing waving good-bye as the *Britannic* slipped from its berth with a shudder that could be felt throughout the massive vessel. The tugs guided it through the inner harbor, past Castle Island—where, for nearly one hundred fifty years, Fort Independence has stood in stalwart defiance of Atlantic storms—and out into Massachusetts Bay and the open sea beyond.

As soon as the tugs disengaged, the *Britannic*'s engines came to life, sending powerful columns of smoke skyward from the four stacks that marched across its upper deck. The ship proceeded on a northeasterly course, skirting the coasts of New England and Nova Scotia toward Newfoundland's grand banks where it would rendezvous with a convoy prior to crossing the Atlantic.

Cooper was inspired by the bracing weather and the visually stunning seascapes. He wasted no time getting to work with his camera, a brand-new 35mm Leica he'd purchased for the trip. Shielded by the rain poncho he kept in his camera bag, his pipe tucked in the corner of his mouth, he left his cabin, went up the gangway to the main deck and made his way forward.

Walls of white-capped fury rose and fell beneath a threatening sky, spattering the deck with seawater. Cooper reached the point of the bow where the port and starboard railings met and, like a gargoyle on the prow of an early explorer's flagship, leaned out over the sea with his camera. He had taken several shots and was advancing the film for another when he felt someone tugging on his sleeve and turned to see a crewman in foul-weather gear standing behind him.

"The captain says you can't be out here in this," the fellow shouted over the gusting wind.

When Cooper protested, the crewman advised he take it up with the captain and led the way to the bridge.

The *Britannic*'s command center was forward of the stacks on the upper deck. The helmsman stood at its center wrestling the ship's wheel, his eyes riveted to a compass that rolled and yawed within its polished brass housing. Nearby, the first officer stood at one of the salt-stained windows, scanning the horizon with binoculars. Off to one side, the navigation officer was hunched over the chart table plotting the *Britannic*'s position under the watchful eye of the captain. The latter had the quiet authority and deeply lined face of someone who'd spent most of his fifty-odd years at sea. He turned at the sound of the bulkhead opening and stopped Cooper with a look as he entered.

Cooper held it with jut-jawed defiance, despite the seawater that dotted his face and dripped from his nose and chin. "I'm quite capable of caring for myself, Captain. I resent being treated like a child."

"As master of this ship, I'm responsible for the wellbeing of its passengers—whatever their age," the captain retorted in a Scottish burr that more than matched Cooper's. "Besides, you're missing supper."

"Aye," Cooper said with a mischievous twinkle. "I chose to feast on the forces of nature, instead."

"Heed my warning," the captain said without a hint of levity. "Or it might soon be the other way round."

Cooper nodded and was trying to appear contrite when the first officer called out, "Convoy on the horizon!" He handed the binoculars to the captain and added, "More than two dozen vessels by my count, sir."

The captain peered through the binoculars, then lowered them and scowled. "Aye, and more than half are rust buckets that'll wreak havoc with our schedule."

Cooper had stepped aside with his camera. He had the captain centered in the range finder and, seizing the moment, fired the shutter. The captain glanced over in response to its precise click. "Sounds like we won't be arriving on time," Cooper prompted.

The captain nodded. "Not every ship in that convoy is as swift as this one or our escort." The latter was a reference to the British warships that helped protect the convoy against attack. "The slowpokes will be easy prey for U-boats if left behind. We'll be proceeding to Glasgow at two-thirds speed . . . and lucky if that."

"How many days late will we be arrivin'?"

"Three . . . if the weather holds."

Cooper's brow furrowed. "Someone's meeting me . . . I haven't seen her in twenty years," he said, as the potential for disaster loomed ever greater in his mind. He had included the date of the *Britannic*'s arrival in a letter to Grace; but now that it had changed, he was concerned she would be there on the wrong day, and—despite Hastings's connections and Joe's generosity and Pastor Martin's prayers—he and Grace would somehow miss each other and spend another twenty years apart.

"Rest assured, the new date will be posted in the *Shipping News* and at the pier where we're to berth," the captain said. Then, sensing the depth of Cooper's anxiety, he added, "Of course, if I could be assured your appetite for adventure has been stifled, there just might be a way to get it to her in advance."

Cooper brightened, then lowered his eyes and nodded. "I promise to behave," he said like a chastened schoolboy.

A short time later, he was in the ship's wireless room sending a telegram to Grace with the new arrival date. He gave the teletype operator the address that Hastings had obtained from Social Services in Edinburgh: Grace Cooper, Faculty Hall, Mary Queen of Scots School for Girls, Forth Valley, Stirling.

Secure in the knowledge that Grace would be on the pier when he arrived, Cooper spent the remainder of the voyage prowling the ship with his camera, and—though his cabin had two portholes and an inviting lounger—relaxing outside in a deck chair with his pipe, blanket, and reading material from the ship's library. He'd just finished one of Somerset Maugham's novellas when he came across a book of poems. The table of contents went from Browning to Yeats, but it was Tennyson, and *Enoch Arden* in particular, that caught Cooper's eye.

Written in 1846, the poem was based on the true story of a sailor believed lost at sea who somehow managed to survive. Sustained by thoughts of his beloved wife, Enoch struggled for nearly a decade to make his way halfway round the world to be with her. He finally succeeded, only to observe from afar that she was blissfully happy with a loving husband and adoring children. Enoch's love for her was so great that he slipped forever away to spare her the emotional pain and legal turmoil of learning he was alive.

Cooper had read it as a student and found it moving; but it was unsettling now. His apprehension wasn't unfounded. Two decades had passed since Grace had lost the baby and returned to Scotland thinking Cooper had been killed in action in France, since he'd gone home to find her and been shunned by her father and since he'd searched for her to no avail. Twenty lonely years, during which he had kept the hope of a reunion alive in his heart and in his correspondence. But the letters he'd written Grace—sent in care of her brother, Colin, because he had no address for her—had gone without a reply; and nearly ten years had passed since he'd sadly accepted the inevitable, and stopped writing altogether.

But why *hadn't* Grace responded? Had the letters not been forwarded? Despite their initial clashes, he and Colin had found common ground in Grace's happiness and made their peace. Furthermore, upon Cooper's return from the war, they had drawn even closer, bonding in tragedy and parting friends. Had Grace met someone else? Had she a husband and children but couldn't bear to tell him? Indeed, at his lowest moments Cooper could easily imagine why. Despite his apprehension, the fact that Grace was registered at the Social Services Office under the name Cooper, her *married* name, bolstered his confidence and made him reasonably certain that Enoch Arden's fate would not soon be his.

Chapter Fifty-Five

The *Britannic* had been at sea for nearly twelve days when Arran, the small island that marks the mouth of the Firth of Clyde, appeared in the morning haze. Cooper was one of the many passengers who had come out on deck and were standing at the rail as the ship navigated the serpentine estuary that funnels traffic into Glasgow Harbour.

Though Cooper had been an American citizen since his WWI military service, the sight of his homeland warmed his heart: the verdant landscape that rolled inland from the sea like a plush carpet; the perfectly scaled buildings with their intricate brickwork and steeply pitched roofs; the bustling shipyards where three-masted schooners of oak timbers had once been built, and where transatlantic liners of welded steel were now under construction.

Cooper's pulse quickened as the White Star Line pier where the *Britannic* would berth—where he would, at long last, be reunited with his beloved Grace—came into view; and by the time the steamer was gliding to a stop alongside it, his heart was pounding.

A crowd of people who were meeting the *Britannic*'s pas-

sengers surged forward. Necks craned upward, they searched
the hundreds of faces peering over the side for friends and
loved ones; and then suddenly, among those above and below,
names were being called out, and fingers were being pointed,
and arms were being waved, and children were jumping up
and down excitedly.

This joyous moment, this instant of recognition and relief, was repeated over and over. Cooper ached to be part of
it as his eyes swept across the faces below. They skipped
swiftly past the men's and darted eagerly from one woman's
to the next and then the next and the next; but after several
minutes of searching, Cooper had yet to find Grace's radiant
features among them.

As soon as the huge liner was tied up, passengers began
clambering down the boarding ramps onto the pier and into
the crowd, which then engulfed them.

Cooper continued his search for Grace among the knots
of people on the pier who were hugging and kissing and
squealing with glee. More than once, if only for a fleeting instant, he thought he'd found her. More than once, his heart
fluttered at the sight of a woman whom he had reason to believe was his long-lost wife. But each time, closer examination proved otherwise. Changing tactics, he retreated to the
fringes of the crowd, hoping to come upon a lone female figure who seemed to be searching, too; one whose posture
seemed tentative, and manner anxious, like his own; but
found none who reflected his demeanor or remotely resembled his beloved Grace.

Cooper waited until the last of the passengers and those
who had come to meet them were gone. He was still waiting
when the *Britannic*'s crew disembarked—still hoping and
praying that Grace had been delayed, perhaps had missed
her train from Stirling, and, at any moment, would come
hurrying down the long wharf, bursting with joy at the sight
of him. But despite the captain's assurances, despite the

postings in the *Shipping News* and on the pier, and the cable sent from the *Britannic,* Grace wasn't there to greet him, to rush into his arms as he had hoped . . . as he had, for so long, dreamed.

Chapter Fifty-Six

Cooper took a few moments to calm his emotions and gather his wits; then he grasped his valise, shouldered his camera bag—which contained his camera, film, travel documents and a copy of his book, *The Christmas Pictures*, which he had inscribed to Grace—and began the long walk down the pier to the White Star Line offices.

The vast space was lined with ticket windows and baggage counters and alive with bustling travelers. Cooper located an information kiosk where a uniformed clerk was filing an assortment of telegrams, folded sheets of notepaper and envelopes into alphabetized pigeonholes. Cooper waited to be acknowledged, then lost patience and called out, "Are there any messages for a Mr. Cooper?"

"Cooper?" the clerk echoed over his shoulder.

"Aye, Cooper. *Dylan* Cooper."

The clerk reached to the pigeonhole labeled *C*, removed a sheaf of papers and began sorting through them. "Constable, Cullan, Colchester, Costigan, Cobb, Carruthers . . . No. Nothing for Cooper."

"You're sure?" Cooper prompted. He was certain that if, for some reason, Grace hadn't received the cable, and had come on the day the *Britannic* was originally due to arrive, but wasn't able to return today, she would have left him a note; or if, having received it, she was taken ill, or had an appointment, or, for whatever reason, just wasn't able to get there, she would have, via phone or telegram, left a message for him with the shipping line. "Perhaps, it was put in another box by mistake," Cooper suggested. "In *D* for Dylan, for example."

The clerk looked insulted. "Not if *I'm* the one doing the sorting, mind you."

"I intended no offense, sir," Cooper said evenly. "But it could've been days ago. Perhaps, someone without your obvious skills was on duty?"

The clerk glared at him, then turned to the rack of pigeon-holes and, with an angry snap of his wrist, snatched the papers from the one labeled *D*. He sorted through them brusquely, then broke into a self-satisfied smile and shook his head no.

Undaunted, Cooper slipped a picture of Grace from his camera bag and showed it to him. "Does she look familiar? I mean, perhaps you've seen her here?"

The clerk glanced at it and again shook his head no.

"You're certain?" Cooper asked. "This was taken twenty years ago. Please, take your time."

The clerk scowled, then studied the photo for a moment. "No, I don't recall seeing her." He smiled in smug appreciation. "I wouldn't forget a woman as fine as that, if I had, believe me."

Cooper emitted a forlorn sigh at the irony, then picked up his valise and walked away. He was drained by the emotional battering he'd taken; but he wasn't beaten by it. He knew where Grace was, knew where she was living and teaching, and knew how to get there. This was Glasgow. Familiar ground. He knew he'd find her. If not today, tonight; if not tonight, tomorrow; if not tomorrow, the next day. Indeed, despite the crushing disappointment, Cooper had no doubt he'd soon be reunited with his beloved wife.

Chapter Fifty-Seven

~

Public transportation in Glasgow was provided by a system of trolley cars that crisscrossed the city from the river to the foothills, and from the mouth of the firth to the River Rutherglen where the River Clyde began to run shallow.

The Clydeside terminal was a short walk from the White Star Line offices. Cooper took the No. 1 into the heart of downtown and got off at the stop opposite Queen Street Station where trains from the north and east terminated. The 19th-century structure with its spired turrets and towering arched windows was typical of the hybrid Victorian-Edwardian style favored by the city's universities, financial institutions, businesses and government agencies.

Emotionally drained and physically exhausted, Cooper spent the night in a traveler's hostel across the street from the station. The next morning, while breakfasting on tea and scones, it dawned on him that he hadn't tasted anything like the latter in decades and bought several more to eat on the train. Then, valise in hand, camera bag slung over his shoulder, Cooper went directly to the train station and bought a one-way ticket to Stirling, thirty miles to the northeast.

Dating to the 10th century, Stirling was not only where the school at which Grace lived and taught was located, but also where Robert the Bruce had annihilated the English in 1314, forever wresting Scotland from their rule. And, as the ancestral home of the Stuart dynasty, it was also where Mary Stuart, at the age of eight months, was crowned Mary, Queen of Scots on September 9, 1543 in the old Chapel Royal.

The Highlands Local proceeded at a painfully slow pace, making stops at Bearsden, Rutherglen, Coatbridge, Cumbernauld, Falkirk, Denny and Bannockburn before reaching Stirling. Cooper stepped from the musty coach into a late-morning sun, checked his valise in the station's baggage room, and walked down St. John Street and across St. Mary's Wynd to Mary Queen of Scots School for Girls.

The school that bore the name of the infant queen was located in the northeastern outskirts of the town beneath a massive volcanic crag from which Stirling Castle dominated the Forth Valley. The collection of stone-buttressed buildings, with arched windows and spired towers, was arranged around a cobblestone quadrangle where students gathered in the shade of centuries-old oaks.

Cooper had little trouble locating Faculty Hall, and anxiously scanned the register for Grace's name. He scrutinized it again and again, his eyes widening in disbelief that Grace Cooper; or Cooper, Grace; or Cooper G; or just Cooper wasn't among the residents listed; nor, to his ever-growing frustration, was her maiden name, MacVicar. Try as he might, Grace's name wasn't there, in any form, to be found.

Reeling at this latest setback, Cooper had just settled on a nearby bench to regroup when a gentleman, carrying a briefcase stuffed with papers and cloaked in a black gown that flowed capelike about his suit, came from the building and began walking toward the quadrangle.

"Pardon me?" Cooper called out, hurrying after him. "This *is* Faculty Hall, is it not?"

"Aye, that it is."

"Might there be more than one faculty residence?"

"No, just this one," the gentleman replied. "I should know, I've been here for seventeen years. Who might you be looking for, if I may ask?"

"A Mrs. Cooper. Mrs. Grace Cooper. I was given this address for her."

"Grace? Grace Cooper?" the gentleman asked, breaking into a fond smile that gave Cooper hope. "Aye, indeed, she *was* in residence here at one time, but not any longer."

Cooper's heart sank. He was stunned and took a moment to recover. "Am I to take that to mean she doesn't teach here any longer, either?"

The gentleman nodded. "It must be at least two years now. Yes . . . Yes, two years this semester end that she resigned."

"Two years," Cooper echoed, staggered.

"Yes, I can't quite believe it, either. I'm sad to say, we've lost touch."

"Makes two of us," Cooper said, deciding not to explain the circumstances.

"Well, someone in the records office might know how to reach her," the gentleman said. "It's in that building there." He pointed across the quadrangle, then added, "Good luck, and, oh, should you happen to see Grace, tell her Charlie Winans sends his regards."

Cooper thanked him and hurried toward a stern-looking building at the far end of the quadrangle. Olde English typography engraved in the limestone blocks above the entrance proclaimed: ADMINISTRATION. The dimly illuminated Records Office was on the ground floor opposite the Headmaster's Suite and Faculty Meeting Room. Its walls were lined with oak file cabinets, racks of small square drawers, like the card catalogue in a library, and floor-to-ceiling shelves, sagging under the weight of leather binders.

The woman behind the desk had an officious manner heightened by rimless spectacles and iron-gray hair kept in a bun by a tortoiseshell clasp—much like the clerk at the school Cooper attended as a child. All bark, no bite, he thought. And he was right. Her icy façade melted at the mention of Grace's name, and she took no pleasure in Cooper's disappointment when she confirmed Grace was no longer teaching there.

"But . . . but . . . Social Services . . ." Cooper sputtered, his frustration getting the better of him. ". . . *the main office in Edinburgh, no less*—has her registered *here!*"

"Government bureaucracies," the clerk said with an understanding sigh. "We notify them within a fortnight, but they're years behind when it comes to updating their records; and now with the war . . ." She looked off in reflection, then said, "Mrs. Cooper was a wonderful person, not to mention a truly gifted teacher. Several of her students are with the Glasgow Ballet. Everyone here misses her."

"Aye, as do I," Cooper replied, letting his burr thicken with charm. "Have you any idea where I might find her?"

"Well, we do make a special effort to stay in touch with our alumni, students and teachers alike," the clerk replied. "I might very well have a forwarding card for her." She turned to the rack of small drawers, opened the one labeled *C,* and began sorting through hundreds of three by five cards.

Cooper sighed, fidgeting with impatience. "Might it be under her maiden name, MacVicar?"

"No, no, here it is, Cooper, Grace," the clerk replied, removing one of the cards with a flourish. "Since vacating her quarters in Faculty Hall, anything sent to her here would have been forwarded by the postal service to this address." The typed card read: 36 Gramercy Park East, Dumbarton/ Strathclyde.

"Dumbarton . . . That's . . . that's where she's from," Cooper said with mixed emotions. Dumbarton was a short trolley ride from downtown Glasgow; and he was more than pleased Grace was nearby; but why would she move back to her hometown? he wondered. Despite the tragic circumstances of her return to Scotland, Grace had long ago rebelled against family oversight. It didn't make sense that she'd risk being subjected to it again, after the autonomous life of a teacher-in-residence.

"It's not surprising she went home," the clerk said, sensing Cooper's uncertainty as she copied the address on a blank file card. "It was hard for her here . . . I mean, socially . . . being a widow and all."

"Aye," Cooper replied, sensing her remark was more significant than she realized, though he couldn't quite put his finger on it. "I don't know how to thank you." He took the file card and turned to leave.

"One moment, please?" the clerk called out. "Just for my records, might I note who's calling?"

Cooper hesitated briefly, then replied, "I'm a friend. An old friend from Dumbarton." He hurried off before the clerk could ask his name, which he knew, all too well, was what she wanted; and which, he had decided, it would be best not to reveal.

Cooper was exiting the building when the significance of the clerk's remark became clear. If Grace was known as a widow, it meant she still believed he was killed in action in France; and that her family had not only impeded his search for her, but also had never told her he was alive. Furthermore, it explained why Grace had never acknowledged the letters he had sent all those years ago. It wasn't because, as he had feared, she had chosen not to reply. No, on the contrary, it was because she had no choice to make. For whatever reason, whether it be postal error or her brother's neglect, she had never received them, not even one. There could be no other explanation, Cooper thought, because the receipt of just one letter would have forever stricken the word "widow" from her vocabulary.

Chapter Fifty-Eight

With Grace's address in hand, Cooper returned to Stirling Station, retrieved his valise from the baggage room and took the train back to Glasgow. In the space of a few hours his emotions had gone from eager anticipation to crushing disappointment to welcome relief.

Now, lulled by the rhythmic clack of train wheels, he was smoking his pipe and watching the countryside glide past when something dawned on him. If he was right about Grace's widowhood, it behooved him to spare her the shock of opening a door and seeing her long-deceased husband standing before her. Indeed, there was no time like the present to resume his letter writing. He took a sheet of paper along with a pen and envelope from his camera bag, and composed a heartfelt note, which gently revealed the truth that had been kept from his beloved Grace for so long.

After completing it, Cooper addressed the envelope, copying it from the file card the clerk had given him. He had just written Dumbarton, Strathclyde—town and district, respectively—when his eyes narrowed at a thought. Although, as the clerk observed, Grace had gone "home," Cooper realized she was living far from the gritty, densely packed neighborhoods of millworkers and coalminers where they'd grown up. On the contrary, with its panoramic views of the Clyde estuary and the firth beyond, the Strathclyde district was Dumbarton's finest, a posh enclave of tree-lined streets with elegant townhouses, similar to Boston's Back Bay, where Glasgow's captains of finance and industry resided.

What would Grace be doing there? Cooper wondered. Had she taken a job with a wealthy family as a tutor? Would she exchange the stature of her teaching position for the subservience of employment in an upper-class household? With growing apprehension, he decided it was far more likely that she would be its mistress. Far more likely, indeed, that, like her employment status, her change of surname had yet to be recorded by an inefficient bureaucracy. He shuddered at the thought that Enoch Arden's dilemma might soon become his, after all, and slipped the letter he'd just written into his camera bag. There was no mailing it now, not until he knew for certain one way or the other.

Dusk had fallen by the time Cooper arrived at Queen Street Station and returned to the hostel. The next morning, taking his belongings with him, he boarded the trolley to Dumbarton. It snaked through congested working-class districts, then climbed to the windswept bluff where Strathclyde perched high above the estuary. Cooper was one of few passengers remaining by the time it reached Gramercy Park. He had little trouble finding Grace's address, number 36, which was emblazoned in polished brass numerals on the door of an impressive townhouse. It was one of many that marched with military precision about a verdant square.

The park's cast-iron fence enclosed stands of trees and manicured lawns edged with beds of blossoming flowers. Here, nannies in starched smocks pushed their privileged charges in wicker prams and kept a watchful eye on their older siblings as they played.

Cooper settled on one of the benches from which he could discreetly observe the townhouse, and lit his pipe. He'd been there for almost an hour when a gleaming maroon and black Bentley rolled to a stop in front of the stately building. A chauffeur got out and opened the back door before taking up his position beside it.

Moments later, a fashionably dressed woman and two children of middle-school age came from the townhouse and got into the car. A butler and a housekeeper, each carrying several grips, followed. They put the luggage in the Bentley's trunk, then returned to the house.

Cooper exhaled a stream of pipe smoke and broke into a knowing smile. A weekend in the country, he thought. They'll fetch the master at his place of business before heading south to Loch Braden or Loch Doon in the Uplands where landed gentry hunt pheasant and ride to hounds on sprawling estates.

Cooper had no doubt the woman was the lady of the house. He didn't get a good look at her face but, despite her couture ensemble, she had neither Grace's statuesque carriage nor dancer's poise; and, thanks be to God, he thought, neither she nor the housekeeper, a tiny woman of approximately Cooper's age, was his beloved wife.

When the car drove off, Cooper left the park with his valise, and crossed the street to the townhouse. He took the letter he had written to Grace from his camera bag and slipped it through the postal slot in the door. He was hurrying off when it suddenly swung open behind him and a man's voice called out.

"Sir? Sir! Excuse me, sir?"

Cooper looked back to see the butler standing in the doorway, holding the envelope. "Are you the one who left this here, sir?" he asked as Cooper returned.

"Aye, guilty as charged," Cooper replied. "May I count on you to see that Mrs. Cooper gets it?"

"I'm afraid not, sir," the butler said, his tone sharpening

as he handed the envelope back to Cooper. "Whoever she is. She doesn't live here."

Cooper's eyes narrowed in puzzlement. "Are you sure?" he asked, feeling foolish as soon as he said it. "I was given this address by Mary Queen of Scots School in Stirling. The clerk there said she—"

"I'm sure," the butler interrupted with a scowl. "Though I joined this household but three years ago, I do know who lives here and who doesn't."

Cooper grimaced and jammed his pipe in the corner of his mouth.

The butler turned to go back inside, then paused, as if struck by a thought. "May I see that again?"

Cooper handed him the envelope.

The butler studied it briefly, then, nodding as if his thought had been confirmed, returned it. "You see, sir, collecting the post is not one of my duties," he said in explanation. "Mr. MacVicar prefers to deal with such personal and private matters himself; but, on occasion, at Mr. MacVicar's bidding, of course, the task does fall to me; and, on reflection, I do vaguely recall seeing a letter addressed to a Mrs. Cooper . . ."

Cooper had nearly bitten through his pipe stem at the name MacVicar. It was the last thing he expected. He was staggered, reeling. At the second mention, the blood began draining from his face.

". . . It was months ago, mind you," the butler went on, not yet aware of Cooper's strife. "Unless my memory fails me, I believe it was *forwarded* here. Yes, yes, I recall the address being scratched out and this one written in its place. Yes, it—" He paused, upon seeing Cooper's distress. "Sir? *Sir,* is something wrong?"

Cooper removed the pipe from between his teeth and swallowed hard. "Did you say Mr. MacVicar?"

"Indeed, I did, sir. Mr. MacVicar is master of this house."

"Mr. *Colin* MacVicar?"

The butler nodded, confirming Cooper's suspicion that

Grace's brother, Colin, was the master of this elegant manse with its butler and staff of domestics, as well as a country squire, owner of a chauffeured Bentley saloon, and vested with all the status that such trappings implied. It was hard to believe this was the same Colin MacVicar who had apprenticed in the mines as a boy; who had been his sister's unhappy and unemployed chaperone when she and Cooper first met in Boston; who, believing Cooper to be unworthy of his sister's affection, had resorted to fisticuffs to defend her virtue; and who, after they had made their peace, had sadly told him of Grace's return to Scotland after losing the baby and being notified by the army that Cooper had been killed in action in France . . . but it was.

More importantly, this shocking discovery answered a question that had been gnawing at Cooper since his arrival on the *Britannic*: Why wasn't Grace there to greet him when the boat docked? Because she didn't know he was coming; because, for over two years, any correspondence that had been posted to her at Mary Queen of Scots School—Joe Clements's letter with Cooper's photo and itinerary, Cooper's recent letter with the *Britannic*'s arrival date and the telegram he'd sent while at sea revising it—had been forwarded *here* . . . to Colin's address; and like the letters he had sent years ago, not one of these had reached Grace, either.

Chapter Fifty-Nine

Cooper was beside himself as he strode to the trolley stop. Every answer led only to another more perplexing question: Why didn't she receive his letters? Because she had resigned her teaching position and was no longer living at the address he had been given. What happened to the letters? They were forwarded to her brother Colin's address. Why didn't he make sure she got them?

It suddenly struck him that none of it mattered. There was one question, and only one, that required an answer; and that question was: Where is Grace? He had no doubt Colin knew the answer; but it was Friday evening. There was no way to locate, let alone confront him, now. No, it would have to wait the weekend and be dealt with on Monday. Furthermore, though he loathed to admit it, Cooper had begun experiencing a slight shortness of breath, and welcomed the time to recover.

As of late, his chronic consumption had been kept in check, not only by Dr. Cheever's insistence that he at least curtail, if not stop, his pipe smoking, and by the fact that he hadn't spent time in his fumed-filled darkroom for weeks; but also by the time he'd spent on the *Britannic* breathing fresh sea air, which proved to be therapeutic. Indeed, on his arrival in Glasgow, he had felt energized and thoroughly rejuvenated; but the events of the last two days had taken their toll and he was feeling every one of his sixty-two years now.

Cooper took the trolley back down the hill into south Dumbarton, the hardscrabble neighborhood where he had grown up, and checked into the Falkirk, a bed-and-breakfast near the trolley stop on Great Western Road. The rooms were sparsely furnished and the carpets threadbare, but it was well located and equally well priced. He spent part of the weekend in the Dumbarton Library, searching phone books and records for Grace's name—both Cooper and MacVicar—to no avail; and spent the rest of it prowling his old haunts with his Leica.

Saturday evening he ended up in Gorbals, a pub named after the infamous 19th-century slums, which had been demolished and replaced with what had since become infamous 20th-century slums. As a young man, Cooper had spent many a night here clutching his tankard with one hand and throwing darts with the other. The faces around the bar were different now; but the smell of beer-soaked wood and tobacco still permeated the air; and scratchy BBC broadcasts still came from the radio tucked amidst the bottles on the back bar.

Cooper settled on a boot-scarred stool in the corner he had always favored, and ordered a Guinness. The barkeep looked vaguely familiar, and for good reason. His hair had gone silver, his face was deeply lined, and he had acquired a girth that ballooned like a freshly stuffed haggis, but his wit was as sharp as Cooper remembered.

At first, the talk was mostly of the war in Europe: of the recent defeat and mass evacuation of British troops at Dunkirk on the French coast just south of the Belgian border; of the growing fear that Germany's Luftwaffe would soon be bombing London and the nation's industrial centers;

and of how U-boats, lurking in the waters outside Glasgow Harbour, had already torpedoed several vessels, bringing the war to their doorstep. Yet, like men in pubs throughout the British Isles, those about the bar in Gorbals had gathered to forget their troubles—to forget the hard work, long hours, meager pay and, now, the demoralizing war; and as the hours passed and tankards were drained and refilled, the complaining stopped and the mood lightened.

Cooper, the barkeep and several regulars were soon reminiscing about the good old days, bursting into hearty laughter as they regaled one another with tales of childhood derring-do and misspent youth. When Cooper injected the name Colin MacVicar into the banter, the others reacted as if the name of a local football hero had been invoked. Indeed, the fierce rivalry between the Scottish Protestant Rangers and the Irish Catholic Celtics had more than once set fists and bar stools alike flying about the pub.

"Aye, Colin MacVicar," the barkeep echoed, rolling the *r* like thunder. "Everyone knows 'im!"

"A powerful man he is," a fellow with coal-tarred fingernails boomed. "And a smart one at that, too."

"Not to mention highfalutin enough to be wearin' a deacon's sash at Strathclyde Presbyterian," a bearded fellow with ruddy cheeks chimed in.

"Well, his name *is* Mac*Vicar*," Cooper said with a grin, knowing it was where members of the wealthy and influential families of Strathclyde, not stars of local football teams, worshipped. "Though he would've been the fellow sweepin' up after the service when *I* knew him."

"Well, *whatever* he was doin' there," the barkeep said, "he met his missus while doin' it; and the rest, as they say, is all pounds sterling."

"So, Colin made the right marriage, then, did he?" Cooper prompted.

"As right as a shot of whiskey on a rainy night, Dylan," the barkeep replied. "His father-in-law is an MP from Strathclyde, a real maverick; made a fortune traffickin' anything and everything during the Great War."

"And now he's got himself another one," the fellow with the ruddy face added. "According to the gossip rags," the barkeep said in a confidential tone, "the old man wasn't keen on the nuptials, but, rather than have his little girl live below her station, he did right by his son-in-law."

Cooper chuckled at what he was about to say. "Aye, those Strathclyde lassies don't fancy coal dust on their bedsheets, now, do they?"

The group erupted with laughter. One of them slapped Cooper on the back. The barkeep winked and topped up his tankard. "You remember Angus Burrell?"

"Angus Burrell . . ." Cooper said, drawing on his pipe. "If memory serves, he had something to do with the miner's union, didn't he?"

"*Everything* to do with it," the barkeep declared. "Just after the war, Burrell set aside his pickax, ran for the leadership and won—with the backin' of MacVicar's father-in-law, of course; and when Burrell needed an assistant . . ." He splayed his hands, implying the conclusion was obvious.

Cooper grunted knowingly. "Colin traded in his coveralls for a three-piece suit and clean fingernails."

"It gets better," the barkeep said with a cackle. "A few years later, Burrell is making one of his podium-poundin' speeches when he grabs his chest and breathes his last. Before you can say rest in peace, papa-in-law is tuggin' his puppets by their strings, and MacVicar takes over the leadership."

"Local boy makes good, eh?" the ruddy-faced man exclaimed with a sarcastic sneer.

"A bloomin' fortune's what he makes!" the barkeep corrected. "Along with his wife's!"

"Is the Union Hall still in that building on Renfrew Street?" Cooper asked.

"That it is," the fellow with the tarred nails said. "I was at a meeting there just last week."

"I'll have to drop by and say hello," Cooper said.

"To Colin MacVicar?" the barkeep challenged with a skeptical cackle. "The way I hear it, most people have to make an appointment, and they're lucky to get one."

"Aye, but I'm not most people," Cooper said with a bit of a swagger. "I'm his brother-in-law."

"Brother-in-law?" the ruddy fellow blurted.

Cooper nodded. "I've been married to his sister for over twenty years."

"Well, Dylan," the barkeep said, as intrigued as he was impressed. "You two go way back, don't you?"

"Aye," Cooper grunted with a wily smile. "Colin and I have a lot of catching up to do."

Chapter Sixty

⌒

The morning sun sat above the horizon burnishing the Highlands' verdant shimmer. It bathed Glasgow's gritty façades in golden light and sent reflections rippling across the Bentley's polished coachwork as the maroon and black saloon sped through streets which were nearly empty at this hour. It turned into Renfrew and came to a stop outside a soot-stained office building. The chauffeur got out and opened the Bentley's back door.

Colin MacVicar folded his newspaper, then rose from the plush leather-piped cushion and, briefcase in hand, sauntered up the broad staircase to the entrance where a brass plaque read: UNITED MINEWORKER'S UNION OF GLASGOW. Colin smiled and tapped it with his newspaper as he did every morning. The gesture suited his bespoke blazer, paisley ascot and straw boater, which gave him a decidedly upper-class rakishness. Indeed, he looked as if he'd just returned from a refreshing weekend in the country, which, of course, he had.

The rotunda as well as the corridors that led off in every direction were, like the streets, nearly empty. His office, with its towering windows, coffered ceiling, chandeliers and massive desk of carved oak, had a grandness befitting the leader of a powerful labor union.

Colin made it his habit to arrive early, before his staff and before the phone calls and rounds of meetings began. In these quiet moments, he would ask God's blessing upon his work, and pray for the strength and guidance to carry it out successfully. He set his boater on a sideboard, and raised his eyes skyward in prayer, causing him to notice the layers of smoke hanging beneath the ceiling. Sunlight streaming through the windows gave them, and the twisting column of smoke rising toward them, a luminous glow. Colin's eyes followed the latter down to the pipe that was tucked in the corner of his visitor's mouth. The man who was smoking it was settled in Colin's chair, his feet propped on the corner of the desk, his back to the windows, and to the daylight that masked his identity.

This placement was no accident. Colin had strategically positioned the desk so that the blinding backlight kept him in stark silhouette. Like a card shark's visor, it shielded his eyes during the pressure-filled meetings and contract negotiations at which *lives* as well as livelihoods were at stake. The tactic had often served him well; but now it was being used against him.

Which of his adversaries could it be? he wondered, squinting into the light. One of the powerful mining barons with whom he'd been battling for higher wages, shorter hours and stricter safety procedures? One of the pro-business politicians with whom he regularly clashed? "Who are you and what are you doing here?" Colin demanded, unable to identify the interloper.

"Aye, 'tis a fine day for questions, Colin," Cooper replied, exhaling a stream of pipe smoke. "Only I'm the one who'll be doin' the askin', and you're the one who'll be providin' the answers."

Though it had been two decades, and Cooper's face appeared as a featureless mask, the pipe and the voice were unnervingly familiar. Colin's mind raced from past to present, seizing on several clues—three of them, to be exact—that had come in the mail, recently. "Cooper? Cooper, it is you, isn't it?" he asked haltingly. "Truth be told, in my darkest moments, I've imagined this day."

"And truth-telling is why I'm here, Colin," Cooper retorted, getting to his feet. "I'm surprised you weren't on the pier to greet me. Grace wasn't, I'm afraid; but you knew that, because you got the post—the letters telling her I was comin' and the telegram that the date had changed; and you kept them, didn't you?"

Colin's eyes were taut with apprehension. He set his briefcase and newspaper on the desk and nodded.

"And after you read them you decided to retain, rather than forward them," Cooper went on, stalking him about the desk. "Just as you did with the letters I sent Grace, all those years ago!"

Colin glared at him, angry at being caught.

Cooper was face-to-face with him now. "Why?" he demanded, his eyes flashing with anger. "You knew I had no address for her, knew I had no choice but to send them in care of you! True, we had our differences, but they'd been long settled when we shared the pain of her tragic loss, when we embraced and shed tears together! Mean-spirited father or no, I had every reason to count on *you*. Every reason to believe you'd forward them to her. I *trusted* you, Colin! I trusted you, and you betrayed me and Grace as well!"

Colin recoiled at the onslaught and moved behind the desk, putting it between them. "What do you want, Cooper?" His tone was impatient, patronizing.

Before Cooper could reply, an aide appeared and handed Colin a typewritten page. He swept his eyes over it, then dismissed the aide, instructing her to close the door after her. "My schedule," he said, filling with self-importance. "Three meetings before noon. Whatever it is, Cooper, be quick about it."

"Aye," Cooper grunted. "No need to be wastin' any of your precious time, Colin. You already know the question, so why not just answer it?"

"Because I can't," Colin snapped, spinning his desk chair in anger. "I don't know where Grace is."

Cooper raised a skeptical brow. "Next you'll be tellin' me pigs can fly, Colin. You don't really expect me to believe that, now, do you?"

"Believe what you like, Cooper. I told you, I don't know where she is."

"All right," Cooper said, biding his time. "Do you know if she still believes I was killed in France?"

Colin winced, then lowered his eyes and nodded.

"As I thought," Cooper grunted. "Shall I take that to mean the 'Widow' Cooper has, or has not, remarried?"

"Has not," Colin replied sharply.

"Well, why hasn't she?" Cooper challenged, his eyes narrowing in suspicion. "Not that I'm sorry, mind you; but an attractive and talented woman like Grace would have suffered no lack of suitors. There must be some reason for it."

"Well, as you might imagine," Colin began in an offhanded tone, "it took her a long time to recover from the loss of the baby. Of course, once she—"

"And the loss of her husband, thanks to you and your father!" Cooper snapped, his burr sharpening with anger. "No doubt he had a hand in this as well!"

Colin sneered with impatience. "I don't have time for this, Cooper. Shall I continue or not?"

Cooper jammed his pipe hard into the corner of his mouth and nodded. "Go on."

"As I was saying," Colin resumed, "once Grace had regained her equilibrium and began teaching, there was always the possibility of a relationship developing. Fortunately, they were few and far between and, in consideration of her circumstances, I took whatever action necessary to discourage them, early on."

"You've become quite skilled at interfering in your sister's private affairs, haven't you?"

"Not really," Colin replied with a casual air. "I just came into timely possession of some information. With one chap it was a question of improper business practices; with another, of improper . . . shall we say . . . behavior? In each case, I merely pointed out it would be wise to avoid having it raised in public."

"I always knew you were spineless, Colin," Cooper said, bristling. "But when it came to Grace, despite your interference, I never questioned your concern for her happiness, or thought you capable of such . . . such cruelty!" Cooper paused, his face a puzzled mask. "But why? It wasn't *my* interests you were protectin', was it? No. No, of course not. So why would you—" He paused again, as if startled by a noise. It wasn't a clap of thunder or a motor backfiring that had struck him, but a chilling insight. "Oh . . . oh, of course! You were there—in Newbury. You got my post from France. Aye, you knew well before I got home that I hadn't been killed, that the notification was in error. And . . . and . . . then, later, when I went off to fetch Grace, you warned your father I was comin', and he turned me away; but it wasn't long before he realized that he'd set a time bomb—of his own makin'—to tickin'. No, and when you came home, he handed it to you for defusin', didn't he?"

"You're mad, Cooper," Colin replied, defensively. He sat at the desk and began shuffling papers. "I've no idea what you're talkin' about."

"Aye, but you will," Cooper went on, his theory crystallizing as he prowled the office. "Grace believed she was a widow and, therefore, free to remarry; and thanks to the lot of you, she went on believin' it! The mere thought of it must've sent shivers up your father's spine. Aye, he was so shaken that he entrusted *you* with the unsavory task of monitorin' her private affairs—of ensurin' none progressed beyond flirtation. Why? Because he knew Grace would be committin' bigamy should she remarry! That's it, isn't it? Isn't it!"

Colin's mouth had become an angry line. He nodded grudgingly. "Bigamy is a crime, not to mention a sin."

"And a deacon at Strathclyde Presbyterian had best be careful about such things, hadn't he?" Cooper taunted, savoring his triumph.

"You've done your homework, haven't you?"

"That I have," Cooper replied coolly. "Enough to know you've done quite well for yourself."

Colin tilted back in his chair. "I've been fortunate," he said, trying to sound humble.

"Aye, no one stood in *your* way, did they?" Cooper erupted at his posturing. "No, as I hear it, they paved it with pounds sterling, instead. Tell me, Colin, this wife of yours with the Strathclyde lineage, was she the lass you were writin' love letters to back in Newbury all those years ago?"

Colin bit a lip and nodded.

"No wonder you were so upset at the thought of losin' her!" Cooper exclaimed, seizing the opening. "It wasn't simply a matter of the heart but a matter of the dowry as well!"

"That's not fair," Colin said, stung by the implication. "We were deeply in love, and still are. Her father was against it at first, but he came round to—"

"Oh, did he now!" Cooper taunted, giving his sarcasm full rein. "Lucky for you he wasn't cut from the same cloth as your own! You're not just spineless, Colin, you're a hypocrite as well!"

"I don't have to take this from you, Cooper!" Colin snapped, losing his composure. He leapt to his feet, face reddened, hair tousled, ascot askew.

"Of course you do, Colin," Cooper said, pleased to have unnerved him. "I'm sure the God you pray to would agree that it's proper punishment for all the pain and anguish you've caused—though hardly sufficient, in my view. You've had a rich and fulfilling life. How could you conspire to keep Grace and I from having the same?"

"I had little choice, Cooper, and you know it," Colin replied, still bristling. "My father believed you to be evil incarnate. He said it to your face twenty years ago, and said it often to mine. You were the devil who convinced Grace to forsake her family and homeland, the devil he believed, *to his dying day,* mind you, had corrupted and destroyed her."

"And you believed that?" Cooper challenged. "It didn't matter what I believed!" Colin retorted, bouncing a fist off the desktop. "He vowed he wasn't going to lose Grace again. Believe me, you had no chance of taking her back, let alone back to America!"

"Nothing's going to stop me this time!" Cooper lunged across the desk and grabbed a fistful of Colin's blazer, pulling him closer. "Now, where is she?"

Colin tightened a fist and cocked it inches from Cooper's chin. Eyes flaring with anger, they were but a heartbeat from coming to blows—as they once had decades ago—when the wisdom of time and sense of decorum prevailed. Cooper's hand opened first. An instant later, Colin's fist dropped to his side. The two men stepped back from their respective sides of the desk, putting some distance between them.

Colin smoothed his blazer and straightened his ascot, then glanced to Cooper. "I've neither seen, nor heard from Grace in over two years," he said, softly. "Not since . . . since our father died. That's when she resigned her teaching position and moved away."

"I can't say I'm sorry Grace is free of his iron-fisted rule; but you're free of it, too, Colin—free of it for two years now. Why haven't you told her the truth? Why haven't you told her that I'm alive? That I'd once come in search of her? That I'd written countless letters, desperate to be with her? Why haven't you told her she can have the life she'd always wanted—now, with me?"

Colin's shoulders sagged, his eyes fell like those of a child caught in an indiscretion. "I was ashamed. I couldn't bear to tell her. I—"

"Agghh," Cooper groaned in disgust. "Spare me the self-loathing. It neither becomes nor exonerates you."

"Perhaps not, but it's the truth. I was ashamed to admit to Grace what I'd done," Colin resumed, his eyes welling with emotion. "Despite bending to my father's will, I care about her, Cooper. Deeply . . . very deeply. She seemed so happy to be going off on her own again, that I . . . I feared, after all she'd been through, the shock of learning you were alive might be devastating. I'm still not sure if she can cope with it. Are you?"

"I'm still her husband, Colin! She's still my wife!" Cooper replied, shaking with frustration. "And, if you're really worried about her committin' bigamy, I'm the best chance you've got of keepin' her from it . . . if it isn't already too late."

Colin looked stunned. He stepped to a window and, in the harsh, unforgiving glare, came to grips with all that Cooper had said, then turned to face him. "I . . . I must admit, I hadn't thought of it quite that way."

"Well, it's time you did. If you've any idea of Grace's whereabouts you'd best tell me now."

"I told you the truth when I said I'd lost contact with her," Colin said, holding Cooper's eyes firmly with his own. "I've made many attempts to locate her . . . failed attempts, I'm afraid. About a month ago I turned to my father-in-law for help, and—"

"Aye, I can only imagine how handy it must be to have an MP from Strathclyde in the family."

"And as I'm sure you *can* imagine," Colin went on, undaunted, "he has many friends in Whitehall." He took a telegram from a desk drawer and handed it to Cooper. "I received this just last week. I haven't had time to verify the information, but it seems Grace is teaching at a private school on Guernsey in the Channel Islands."

Cooper looked baffled. "Channel Islands . . ." he echoed, unable to make the connection. They could have been in one of the distant British colonies for all he knew. "Have you any idea where they might be?"

"About as far from Glasgow as one can go and still live in the U.K." Colin's face reddened with remorse. "Not that I blame her."

"Nor I." Cooper took a deep drag of his pipe and exhaled slowly. "Well, wherever they are, I guess I know where I'm going next, don't I?" He swung his bag over his shoulder and started for the door.

"Cooper? Cooper, wait," Colin called out, stopping him. "I have something for you."

Cooper watched with impatience as Colin stepped to a decorative screen that zigzagged across one corner of the office. He folded it aside, revealing a large safe, then spun the combination dial several times and opened the door. From among the folios, documents and neatly banded bricks of currency, Colin removed a thick stack of envelopes tied with string. "These are yours," he said, offering them to Cooper. "It's only right you should have them."

Cooper's eyes widened in recognition and amazement as he sorted through them. The cable he'd sent from the *Britannic*, his recent letter from Newbury and Joe Clements's letter with his snapshot were on the top; and below them, in envelopes that had been opened and that had yellowed with age, the scores of letters he'd sent Grace years ago. "My letters . . . my letters to Grace?" he whispered, almost afraid to believe it. "You . . . you kept them all these years?"

Colin nodded apprehensively. "As I said, I sensed this day might come, and thought Grace would find them heartening. They'll prove beyond any doubt that your love for her has endured and never diminished. I can only hope that knowing I kept them will prove the same of mine; and perhaps, in some small way, deliver Grace from anger to forgiveness as the good Lord teaches."

Cooper groaned in disbelief. "For two decades, you conspired to keep us apart, thwarting our happiness, and ruining our lives, and . . . and . . ." He shook the letters in his fist. "And now you expect *these* to redeem you!"

"The issue of my redemption is in *God's* hands," Colin replied, his voice ringing with indignation. "We're all forced to make choices in life. I made mine, and . . . and . . ." He emitted a forlorn groan, his protests ringing hollow in his own ears, his words catching in his throat like rising bile. He swallowed hard, again, and then again. Finally, his eyes moist with remorse, Colin raised them and resumed: "In my heart, I . . . I know the good Lord would never approve of my . . . my deceit. I chose wrongly, Cooper. *Wrongly*. I admit it. I should have been truthful, and . . . and I'm truly sorry that I—"

"Aye," Cooper interrupted. "And if God is, indeed, wise and just, He'll have no trouble comin' to the same conclusion."

"I've no doubt of it," Colin said in a penitent rasp. "I can only hope He'll understand that it was impossible to be a good son and a good brother at the same time." He bit his lower lip, which had begun to quiver, then steeled himself and locked his eyes onto Cooper's. "Have you any idea what that was like?" he went on, tortured by the memory. "To be forced to choose between a father and a sister? Have you any idea of the wrenching anguish? Of the heartache that comes from knowing that there is no right answer? From knowing that you are going to deeply wound a loved one, regardless? Do you?" He paused and shook his head despairingly. "I've lived with it every day for twenty years. Thanks be to God, that—"

"As have I," Cooper interrupted softly, moved by the emotional outpouring.

"Thanks be to God that I have no such conflict now," Colin concluded.

Cooper studied him for a long moment. "I suppose we all suffer at the hands of others, don't we?"

Colin nodded in agreement. "Condemn me if you will, Cooper, but you have my apology and my sympathy; and, for Grace's sake, I hope, I yours."

Cooper was drawing thoughtfully on his pipe when he recalled Pastor Martin's advice that he trust the Lord to make his reunion with Grace come out right. "Aye, for Grace's sake," he conceded, taking heart in the pastor's wisdom. "Knowing her as I do, I've little doubt she'll be of the mind that it's not her judgment you'll, one day, be facin', but God's."

Colin's expression seemed to brighten. "Good luck," he said, clearly relieved by Cooper's reply. "And please give my love to Grace when you see her."

Cooper responded with a thoughtful nod, then a smile softened the line of his mouth. "I'm afraid there might not be time for that, Colin, because I'll be usin' every minute of every day to give her mine."

Chapter Sixty-One

After leaving Colin's office, Cooper went in search of a bookstore that he vaguely recalled was on the corner of Hope and Regent. The city had changed in many ways, but Warwick's, with its musty air and rickety shelves, was still there. Cooper went directly to the stacks labeled GEOGRAPHY, found an atlas of Great Britain and carried it to one of the library tables. It took a few minutes to locate the Channel Islands; and when he finally did, his eyes widened in amazement on seeing that, though they were part of the United Kingdom, they were much closer to France than to England.

As Colin had said, they were indeed as far from Glasgow as one could imagine and still be on British soil. Like a handful of leaves scattered across a vast pond, the five islands that made up the tiny archipelago—Jersey, Guernsey, Sark, Alderney and Herm—were in the English Channel fifty miles from the British mainland and just ten miles from the northwestern coast of France where war was raging.

Thanks be to God, Cooper thought, on seeing that they weren't off in one of the distant corners of the Empire that touched every continent and hemisphere, as he had at first feared; though on second thought they might just as well have been.

Getting to the Channel Islands meant traveling by rail across nearly the whole of Great Britain, and by boat across nearly the entire English Channel at its widest point. The five-hundred-mile journey would take Cooper from Glasgow in northwestern Scotland to the port city of Bournemouth on England's southern coast, where one of several ferry terminals that serviced the islands was located. An accompanying railway map indicated that he'd be required to change trains at Manchester, Birmingham and London; and, calculating the waiting time between trains, that it could take at least several days to get there . . . if every train kept to schedule and the ferries ran on time.

Cooper quickly realized that before embarking on such a lengthy and undoubtedly costly journey, he'd be wise to confirm that there was indeed a reason to make it. It could be easily accomplished with a telephone call—a long-distance telephone call. Rather than take the trolley back to Dumbarton and place the call through the Falkirk's switchboard, he walked several blocks south to the Glasgow Telephone Building on Buchanan.

Here, in a vast room on street level, operators worked at switchboards, placing long-distance and international calls for local residents and travelers who came there for assistance. After giving one of the operators the number to be called and paying a flat three-minute rate, the caller would take a seat until the connection was made. Once this was accomplished, the call would be transferred to one of the numbered booths that lined the busy room, to which the caller would be directed.

The telegram Colin had given Cooper stated that Grace was a teacher-in-residence at St. Anne's School on the island of Guernsey, and nothing more. An operator helped get the school's telephone number, then, with an apologetic sigh, explained, "We've few lines to the Channel Islands. The ones to Guernsey are already in use, and there are a number of calls before yours. So, it will be a while."

"Aye," Cooper grunted. "It wouldn't be surprisin' if they were still usin' carrier pigeons."

"They might be faster these days," the operator joked with a chuckle.

"So what is it that has so many people callin' these islands in the middle of nowhere?"

"The war," the operator replied. "People are worried with them being so close to France 'n all."

Cooper nodded and thanked her with a smile, then took a seat. He spent almost an hour waiting, fidgeting with impatience and smoking his pipe. He was relighting it for the second time when the operator summoned him to her station and said, "Booth eight, Mr. Cooper."

Cooper hurried toward it and slipped inside, then lifted the phone from its cradle. "Hello? Hello? St. Anne's School?" he asked in an anxious voice.

"Yes, yes, this is St. Anne's," a woman's voice replied. "I'm the switchboard operator. How may I help you?"

The line was rampant with buzzing noises and scratchy static, and Cooper winced, straining to hear her. "I'd like to speak with someone in the records office," he replied, raising his voice.

"Please hold while I connect you," the operator said. She studied the tangle of connectors on her switchboard, then frowned on seeing the port she wanted was already occupied. "I'm afraid that extension is busy, sir," she said, coming back on the line. "It was a Glasgow operator who placed your call, wasn't it?"

"Aye, indeed it was."

"You're quite a ways from us, aren't you?" the operator observed in a sympathetic tone. "Is there any way I might be of help? I mean, it might spare you the expense of having to ring back."

"Perhaps there is," Cooper replied, sparking to her offer. "I'm trying to confirm that a Mrs. Cooper, a Mrs. Grace Cooper, is a teacher-in-residence at your school. Are you able to do that?"

"Yes, sir, I am," the operator replied. "Teaches dance here, she does. That and its history. Mrs. Cooper's been with us for about two years now, if I'm not mistaken. I doubt she's in her quarters at this hour, but I can ring her if you like?"

"No, no please don't," Cooper replied, unnerved by all that her well-intentioned offer implied. "No, I wouldn't want to be disturbin' her even if she is."

"May I give her a message?" the operator asked.

"No, no message, either, thank you," Cooper replied. "You've been most helpful." He hung up before she could ask his name or why he was calling.

Despite the unsettling moment, the knowledge that Grace was definitely there brought a relieved smile to Cooper's face, and there was a spring in his step as he left the telephone building; but his thoughts soon turned to the rigors of his upcoming journey, tempering his cheerful mood.

Chapter Sixty-Two

That same day, in a dance studio at St Anne's School for Girls on Guernsey in the Channel Islands, Grace Cooper stood in front of her class, demonstrating a ballet exercise. "To attain speed and lightness of movement, and maintain line and balance, remember"—Grace paused *en pointe,* her students hanging on her every word and gesture—"tighten buttocks, draw abdomen in, lift diaphragm . . . then, in adagio, slow, sustained movements from one position to the next."

There were about a dozen students in the class, all girls in their teens, poised at ballet bars that ran along three of the walls, which were mirrored. The fourth had a row of leaded-glass windows, through which daylight bathed the vast white space. Following Grace's lead, the students performed the exercise in unison, studying themselves in the mirrors.

"Working-leg straight and stretched to maximum from thigh to toe . . ." Grace went on, continuing to demonstrate. Then she stepped out of the position and began moving from one student to the next, observing, encouraging, correcting, adjusting posture, modifying positions. "Back well arched . . . arms extended in a flowing line . . . Good, and again . . . and again . . ." she instructed them. "See the arabesque spiral in your mind, feel it moving through your limbs to the very tips of your fingers and toes . . ."

In ballet slippers, tights and leg warmers, her hair swept back severely in the traditional bun, Grace looked very much like her students. Indeed, with her radiant features and lithe body she could almost have been one of them. It was the fine laugh lines around her eyes and mouth, and strands of gray streaking her amber-colored hair that hinted at her age. What's more, the exquisite technique and poise with which she executed each dance movement left no doubt she was the teacher here, the inspiring and demanding mother-instructor whom these young women would do anything to please, and whose advice they eagerly sought.

Grace stopped in front of one student and frowned, then adjusted the extension of her leg. "Your body may be here, today, Christiane," Grace said wryly, "but it seems your mind is elsewhere."

Christiane straightened and held the extension to perfection. Tall and lithe like her teacher, Christiane Devereaux had auburn hair, sparkling green eyes and an open face that displayed her emotions. She also had exceptional talent and determination.

Grace knew her lapse was not from lack of interest or ability, and took her aside after class. "You weren't yourself this morning, Christiane," she prompted gently.

Christiane lowered her eyes in contrition and nodded. "*Oui*, Madame Cooper, I know. I am so sorry." She was one of several students from France who were enrolled at the school. Her English was excellent but her pronunciation and phrasing were sometimes awkward.

"Are final examinations of concern?" Grace asked, aware of the inevitable pressure at this time of year.

"*Non, non,* I am prepared," Christiane replied with conviction. "But I *am* having a distraction."

"Well, we'd best get it cleared up before Saturday," Grace said, referring to an upcoming dance recital.

"*Oui*, that is what causes me my worrying."

"Oh, you'll do fine, Christiane. Besides, your father will be there. He'll be so proud of you, and—" Grace paused, sensing she'd touched a nerve. "He *is* coming, isn't he?" she asked, sounding as if she'd touched one of her own nerves as well.

Christiane shrugged. "I have not had any post in weeks . . . *trois semaines, trois* . . . since I wrote reminding him to come. I can't believe he isn't, but what if . . ." she trailed off, her face rife with uncertainty.

"That *would be* very disappointing for . . . for both of us, wouldn't it?" Grace asked, knowing Christiane was aware she, too, looked forward to her father's visits.

Christiane nodded sadly.

"But why jump to conclusions?" Grace wondered rhetorically. "He hasn't missed a visit yet, not one, has he? And he came to last year's recital. Why wouldn't he be coming to this one?"

"*C'est la guerre*," Christiane replied. "I think it is more and more dangerous now, at home, you know?"

"Yes, I'm afraid I do; and I've no doubt it's why the post from France has been delayed," Grace said, in poignant reflection. "That's what war does, it . . . it . . . changes things. You'll get a letter, you'll see."

Christiane pouted, clearly unconvinced.

"I've an idea," Grace enthused, trying to get past her feelings and brighten Christiane's mood. "I'm stopping off at Main Hall to collect my post. Why don't you come along and do the same?"

The stone structures of St. Anne's School were arranged about a cobblestone square like a medieval village. Perched on a bluff above L'Ancresse Bay in Vale parish, it was approximately five miles north of St. Peter Port, Guernsey's capital. Main Hall was where assemblies and recitals were held and where the administrative offices were located. One wall of the lobby was lined with faculty and student postal boxes.

Christiane ran ahead as they entered and opened her box. *"Regardez!"* she called out to Grace, waving an envelope with French postage and a return address, which meant it was the one she wanted. She tore it open anxiously, eyes widening as she scanned the handwritten letter. "He is coming!" she exclaimed, barely able to contain herself. *"Mon père* is coming! He says, here, despite Dunkerque, your British troops are still in Granville and Saint-Malo, so . . . He is coming!"

"See, I told you," Grace said, equally pleased, if not as demonstrative.

"Ah, Madame Cooper, *vous êtes mon ami et ma mère!"* Christiane said, hugging Grace with girlish enthusiasm. "I don't know what I am doing without you!"

Grace chuckled at her unabashed expression of affection. "You'll do just fine, Christiane. That's what you'll do. I've no doubt of it."

Christiane tucked the letter into her schoolbag and hurried off. Grace watched as she sauntered down the corridor, then opened her own post box and found a dance magazine, a copy of the *Star,* which was Guernsey's daily newspaper, and a note from the school's switchboard operator suggesting she drop by when she had a moment.

"Ah, Mrs. Cooper," the operator said as Grace entered the telephone office. The switchboard buzzed, and she held up a hand as she answered the call and made the connection, then smiled in apology. "I thought you should know you had a call this morning."

"Oh," Grace said, looking puzzled. "I'm afraid your note has neither name nor number."

"Precisely, the gentleman who called didn't leave them.

He wanted to know if you were a member of the faculty. He didn't explain why, either, I'm afraid."

Grace shrugged. "Maybe it was someone from Social Services. Though I did register in the local office when I arrived. Perhaps they were just—"

"Pardon me, Mrs. Cooper," the operator interrupted as her switchboard buzzed again. She took care of the call, then tilted her head in thought. "You know, now that you mention it, it wasn't a local exchange. No, no, it came over the long-distance line. Placed by a Glasgow operator, it was."

Grace's eyes clouded with concern. "Glasgow . . ."

The operator nodded. "He asked for the records office. Had a crisp burr just like yours, he did."

"I see . . ." Grace whispered, her concern growing.

"To make a long story short," the operator went on, "the line was busy, so I offered my assistance . . . to spare him the expense of ringing back, you see? That's when he asked about you being on the faculty, and . . . and I said, you were. I hope that was all right?"

"Of course, it was very thoughtful," Grace said, fairly certain she now knew the caller's identity. Who else with a South Dumbarton burr would be calling from Glasgow and secretly checking up on her but Colin? she thought. She had purposely not written him and had not told him, nor anyone else, for that matter, where she had gone. And for two years now, she'd been thoroughly enjoying the freedom of mind and movement it afforded her. Indeed, she wasn't at all pleased by the thought of Colin tracking her down, and was concerned no good would come of it if he had.

Chapter Sixty-Three

~~~~

After making the call that confirmed Grace was teaching in the Channel Islands, Cooper headed across town to Central Station from where trains to all points south in Scotland, Wales and England departed. It was on Oswald Street, near the river, a short walk from the Glasgow Telephone Building. Cooper queued at one of the ticket windows, and told the agent he wanted to go to Bournemouth—the port city on England's southern coast where the Channel Islands ferry terminal was located.

The ticket agent raised a brow. "Bournemouth? That's a costly routing." He spread several train schedules across his counter, and added, "A complicated one, too, I'm afraid." The station was stifling hot and crowded with travelers. Those queued behind Cooper soon became impatient and moved to other windows. It seemed like an eternity passed before the agent figured it out and issued the ticket. As Cooper expected, it required he change trains in Manchester, Birmingham and London.

* * *

Cooper took the trolley back to South Dumbarton and checked out of the Falkirk, then returned to Central Station and caught the afternoon train to Manchester, the first leg of his five-hundred-mile journey.

Like the station, the coaches were stifling and crowded with passengers: military personnel who were reporting for duty, foreigners who were anxious to leave the country, and citizens evacuating cities and industrial centers in danger of being attacked by Hitler's vaunted Luftwaffe.

The train from Glasgow arrived in Manchester on schedule, but Victoria Station was in a state of chaos due to a derailment on the southern spur that was having an impact on both arrivals and departures.

Cooper made his way to the central hall and came upon a large crowd of travelers milling about unhappily beneath the departure board. Neatly lettered signs that proclaimed CANCELLED had been posted next to all trains destined for points south including Birmingham, where Cooper was headed.

Cooper spent the night in the station along with hundreds of other stranded travelers. He slept fitfully on a bench, afraid of missing the departure announcement, which never came. By the time service was restored, his departure from Manchester had been delayed by more than a day. He finally boarded the night express to Birmingham, on which he'd been originally ticketed.

Now, nearly two days after embarking, Cooper had traveled a distance of barely two hundred miles. Each day had been arduous and exhausting, and the nights even more so. Despite it, Cooper had found artistic inspiration in his fellow travelers. Like him, most were just simple folks struggling to survive. They reminded him of the immigrants he had photographed at the train station in Boston so many years ago; and he made good use of his Leica, recording many powerful and poignant images.

To make up for the lapse in service, the express—which had been scheduled to make three stops—had run as a local instead, picking up passengers at every station en route. Cooper spent the journey sleeping in his seat. The train arrived in Birmingham midmorning, several hours late, just minutes before Cooper's train to London was scheduled to depart. Lugging his camera bag and valise, he jogged the length of the platform into the rotunda and searched the departure board for the track number. Then, chest heaving, brow dotted with sweat, he hurried back across the rotunda, jogged nearly the length of yet another platform and boarded the train.

The coach was packed with travelers and their belongings, which were stuffed into luggage racks, piled in the aisles and balanced on their laps. The seating was two abreast and configured to allow four people to sit facing each other. Every seat seemed to be taken, but Cooper finally spotted one that was available. He shoved his valise into the overhead rack, then dropped into the empty seat, joining three young men in military uniforms. The cushion was still compressing under his weight when the train suddenly lurched forward and started rolling from the station. Cooper took a few moments to catch his breath and recover from his ordeal.

A short time later, the train had snaked its way out of the Birmingham yards and was picking up speed when something caught Cooper's eye. He glanced to the young man next to him, who was staring out the window at the tableaux of steels mills and factories racing past. His elbow was propped on the ledge, his chin was resting in his hand, and his silver pilot's wings were reflecting the sunlight, which was what had attracted Cooper's attention.

"So, you're RAF, are you?" Cooper prompted, trying to strike up a conversation.

The young pilot responded with an imperceptible nod and kept staring out the window.

"Aye, is it a Spitfire that you're flyin'?"

The pilot shook his head no and, still staring out the window, mumbled, "Hurricane."

Cooper smiled at the two flyers seated opposite him, then shrugged and splayed his hands in a "Well, I was just trying to be friendly," gesture.

"Oh, don't mind him," the boyish one with the freckles said with a cackle. "He's just a lovesick bloke who'd rather be doing his barrel rolls beneath a quilt, if you get my meaning?"

"A true hero of the British Empire, he is," the one with the moustache chimed in. "I mean, it's not every man who'd leave his blushing bride to fight for his country."

"*I* did," Cooper said with a wily grin.

"You?" the boyish flyer exclaimed with a laugh. "The Germans still haven't crossed the Channel and we're conscripting pensioners! It'll be women and children next!"

Cooper laughed good-naturedly. "That's what they said twenty years ago when you were but a gleam in your father's eye."

"You fought in the Great War?" the one with the moustache asked, becoming intrigued.

"*Flew* in it," Cooper corrected smartly, slipping the Leica from his camera bag. He raised it to his eye and snapped a picture of the two flyers opposite him. "I was in aerial reconnaissance."

The lovesick flyer suddenly came to life and turned from the window, facing Cooper. "Biplanes? Open cockpits? The Red Baron?"

"Aye," Cooper grunted.

"My father flew with the RAF in that war," the flyer went on. "Had three kills, he did."

"None for me, I'm afraid," Cooper replied. "Not official ones, anyway. I handled the machine gun once in a while, but most of the time it was my camera that I was aimin'. A great big Graflex, it was . . . not this itty-bitty thing here."

The flyer looked serious again and locked his eyes onto Cooper's. "Did you really leave your bride behind?"

Cooper nodded apprehensively, sensing what the next question would be.

"So . . . so was she waiting with open arms when you got back?" the flyer asked, as Cooper knew he would.

Cooper tilted his head in thought. "No, I'm afraid not. Though not for the reasons you're thinkin'. It's a long story and I won't be borin' you with it; but I'm hopin' that's exactly what she'll be doin' when I finally get to Guernsey."

"Guernsey," the lovesick pilot echoed. "In the Channel Islands?"

"Aye. That's where I'm headed. Why?"

"My brother was stationed there. About a week ago, his entire air group was recalled to Ramsgate."

Cooper looked puzzled. "To the mainland?"

The lovesick pilot nodded. "He said all other military personnel were withdrawn as well."

"By order of the king himself," the boyish flyer with the freckles chimed in. "It seems he's decided the islands 'ave no strategic importance."

The flyer with the moustache nodded. "It came over the radio. What's the point of keepin' men and equipment deployed against an attack that's not likely to come?"

"Aye," Cooper said, with a reflective smile. "I lost my wife fightin' a war. I wasn't plannin' on fightin' another to get her back . . ." Then with jut-jawed determination added, "But I would."

Chapter Sixty-Four

It was midafternoon when the train from Birmingham arrived at London's King's Cross Station. The train to Bournemouth, on which Cooper was ticketed, wasn't scheduled to depart for several hours. So, he made his way through the surging crowds to a steamy fish and chips parlor across from the station, and had supper before boarding the train.

True to its name, the Bournemouth Local stopped at Staines, Chertsy, Frimley, Basingstoke, Winchester and Christchurch before arriving in Bournemouth. It had taken Cooper nearly three days to travel the four hundred miles from Glasgow. The station clock was nearing midnight when he stepped from the coach. The night air was cool and moist, and smelled of the sea. Cooper spent the night in a nearby traveler's hostel.

Early the next morning, he set off for the Channel Islands ferry terminal.

The taxicab followed the road that encircled the waterfront. Quaint houses and floating wharves dotted the horseshoe-shaped inlet where fishing boats were putting to sea.

The taxi snaked between the piers and rumbled to a stop in front of the terminal.

The ferry from Guernsey had just arrived. Like the trains on which Cooper had been traveling, it was crowded with passengers who had been uprooted because of the war: businessmen who were moving to mainland offices, vacationers who were cutting short their holiday, residents who were evacuating despite the government's conviction that the islands wouldn't be attacked. Conversely, there were few passengers waiting to board departing ferries; and Cooper had no trouble finding a ticket window without a queue.

The agent, a young woman with a friendly face, was wearing a brand-new uniform. Like many housewives, she had been pressed into service because the workforce was being depleted by the need for military conscripts and volunteers. "May I help you, sir?" she asked cheerily.

"Aye," Cooper replied. "I'd like to purchase passage to Guernsey."

"May I see your passport, please?"

Cooper looked puzzled as he slipped it from his camera bag. It was odd to be asked for it, he thought, since he wasn't leaving Great Britain.

After hearing Cooper's Scottish burr, an American passport was the last thing the agent expected. She scanned the title page and frowned, though her reaction had nothing to do with citizenship. "I'm sorry, sir, but passage to Guernsey is out of the question, I'm afraid."

"And why might that be?" Cooper challenged.

"Because passage to all the islands has been restricted to residents only." The agent turned to the wall behind her, which was covered with copies of official-looking documents that overlapped each other. She stabbed a finger at one titled TRAVEL RESTRICTIONS, and said, "Came straight from Whitehall, a fortnight ago. I'm sorry."

Cooper's heart sank. Since his departure from Birmingham things had, finally, been going according to plan. Now, yet another problem had surfaced. "Well, I'm afraid you're right," he said, letting his burr thicken with charm. "I'm not a resident of Guernsey . . . but my wife is."

"Oh, I see," the agent said, looking confused.

"Aye, Scottish born and bred . . ." Cooper rushed on, ". . . as am I, which I'm sure you can plainly detect." Then, seeing the question in her eyes, he decided to answer it, unabashedly, knowing the heart-tugging truth would serve him best. "I know what you're thinkin'. Why is she living on Guernsey if her husband, the love of her life, is in America? Because terrible things happen to decent people all the time. It's a long story. You see, we've been—"

"Oh, indeed," the agent interrupted with obvious empathy. "I know all too well what you mean, sir; but I'm not authorized to make exceptions, I'm afraid."

Cooper sighed, then, in a voice trembling with emotion, resumed. "Of course you're not; but, you see, we've been apart for twenty years," he said, going on to explain the tragic sequence of events and ongoing conspiracy that had been responsible for it; and that, after two long and lonely decades, had brought him to her ticket booth.

The agent sighed mournfully. "Oh dear, I'm so sorry."

Her eyes were glistening with emotion now. Cooper held them with his own and, pleading with her, added, "I've been waitin' for so long . . . and I've come so far . . . and, thanks be to God, I've finally found her. The only thing keepin' us apart now is the ferry to Guernsey. It's just not fair, not fair a'tall, is it?"

The agent brushed away a tear, then glanced to the directive on the wall and winced, torn by conflict.

"Please . . ." Cooper said, imploring her. "I know these are tryin' times, and Whitehall's counting on you to carry out your orders; but, after all my wife and I have been through, I can't believe they're countin' on you to keep us from being reunited now. Can you?"

The agent bit a lip and brushed another tear from her cheek. "No. No, I can't." She removed a ticket from her drawer and put it on the counter with Cooper's passport.

"Thank you," Cooper said with an emotional timbre. "Thank you from the bottom of my heart." He took a deep breath, then glanced to a tariff board on which the fares were posted. "Two and six, is it?" He took a five-pound note from his wallet and put it on the counter. "I've no need for any change."

The agent thanked him with a smile. "I almost forgot," she said, returning the five-pound note to Cooper. "It's Thursday. There's no fare on the ten o'clock crossing today." She turned to the wall of official-looking documents behind her and pretended to be searching it. "I'm sure that directive's up there somewhere."

Chapter Sixty-Five

Dusk was falling when the island of Guernsey rose in the sweep of blue-purple twilight. The ferry cut through the swells and angled toward the clusters of incandescent lights twinkling in the distance.

The crossing from Bournemouth usually took between nine and twelve hours, depending on the currents and wind direction. Cooper had gotten lucky on both counts and it was well before 7:00 PM when the ferry nosed into the slip in St. Peter Port, Guernsey's capital.

Its stately homes and densely packed row houses, with their dormered roofs and cast-iron balconies, had been built on terrain that rose from the sea. Along with a variety of quaint shops, pubs, restaurants and hotels, they were connected by steep staircases and narrow streets that were shaded by centuries-old trees and illuminated by bishop's crook streetlights. The finest of these fronted on the Esplanade, a roadway that snaked along the harbor behind a stone seawall.

Almost three weeks had passed since Cooper's departure from Boston. The voyage on the *Britannic,* the search for Grace in and around Glasgow, the train journey to Bournemouth and the ferry crossing had taken longer than expected, or hadn't been expected at all. Nor had he anticipated that his journey would be so stressful and exhausting. Now, having arrived on Guernsey, Cooper craved a hot bath, a hearty meal and a decent night's sleep. So, instead of staying in a traveler's hostel as he'd done previously, he checked into the Royal Hotel on St. Julians Avenue, a short walk from the terminal. With its porticoed entrance, plush lobby and richly furnished rooms, The Royal catered, in the finest European tradition, to wealthy guests, who appreciated the island's mild climate and French-based cuisine.

Cooper had spent the time on the ferry thinking about Grace and what her reaction might be. During his transatlantic crossing excitement, not uncertainty, had been his primary emotion because he believed Grace knew he was coming. But having learned that it had been, and still was, quite the opposite, this voyage had been rife with anxiety.

Despite his desire to be with Grace, Cooper still planned to keep his distance and gently reveal the truth in a letter. Indeed, nothing had changed since he'd visited Mary Queen of Scots School and learned that she still believed herself to be a widow. If anything, his subsequent confrontation with Colin, and Colin's concern about his sister's reaction to the truth, only confirmed the importance of sparing Grace the shock of opening a door, or turning a corner, and coming face-to-face with her "long-deceased" husband without prior warning. Cooper still had the letter he'd written on the train back to Glasgow from Stirling, the one that he'd delivered to Colin's townhouse and that had been returned by the butler. However, rather than sending it to Grace, he thought it would be best to rewrite and expand it to reflect recent events.

* * *

Early the next morning, he awakened in his hotel room, intending to do just that; but as he took the letter from his camera bag and settled at the writing desk, he was suddenly gripped by an overwhelming compulsion to see Grace first; not only to confirm her presence, but also to realize the emotional uplifting that even a distant glimpse of her would provide.

Camera bag slung over his shoulder, Cooper went down to the lobby and obtained a map of Guernsey from the concierge, who also rented him a bicycle. They were a common mode of transport on the island, which measured barely nine miles long and five miles wide. Far across the channel, the rising sun hovered above the French coast, sending long shadows across St. Peter Port's empty streets as Cooper pedaled north on the Esplanade in the direction of St. Anne's School.

It had been many decades since Cooper had ridden a two-wheeler but the old adage proved true, and he had no trouble keeping his balance. He coasted along, his face reddening in the wind, his head filling with the scent of brine, his mind drifting joyously to thoughts of biking about the island with Grace.

The brick and limestone façades of St. Peter Port soon gave way to the glass-enclosed greenhouses of tomato farms, and then expanses of rolling countryside. The road, like the branches of the centuries-old trees that shaded it, forked again and again; and more than once the map saved Cooper from taking a wrong turn. Finally, he came through a small forest spread across the crest of a hill, and there, below, like a tiny village by the sea, were the stately stone buildings of St. Anne's School for Girls.

Cooper leaned the bike against one of the trees, then made his way to an outcropping of rocks from where he could observe the school without being seen. Most of the buildings were clustered on narrow streets, but two of them were set off by themselves. These had the repetitious, multi-story façades of dormitories; and Cooper deduced that they were the student and faculty residence halls.

And they were. He'd been there about half an hour when teenage girls with schoolbags began emerging from the larger one, and teachers in billowing cloaks from the smaller. Alone and in groups, they crossed the campus en route to other buildings where morning classes would soon commence.

Cooper's pulse had quickened with anticipation when he first came upon the school, but it accelerated exponentially when Grace suddenly appeared, bursting from the faculty residence in full stride. Her gray-streaked hair was pulled back severely in a chignon, and her dance-class attire peeked from beneath a billowing cloak. Cooper knew it was Grace the instant he saw her—even before her head had turned, revealing her radiant features. Indeed, he knew just by the way she carried herself, by her poise and perfect balance, and by her quick, splay-footed stride; and at this moment, he knew beyond any doubt, that he had at long last found his beloved Grace, and was actually *seeing* her for the first time in twenty years.

Cooper watched as she hurried toward the building that housed the school's dance studio. He took some time to savor the moment and catch his breath. Then, with Grace safely inside, he walked down the hill to the building, circling it until he came upon a row of leaded-glass windows. Cooper stood behind one of the stone columns that separated them, and served to conceal him; and suddenly, there, just beyond the diamond-shaped panes—there, almost within arm's reach, was his Grace. Cooper's heart fluttered as she went gliding past, demonstrating a dance movement to her students.

Though his feelings for her had never diminished, two decades of suppressed emotions came rushing to the surface. His face flushed, his eyes brimmed with tears, his stomach flip-flopped and tingled as it did when he first saw her that day at the Van Dusen Gallery more than twenty years ago; and he fell in love with her all over again. Then, all too aware that the outcome could be disastrous if Grace caught even a glimpse of him now, he moved away from the window and hurried off.

Cooper had just returned to his rocky perch when the sound of an internal combustion engine rose in the distance. Moments later, a black sedan appeared on the road that wound through the trees. It came roaring over the crest of the hill, and continued down toward the school. It was going too fast for Cooper to see the license plates from France, or the caduceus medallion affixed to the rear bumper; but he had spent enough time there to know a Citroën when he saw one.

Cooper watched as it slowed and parked along the curb in the cobblestone plaza, the crossroads of the campus from which narrow streets lined with school buildings went off in every direction. The driver, a tall, well-dressed man, in his midforties with dark hair and chiseled features, got out from behind the wheel on the left side. He glanced at his watch, then walked to a stone wall across the square, and leaned against it as if waiting for someone.

Having finally seen his beloved Grace, Cooper was anxious to return to the hotel, revise the letter as he'd been planning and mail it to her as quickly as possible. He was about to mount his bicycle when a clanging bell signaled the end of the first hour of classes. Teachers and groups of students began emerging from the buildings. Grace came from the one that housed the dance studio. Cooper brightened at the sight of her and set the bike aside. She was in the midst of about a dozen teenage girls wearing leotards. They all walked in the same splay-footed stride, and they all seemed to be talking at once, to her and each other. Indeed, they were chatting excitedly about tomorrow's dance recital—all except one, who seemed distracted and was looking about anxiously.

"Christiane!" the gentleman leaning against the wall called out, waving to her. "Christiane, *regarde!*"

"La! There! He is there!" Christiane exclaimed, turning to Grace. She ran across the square and lunged into the man's arms. "Papa!" she squealed with a relieved giggle.

Lucien Devereaux enfolded his daughter in a fatherly embrace, then broke into a charming smile as Grace caught up and joined them. *"Ah, Grace, bonjour! Comment va-tu? Ça va?"*

"Oui, Lucien, très bien," Grace replied, beaming with delight as they hugged each other, kissing on both cheeks. "Your letter to Christiane came but a few days ago," Grace went on and, with a demure smile, added, "She was quite concerned you might not be coming."

"Je comprends," Lucien said, his eyes suggesting he knew Grace was speaking for herself as well. "As you know, things at home are not good, but I am here! And *nous nous amuseront bien! Oui?"*

"Mais oui!" Christiane replied as the three of them sauntered off, hand in hand, in the direction of the residence halls. "We will have a *very* good time!"

From his distant vantage point, Cooper hadn't been able to hear what they were saying, nor had he been able to discern what was being communicated by their facial expressions or the looks that passed between them; but he *could* see that the man—who had hugged and kissed his wife with undeniable affection, albeit on the cheeks, and was now holding her hand—was not only ruggedly handsome, but also of Grace's generation, not his. Was this dashing fellow her colleague, friend or lover? Was it possible that Colin's worst fear, not to mention his own, had come true? That Grace had remarried? Or was intending to?

Cooper sagged under the weight of it as he watched them walking off. He felt suddenly hollow as if the air had been sucked out of him. Indeed, what he had just witnessed crushed his spirits and made him all the more uncertain as to how to proceed. Overwhelmed, he climbed aboard his bicycle and began pedaling back toward town, beset by powerful emotions that had suddenly set entire stanzas of *Enoch Arden* racing through his mind, intensifying his dilemma.

Chapter Sixty-Six

The sun was directly overhead by the time Cooper returned to the hotel and took refuge in the welcome coolness of his room. The divan opposite the window provided a comfortable respite from the seat on his bicycle. He settled into the cushions and went about meticulously cleaning his pipe, then thumbed fresh tobacco into the bowl and lit it. A short time later, the space overhead was filled with wispy layers of smoke, and his dilemma, if not yet resolved, had been fully contemplated.

Enoch Arden's example notwithstanding, Cooper had little trouble in deciding that he had waited too long and had come too far to simply slip, forever, away. He also realized that Grace's apparent, if frustratingly unclear, circumstances made it all the more important that he forewarn her and not appear unannounced.

Decision made, Cooper stepped to the writing desk where, earlier that morning, he'd left the letter he'd been planning to revise. The drawers of the graceful antique were well stocked with postcards and hotel stationery; and on several sheets of the latter, he copied the sensitively worded paragraphs, which revealed the truth that had been kept from Grace by her family. In addition, Cooper wrote briefly of his recent search for her and his presence on Guernsey.

When finished, he fetched his camera bag, removed the stack of letters Colin had given him and selected two envelopes that had been sent to Grace at Mary Queen of Scots School in Stirling. One contained both the letter Joe Clements had written informing her Cooper was coming and the snapshot of Cooper leaning against his camera; the other, Cooper's letter with the date of the *Britannic*'s arrival in Glasgow. He slipped both of them along with the letter he'd just written into an envelope, addressed it to Grace at St. Anne's School, then sealed it and hurried from his room.

The St. Peter Port Post Office, a stalwart stone building with the Union Jack flying over the entrance, was on Smith Street, a short walk from the hotel.

Cooper stood at the window, watching as the clerk weighed the envelope and affixed proper postage. He knew he would be on pins and needles waiting for a reply and wanted to determine when he might realistically expect one. "When might it be delivered?" he asked, trying not to sound impatient.

"In tomorrow's post," the clerk replied genially.

"Aye," Cooper grunted, brightening at the news. "I can't be hopin' for better service than that, now, can I?"

"We weren't always quite so efficient," the clerk replied with a wry smile that bordered on melancholy. "Ever since the telephone service came in . . . Well, people just don't write as many letters anymore. So whatever post there is gets delivered straight away."

The sun was falling to the horizon as Cooper left the post office and walked through the narrow streets to the harbor, where he treated himself to a proper supper at Poissons de Normande, one of the many restaurants that specialized in fresh seafood.

*   *   *

The next day was Saturday.

Cooper awakened late morning, having enjoyed his second decent night's sleep in as many weeks, and spent the afternoon bicycling about the harbor with his camera. After what he'd seen at the ferry terminal in Bournemouth, he wasn't surprised that St. Peter Port's terminal was crowded with residents of Guernsey who had decided to evacuate.

Bicycling south on the Esplanade, Cooper came upon a bay where scores of fishing boats were bobbing in their slips. He had taken several shots of some fishermen repairing their nets when another boat came gliding toward an adjacent slip. Cooper was surprised to see that its cargo wasn't the day's catch but, in an ironic twist, several dozen refugees from war-torn France. Lugging suitcases and bundles of personal belongings they had salvaged, they stood on the deck, their shoulders slumped in defeat, their eyes wide with fright and blank with disorientation, their wounds seeping crimson through white gauze bandages.

Cooper instinctively raised his camera, but the gut-wrenching reality of war struck him with jarring impact; and, instead of taking pictures, he set the Leica aside and joined the group of local fishermen who were helping the refugees disembark.

Once ashore, they explained that the Germans had recently taken the major shipping ports of Dieppe and Le Havre. Just the night before, French and British troops had been overrun and driven back to the sea, most of the latter evacuating as they had at Dunkirk. Now, the German Army, led by several panzer divisions, was moving east toward Caen and the Cherbourg Peninsula. This section of the French coastline was closest to the Channel Islands, a mere ten miles at some points, and was dotted with a number of smaller ports that provided them with ferry service.

"I suppose the bloody Jerries'll be bombing us next," one of the fishermen said.

"Poppycock," another retorted smartly. "Whitehall says we're of no strategic importance at all."

"Aye, so I've heard," Cooper said with a skeptical frown. "Let's hope they told that to the Jerries."

Chapter Sixty-Seven

Six miles to the north, at St. Anne's School, Grace spent the day in the dance studio rehearsing her students for the recital that evening. It was late afternoon by the time she finished. She was crossing the grounds toward the faculty residence when she detoured to Main Hall to collect her post from the wall of boxes in the lobby. Cooper's letter was amidst the advertising flyers and copy of the daily newspaper.

Though Grace had no idea who the letter was from, her brows arched in surprise at the sight of it. Not only was it thicker and heavier than most envelopes addressed by hand, which usually contained a few pages of personal correspondence; but, since she had neither informed anyone of where she had gone, nor had been corresponding with anyone, it was also unexpected.

On first glance, the handwriting seemed vaguely familiar, and she gasped as her mind jumped to a bone-chilling conclusion. Colin! Grace thought, reflecting on the mysterious caller from Glasgow whom she had feared all along was her brother. The idea of it had been so unnerving that she'd talked to Lucien about it over dinner the previous evening. But the local postmark, not to mention the typography on the flap—which spelled out Royal Hotel in bright blue script—powerfully contradicted the idea it had come from Glasgow.

Far from comforting, this moment of insight sent a second, and even more chilling shiver through her. Had Colin not only tracked her down, but also come to Guernsey in search of her? Was he here? On the island? At the Royal Hotel? This unsettling notion was quickly dispelled by further examination of the handwriting on the envelope, which, Grace realized, wasn't her brother's. It *was* familiar, however, which made it all the more intriguing.

Grace's mind was racing in search of a connection when she detected an equally familiar, if faint, aroma that was coming from the envelope. She couldn't quite place it, either, at first, and was staring at it with a puzzled frown when it suddenly struck her, struck her with unnerving clarity, that it was the scent of smoke, the scent of *pipe* smoke, the scent of pipe smoke she recognized! Indeed, her sense of smell—our most powerful memory trigger—had made the connection that her eyes, upon scrutinizing the handwriting, could not. And now, as absurd, impossible and confusing as it seemed, Grace was almost certain that, even before opening the envelope and reading its contents, she knew who it was from, and all that it meant.

She stood in the corridor in front of the wall of postal boxes, rocked to her core by its astonishing implications and the fear that opening it would confirm them. Her chest heaved in deep breaths that ended in an involuntary sigh each time she exhaled. Finally, she regained her composure and hurried from the lobby with the envelope. The faculty residence hall was just across the cobblestone square. She had no memory of whether she had walked numbly, stumbled clumsily or ran frantically as she pushed through the entrance and climbed the stairs to her quarters.

The cozy flat had a bedroom, as well as a sitting room with an alcove where a small icebox resided along with a hotplate and small sink. Like most faculty quarters, it had come fully furnished with a mixture of pieces of no discernable pedigree. Grace preferred them to the stuffy Edwardian reproductions used to furnish the dormitory's common rooms. They were set against a variety of floral-patterned wallpapers, which she concealed with her collection of dance posters—Isadora Duncan, Ruth St. Denis, Nijinsky, Sergei Diaghilev, and Martha Graham prominent among them. On the vanity, along with her toiletries, flacons of perfume, hairbrushes and clips, was a tarnished silver picture frame with a snapshot of Cooper in his military uniform that he had included in one of his letters from France.

Moments later, Grace found herself sitting in the overstuffed chair in the corner between the bookcases, staring at the unopened envelope. She seemed paralyzed by the mere existence of it—the whole of her unmoving except for the trembling hand that held the letter—and threatened by its implications. Finally, she gathered her courage, slipped a fingernail beneath the flap and carefully tore it open, pausing briefly before removing its contents.

The pages of Cooper's handwriting along with his signature confirmed what the writing on the envelope and scent of pipe smoke had presaged. Grace's husband, the love of her life, the man she thought had been killed in action twenty years ago, the man whose tragic death had taken her decades to overcome, was not only alive but there on Guernsey! Grace shuddered and sighed loudly, overwhelmed by a flood of memories. Her mind raced in fragmented bursts as if reliving every moment of her life with Cooper in a matter of seconds. Her lower lip began to quiver, then her eyes welled and overflowed, sending tears streaming down her cheeks.

Grace brushed them aside several times, then steeled herself and read Cooper's letter. Staggered by its contents, she read it again, unable to comprehend or accept what it revealed. Whereas Cooper's heart had fluttered at the sight of her, at this moment, Grace's felt as if hers was trying to fight its way out of her chest. Driven by emotions that had run the gamut from momentary delight to shocking disbelief to growing anger and fear, her heart pounded and stuttered and raced intermittently as if uncertain about its mission.

A short time later, she had read the two letters that Cooper had included with the one he'd written at the hotel. Now, the pages were scattered across the cushions next to her, and she was staring at Joe Clements's snapshot of Cooper, his face lined with age, his head a mass of unruly white curls, his fist planted defiantly against a hip, his jaw set firmly but unable to conceal a trace of mischief in his smile. Right down to its serrated edges, the snapshot perfectly captured Cooper's personality, captured that mixture of crusty defiance and zest for life that Grace had found so compelling and appealing. Several times she glanced from it to the framed picture of him in uniform on her vanity that had captured those very same qualities, and had helped keep the memory of Cooper alive for her all these years.

Grace had no idea how long she'd been sitting there staring at the snapshot—her emotions alternating between overwhelming joy and growing anger at the bittersweet unfairness of it all—when the clock on the side table chimed. She leapt from the chair, realizing she had barely enough time to bathe, dress and get to the recital hall to make certain everything for the performance was in order. Unsettled, trying to catch her breath, she gathered herself and accepted the fact that whatever she was, or wasn't, going to do about Dylan Cooper would just have to wait.

Chapter Sixty-Eight

~⌒~

Though the days were longer at this time of year, and the sun was still high above the horizon, the windows of Main Hall were ablaze with orange light; and the cobblestone square at the center of the campus was filling up with vehicles as students, family members, school administrators and faculty, and local residents arrived for the dance recital, and began streaming into the auditorium.

Backstage, Grace was flitting about her student corps de ballet like a mother hen, tending to last-minute details, fussing with costumes, adjusting hair fashions and managing cases of stage fright.

Christiane was putting on a ballet slipper when one of its ribbons, which she was tying about her ankle, tore loose from the edge of the slipper where it had been sewn. *"Ah, mon Dieu!"* she shrieked, hurrying toward Grace, her eyes wide with panic, the length of satin ribbon in one hand, the slipper in the other. *"Madame! Madame Cooper! C'est une catastrophe! Regardez!"*

"Oh, Christiane, no!" Grace exclaimed, sounding unnerved. "How did you manage that?"

Christiane shrugged and emitted a whimper.

"Well, you'll just have to borrow someone else's," Grace said matter-of-factly. "Find someone who's not in your ensemble who's the same size."

"But these are my favorites," Christiane whined in protest. "I can't dance in someone else's. I just can't."

"I've no time for this!" Grace snapped.

Lucien, who had been observing from a discrete distance, came forward. "Christiane, *donne moi le chausson,*" he said with characteristic aplomb.

Christiane gave the ballet slipper to her father as instructed, then watched with bated breath as he took a pocketknife from his jacket. It had several blades, one of which had been sharply honed. With the skill of the surgeon he was, Lucien cut a slit in both the sidewall of the slipper just below where the satin ribbon had been sewn and in one end of the ribbon itself, which was approximately one and one-half inches in width. Next, he threaded the uncut end of the ribbon through the slit in the slipper, then through the slit in the other end of the ribbon, making a loop, which he pulled tight against the leather sidewall.

Christiane slipped it on and tied the ribbons about her ankle, securing it. After testing it with several pirouettes, she sighed with relief, then thanked her father with a hug and hurried off, joining the other girls who were assembling in the wings.

"Are you all right?" Lucien whispered, joining Grace, who had stepped aside.

"Of course I am," Grace replied defensively. "Why?"

"Well, it's not like you to lose your composure," Lucien said gently. "I have never seen you so upset."

"That's because you've never been backstage just before curtain!" Grace snapped. "Truth be told, that's why I prefer parents to refrain from doing so."

Lucien's hand went to his heart as if he'd been wounded. "I wasn't here to be with Christiane," he scolded gently.

Grace lowered her eyes and sighed with remorse. "I'm sorry. You're so sweet . . . so understanding."

"*Mais oui,* I know . . ." he said with a charming smile. "And I fully expect you will have dinner with me so you can continue making your apology."

Grace forced a smile, and nodded.

Lucien kissed her cheek and hurried to take his seat in the audience, still troubled by her demeanor. Despite Grace attributing it to precurtain jitters, he was certain something else was wrong, but couldn't put his finger on it, and found it difficult to put it out of his mind during the recital—which went extremely well.

Indeed, but for a missed step or two that only Grace had noticed, the students danced beautifully. Christiane's repaired ballet slipper remained firmly in place, and the audience applauded with appreciation and enthusiasm.

After the curtain calls and backstage ceremonies had been concluded, all the students—dancers and spectators alike— returned to their dormitory rooms. Just one week of school remained—examination week—and, despite it being Saturday night, they wasted no time getting back to their studies.

Lucien's car was one of many parked in the square. He and Grace drove a short distance to an inn perched high above Fontenelle Bay that had a small, romantic restaurant with a view of the sea. But for reasons that only Grace knew, and which Lucien still couldn't fathom, she was distracted throughout, and was far from the vivacious and engaging dinner partner Lucien had enjoyed on previous visits. By the time they left the restaurant, the sun had fallen to the horizon, painting both sea and sky with an iridescent shimmer.

"Shall we take a walk?" Lucien prompted, gesturing to the stunning vista.

"It sounds lovely, Lucien," Grace replied wearily. "But I

think it best if we go back now." She forced a smile, then turned and began walking toward his car.

"Grace?" Lucien called out, stopping her. "Forgive me for being so . . . so forward, but you haven't been yourself all evening. I don't know what's troubling you but, perhaps it would help to talk about it."

"That's quite thoughtful of you, Lucien. But, no, no, I'm . . . I'm fine. I'm just tired."

"Ah, oui, fatiguée," Lucien conceded, splaying his hands in a gesture of endearing charm that only the French can manage. "But it is not like you to be so . . . so . . . as we say *en Français . . . froide et renfermée."*

"I'm sorry," Grace said with a contrite sigh. "I haven't been very good company, have I? As I said, recitals are always quite stressful, I'm afraid."

"But it is finished, and a wonderful success," Lucien countered, undaunted. "Therefore, such stress has been removed, *non?"*

"It always takes me a wee bit of time to recover."

"Perhaps," Lucien said, still unconvinced. He captured her eyes with his, and said, "No. No, there is something more. All during the recital, and dinner as well, I've been wondering what could have happened to so upset you. And, as you would say, 'I'm afraid,' the only thing that came to mind is this mysterious caller whom you mentioned."

Grace stiffened. Her lips tightened into a thin line. She walked toward the edge of the bluff and looked out over the sea, deciding whether or not she would share it with him. A strong breeze was coming off the water, and her amber tresses, gray-streaked and long, were blowing in the wind as Lucien followed. He wrapped his arms around her from behind and prompted, "That is it, isn't it? The caller. *N'est-ce pas?"*

"Yes, I'm afraid," she said with a rueful smile, knowing she couldn't keep the truth from him forever.

"So, it was your brother as you thought, *non?"*

"Non," she replied, wincing as she turned to face him. "There's no easy way to say this, Lucien, so I best just say it straight off. It was my . . . my husband."

Lucien looked incredulous and confused. A long moment passed before he cleared his throat and said, "Your husband? But . . . but I'd thought he was killed in the Great War . . ."

Grace nodded and raised her shoulders in a helpless shrug. "As had I. I still have the telegram."

Lucien sagged as the implications and wrenching complexities struck him. "Then . . . Then it was a mistake."

Grace nodded. "A twenty-year mistake." She paused, gathering her courage, and in a whisper added, "He's . . . he's here . . . in St. Peter Port."

"Ohhhh . . . Je suis désolé . . ." Lucien said, running the words together into a distraught sigh that blended with the wind. He took Grace's hand and led her to one of several benches that had been positioned to take advantage of the view. For a moment they sat, hugging each other. Then, his voice quavering with remorse, Lucien said, "Grace, I am so sorry. I had no right to be so . . . so insistent, so demanding. It was terribly insensitive of me."

Grace responded with an absolving smile. "It's not your doing, Lucien. It's his. *My husband's,"* she said, her voice taking on an edge. "It's not a'tall fair. How could he just suddenly appear! How could he let so much time go by before trying to find me?"

"You heard nothing from him for twenty years?"

She shook her head no. "Nothing," she snapped, as she got to her feet, unable to control her anger. "He claims he's written but I never got a single card or letter, not even one! Why would he say that? Why!"

Lucien stood and embraced her, consolingly. "Grace . . . Grace, try to calm yourself. You will need a clear mind and . . . and heart . . . to think this through. There are *many* questions to be answered. If I may, it seems it would be best to ask them of him."

"Oh, Lucien, I don't know if I can," Grace said, her voice rife with conflict. "I don't know if I can even bring myself to see him. I'm . . . I'm betwixt and between. Bursting with joy one minute and in absolute shreds the next. It's been my undoing all day. I can't imagine how I got through the recital."

"Oui, je comprends," Lucien said, nodding with understanding. "From what you've told me about him, he sounds like a decent fellow who loved you deeply . . ."

"Yes," Grace whispered.

". . . And therefore not the kind of person to conduct himself in such a callous manner. *Non?*"

"No, no, not a'tall. He's quite a gentleman, actually," Grace replied, brightening in reflection. "Truth be told, I'm just . . . just frightened, and quite disappointed, too. I mean, what will become of our plans? It would be the first real holiday I've had in decades. I even went to the safe deposit at the bank for my passport. I don't know what I'm doing anymore."

Lucien's eyes softened with empathy. "Nor do I, not as of late. Ours is not the only holiday *en Provence* facing uncertainty, Grace. Whatever happens, it will be the Germans, not your long-lost husband, who will be responsible for ruining it. It doesn't look at all promising."

"Yes, I know. I just didn't want to face it," Grace said sadly. Then, struck by a thought, she added, "Maybe you and Christiane could stay here? It would be safer than going home, wouldn't it?"

"Perhaps, but I have many responsibilities, Grace. My patients, my staff, even my countrymen now, for that matter. Every surgeon will be needed. Not to mention my parents, siblings, aunts, uncles, cousins—all of whom are looking to me for guidance in these times. Why? Because I am a doctor and therefore I must know everything. No, as planned, I must return to Brittany as soon as school is finished, and so must Christiane."

"But the newspapers say the Germans may soon be

threatening Brittany," Grace protested. "You could be taken prisoner or even killed."

Lucien nodded gravely. "Yes, but we are a large family; and there are many homes, cottages, villas and farms scattered throughout the region, even a winery or two. So, if one is not safe, perhaps another will be. Of course, there are no guarantees." He studied her face. Then, holding it gently between his hands, said, "It would be *difficile et dangereux;* but I would be very happy if you came with us, Grace."

"So would I, Lucien," Grace replied with heartfelt sincerity. "It would solve my dilemma, wouldn't it?"

Lucien smiled and shook his head no. "That would be my hope; but in truth, I don't really think it would. With time you will have more questions, more uncertainty, more ... more emotional turmoil, not less. No, you must resolve this first, Grace. Please, take the rest of the weekend and give some serious thought to seeing your husband. I think it best you do."

"I wish I had your certainty, Lucien," Grace said meekly. "I've managed all these years alone, without him. Why change now? Why not just go on with my life, with *our* lives?"

"Because, as I have learned from my own travails, it is impossible to embrace the future while living in the past ..." Lucien replied evenly. "When I lost my wife, well, as I have said ... for many years after, I was unable to function until I stopped blaming myself for not saving her, for not using all my training and experience to perform what would have amounted to a miracle." He splayed his hands, in a helpless gesture, then let a smile soften his expression. "If not for you, for your ... your spirited support ... your willingness to share your own tragedy with me, I would still feel responsible. Sometimes, for whatever reason, we blind ourselves to truths that others can plainly see. Even Christiane, a mere child at the time, saw more clearly than I ..." Lucien paused, misty-eyed in reflection. Then, his voice taking on a more forceful timbre, he concluded, "All things considered, I think it behooves you to see him. Please, Grace, for us. Face your husband. Don't flee from him. I implore you."

Grace stood shivering in the cool night air, both touched and troubled by Lucien's impassioned plea. "You're right, Lucien, and I will. I promise . . ." She looked off into the hazy twilight that had settled over the sea, then realized her answer was ambiguous, and added, ". . . to think about it."

Chapter Sixty-Nine

⌒

That same evening, Cooper had dinner in the Royal Hotel's restaurant, then settled in the lounge with a Guinness, listening to news of the war on the radio with some of the other guests. The BBC reported that the French government was being pressured by Germany to negotiate terms of surrender. Whitehall was convinced that if France fell, Great Britain would be attacked; and, despite the ongoing evacuation of British troops from France, Churchill was urging General de Gaulle, who had already been exiled to London, to call upon French citizens—civilians and soldiers alike—to keep the resistance alive.

The chance that Great Britain might soon be invaded intensified Cooper's anxiety about Grace. He wanted nothing more than to reunite, affirm their love for one another, and return to Newbury before they became caught up in the hostilities and trapped in England. Barely a day had passed since he had mailed his letter, and he was already wondering when, or, at his lowest moments, *if,* he would hear from her. Having spent the day bicycling about the waterfront with his camera and assisting the war refugees from France, he felt drained of energy and decided to retire early.

He was crossing the lobby intending to pick up his room key at the check-in desk when a tall, ruggedly handsome gentleman, whom he thought he recognized, entered the hotel. Cooper reversed direction, returning to the lounge, and watched from a distance as the man fetched his key and crossed to the elevator. As soon as he had stepped inside and the uniformed operator closed the door, Cooper approached the desk clerk.

"Excuse me? That gentleman who just left," Cooper began casually. "I'm quite certain I know him from somewhere, but his name escapes me."

"We're not supposed to give out information about our guests, sir," the clerk said. "I'm sorry."

"Aye," Cooper grunted with a genial smile. "But one day, when your hair turns to snow and your brain's gone fallow like mine, *you'll* be on this side of the desk, prayin' a helpful lad like yourself is on the other."

The clerk's head bobbed with uncertainty, then, taken by Cooper's self-deprecating charm, he whispered, "His name is Devereaux. Dr. Lucien Devereaux."

"Aye, Dr. Devereaux, of course!" Cooper exclaimed. "As I recall, he drives a black Citroën, doesn't he?"

"Indeed. You're quite right about that," the clerk replied, accepting it as proof that Cooper knew Devereaux as he'd claimed. "He comes over on the car ferry from Brittany. One of our regulars. Lovely chap."

All too lovely, I'm afraid, Cooper thought. He resisted the temptation to say it and, instead, remarked, "Aye, that he is. A fine chap, like yourself." He slipped a few coins into the clerk's palm, then obtained his key and headed upstairs to his room.

The next day was Sunday.

A heavy rain had started falling during the night, varnishing the stone pavers and enriching the city's tones and textures. Cooper had always found such weather inspiring and, on any other day, he would have been roaming the streets with his camera; but, despite the creative impulse, he remained at the hotel, waiting for Grace to reply to his letter—whether by message, phone or, should his fondest wish come true, in person.

By midday Monday, there was still no word, and Cooper was pacing his room like a caged animal. When the rain turned into a misty drizzle, he donned the poncho he kept in his camera bag, then left the hotel and went bicycling about St. Peter Port, taking pictures with his Leica. There were a number of phone boxes scattered about the city; and Cooper called the Royal several times, checking for messages, to no avail. Dusk was falling when the sky darkened and the light rain turned into a downpour, prompting him to return to the hotel.

Cooper deposited his bicycle with the garage attendant, as he did at the end of each day, and went inside, shaking the rain from his poncho. He was walking toward the lounge to quench his thirst when a voice called out, "Mr. Cooper?" He turned to see a bellman coming toward him. "Someone is waiting to see you, sir. If you'll come with me, please?"

Thanks be to God, Cooper thought, *she's here!* At long last he was not only going to see but actually, *be* with his beloved Grace. Cooper took a moment to remove his poncho, which he stowed in his camera bag, then smoothed his clothes and ran his fingers through his damp hair. His heart was pounding with anticipation as he followed the bellman down the corridor to a glass-paneled door that opened into a sitting room off the lobby; and his spirits soared as he entered, trying to gather his wits and decide how he would greet her.

The sitting room was furnished in the style of a London

men's club, with tufted leather sofas and chairs arranged about a fireplace, which, at this time of year, was filled with an arrangement of fresh flowers. A large ceiling fan whirred slowly overhead. Rain pelted the windows in a steady rhythm. But Grace was nowhere to be seen. Indeed, the only person there was a man seated in one of the club chairs, reading a newspaper.

"Dr. Devereaux?" the bellman called out. "Pardon me, Dr. Devereaux. Mr. Cooper has arrived."

Lucien glanced up at Cooper over the top of his newspaper; then he set it aside and got to his feet, extending a hand as the bellman left, closing the door after him. The sight of Lucien had so shocked and disappointed Cooper that a long moment passed before he collected himself and grasped it.

"Ah, Monsieur Coupaire," Lucien said as they shook hands. "My pleasure to meet you. I am Lucien Devereaux. Your . . . your wife, Grace, and I are friends."

"Aye, I'm afraid so," Cooper quipped with a nervous smile, camouflaging his fear that Grace had decided against seeing him and had asked Lucien to deliver the bad news. His anxiety was intensified by the fact that Lucien's accent caused him to pronounce Cooper "Coupaire," as had Georges Latour, the conniving fashion mogul he had worked for in Boston all those years ago, the memory of which still rankled him.

"Please make yourself comfortable," Lucien said, gesturing to one of the club chairs. "Grace asked me to tell you that she received your letter," he explained as they settled opposite each other. He took a pack of cigarettes from the table next to his chair and offered one to Cooper, who, beside himself with suspense, barely managed to shake his head no and produce his pipe in reply. Lucien slipped a cigarette from the pack, then lit it and exhaled, filling the space between them with smoke, before resuming. "Furthermore, after a most tormenting period of uncertainty, she has decided she would like to see you."

Cooper emitted an audible sigh of relief. Many exclamatory responses came to mind but he could only utter an enthusiastic, "When?"

"Tomorrow," Lucien replied, making an apologetic gesture with his hands. "Grace hopes you'll forgive her for the delay and for not responding sooner. I'm sure you can understand how overwhelming it was to receive your letter and to . . . to learn the truth, after all this time."

Cooper's eyes clouded with concern. "Aye, I'm sure she was quite unsettled by it."

"It was more than unsettling, Monsieur Coupaire, I assure you," Lucien said gravely, leaning forward in the chair. "And it has taken her several days to . . . to . . . as you would say, come to grips with it. Also, this is the last week of school, which makes more stress for her."

"Well, I've been waitin' for more than twenty years, Dr. Devereaux," Cooper said, rolling the *r*'s as he emphasized the syllables of his name. "One day more or less shouldn't matter but, truth be told, I can't be waitin' much longer to see her."

"Mais oui, je comprends," Lucien said with evident sincerity. "Of course, I understand." Then, after a thoughtful drag on his cigarette, he said, "I would like to make a suggestion in that regard, if I may?"

Cooper tilted his head as if considering it and took a moment to light his pipe. "You seem to be a rather decent lad and quite keen, too," he said, his face veiled by the smoke. Then, chuckling at what he was about to say, concluded, "Lord knows, Grace wouldn't be givin' you the time of day if you weren't. So, please, speak your mind."

"Merci beaucoup," Lucien said, making a little bow from the chair. "May I say, in kind, it seems you're every bit the gentleman Grace said you were. Now, as I've explained, she is coping with what can only be described as wrenching emotional turmoil, and—"

"As am I," Cooper interrupted. Then, emitting a stream of pipe smoke, he studied Lucien out of the corner of his eye, and said, "And you as well, I've no doubt."

Lucien cocked his head as if making a decision, then stood and crossed to a window where the rain ran in sheets, distorting the view beyond. The rhythmic whirr of the ceiling fan seemed to be counting the seconds until he turned back to Cooper, and nodded. "Yes, it is true. My feelings for Grace are strong . . . an *affaire de coeur,* as we say *en Français;* but she is in a far more fragile state than either of us; and I urge you to proceed with caution, not to mention extreme patience and sensitivity."

"Do you now?" Cooper challenged as he pushed up from the chair to face him. "I should think contactin' Grace through the post, instead of showin' up on her doorstep unannounced, is crystal-clear evidence of my bein' committed to all three."

"*Touché*, sir," Lucien replied with a thin smile. "I intended no offense, believe me. My concern is only for Grace."

"As is mine," Cooper countered, gesturing with his pipe for emphasis. "Suffice to say, concern for her happiness is our common ground."

"Unfortunately, there is only ground enough for one of us," Lucien retorted softly. "My circumstances are such that, despite my advice to you, Grace has little time to decide which of us shall occupy it; and I am hoping that seeing you tomorrow will enable her to do so. In that regard, it so happens that I have a car here, and—"

"Aye, a black Citroën, I know," Cooper interrupted, tucking his pipe into the corner of his mouth with a certain satisfaction.

"I see," Lucien said curiously. "Well, I was about to say, I'd be happy to give you a lift tomorrow, if you like?"

"My bicycle suits me fine, thank you."

"Whatever you wish, Monsieur Coupaire. There is a pavilion on the north shore not far from the school—"

"Aye," Cooper grunted. "I took some pictures of it while ridin' about the island the other day."

"*Bon. Demain, la dernière classe de Grace finit à trois heures, et*"—he paused, then smiled in apology—"Pardon. Tomorrow, Grace's last class is finished at three o'clock, and she will go there immediately."

"I'll be waiting," Cooper said resolutely.

"Feel free to let me know if there's anything else I can do to be of assistance."

Cooper's eyes came to life with a mischievous twinkle. "Well, there *is* something, now that you mention it; but you won't be vanishin' into thin air anytime soon, now, will you?"

"Not anytime soon, no," Lucien replied with a good-natured smile before tilting his head to one side, as if reconsidering it. "On second thought, perhaps . . . if it was Grace's wish . . ."

"It's quite clear it isn't, I'm afraid," Cooper said, loath to admit it. "Not yet, anyway."

"And it may never be . . ." Lucien said. Then, holding Cooper's eyes with his own, he challenged, "For Grace's sake, should that be true, I hope you would be of similar mind."

"I've never been one to believe that the key to success lies in contemplatin' failure, Dr. Devereaux," Cooper retorted. "And I see no point in startin' now. Grace was the one and only love of my life, and . . . and, as far as I know, she would say the same of me. We were—"

"*Oui,* as she has told me," Lucien conceded.

"I'm not a'tall surprised," Cooper said, matter-of-factly, concealing that he was more than pleased, not to mention relieved, to hear it. "I was about to say, we were sublimely happy and just beginnin' our life together when, due to a combination of pure happenstance and malicious intent, it was all . . . all . . ." Cooper paused, his voice breaking with emotion; he drew deeply on his pipe as if it were a source of sustenance, then concluded, ". . . *stolen* from us."

"Yes, I know," Lucien said, reflecting on his own painful loss. "I am personally able to empathize where life's tragedies are concerned, I assure you." He emitted a reflective sigh and added, "Not to mention my country, yet again ravaged by war."

"Aye," Cooper grunted, anger rising at the memory of it. "I served in the Great one, in your country. It didn't cost me my life . . . just my life with Grace."

Lucien nodded with empathy. "I was a medic . . . in the field. I was devastated by the things I saw."

"As was I," Cooper said. "But ever since, I've been keepin' the memory of the good times, the times I had with Grace before it, alive in my heart, wanting nothing more than to recapture whatever might be left of them."

"I've no such hope, unfortunately."

"Well, thanks be to God, *I* do," Cooper said softly. "And, now . . . Now that I've finally found her, I'm hopin' and prayin' Grace wants the same."

"And if she doesn't?" Lucien asked gently.

"Well, as I said, Dr. Devereaux, I've never been one to concede defeat before the battle's even begun. And if you know Grace a'tall, you know had the tables been turned, she'd be standin' here telling herself, 'If at first you don't succeed . . . well, lass, then you had best try, try and try again.' And I've no doubt she's expectin' the same of me."

"Absolument," Lucien conceded with a reflective smile. "She is a most highly spirited and fiercely independent woman, isn't she?" he asked, enthralled by the image Cooper's words brought to mind.

"That she is," Cooper replied, matching Lucien's appreciative fervor.

"In that regard," Lucien said, "I urge you to consider the possibility that Grace might decide her happiness wouldn't be well served by that adage."

Cooper nodded grudgingly, unable to deny that the outcome was, at least, uncertain. "Suffice to say, if she so decides, I'd have little choice than to be the one vanishin' into thin air, now, wouldn't I?"

Chapter Seventy

~

The next afternoon, camera bag over his shoulder, Cooper left the hotel on his bicycle, taking the same route out of St. Peter Port that he did the morning he had gone to St. Anne's School. With each rotation of the pedals his emotions alternated between excitement at the idea of finally reuniting with his beloved Grace and fear at the thought of being rejected by her.

About half an hour later, Cooper reached the point where the main road forked. Instead of continuing up the hill and down the other side to the school, he took the turnoff into a gravel-paved side road. It meandered through fields of wildflowers to the coastline where it ran atop the palisades that rose from the beaches below. A light haze drifted over the Channel, filtering the sunlight and, though the rain had stopped, the landscape was still saturated with water, infusing every flower and pebble and blade of grass with arresting brilliance.

In the distance, Cooper could see a long, narrow pier built atop a forest of pilings that grew out of the surf. Sheathed with wooden decking, it had waist-high railings, and was furnished with clusters of cast-iron benches. At the far end stood an airy, Victorian-era pavilion with a glass and steel roof. On weekends, it was crowded with fishermen, strollers and tourists taking the sun; but, on this midweek afternoon, a few seagulls seemed to be its only occupants.

Cooper coasted down the sweeping curve that led to the pier. The wind was brisk. The air was rich with the scent of brine. Seagulls were hovering and swooping in graceful arcs above the expanse of shimmering sea—much like the day, twenty years ago, Cooper and Grace had strolled the waterfront in Boston and realized they wanted to spend their lives together. *Aye, it's a good omen,* he thought as the bicycle rolled onto the pier and his eyes detected a figure inside the pavilion. It appeared to be a woman in a black cloak, but the glare coming off the water masked her identity.

Cooper dismounted and walked the bicycle toward her. She heard the *click-click-click* of the derailleur and turned to face him, filling Cooper with overwhelming joy. His beloved Grace had apparently come straight from teaching class, as Lucien said she would, because she was wearing leotards beneath her billowing academic gown, and her hair was swept up into a chignon, making her look haughty and unapproachable; but her expression seemed to soften with warmth as Cooper approached.

Indeed, with his ruddy complexion, wind-blown snarl of white curls and jut-jawed bearing, Grace thought he looked handsome, almost dashing; though, like Cooper, she could hardly breathe, let alone speak, and an awkward silence ensued as they stood, staring at each other as if at aliens.

"Look at you, Grace," Cooper finally said. He was all nerves, which made his throat dry, and it came out in a whispered rasp. "You haven't aged a day, lass. I've been dreamin' of this moment, of our . . . our reunion for so long, I . . . I can hardly believe we're actually standin' here, face-to-face after all this time."

"I was about to say the same, Mr. Cooper, as you might very well imagine," Grace said, finding her voice, which simmered with anger as she continued. "How?" she asked in a distraught moan. "How, Dylan Cooper, could you not have come for me sooner? Not contacted me sooner, for that matter!"

Cooper flinched at the onslaught and stammered, "But Grace . . . Grace . . . I did . . . I—"

"For so many years," Grace rushed on, "I grieved over losing you and the loss of our baby. Have you any idea what it was like? Any idea what I lived through? Lived through alone, mind you? I would have cried with joy to learn the army had made a mistake! I would have danced for days on end to have taken comfort in your arms!" She groaned, throwing up her hands at the futility of it, and turned back toward the railing.

"But not anymore," Cooper said, finishing the thought as he set the bicycle aside and joined her. "That's what you're saying, I'm afraid. Isn't it?"

"God knows there's still a part of me that wants to, Dylan," she said with a fiery glance. "But it's so much more difficult now. For the first time in years I'm finally feelin' secure, finally makin' a life for myself! Why couldn't you have come twenty years ago? Ten years ago! Five years ago!"

"I did, Grace," Cooper replied gently. "I came for you then, as I've come now. When I returned from the war to find you gone and Colin in your place, I booked passage as soon as he told me what happened; but when I got to Dumbarton, you weren't there, and your—"

"No, I wasn't," Grace retorted. "I was in Galloway. My parents sent me to an uncle's farm, thinking the peace and quiet would help me recuperate. All you had to do was ask them, and they'd have told you."

"Ask them!" Cooper exclaimed, bristling with incredulity. "I begged and pleaded with them; but your father turned me away! Not before equatin' me with the Devil and accusin' me of destroying you, of course. No, on the contrary, he did everything possible to keep us apart, Grace. You see, when

Colin warned him I was comin' for you, he—" Cooper paused, seeing Grace's reaction. "Aye. You didn't know that, did you? The real reason your father sent you off to that farm was to keep you from learnin' the truth—from finding out I was alive!'"

Grace looked stunned and took a moment to collect her thoughts. "But . . . but why? I don't deny my father had his faults—Lord knows, more than most—but he loved me in his way; and I've no doubt he knew learnin' the truth would have made me happy. Why wouldn't he tell me you were alive? That you had come for me? Why!"

"Because he cared more about his own happiness than yours, Grace," Cooper replied sharply. "Have you forgotten he so disapproved of your wantonness, of . . . of your traveling the world and your life on the stage, that he assigned Colin to be your minder! Needless to say, he disapproved mightily of me as well! There was no doubt of it when I finally met the man, I assure you." Cooper paused, giving her a moment to digest it, then concluded. "He wanted you back home, Grace. Wanted his daughter to know her place, to stand, dutifully, off to the side and two steps behind—and that's what he got, wasn't it?"

"No," Grace said, sounding trapped and defensive. "No, I lived my life, despite him, as I always had. Teaching was my way to continue dancing, to somehow satisfy him and myself at the same time. If his intention was to destroy me, he failed."

"But he succeeded in destroyin' *us,* Grace," Cooper retorted softly. "He turned the war's horrible mistake into a lie—a twenty-year lie that he used Colin to perpetuate. Aye, they conspired to keep the truth from you, Grace, because as long as you believed I'd been killed, your father could command your subservience."

Grace glared at him for a long moment, then nodded in concession. "Truth be told, my father was more than capable of it. It was my punishment for defying him, I imagine; but not Colin. No. No, I won't believe it of him," she declared, her eyes flaring in anger. "Despite his sanctimony and over-bearing ways, my brother cared about me . . . cared about my happiness. He would have told me the truth, Dylan. He would have! I know it!"

She turned away, collecting herself; then, raising her chin to the wind that was loosening long locks of hair from her chignon, and blowing her gown about her lithe figure, she turned back to Cooper and captured his eyes with her own. "I wasn't sure whether or not I could even see you, Dylan. I agreed only because my friend Lucien urged me to . . . im-plored me to, actually, because he was afraid I'd forever be wondering what would have happened if I hadn't, and—"

"Aye," Cooper interrupted. "I judged him a bright lad and, it seems, he proved me right. You can't embrace the fu-ture while denying the past, Grace. No, you have to face it straight on, I'm afraid."

Grace emitted an exasperated sigh. "Where might I have heard that before?" she wondered sarcastically. "No matter which way I turn, there seems to be a man waiting to dis-pense the same advice."

"The same *good* advice," Cooper countered. "Suffice to say, you'd be wise to take it to heart."

"Well, thanks to you, Mr. Cooper, I've had little choice in the matter!" Grace retorted. "*Suffice to say,* though your letter was terribly upsetting, this . . . this *reunion* as you call it, has been nothing less than unnerving. Not only have you tres-passed on my little island of tranquility, you've . . . you've dredged up all the pain and misery that I'd finally banished from my life and deposited them in the center of it!"

"I wasn't intendin' to hurt you, Grace," Cooper said, lower-ing his eyes in contrition. "And you know in your heart, I never would. No, lass, if there was any other way of revealin' the truth . . . of tryin' to . . . to reclaim the life we once had, I'd have found it, believe me."

Grace's eyes moistened with sadness. "That life is gone, Dylan. Gone long ago. And there's no reclaimin' it, I'm afraid," she said in a trembling whisper. "I'm sorry, but there's no more to be said on the matter. I think it's time for you to go back home. Please, just go and leave me here in my place. As well intended as I know you to be, I wish you'd never found it." She inhaled deeply, blinking back tears, then turned and began walking from the pavilion.

Chapter Seventy-One

As Cooper had feared, his beloved Grace had broken his heart and sent him reeling. His posture slackened as he watched her go. The color drained from his face. He felt hollow, as if the breath had been knocked out of him. It had taken decades to find her and now, within minutes, it had all come crashing down, and he had lost her again. He was about to mount his bicycle and pedal off in abject despair when he reflected on his meeting with Lucien the previous day, reflected on what he'd said to Lucien about Grace, and decided to try, try, and try even again, if need be.

"Grace? Grace, wait!" Cooper called out, leaving the bicycle behind as he hurried after her. She had emerged from the pavilion and was striding purposefully down the pier when he caught up, walking alongside her. "Grace, Grace, believe me, at this moment, I . . . I wish I'd never found it, either," Cooper said, his voice breaking with emotion. "I'm afraid it would've been far better to spend the rest of our lives embracin' the joyful memory of what we had, than the pain that seems to be comin' from my wantin' more, but you're—"

"Good," Grace interrupted. She stopped walking and turned to face him. "I'm glad you understand."

"Aye, but you're still my wife, Grace, my soul mate, the love of my life, and for all these years the flames have burned brightly in my heart," Cooper rushed on, trying to prevent her from taking flight again. "Lord knows, the sight of you has only served to fan, not dampen them. I've waited so long and come so far, and there's so much more I want to tell you. I'm begging you, lass, please, please don't turn me away before hearin' me out. Don't let the torment of this moment be what we remember for what's left of our lives. Not after all we've been through."

Grace's lips tightened into a thin line. Her eyes narrowed, staring him down as she folded her arms across her chest as if making a decision; then, as if a switch had been thrown, the emotional dam she had constructed cracked. She shuddered and burst into tears, clearly moved by Cooper's presence and plea. "I'm . . . I'm sorry if I hurt you, Dylan . . ." she said haltingly, ". . . truly sorry; but . . . but this has been too painful to endure, I'm afraid . . . too . . . too painful and frightening."

Thanks be to God, Cooper thought. He desperately wanted to take Grace in his arms and comfort her but thought the better of pressing his advantage, and guided her to one of the benches instead. The wind had all but unknotted her chignon, and her hair tumbled about her face, making her look waiflike and vulnerable.

Grace wiped the tears from her cheeks and took a few moments to compose herself, then looked up at Cooper, who was leaning against the rail opposite her. "So," she began, as if trying to get things straight in her mind. "You came for me, only to be turned away by my father; then . . . then searched the whole of the Highlands to no avail, and returned to Newbury broken-hearted and alone. Two decades later, you tracked me down, and wrote me the letter I received on Saturday, and here we are . . ." She paused, a question forming in her eyes as Cooper nodded curiously, wondering what the point of it might be. "There's just one thing I don't understand," Grace resumed, cocking her head to one side and wincing as if she had tried and failed to answer it herself. "Why didn't you send the letter twenty years ago?"

"Oh, you poor child," Cooper said with a dismayed sigh. He settled on the bench next to her, his eyes moist with empathy. "You've no idea, do you?"

"No idea of what?"

"Not only had I come for you, lass, I'd written more letters than you have years," Cooper replied, touched by her innocence. "I wrote you a letter the day I returned to Newbury. Indeed, I wrote one every week—every *day,* sometimes— and on holidays and birthdays, and . . . and sunny days and rainy days; but I had no address for you, Grace. And, since sending them in care of your father would've been the same as not sendin' them at all, I sent them in care of Colin."

Grace's eyes seemed to be widening in shock with every phrase, and now they were darting about in confusion. "But . . . But I never got any of them—not even one."

"Aye, I'm afraid not," Cooper replied. "Though Colin and I had made our peace, it was an uneasy one, as you know; and, it seems, I was a fool to have counted on him. But when I returned from the war, we became tightly bound by what had happened to you and . . . and the baby." Cooper emitted an anguished sigh. "He was as crushed by the tragedy as I. Truth be told, we were like brothers, comforting each other. So, once he returned to Dumbarton, I had every reason to believe he would forward my letters—but he didn't."

"Why not?" Grace challenged, sounding indignant. "Why wouldn't he?"

"Suffice to say, your father demanded it," Cooper replied, his burr rolling like thunder. "Time and again, he forced Colin to choose between being a good brother and a good son— and each time Colin chose the latter. Aye, he retained all my letters, keepin' the truth from you." Cooper's eyes softened with compassion as he added, "Don't judge him too harshly, lass. He's a tormented soul who couldn't help himself; but he cares about you deeply . . . very deeply; and, despite my anger, I'm afraid he's to be pitied rather than condemned."

"But you *are* condemning him—with innuendo and unsubstantiated accusations," Grace retorted as she sprung to her feet, bristling with renewed energy. "I can't believe Colin would do such a thing."

"He didn't think you would, Grace," Cooper said, taking the camera bag from his shoulder. He set it on the bench next to him, then threw back the flap and removed the letters Colin had given him. "That's why he gave me these."

"You saw him?" Grace asked, surprised, staring with disbelieving eyes at the thick stack of envelopes that was bound tightly with twine.

"Aye, but a week ago." Cooper replied, "They're all here, Grace. Every last one, along with birthday cards, Christmas cards, telegrams, and—"

"Enough," Grace moaned. She whirled to the railing and, head thrown back in anguish, drank in the sea air in an effort to comprehend it. "It's . . . it's evil," she exclaimed, turning back to Cooper. "Evil and . . . and . . . unconscionable!"

"Aye," Cooper replied, getting to his feet and joining her. "Their entire scheme would've come undone if you'd received even one. They had complete control . . . *almost,* any way. There was just one thing that worried them."

The pain in Grace's eyes turned to intrigue. "And what was that, pray tell?"

"Well," Cooper replied, unable to suppress a thin smile of satisfaction, "the unintended consequence of concealing the truth was that you went on believing you were a widow, wasn't it?"

Grace was stunned to silence. The implication was painfully clear and, through trembling lips she finally whispered, "A widow who could . . . could . . . remarry."

Cooper nodded smartly. "Now we're getting to work on the crust of the bread, aren't we? For two long decades they were haunted by the spectre of it. Fearin' you'd commit not only the crime, but also, as Colin, exalted deacon of Strathclyde Presbyterian Church, explained, the *sin* of bigamy as well."

"Oh, dear Lord," Grace sighed, awestruck. "That . . . that had never occurred to me, I'm afraid."

"Aye, and with good reason, Grace. Widows may have concerns when it comes to remarryin', but committin' bigamy isn't one of them," Cooper said wryly, sensing he'd finally reached her. "Our old friend, Doubtin' Colin, also admitted to interferin' in your personal affairs, to forcin' suitors to curtail their pursuit." He allowed himself a mischievous grin, and added, "I should thank him for the favor, I suppose."

Grace had looked dismayed, then enlightened and finally amused as Cooper spoke. "I sometimes wondered what I had said or done to offend this lad or that," she said, forcing a laugh. "After a while, I sensed it might've been Colin's hand at work, but I didn't attach any special significance to it because he never thought anyone worthy of me, anyway."

"Yours truly included," Cooper said with a self-deprecating chuckle. "But thanks be to God, Grace, you trusted your heart and decided otherwise. I'm hopin' and prayin' you'll do the same again . . ."

Grace sighed and lowered her eyes momentarily. "I wish it were that simple, Dylan," she said, moved by the honesty and undying love she saw in his.

"Dr. Devereaux, I presume," Cooper said with a nervous smile. "You referred to him before as your friend, as did he; but I've a feelin' *close* friend would, at the least, be more accurate, wouldn't it?"

Grace responded with a demure nod.

"Aye," Cooper said resignedly. "He spoke of strong feelings. An *affaire de coeur,* I believe he called it. Tell me, Grace, might it be even more than that?"

"If you're referring to intimacy, the answer is no," Grace replied, her eyes leaving no doubt of it. "Though I've been expecting it would happen in its time. In truth, there's a certain . . . certain *spark* between us that I can't deny; and we've come to realize we've much in common including the loss of a spouse—or so I thought, until your letter arrived."

"Aye, he spoke of personal tragedy."

"Yes, Lucien's wife passed away several years ago. He was so distraught, so unable to cope, he thought it best for his daughter to be away, and enrolled her in St. Anne's. Sometimes, Christiane would go home during hiatus and on weekends; but, now that the war has spread to France, Lucien's been coming here instead."

Cooper looked relieved. "So it's a fairly recent, dare I say, infatuation, then?"

Grace responded with a rueful smile and shook her head no. "We met a little over a year ago, I'm afraid."

"I see . . ." Cooper mused unhappily.

"He'd come to attend the dance recital, as he did now," Grace explained matter-of-factly. "Gradually, his visits became more frequent. We were planning to spend the summer in Provence with Christiane . . ." She sighed and shrugged with uncertainty.

"As you might imagine, Grace, I've been plannin' to spend the summer with you, too . . ." Cooper said with a hopeful smile, ". . . back home in our cottage in Newbury. Many people there are anxious to see you. You remember Pastor Martin?"

Grace's eyes clouded with sadness. "Of course I do, Dylan," she said, her lips trembling. "He held a service when I . . . I lost the baby, and prayed with me to thank the Lord for taking him to Heaven."

Cooper eyes welled with remorse. "I'm so sorry, Grace.

I . . . I was thinkin' of the day . . . the day the good pastor married us."

Grace nodded, biting a lip to maintain her composure. "It's all right. I'm fine. I remember that day, too . . . the happiest of my life."

"And mine as well," Cooper said, sounding wistful. "I was about to say, Pastor Martin is ready, willin' and able to marry us again. With a wee bit of luck, we'd be returnin' just in time for our anniversary."

Grace's expression brightened. "It would be our twenty-second, wouldn't it?"

"Aye, lass, at which time I was thinkin' we'd celebrate with the proper ceremony and reception that had been denied us so long ago."

Grace sighed at the mention of it, which opened a floodgate of memories that stirred her heart. Her eyes welled over, sending tears streaming down her cheeks. "Oh, Dylan," she wailed, leaning against him in search of comfort. "I'm so sorry . . . so, so sorry . . ."

"For what, lass?" Cooper asked, not hesitating to embrace her this time. A surge of joy went coursing through him as she buried her face in the curve of his neck. He stood there enfolding her in his arms, her willowy body pressing against his, her sweet fragrance, the memory of which he'd savored all these years, filling his head. "None of this is your doin', now, is it? No, lass, no . . ." he said in as soothing a tone as his smoke-and-whiskey-coarsened voice could manage.

"I . . . I just feel so overcome with sadness," Grace said with a weary sigh. "So . . . so remorseful for being angry, for doubting you, for . . . for not being able to just take up where we left off." She drifted off in reflection then looked up at him. "How many times I've thought of that day . . . of standing outside the gallery and waving as the trolley took you away from me . . . watching long after it was out of sight, and wondering if I'd ever see you again."

Then, her eyes clouding at a thought, she leaned away and gently disengaged from his embrace. "But . . . but I've a terrible dilemma, I'm afraid. My emotions are all topsy-turvy. My heart has no . . . no certainty," she rushed on, wrestling with the conflict. "As you were saying before, you've come so far, and been waiting so long that it's hard for me to . . . to . . ." She paused, groping for the right words. "I mean, it's not a'tall fair to be asking this of you, Dylan, but please be patient with me. I need some time to make sense of my feelings, and know, beyond any doubt, where I belong."

Cooper took a deep breath, then nodded and smiled with understanding. "You remember the day in Boston we were walkin' along the harbor, and I started goin' on about spending the night together?"

Grace smiled alluringly. "Indeed, as I recall, I rather cleverly managed to both postpone and intensify your ardor by promising you that good things come to those who wait."

"Aye, and indeed, they did," Cooper conceded with a reflective smile. "So, why wouldn't I do the same now?"

Grace sighed with relief and thanked him with a smile.

"Do you recall my reply as well?" Cooper prompted.

"I certainly do, Mr. Cooper," Grace replied smartly. "You looked deeply into my eyes, so deeply that I felt you were seeing into my soul, and said, 'I'd wait a lifetime for you, Grace . . .'"

"Precisely," Cooper declared, caught up in the reverie. "And as you can plainly see I meant every word of it, didn't I?"

Grace lowered her eyes demurely, and nodded. "I recall saying the same, Dylan."

"And I've always believed it, but history seems to be repeatin' itself; and, once again, thanks to Whitehall, who've announced they'll not be defendin' the islands against German attack, we've little time, I'm afraid."

Grace nodded matter-of-factly. "So I've heard; but I've also heard they so decided because the islands are of no strategic importance, and *won't* be attacked."

"Aye, but some of the lads doin' the decidin' are from the same bunch who decided Hitler's appetite for conquest could be satisfied by allowin' him to nibble on Eastern Europe. Keeping that in mind, lass, it'd be best not to take too long resolvin' your feelings. Otherwise, whatever you decide, the happy couple might never make it off the island— whether the coast of New England or the coast of Brittany be their destination."

Grace smiled at the deftness of his metaphor. "Yes, Lucien's under enormous pressure to get back home, too."

"Aye, I'm hopin' you'll forgive me for creatin' this dilemma. I'm also hopin' these will prompt you to resolve it in my favor," Cooper said, handing her the stack of his letters. "Better late than never," he quipped. As Grace took them, he reached into his camera bag and presented her with a copy of his book: *The Christmas Pictures*. "If they don't, perhaps this will."

Grace hugged it and the letters to her chest as her students did their schoolbooks, and thanked him with a smile; then, eyes welling, she did a little ballet-like turn, and hurried down the pier.

It was an emotionally charged moment for both of them, especially for Cooper, who wanted to run after her and steal her away before she decided in his rival's favor. Instead, he remained where he stood, drinking in the sight of her through eyes brimming with tears. When Grace reached the end of the pier, he slung the camera bag over his shoulder, intending to return to the pavilion and retrieve his bicycle, but a flicker of sunlight, reflecting off the windshield of a vehicle racing atop the palisades, caught his eye, stopping him.

Cooper sagged as the black Citroën emerged from behind the tall grasses along the roadway, which had obscured it. Lucien greeted Grace with a little wave as he pulled to a stop in front of the pier where she was waiting. Grace opened the door and got in beside him.

Cooper stood there crestfallen as the car drove off. His long-sought-after reunion with his beloved Grace had left him with misty eyes and a growing emptiness. The possibility that he might never see her again, that *he,* not Lucien, might be the one to be disappearing into thin air, loomed ever greater and plunged him to the depths of despair.

Chapter Seventy-Two

During the drive back to St. Anne's School, Lucien was more than curious about Grace's meeting with Cooper; but she was too emotionally drained to discuss it, and had him drop her off at the faculty residence hall. She spent the evening in her quarters with Cooper's letters, reading late into the night. By the time she finished, scores of envelopes and countless pages—covered in Cooper's energetic hand—were spread across her desk, sofa and bed covering.

More than once, Grace had been moved to tears by Cooper's declarations of love, by his outpouring of emotion, by his imploring her to respond, by his pleas for news of her whereabouts and by how desperately he missed her; and, every so often, moved to admiration by his acute observations, and to hearty laughter by his wry sense of humor. She was also deeply touched by Cooper's book, with its moving and heartwarming images of New England's people and places—images of Cooper's rambling cottage blanketed in snow, of children skating on a frozen pond, of a youthful and radiant Grace bundled against the cold, of the Newbury Community Church glistening in an icy rain, of immigrants arriving at a bone-chilling Boston train station, and of the young woman cradling her infant, the photograph that became the first Christmas picture among them. Along with Cooper's letters they triggered a surge of nostalgia that powerfully stirred Grace's heart but, to her dismay, only intensified rather than resolved her conflict.

For the next few days, Grace lived with the troubling uncertainty while dealing with the demanding schedule of exam week, which included grading dozens of papers on the History of Dance, which she also taught.

Thursday, June 27, was the last day of classes, and marked semester end. Friday was designated as packing day for the students who would be moving out of their dormitory rooms over the weekend.

On Thursday Grace was up half the night wrestling with her dilemma. At sunrise the only decision she had made was to seek independent counsel. She knew just the person who could provide it; but it meant going to St. Peter Port. Lucien would be arriving shortly to help Christiane pack her belongings prior to taking her back to Brittany on the car ferry Saturday morning; and he would have gladly given Grace a lift into town had she asked. But she preferred to keep this to herself and decided on public transportation instead.

One of the city's bus lines circled the island hourly, stopping wherever and whenever someone flagged it down. Grace dashed from her flat, hurrying across the square and down one of the narrow streets to the main road, arriving just as the bus was approaching.

About forty-five minutes later, the lipstick-red coach had reached the heart of St. Peter Port. As it turned south on High Street, Grace was surprised to see long queues of residents outside the banks, which had yet to open. Apparently, the recent fall of France and presence of German troops on the coast of Normandy had prompted anxious residents to withdraw their savings in case evacuation to the British mainland became necessary.

Indeed, moments earlier, as the bus came down the Esplanade past the harbor, it seemed many had already decided to do so, and had gathered on the long wharf where crush barriers had been erected to control the flow of evacuees to the ferry terminal. At an adjacent pier, the *Antwerp,* one of several ships dispatched by Whitehall, was taking on hundreds of children, who were being sent to live with relatives on the mainland.

The bus deposited Grace at the southernmost end of High Street directly opposite the carved wooden doors of a medieval stone church that had stood on that spot for nearly nine hundred years. Town Church, as it had been called since being rebuilt in the 15th century, was one of the city's oldest structures. Grace often attended Sunday services there, and had become active in organizing cultural and theatrical events.

Each morning at this hour, the long shadow of its steeple fell across the church's beautifully landscaped gardens; and as Grace approached, it seemed to be pointing the way to Pastor Highsmith, who was bent over a gnarled rosebush that he was pruning.

"Grace!" he exclaimed when he saw her on the garden's winding path. He had a friendly, friarlike demeanor and expressive eyes that made his thick brows twitch as he spoke. "I hope you've brought your shears along, this garden is getting the better of me."

"I've brought you a dilemma instead," Grace said. "It's a horribly tangled matter of the heart that has me in shreds. I was hoping we could have a word."

"Of course," the pastor said as he snipped a withered branch. "You fancy a cup of tea?"

"That would be lovely, Pastor Highsmith," Grace replied,

trying to sound appreciative. "But today is semester end. I shouldn't even be here, let alone—"

"Well, you *are*," the pastor said decisively. "And since it's just brewing . . ." He turned, preempting her protest, and began walking toward a stone patio where a wrought iron table and chairs stood beneath a wisteria-covered trellis. Grace took a seat as the pastor went inside to the parsonage's kitchen.

Moments later, he returned with a tray that held a lovely tea service. "When it comes to unraveling tangles, I've found that pulling on the wrong thread can tighten it into knots," Pastor Highsmith said, filling two cups with steaming tea. "No, it's best to study its twists and turns to see how they came about before trying to undo them. So, why don't you start from the beginning?"

"It's a long story, I'm afraid," Grace replied, pausing to take a swallow of tea before explaining its genesis in Boston, twenty years ago; its zenith with Cooper's purchase of the cottage and their marriage in Newbury; its tragic end with Cooper's mistaken death notice and her loss of their baby; and its recent and shocking resumption with Cooper's arrival on Guernsey just as she was considering a new life with Lucien.

"A dilemma, indeed," Pastor Highsmith mused while stirring sugar into his tea. "Discovering the truth, the ugly truth, unfortunately, doesn't make resolving your emotional conflict any easier, does it?"

Grace shook her head in dismay. "No, learning it has been quite painful; and deciding what to do about it even more so."

"Well, regarding the latter, like Solomon, I could decree that you're to be split in two and see which of these gentlemen pleads for your life," the pastor joked with a mischievous twinkle. "But since you're not trying to discern which of them *truly* loves you . . ." He trailed off and sipped his tea, entertaining a thought. "You said you and your husband married just before he went off to war . . ."

"Yes, we were forced to advance the wedding date," Grace said curiously. "Even then, we had but a few days together for a honeymoon. Why?"

"Well, sometimes the nastiest tangle can be easily undone by pulling on just the right thread," he said, sounding sagacious. "The trick is finding it. Though, thanks to the Almighty's infinite wisdom, the one we're looking for seems to be in plain sight."

"Thanks be to God, indeed," Grace said, unable to conceal that she'd drawn a complete blank. "In plain sight or no, I'm afraid, I'm blind to it."

"Perhaps, if I point you in the right direction . . ." the pastor offered, leaning back in his chair. "Does Matthew, Chapter 19, verse 6, ring a bell?"

Grace winced, then reddened with embarrassment. "No, I'm stone deaf as well, I'm afraid."

The pastor smiled as if tolerating the ignorance of a favorite child. "'What therefore God hath joined together, let not man put asunder,'" he said, reciting it gently. "I'm sure you recall it now."

Grace nodded contritely, toying with her teacup.

"You see, Grace," the pastor concluded, "despite your abbreviated honeymoon and the long interlude which followed, in God's eyes, you're still married."

"Yes, and in my husband's as well," Grace said with a reflective sigh. "Truth be told, I loved him once. Madly, and with every fiber of my being. I wanted nothing more than to spend every minute of my life with him." She paused, her brow knitting in frustration. "But I've spent decades recovering from devastating tragedy—not one, but two, mind you; and now that I've finally managed it, he's brought all the painful memories back."

The pastor's brows arched with understanding. "Which has made you angry and resentful . . ."

"Yes, I've been quite cross," Grace said with a forthright nod. "Is that so wrong?"

"Not at all. It's only human to have such feelings, Grace; and quite healthy to express them," the pastor replied. He drained his cup and set it back in its saucer. "Of course, it's not the best state of mind to be in when making such decisions, is it? Perhaps, it would help if you accepted this latest turn of events as part of God's plan for you."

"Which plan?" Grace asked, looking puzzled. "The old one or the new one?"

"Ah," the pastor said, sounding as if he'd had an insight. "His old plan or His new plan . . . I see. And the latter involves this chap Lucien you mentioned."

"Precisely," Grace said crisply. She lifted the teapot and went about refilling their cups. "But as soon as I was about to embrace it, He . . . he switched back to the old one." The anger rose within her, and she set the teapot back onto the table harder than she intended. "It's confusing and unfair!"

Pastor Highsmith flinched at her outburst, then his eyes hardened and he leaned across the table toward her. "I doubt the good Lord engages in sleight of hand when drawing up His plans for us, Grace," he scolded forcefully. "I strongly suggest that instead of separating the events in your life into His old plan and His new plan, you think of them as all part of His *original* plan. He *does* often work in mysterious ways, you know?"

"So I'm learning, Pastor Highsmith," Grace said with a humbled expression.

"That's why you must trust in Him to show you the way Grace, and not allow your anger to—"

The remainder of Pastor Highsmith's sentence was obliterated by the sudden scream of German warplanes that had come in low across the channel from France. The roar of their engines thundered overhead, pounding the earth with turbulence that rattled the parsonage's windows and set the teacups to dancing in their saucers.

The lead plane had flown directly over the church at such a low altitude that it would have clipped the steeple had it been but a meter or two taller. It was one of at least a dozen Me-109 fighters that were in escort of a squadron of Stuka dive-bombers. Along with machine guns, cannon and racks of bombs beneath their bellies, each plane brandished the bold Luftwaffe cross on its fuselage and wings, and the chilling Nazi swastika on its tail.

Flying at attack speed in the direction of St. Peter Port's harbor, the planes were almost out of sight by the time Grace and Pastor Highsmith had leapt to their feet in reaction. They were still frozen in place, their eyes wide with shock and surprise, when the distant chatter of machine-gun fire erupted and the whistle of falling bombs ended with the whomp of massive explosions that stirred the air.

Chapter Seventy-Three

A short distance away, at the Royal Hotel, the dining room was in the midst of breakfast service when the entire building shook violently as if an earthquake had struck the island.

Cooper was at a table by himself, enjoying his favorite breakfast—a pot of tea and a basket of fresh scones and Devonshire cream—when the shock wave from the bombs set the chandeliers to swaying. Seconds later, it was followed by another and then another that toppled glasses and flower-filled vases, and intensified the screams of panic-stricken guests and hotel personnel, who were diving beneath tables and dashing about in search of safety.

The explosions went on for what seemed like an eternity, though barely five minutes elapsed from first to last. It was followed by a tense silence that, as if on cue, was suddenly broken by the sounds of tumbling furniture as the people who had taken cover behind and beneath them began getting to their feet; and by their loudly voiced condemnations of: "Those fools in Whitehall!" and "Those rotten Jerries!"

Cooper and several of the other guests left the dining room and hurried outside to investigate. "The harbor!" someone shouted at the sight of smoke rising from the waterfront. "They've bombed the harbor!" They were standing on St. Julian's Avenue in front of the hotel when several German fighters that had circled over the channel came flying back across the city, strafing the harbor with their machine guns.

It had been more than twenty years since Cooper had heard their jarring chatter; since he'd hunched, terrified, in the open cockpit of a Breguet-Bristol biplane and set aside his camera to fire its machine gun at an attacking Fokker. The sound of it raised his pores and set his stomach to churning; as did the deafening shriek of sirens and clang of bells echoing in St. Peter Port's narrow streets as Cooper joined a group of men running down the avenue, which curved around the north end, leading directly to the long wharf and ferry terminals.

They arrived to find the pier awash in flames and littered with the bloodied bodies of the wounded and dead. People were running through the choking smoke in every direction. Emergency vehicles were converging on the scene and driving down the long wharf amidst the chaos. Firemen were working frantically to hook up hoses and battle blazing infernos that seemed to be raging everywhere. Police officers were searching for victims trapped in the wreckage. Medical personnel were moving swiftly among the casualties, leaving the dead where they lay and tending to the wounded.

At the time of the attack, along with the residents being evacuated by ferry, and the children disembarking on the *Antwerp,* several dozen farmers, delivering their crates of produce for transport to the mainland, had queued their lorries along one side of the long wharf. When the machine-gun fire erupted, many of the evacuees had taken cover under the vehicles and were now crawling out from their hiding places beneath them.

A screaming child with her clothing afire emerged from beneath one of the lorries. It had been stitched by bullets that punctured its gasoline tank, spraying her dress with fuel. Panic-stricken, she got to her feet and began running down the long wharf, unintentionally fanning the flames that threatened to engulf her. She nearly collided with Cooper who, along with the other men from the hotel, were hurrying onto the long wharf.

As the little girl ran past, Cooper scooped her into his arms and swiftly placed her on the ground, smothering the flames with his jacket; then, cradling the child to his chest, he ran toward a triage area that had been set up within a circle of ambulances. Medical personnel were working at a frenzied pace to stabilize the overwhelming number of casualties.

As Cooper approached, the traumatized child suddenly began screaming "Mummy! Mummy! I want my mummy!"

Nearby, Pastor Highsmith—who had wasted no time driving the short distance down the Esplanade from Town Church— was ministering to the victims in the triage area, and heard the child's screams. He turned in reaction, revealing Grace, crouching behind him. She was holding a compress, now bloodied, to the chest of a badly injured victim while a medic prepared a proper bandage.

Cooper stopped in his tracks. "Grace!" he called out, his voice ringing with concern over the cries of the terrified child he was carrying. "Grace, are you all right?"

Grace whirled at the sound of his voice. The sight of Cooper, holding the crying child, propelled her to her feet. Her hands, face and clothing were spattered with crimson grime and her eyes were wide with concern; but no words were necessary. Her reaction was all the reply Cooper needed. Nor were there any need for words now, as Grace held out her arms, prompting him to place the terrified child into them. The little girl nestled her head on Grace's shoulder and curled up against her, seemingly reassured by her embrace. Cooper hurried off and fetched a blanket. They wrapped it about the frightened child and carried her to the triage area, remaining at her side until Pastor Highsmith arrived with a medic, who began ministering to her.

Cooper and Grace were hurrying off in search of other victims who might be in need of assistance when two German warplanes came screaming across the harbor. Everyone who was capable of movement, including police, fire, and medical personnel ran for cover, expecting that the planes would strafe the long wharf with bursts of machine-gun fire before dropping more bombs as they had done previously.

All in one motion, Cooper lunged toward Grace, wrapped his arms about her torso and swept her to safety behind a pallet of shipping crates, shielding her with his body. She burrowed into him and covered her ears in anticipation of the deafening racket that was about to erupt. They clung to each other like frightened children, wincing, waiting, the suspense building; but to their relief, they soon realized that, instead of bombs, these planes were dropping leaflets, thousands of them, that came floating down over the harbor and the center of the city like massive flakes of snow. Cooper snatched one out of the air as he and Grace came out from behind the packing crates. In bold, bulletin-style typography, the leaflet declared:

ORDERS OF THE COMMANDANT
OF THE GERMAN FORCES IN OCCUPATION OF
THE ISLAND OF GUERNSEY

1. The island will be occupied by troops of the German Reich and governed by its Military Authority.
2. All orders given by the Military Authority are to be strictly obeyed.
3. Residents will be treated with respect provided they do not resist, cause trouble, or break the curfew, which will be in force between the hours of 11 PM and 6 AM.

4. All rifles, pistols, sporting guns, ammunition, daggers and other weapons must be surrendered.
5. The use of boats and motor vehicles of any description for personal use is prohibited.
6. British military personnel must report to the Military Authority for processing to POW camps.
7. Citizens of nations at war with Germany, other than Great Britain, will be deported to detention centers in Germany where they will be processed.
8. All non-resident British civilians and all citizens of nations not at war with Germany will be evacuated to the British mainland.
9. Passports will be required to establish all claims of national identity and residency.
10. Banks, shops and houses of worship will be open as usual.

Cooper and Grace were staring wide-eyed at the leaflet when another victim, his clothing soaked with blood, came limping toward them. They hurried to the man's side, taking hold of him just as he was about to collapse; then, without a word between them, they swung his arms over their shoulders and carried him until they came upon an empty stretcher. After placing the wounded man on it, Grace lifted one end and Cooper the other.

"What are you doing here, lass?" Cooper finally asked as they carried the stretcher toward the triage area. "I thought you'd be at the school."

"I came into town to . . . to work on the cultural program at my church," Grace replied, deciding to keep the real reason to herself. "It's just down the road. The pastor and I heard the explosions and . . ." She sighed, suggesting the rest was obvious.

"Aye," Cooper grunted as they set the stretcher next to one of the ambulances. "I was in the midst of a lovely breakfast."

For the next several hours, they continued to help stabilize the injured, comfort those in pain, carry stretchers to the triage area and ambulances, and console the grief-stricken families of victims. Throughout the gruesome task—rife with human suffering, emotionally draining stress and the frightening reality of war—Cooper and Grace had worked together like a well-practiced team, requiring only looks rather than words to communicate. It was as if each knew what the other was thinking, or was about to do; as if, after all these years, they had, somehow, just clicked.

Now, on the verge of exhaustion, they stood on the charred, bullet-pocked long wharf, cooled by the breezes that came off the sea, leaning on each other for support, their faces glistening with sweat and dotted with grime, their clothes stained crimson—their eyes aglow with mutual admiration one minute . . . clouded with uncertainty and unspoken questions about what the future might hold for them the next.

Chapter Seventy-Four

When the remains of the deceased had been removed and all the wounded had been treated or hospitalized, the long wharf was left to police, fire and clean-up crews. Brigadier Ambrose Shaw, Guernsey's administrator, who had spent hours at the scene overseeing the operation, announced that there would be a meeting within the hour at Town Church.

Cooper and Grace joined the overflow crowd of residents that assembled. All were shaken and fatigued. Many were bloodied and bandaged.

Pastor Highsmith stood in the 12th-century pulpit—all that remained of the original wooden structure—and in a comforting but authoritative voice, said, "This has been a painful day for us all; and we undoubtedly face many more such days ahead; but, in the end, with our faith in Jesus Christ, we will survive this malicious act and frightful occupation, and freedom will prevail. I have been in touch with clergymen from all the other churches on Guernsey, and am pleased to report that they, along with those on our sister islands, have voted, unanimously, to remain in their pulpits to serve the vast majority of Channel Islanders who have chosen not to evacuate." The pastor finished with a prayer, then gave the floor to Brigadier Shaw.

"I've just received a cable from Whitehall," the brigadier began, holding it aloft. A country gentleman in houndstooth tweeds and ascot, and a waxed moustache that turned up on the ends, befitting his rank, he had a commanding presence. "Immediately following the attack on our island, a protest was lodged with the German government, deploring the slaughter of civilians and innocent children. Furthermore, to Whitehall's surprise, an immediate expiatory and explicative reply was received. In a nutshell, the enemy had identified the crates of farm produce on the lorries as boxes of munitions, causing our long wharf to be designated a legitimate military target in error. Evidently, they either did not know, or did not believe that the islands had been demilitarized." He paused, shuffling through the pages he was holding, and found the one he wanted.

"Just prior to coming here," the brigadier resumed, "I received a call from the airport. Apparently, two German military transports have landed, carrying the commandant of the Military Authority and members of his staff. So, I urge all residents to become familiar with these leaflets that, along with the bombs, rained down upon us today." He went on to review the ten-point directive, noted its reasoned tone, cautioned against panic and—since the islands had indeed been demilitarized—advised compliance.

After announcing that some ferry terminals and boat slips were still in working order, he urged residents to remain rather than evacuate, and to continue working at their jobs and operating their businesses.

Grace had looked preoccupied throughout, and when Brigadier Shaw opened the meeting up to questions, she took Cooper aside. "I can't stay any longer," she said, sounding frantic as she hurried from the church with Cooper in pursuit. "Lucien and Christiane must be beside themselves with worry by now. They'll never get home once the Germans arrive."

"Aye," Cooper grunted, following her into the churchyard. The day had taken its toll and his breaths were coming in short, tight puffs as he hurried to catch up. "Accordin' to the directive, if captured here they'll be sent to detention camps for processin'."

"Whatever that means," Grace said, hugging herself as if chilled at the thought. She sensed Cooper's distress and stopped walking amidst the garden's colorful flora. "Dylan, are you all right?"

"I'm fine," Cooper replied, making light of it. "Nothing that heartier pipe tobacco and a week or two in the darkroom wouldn't cure. You'd best stick to worryin' about your friend Lucien and his daughter."

Grace nodded. "I have to get back to them," she said, her voice breaking with concern. "Lucien said they're planning to leave in the morning, and . . ."

"As am I," Cooper interrupted. "I imagine you'll be doing the same as well—with one of us or the other."

Grace emitted a distraught sigh, clearly torn by conflicting emotions. "Oh, Dylan . . . I'm sorry . . . I . . ."

"It's all right, lass," Cooper said, absolving her with a smile. "If your heart's with him, so be it. You've a right to be happy after all your sufferin'. Besides, I'm almost sixty-three. How much time have I left?"

"Oh, don't say that, Dylan . . ."

"If truth ever be told, now's the time, lass," Cooper said with a heavy heart. "He's of your age, Grace, and you'll have many more years with him than you'll ever have with me."

Grace's eyes clouded with sadness and filled with tears. She lunged into his arms in search of comfort, hugging him tightly as if not wanting to let him go. Despite her ambivalence, there was an air of finality about it, Cooper thought as he embraced her. It pained him terribly to acknowledge it, but it was almost as if she knew they would never see each other again.

Grace slipped from his arms and ran off across the churchyard. Cooper impulsively pulled the Leica from his camera bag and called out. "Grace!"

She pirouetted about in reaction, her chin raised, her arms gracefully extended, her crimson-stained dress flaring up around her torso, looking like an angel of mercy about to take flight. Cooper fired the shutter, capturing this last moment with his beloved Grace for all eternity. Her momentum carried her around in the direction she'd been hurrying and, with a few quick steps, she was gone.

Chapter Seventy-Five

Darkness was falling by the time the bus from St. Peter Port came down the hill toward St. Anne's School. It creaked to a stop and deposited Grace on the main road at the same intersection where she had boarded that morning. Despite Pastor Highsmith's counsel, her determination to resolve her emotional dilemma had been both eclipsed by the harsh reality of war that had erupted on her doorstep and revived by the impending occupation that intensified the pressure to make a decision. She spent the time on the bus reflecting on the pastor's advice and praying for divine guidance.

The grounds were bustling with semester-end activity and news of the attack as Grace hurried between the buildings to the dimly illuminated square. Students, parents and faculty members were scurrying back and forth from dormitory buildings with footlockers, suitcases, duffel bags and boxes of belongings, which they were loading into the trunks of cars, the cargo holds of lorries, and even onto the luggage racks of bicycles and motor scooters. Though this was packing day, and the premises were traditionally vacated the next, everyone seemed in a frenzy to depart before the Germans arrived and enforced the rules of occupation.

Grace spotted Lucien's Citroën among the vehicles in the square, and emitted a relieved sigh at the sight of him loading Christiane's belongings into it.

"Grace! Where have you been?" Lucien scolded when he saw her approaching. "We've been beset with worry. We spent half the day looking about the school for you."

"I'm sorry," Grace said with a contrite sigh. "I'm afraid I was in town when the harbor was attacked, and—" She splayed her hands, gesturing to her clothing that was soiled with crimson grime. "There were so many casualties . . . I . . . I had no choice but to remain—"

"Madame Cooper!" Christiane exclaimed, running toward them with a box of schoolbooks. She handed it to her father, then recoiled at Grace's disheveled appearance. "Are you all right?"

"Yes, I'm fine," Grace replied. She removed a copy of the ten-point directive from her purse and handed it to Lucien. "I've been worried about you, too. Have you seen this?"

Lucien nodded grimly. "Yes, everyone who'd been in town returned with one, and with news of the attack, of course. The BBC has been broadcasting reports throughout the day."

"There are also reports that the German commandant and his staff have arrived on the island," Grace said, her voice taking on a desperate timbre. "You and Christiane must leave as soon as possible."

"Mais oui," Lucien said, resolutely. "We've already had a change of plans. A car ferry for Brittany is departing later this evening. I was able to secure passage for us—"

"Oh, thanks be to God!" Grace exclaimed.

". . . For the three of us," Lucien went on, arching a brow in anticipation of her reaction.

Grace seemed a little taken aback. "I haven't even started to pack," she said, sounding overwhelmed.

"The ferry doesn't depart for several hours," Lucien explained. "There is plenty of time."

"Several hours?" Grace echoed wearily. "It'll take me half the night, and I'll be lucky if that."

"We'll help you," Christiane offered with teenage enthusiasm. "The three of us—how do you say—can make short work of it. *Non?*"

"*Non.* You go on ahead," Grace said decisively. "We can't be taking any chances you'll miss the ferry. I'll . . . I'll come soon as I can. Don't worry, I'll . . ." She saw the look in Lucien's eyes and bit off the sentence.

"You're not coming with us, are you, Grace?" Lucien prompted knowingly.

Grace lowered her eyes and motioned Lucien aside, leading the way to a stand of trees that arched above them in the darkness. "My . . . my husband happened to be there today, too," she said haltingly. "We were just swept up by this . . . this tragedy . . ."

Lucien nodded grimly. "The BBC reported it was some kind of mistake."

"Yes, a horrible one that plunged both of us into a world of unimaginable pain and suffering," Grace went on in a breathless rush. "Yet, despite the chaos, Cooper and I somehow found each other and, together, began helping those in need. It was uncanny the way we . . . we . . . harmonized. It was as if we had instantly become one." She paused, capturing Lucien's eyes with her own, and added, "In those moments, and in the others I've shared with him these few days, I've . . . I've had feelings that I haven't had in decades."

Lucien sagged with disappointment. "I see."

"It's hard to put into words," Grace went on. "But I'm feeling *whole* again, Lucien. It's as if all these years I've been somehow . . . incomplete; and now, now that I've finally found the part of me that's been missing, I can't afford to ever lose it again."

"Of course," Lucien said, with an ironic smile. "My advice was very good for him . . . very bad for me."

"Yes, Lucien, I know," Grace said, her eyes moist with

empathy. "Fortunately or unfortunately you were more than right to encourage me to see him. Had I not—had I not faced my past as you advised—I would have never found my future. I'm sorry . . ."

"*Oui, un*fortunately, you found it . . . without me," Lucien said, sadly, inviting her into his arms.

Grace sighed and lunged into them. "Take care of yourself and Christiane," she whispered, as they embraced. "I'll never forget you."

"*Au revoir et bonne chance,*" Lucien replied. "I wish much happiness for you and your husband." He released her, took a step back, then forced a smile and returned to the car. "Come, Christiane, we're going now."

"Madame Cooper will come later?" Christiane asked. She whimpered at the answer she saw in her father's eyes, then dashed across the square, throwing herself into Grace's arms. "I thought you wanted to be with us?"

"I do, Christiane," Grace replied with heartfelt sincerity. "I care about you, and your father, deeply. You know I do. But my husband is the love of my life, and I must spend what is left of it with him."

"Why?" Christiane sighed. "I don't understand . . . I . . ." she began sobbing, unable to continue.

"You will," Grace said reassuringly. "One day, you'll find your special man and you'll understand."

"We will never see each other again, will we?"

"Of course we will," Grace replied with as much certainty as she could muster. "We'll find a way to reunite when the war is over. I promise."

Christiane hugged her tightly, then suddenly ran back to the car and got in next to her father.

Grace remained in the stand of trees and watched them drive off. She waited until the Citroën's taillights were like dying sparks in the darkness, then, eyes brimming with tears, hurried across the grounds.

Chapter Seventy-Six

❧

The faculty residence hall echoed with surprising empti- ness as Grace bounded up the stairs and through the door of her flat. She pulled a battered suitcase from beneath the bed and set it atop the covers; then began removing arti- cles of clothing from her closet and dresser, piling them next to it. She swept the items atop the vanity into a cloth sack, all except the framed snapshot of Cooper. Her eyes lingered on it until her cheeks dimpled with affection. She gently tucked it in her suitcase, then went to the phone and placed a call to the Royal Hotel, asking to speak with Cooper.

"I'm sorry," the desk clerk replied, curtly. "I'm not able to connect you."

"Why not? Has Mr. Cooper checked out?"

"No, Madame," the clerk replied, in a tense whisper. "But *they* are here. Do you understand?"

"The Germans . . ." Grace declared.

"Precisely," the clerk said, eyeing the contingent of offi- cers and armed soldiers that was marching into the hotel. "They're arriving as we speak."

The commandant, resplendent in a finely tailored uni- form with jodhpurs and riding boots, stood in the center of the lobby and looked about haughtily, as if making an assessment, then nodded in satisfaction.

"Greetings from the *Führer*," he announced to the guests and staff members who had responded to the commotion. "I am Major Brukmann, commanding officer of the German Military Authority in occupation of the Island of Guernsey. As of this moment, this establishment will serve as living quarters as well as official headquarters for its officers and staff." A striking figure with precise gestures and crinkly eyes that softened the sharp planes of his face, he spoke in lightly accented English that sounded as if he had learned it from listening to the BBC.

Grace still had the phone pressed to her ear and heard the major's announcement. "They're taking over the hotel?"

"Yes," the clerk whispered, cupping the mouthpiece as German troops began marching down corridors, up staircases, and into the dining and sitting rooms.

"Furthermore," Major Brukmann went on, "all guests are required to vacate their rooms immediately, and to assemble in the ballroom with their personal belongings and travel documents—at which time their status will be determined."

"Are you still there?" Grace prompted anxiously.

"Yes," the clerk replied as a German officer came striding purposefully toward the desk. "The guests are being forced to vacate their rooms and—" The line clicked and went dead.

Grace hung up the phone. Her concern for Cooper's safety was assuaged by the knowledge that he was neither a resident of the island nor, as an American, a citizen of a nation at war with Germany and, as per the ten-point directive, wouldn't be detained—assuming the Germans adhered to it.

Grace finished packing her clothing and personal items, then began taking down the dance posters, which she rolled up and slipped into the cardboard tube in which she'd brought them. She glanced about the flat with a wistful sigh and headed out the door and down the stairs to the street.

The frantic rush to vacate the dormitories had abated, and a taut silence had replaced the chattering bustle of departing students. Grace hurried across the grounds, lugging the suitcase, cardboard tube and a carpet bag slung over a shoulder, continuing on through the square where few vehicles remained. Nearly the last to leave, she strode swiftly down the darkened streets to the main road to catch the bus to St. Peter Port.

In less than thirty minutes, it would deposit her directly opposite the Royal Hotel. Despite what the clerk had said about it being taken over by German troops there was a chance Cooper might still be there. If he wasn't, she would seek shelter at Town Church with Pastor Highsmith. She knew Cooper was planning to depart in the morning and, immediately upon rising, she would go to the ferry terminal in search of him.

Grace stood along the side of the road, her eyes fixed on a distant hilltop where it converged to a pinpoint. At any moment, she expected the darkness would be broken by the distant glow of headlights and of the illuminated route number that would identify an approaching vehicle as a bus. Ten minutes later, there was still no sign of it. Weary to the bone from the day's events, she sat on her suitcase for nearly ten minutes more, then glanced to her watch, and gasped. It was nearly midnight. Caught up in the frantic pace of the evening's events, she had lost all track of time and had no idea it was that late.

Indeed, to her dismay, it dawned on her that there would be no bus on this night. Nor on any night at this hour, now that the Germans had arrived. No, the fact that they had already taken over the hotel meant the curfew was being enforced, which meant bus service had been suspended at 11 PM. She had little choice but to return to her flat until morning. Indeed, little choice but to wait until the curfew had been lifted and the buses began running again—*if* they began running again.

Chapter Seventy-Seven

$\sim$

At the Royal Hotel, Cooper and the other guests had assembled in the ballroom in response to Major Brukmann's order. One by one they were brought to the manager's office, an antique-filled room with silk drapery and vases of fresh flowers, and interviewed by Brukmann, who scrutinized their passports and determined their travel status. As Grace had hoped, Cooper and all guests who weren't residents of Guernsey or citizens of nations at war with Germany were cleared to leave the island. Brukmann stamped their passports with the seal of the Third Reich, a fierce-eyed eagle with a Nazi swastika in its claws, giving the bright green ink a moment to dry before writing his signature across it.

The next morning, as shafts of sunlight streamed down St. Peter Port's narrow streets, Cooper left the hotel and went straight to the harbor. The previous afternoon in the churchyard his emotional farewell with Grace had left him convinced that she had decided to go with Lucien, and he had no reason to linger.

He arrived at the terminal expecting to board a ferry that was scheduled to depart for Bournemouth within the hour; but long queues of evacuees snaked the entire length of the pier. Crush barriers funneled the endless lines of people to a narrow gateway that led to the ferry's boarding ramp. It was a disheartening sight; but Cooper soon made another unexpected discovery that brightened his outlook: there wasn't a German soldier in sight. Evidently, despite what had happened at the hotel, the main occupation force hadn't landed yet, because the only men in uniform were local police officers who were keeping order amongst the burgeoning crowd and controlling access to the boarding ramp.

That same morning at St. Anne's School, after a restless night in her flat, Grace had little trouble rising at the crack of dawn. Had the curfew been lifted? she wondered as she hurried to the main road, lugging her belongings. Had bus service resumed? If it had, she had plenty of time to catch the first one to St. Peter Port. To her relief, it wasn't long before a lipstick-red coach emerged from the morning mist.

A half hour later, when the bus arrived at the waterfront, Grace went directly to the long wharf to find Cooper. More than merely disheartening, the long queues leading to the ferry terminal were daunting. She took a moment to comprehend the enormity of the task before her, then began searching for him amongst the dense queues and clusters of evacuees.

Far ahead, in a queue that had come to a standstill, Cooper was lighting his pipe when he happened to glance behind him and saw a woman with a suitcase and other belongings, darting between groups of evacuees as if searching for someone. She was there, then gone in an instant, swallowed up by the crowd. She bore a strong resemblance to Grace, he thought. And his eyes had widened at the sight of her; but it was a fleeting glimpse at best, and she was a distance away, making it difficult to be certain. He was reluctant to give up his place in the line, but was on the verge of doing so in order to eliminate the slightest possibility that the woman he saw might have been Grace. Despite the compelling impulse, his mind won out over his heart, and he remained in the queue. It was just wishful thinking, he thought, reflecting on the bitter truth. His beloved Grace was gone . . . gone with Lucien, and he'd be a fool to allow himself to think otherwise.

Somewhere within the surging crowds, Grace was searching for him frantically. Heart pounding, face slick with perspiration, she was gripped by a growing fear that time was running out; that Cooper would board a ferry and be gone before she could find him. Indeed, it might all be for naught, anyway, she thought, because Cooper could have already boarded a ferry—a ferry that had since departed—and be well on his way across the channel to the mainland.

Cooper had been inching forward with his camera bag and valise, drawing heavily on his pipe for comfort. Despite his self-admonition, he couldn't help looking over his shoulder every now and then, on the off chance that the woman he'd glimpsed would somehow reappear and miraculously turn out to be Grace; but each glance only sent his spirits plunging. They were buoyed somewhat when the queue suddenly began advancing, and the gateway to the ferry's boarding ramp came into view.

Grace was frantic, verging on despair at not being able to find him. She was weaving between the queues of evacuees when her eyes darted to an unruly mane of white curls glowing in the sun like the globe of a streetlight. Could the thin layers of haze streaming alongside it be smoke? Could they be pipe smoke? Now, despite the burden of what she was carrying, Grace began pushing and elbowing her way through the crowd, closing the distance to her target. Yes, it was Cooper! she thought, as she drew nearer. She had no doubt of it now.

And her eyes were already brimming when Cooper glanced over his shoulder, yet again, and gasped at the sight of his beloved Grace rushing toward him. She was still a few steps away when their emotional dams burst. They released their suitcases and belongings, and lunged into each other's arms, emitting cries of relief and unrestrained joy.

Cooper, having accepted the fact that he would never see her again, was weeping unabashedly. Grace, having feared she'd never find him, was hugging him as if she was afraid he'd somehow escape, nearly squeezing the breath out of him. "I said you'd always have my heart, Mr. Cooper," she finally said, her reddened cheeks glistening with tears. "And I'm afraid you do."

"Aye, and . . . and you mine, lass," Cooper replied, his voice breaking with emotion. "Always. There's never been anyone. Never, not one person."

"Nor for me."

Cooper and Grace kept staring at each other through tear-filled eyes—overwhelmed at having finally, with heartfelt emotion and commitment, reunited after all these years. They were oblivious to what was going on around them and, when the queue began moving, it took them a few moments to sense the pressure from those behind them to close the gap. Indeed, they had finally reached the narrow gateway that led to the boarding ramp and ferry beyond. Under the circumstances, the fare was being waived, and the police officers, controlling the flow of evacuees through the checkpoint, were giving passports and travel documents cursory glances, if that. The ferry was overflowing with passengers, and Cooper and Grace were counting themselves lucky that they would be among the last to be allowed aboard when an announcement was made that it was loaded to capacity.

Several police officers rushed forward and prevented the

jostling passengers who had reached the mouth of the ramp from boarding. The officers posted at the checkpoint moved quickly to seal the narrow gateway with a steel barrier that slammed shut in front of Cooper and Grace with a chilling clang of finality.

Chapter Seventy-Eight

As the ferry departed, a forlorn groan rose from the crowd that surged forward, threatening to breech the restraining crush barriers; but within a matter of minutes, the disgruntled ranting was replaced by an enthusiastic roar as an empty ferry nosed into the slip that the other had vacated, and began taking on passengers.

Cooper and Grace were among the first to approach when the gateway reopened. They presented their American and British passports, respectively; but the officers manning the checkpoint merely glanced at them and nodded as they passed. Despite all that they were carrying, Cooper and Grace almost sprinted up the boarding ramp onto the ferry that would take them—and the passengers boarding, after them, by the dozens—to the mainland.

Giddy with relief and overcome with joy at the prospect of finally resuming their lives together, they were settling down for the nine-hour journey to Bournemouth when the blaring honk of klaxons heralded the arrival of German patrol boats. The fast-moving vessels seemed to have come out of nowhere as they cut through the waters of the channel, sealing off the harbor.

The ear-piercing racket was intensified by the scream of a siren mounted in the cowling of a German staff car. It was an open-topped, Daimler-Benz saloon. Nazi flags fluttered above its rolling fenders. Military bodyguards perched on its broad running boards. Major Brukmann sat in the command position next to the driver, watching as a line of trucks, their massive tires rumbling thunderously on the long wharf's decking, came racing toward the ferry terminal.

A company of German shock troops, whose presence did just that to those gathered on the pier, piled out of the trucks and deployed in lockstep formation across the long wharf. Their precise movements, black uniforms, and bristling weapons were unnerving precursors of the coming occupation. One group lowered the Union Jack from the terminal's flagpole and ran up the Nazi swastika. Another discharged the St. Peter Port police officers who were controlling the queues of evacuees and access to the ferry. A third shut down the terminal, taking over the gateway checkpoint and boarding ramp. The remainder swarmed onto the ferry that had been boarding, and began forcing the passengers to disembark.

Major Brukmann, his Iron Cross sparkling against the dark green of his crisply pressed uniform, stood in the well of his staff car with a bullhorn and, in his British-inflected English, announced: "All passengers are required to disembark immediately. Furthermore, per the Military Authority's ten-point directive—with which you should all be quite familiar by now—only British citizens who are not residents of Guernsey and citizens of nations not at war with Germany will be permitted back on board."

Grace swung a forlorn look to Cooper. "Well, that leaves me out," she said, crushed that they were being forced to disembark after having come so close to making their escape. "As we both very well know, I'm neither."

Cooper was equally devastated by the disheartening turn of events; but as they came back down the boarding ramp and through the gateway into the terminal, his eyes came to life with an idea. "Aye, truth be told, you may be neither, lass; but there's no need for concern," he said, his burr ringing with confidence. "Because you're somethin' else that's even better . . ." He waited until Grace looked appropriately bewildered, then concluded, "You're an American."

Chapter Seventy-Nine

‿‿‿

After making his announcement, Major Brukmann left his staff car to oversee the goings-on and inspect the terminal. Informed that the passengers had been removed from the ferry, the major ordered his officers—posted at the gateway checkpoint and the mouth of the boarding ramp—to resume the boarding process. What had been a merely casual review of passports and travel documents now became an intense, anxiety-ridden inquisition.

The officer in charge either couldn't or wouldn't speak a word of English. Furthermore, he was purposely brusque and rude as he went about his task in an effort to intimidate those who sought to leave illegally—and with good reason: There weren't any German troops present when the residents seeking to evacuate had arrived. Indeed, many, who knew they were forbidden to leave were trying to do just that before the island was occupied and the restrictions outlined in the ten-point directive were enforced. As a result, many of those who had been forced to disembark were now being denied passage. Some were being detained for further questioning. Others were being arrested on the spot.

Having been within arm's reach of the barrier when it slammed shut, Cooper and Grace were among the first to be processed. Cooper handed both his American passport and Grace's British passport to the officer, thinking it would reinforce the idea that they were husband and wife, traveling together. "We're the Coopers. We're married. Mr. and Mrs. Cooper. Same name, see?" he said, pointing to the name Cooper in both passports. "Furthermore, I'm an American, which makes my wife an American, too. Do you understand?"

The officer glanced from one passport to the other and back. His eyes widened at the sight of the major's stamp inside Cooper's. He managed a crooked smile as he returned it and nodded, giving Cooper permission to board the ferry. Cooper hesitated, and gestured to Grace's passport, as if reminding the officer to return it so she could do the same. The officer's eyes flared with anger. He shook his head no, and shot an arm out in front of Grace, holding her back; then, still clutching her passport in his fist, he shouted, *"Nein! Nein! Wohnen Sie hier! Auf der insel! Nein!"*

Cooper stiffened as if he'd been punched. Grace shuddered, fighting for composure. Neither understood German but it sure sounded like the officer had said, *"No! You live here! On the island!"*—as indeed he had.

"Yes, I *am* a resident," Grace conceded evenly. "But as my husband just explained, he is an American citizen. I am his wife, which makes me an American, too. Therefore, I should be allowed to depart with him."

It wasn't clear if the officer understood what either of them had said; but it was obvious he now not only looked angry, he looked both flummoxed and angry. Like a prosecutor presenting evidence at a trial, he brandished Grace's passport and growled, *"Engländerin! Wohnen Sie hier! Sie haben kein richtigen pass! Nein!"* He stuffed the passport into Grace's hand, then signaled the soldiers guarding the gateway with a jerk of his head. They charged forward, rifles held high across their chests, driving the Coopers back from the narrow opening.

Cooper shepherded Grace aside. They walked a short distance along the crush barrier to an open area between the queues, and took a few minutes to regroup.

"*You* can still go," Grace said, trying to sound courageous and conceal her disappointment. "I'll stay at the school. I'll be fine."

"Grace," Cooper scolded gently, his eyes widening in disbelief. "We're the Coopers, remember? No. No, I'm not leavin' without you, lass. And there isn't anything on God's good earth that'll be convincin' me otherwise." He caressed her face and softly added, "So, we'll have no more talk of that, now, will we?"

Grace smiled and shook her head no. "Then, what?"

Cooper shrugged, seemingly stymied. They were sitting on their suitcases, pondering the dilemma when Cooper noticed Major Brukmann striding across the long wharf with his entourage. "Perhaps, we'd be wise to appeal to a higher authority."

"I didn't know Hitler had arrived yet," Grace joked, trying to lighten the moment. "Who, pray tell, Mr. Cooper, do you plan to make your appeal to?"

"Him," Cooper replied, gesturing to the major, who had completed his inspection of the ferry terminal and was heading in the direction of his staff car.

Grace glanced over her shoulder, then looked back to Cooper and arched a brow with uncertainty. "Aside from the fact that he speaks English, what makes you think he'll do any more than turn us down in a language we understand?"

"Aye, that he might," Cooper replied. "But the major and I had a lovely chat at two this morning while he was decidin' my fate. It seems he was on the Harbor Police in Hamburg before the war, and learned his English from British sea captains, many of whom he still counts among his friends."

"Just one of the lads, eh?" Grace prompted, giving her skepticism full rein. "Well, I guess it couldn't hurt," she concluded.

They gathered up their belongings and hurried in the direction of the German staff car. The major's driver had just opened the door. Brukmann had one foot on the running board and was but a step from getting in when Cooper and Grace approached.

"Major Brukmann?" Cooper called out. "Major? Might we have a word? It will only—" He cut the sentence short as two of the major's bodyguards sprung into action and began hustling him and Grace aside.

"It's all right," Brukmann said sharply in German, calling off the bodyguards. He stepped from the running board and came toward them, squinting at Cooper with an air of recognition. "The Royal Hotel. Herr . . . Herr . . ." Then he snapped his fingers. "Cooper."

"Aye, Herr Cooper," Cooper echoed with a relieved sigh. Then, setting the stage for his appeal, he gestured to Grace and added, "And *Mrs.* Cooper. It's a rather simple matter that will take but a moment to explain."

The major cocked his head, then nodded. "Why not? Consider it compensation for relinquishing your accommodations and keeping my staff from sleeping in the street." He laughed at his own joke then, shaking his finger at Cooper, ordered, "Make it a *brief* moment."

Cooper wasted no time making his case. As he had with the officer at the checkpoint, he presented both passports, pointed out the name Cooper in each, and explained: He is an American citizen. By law—despite her British passport and Guernsey residence—so is his wife. Germany isn't at war with the United States. Therefore, like him, she can't be detained.

The major nodded as if he was impressed. "A rather technical analysis, Herr Cooper, but a most compelling one, I must admit."

Grace suppressed a smile and exchanged a hopeful glance with Cooper.

"However," the major went on, his tone sharpening, "a shared surname doesn't prove this woman is your wife, does it? No, it could simply be a coincidence. She could also be your cousin, or your sister, or"—he paused, and swept his eyes over Grace appreciatively—"since she's quite obviously fifteen to twenty years your junior, even your daughter, couldn't she?"

"Aye, that she could," Cooper said, deciding it would be wise to make a strategic concession and ignore the barb. "But truth be told, Major, she's neither. She's my spouse of twenty years, and—"

"Then how do you explain that she has a British passport?" Brukmann challenged. "That you don't even live in the same country, let alone the same residence? Very suspicious, indeed. Furthermore"—he angled his hand, as if admiring his wedding band that caught the sunlight—"observant chap that I am, I just happened to notice that neither of you are wearing one of these. So, why should I believe you?"

Both Grace and Cooper winced and shared anxious glances, fidgeting with bare ring fingers. Cooper knew the answer would sound like a convenient story, but had little choice, and explained: "We were married twenty years ago in the United States; but we were separated by the Great War; and now, after decades apart, we have finally reunited. It's a very long story, and—"

"Yes, and such a touching one, too," Major Brukmann interjected sarcastically. "I'm afraid you could claim any woman on the island is your wife to help her get to the mainland, couldn't you, Herr Cooper?"

"Aye, I suppose so," Cooper replied, sensing the battle was lost. "But why would I do that?"

"To sneak out a spy, perhaps?" the major replied with a sly grin. Then his expression darkened, and he prompted,

"Or a Jew?" He locked his eyes onto Grace's, and asked, "Are you a Jewess, madam?"

Grace shook her head no imperceptibly, suppressing her anger at being forced to make such a declaration. "I'm a Christian," she replied softly.

"Good," the major said, seeming relieved. "As am I. Now, can you prove that you're married, or not?"

Cooper and Grace exchanged forlorn glances, their minds racing in search of a way to do so, but to no avail. They both shrugged and shook their heads no.

"I'm sorry," the major said, sounding as if he meant it. He climbed into his staff car and perched straight-backed in his seat. The driver closed the door, went round to the other side and got in next to him. Major Brukmann nodded smartly. The bodyguards had barely taken up positions on the running boards when the engine started with a throaty growl. Then, with the whine of its siren scattering people in the queues, the staff car raced off down the long wharf, leaving Cooper and Grace standing in the blue-gray haze of its exhaust.

Chapter Eighty

〜

Cooper was devastated. All was lost, he thought. Despite finally reuniting with his beloved Grace, his twenty-year quest *de coeur,* as he imagined Lucien would call it, had backfired, terribly. Instead of taking his wife home to America, the land of the free, where quaint, peaceful Newbury nestled in the cradle of democracy, he had condemned Grace to the totalitarian horrors of Nazi domination, quite possibly for the rest of her days.

Indeed, despite the crushing blow, Cooper had no doubt that Grace's need for comfort and reassurance was far greater than his own; and he turned to her with open arms, intending to provide them; but to his shock and utter confusion, the radiant smile that was breaking across her face suggested she had no need, whatsoever, of either. "Would it be too much to ask what it is that you're smilin' about, lass?"

"We have proof," Grace said in a voice that rang with absolute certainty.

Cooper looked baffled. "We do?"

Grace nodded. "I took our marriage license and the church certificate with me when I left Newbury."

Cooper's brows twitched as if electrified; then his pace

quickening, he asked, "You mean, the ones signed and dated by the Massachusetts secretary of state and by Pastor Martin and various witnesses, not to mention the two of us, twenty years ago?"

Grace nodded again. "The very ones."

"Thanks be to God, lass! Thanks be to God!" Cooper exclaimed, as his fervor turned to confusion. "Where are they? Why didn't you show them to the major?" His eyes widened in horror at the answer that occurred to him. "Oh, Lord, no. No, you're not goin' to be tellin' me they're back home in Dumbarton, now, are you?"

"Well, they *are* in the Royal Bank of Scotland . . ." Grace replied with an enigmatic smile. "The one here, on High Street, in the safe deposit along with my teaching credentials and a few other documents."

"What are they doin' there, lass?" Cooper asked, beside himself. "Why didn't you fetch them when you fetched your passport?"

"Because I fetched it well more than a fortnight ago," Grace replied smartly. "I *was* planning to spend the summer in France, and return to St. Anne's, as you may recall. With all that's happened since, I forgot about the safe deposit, and my savings, for that matter."

"Dare I ask if you're in possession of the key?"

Grace raised a brow in reply, then, plucking the key from somewhere within the darkest recesses of her carpet bag, dangled it in front of him.

"Well, let's go, lass," Cooper said, his voice charged with urgency. "Lest we spend this summer and the next, and God knows how many more, being squashed beneath the Jerries' jackboots."

The long wharf was a short walk from High Street where all the island's banks were located. The Coopers were hurrying down the Esplanade when they realized that it was Saturday. The banks would be closed! And by Monday, when they would normally reopen, they might have been taken over by the Germans and closed permanently! Even if they weren't, and even if the Coopers could eventually get their marriage certificate from the safe deposit box, the ferries might no longer be running, and they'd be trapped on the island. They were still reeling from the crushing blow when they turned onto High Street to see lengthy queues extending from the entrance to every bank; and, to their profound relief, learned that, despite it being Saturday, and despite limiting withdrawls to twenty-five pounds as they had done the day before, the banks had opened at the crack of dawn to allow anxious depositors access to their savings.

The Coopers joined the daunting queue that led to the Royal Bank of Scotland, acutely aware that they were running out of time. Indeed, the ferry on which they had been denied passage would soon be departing and, with German troops in control of the terminal and harbor, it might very well be the last one allowed to leave St. Peter Port.

Cooper's mind raced to find a way to accelerate the process. "Do you have substantial funds on deposit here, lass?" he asked, an idea forming.

"Quite the contrary, I'm afraid. Why?"

"Good," Cooper replied. "Leaving them behind will be worth it, if I'm right in what I'm thinkin'." He left Grace in the queue and went to the entrance where a guard was controlling the flow of customers. "Pardon me, sir," Cooper called out, getting his attention. "Must I wait in this queue to gain access to a safe deposit box, if I'm not withdrawin' funds?"

"You're wise to ask, sir," the guard replied. He opened the door and pointed into the lobby where about a half dozen people were lined up in front of a desk. "The safe deposit queue is that one right there."

Within ten minutes, Grace had signed the signature card at the desk, descended to the basement vault and retrieved the documents from her safe deposit box. She hurried up the stairs to the lobby where Cooper was waiting with their suitcases and belongings. "I've got them," she said, clutching an envelope. "We'd best hurry. We've little time to make the ferry."

"Aye," Cooper grunted. "But there's no guarantee that mindless Nazi at the checkpoint will be able to make heads or tails of those documents, is there?"

Grace looked crestfallen.

"No," Cooper went on. "We'd be wise to take a few minutes and ensure that he can."

"And how, pray tell, do we do that?"

"By having them officially authorized . . ." Cooper tugged his passport from his camera bag and pointed to the page that had been stamped and signed by Major Brukmann. ". . . by the major himself."

In a matter of minutes, they had climbed the steep steps on Lefebvre Street to St. Julians Avenue where the Royal Hotel was located. German staff cars and troop transports lined both curbs. Heavily armed soldiers were stationed on every corner. Cooper led the way beneath the large Nazi flag, hanging between the columns of the portico, to the hotel's entrance where two soldiers with rifles were posted.

Cooper presented his passport to one of them. "We're the Coopers. We're here to see Major Brukmann," he said smartly. The guard's eyes widened at the sight of the major's signature and stamp. He nodded and stepped aside, allowing them to enter the hotel. They hurried through the lobby to the hotel manager's office that Major Brukmann was now occupying, along with the rest of the island. The door was somewhat ajar, but it was flanked by two soldiers with rifles who stepped in front of it, blocking their way. Once again, Cooper presented his passport; but this time, despite the major's imprimatur, the guard shook his head no, and grunted, *"Nein."* In hesitant English, he explained, "Major is busy—too busy—Major Brukmann busy, *ja?*"

And indeed he was. On returning from the harbor, Brukmann had the hotel manager remove his belongings from the office. Now, comfortably ensconced amidst its fine antiques, the major was personalizing it with items he had taken from his briefcase: a brass plate engraved with his name and rank, an ornate pen and pencil set, a crystal inkwell, and a miniature flag set with three poles to which were affixed the banners of his country, hometown, and military unit.

There was a sliver of space between the two guards which allowed Cooper to catch a glimpse of the major through the partially open door. He imagined Brukmann would grant them an audience, eventually; but they had to see him now, right now, which meant they had to find a way past the guards right now. Under the circumstances, only one came to mind.

Cooper nodded in meek compliance; then, pretending he and Grace were departing, he took her arm and began walking off, prompting the guards to return to their positions on either side of the door. After taking a few steps, Cooper abruptly reversed direction, darting between the startled guards and through the partially open door into the office.

Brukmann was replacing the picture of King George VI that hung behind the desk with one of Adolph Hitler that he'd taken from his briefcase when Cooper came charging into the office with the guards in pursuit. "Herr Cooper!" the major erupted, his eyes flaring with anger as the guards took hold of Cooper. "It seems you've forgotten that item three of the directive states: Residents will be treated with respect provided they do not resist or *cause trouble!*" He shifted his look to Grace, who was standing in the doorway, fearing Cooper would be hurt. "I told you, without proof, there's nothing I can do! Now go, before I—"

"We have it," Cooper interrupted, resisting the guards who were dragging him toward the door. "We have the proof. We've brought it with us."

Brukmann recoiled slightly as if taken by surprise and, with a skeptical scowl, hissed, "Proof—"

"Aye," Cooper grunted, pressing the advantage. "We were

hopin' you'd be kind enough to give it your stamp of approval, so to speak."

"I see . . ." the Major mused, taking a moment to recover and consider the request. Finally, he nodded, signaling the guards, who released Cooper and left the office. "I don't see why not," Brukmann conceded, ". . . assuming it turns out to be genuine."

"The documents are in here," Grace said as she came forward and handed the envelope to the major.

Brukmann glanced at it, then stepped to his newly appropriated desk chair and sat down. He made a ritual of cleaning the lenses of his reading glasses before putting them on, then removed the documents from the envelope and unfolded them. His crinkly eyes widened at the sight of the marriage license. He leaned back, studying it, then set it aside and turned his attention to the church certificate. Looks that crackled with tension were darting between Cooper and Grace now. It seemed as if an hour had passed when the major finally looked up. "Well, Mr. and Mrs. Cooper," he said, with an amused smile. He removed his glasses, set them on the desk and leveled his gaze at Cooper. "I still have no idea, whatsoever, if this lovely lady is a spy, or a Jew, or both; but I do know, beyond any doubt, that she is your wife, sir."

"My *American* wife," Cooper said, hastening to make the clarification.

"Yes, yes your *American* wife," the major said with a good-natured chuckle. He inked his official stamp, and brought it down on each document, making a perfect impression. When the ink had dried, he plucked his fountain pen from its holder and signed his name across the Third Reich's eagle insignia. "There," he said, admiring his handiwork. "Now, you not only have the signature of your pastor and your secretary of state attesting to your marriage; but, more importantly, you also have the signature of Major Klaus Brukmann, commandant of the Military Authority on the Island of Guernsey." He folded the documents carefully, slipped them into the envelope and handed it to Grace as he got to his feet. "You should have no trouble with any of my officers at the ferry terminal now."

Two audible sighs of relief applauded the major's remarks. "I don't know how to thank you," Grace said softly, taking the envelope from him.

"Nor I," Cooper said.

Brukmann forced a smile, then removed several framed photographs of his wife and children from his briefcase, placing them on the desk so Grace and Cooper could see them. "Well, perhaps, you could say a prayer that we will all, soon, be back home with our families."

Chapter Eighty-One

The dramatic takeover of St. Peter Port's ferry terminal and harbor by German troops and high-speed patrol boats stunned evacuees and harbor police alike. The word spread swiftly across the island. Now, every resident knew that Guernsey was officially occupied, and that the restrictions in the ten-point directive were in force. As a result, when Cooper and Grace returned to the long wharf they found the endless queues and clusters of evacuees had dispersed. Few passengers were at the terminal waiting to board the ferry, which, in stark contrast to those that had departed earlier, was far from overcrowded.

Furthermore, as Major Brukmann had promised, the officer at the checkpoint, who had turned Grace away earlier, saw the official stamp and signature on their documents and waved them through without question. Cooper led the way up the boarding ramp, which was withdrawn just moments after he and Grace were aboard.

They were still stowing their suitcases and belongings when the ferry's engine came to life with a series of startling thumps, sending a plume of black smoke skyward; then, with several blasts of its air horn, the vessel eased from its slip and angled into the channel's choppy waters.

A loud cheer went up from those aboard. They had escaped the frightening German troops, the restrictive rules of occupation and the horrors of war; and would soon be enjoying the safety and comfort of the British mainland—or so they thought.

In truth, ever since the German Enigma code had been cracked, Whitehall knew that the Day of the Eagle—as the Luftwaffe's hierarchy had code named the bombing raids they were planning to unleash on London and other industrial centers—would soon begin. In the interim, the enemy had been attempting to cripple the British naval bases at Plymouth, one hundred miles west, and Portsmouth, forty miles east of Bournemouth. German fighters and dive-bombers had been attacking these targets nightly, and were engaged by RAF Spitfires in fierce air battles over the English Channel.

Now, nearly ten hours after the ferry had departed St. Peter Port, the British mainland appeared on the horizon. Most of the passengers, Cooper and Grace among them, came out on deck to see the lights of Bournemouth Harbour twinkling at the edge of the star-dotted sky. It wasn't long before the darkness was broken by the distant flash of explosions, the bright orange spatter of machine-gun fire, the arcing streaks of incendiary tracers and the death spirals of flaming aircraft.

From the ferry, the distant pyrotechnics seemed like a spectacular fireworks display. Indeed, the Fourth of July was less than a week away, and to someone like Cooper, who'd spent more than thirty years in America, it was reminiscent of Independence Day celebrations; but there was nothing to celebrate on this night. On the contrary, despite the guise of distance, this was the cruelty of war in all its ugliness; and, somewhere on the ground, British civilians and military personnel were being maimed and killed as were pilots from both sides in the blackened skies above.

Grace was standing at the railing with Cooper, watching the distant spectacle. "Truth be told," she said, feeling anxious at what it portended, "the Coopers had best be heading for home as soon as possible."

"Aye, but everyone will be fleeing the southern cities now," Cooper cautioned, automatically connecting the word "home" to Scotland, as he always had whenever Grace was concerned. "Train tickets to Glasgow will be hard to come by, I'm afraid."

"Oh, I've no doubt of it," Grace agreed, smiling demurely at what she was about to say. "But we both left Scotland a long time ago, didn't we, Mr. Cooper? It's our home in America that I'm speaking of."

"You mean, our cottage in Newbury," Cooper said, with a broadening smile.

Grace nodded. "If we're going to be taking up where we left off, I think we'd best be taking up where we left off, don't you?"

"Aye, it'd be the dream of a lifetime come true."

"Assuming, of course, it's still in the family," Grace added with a mischievous smile.

"It certainly is, lass," Cooper replied. "Of course, it could use a woman's touch here 'n there . . ."

"Well, then I'll . . . just take up where I left off, won't I?" Grace asked with a giggle that ended with a curious tilt of her head. "Tell me, Mr. Cooper, is that lorry still in the family as well?"

"You wouldn't be referrin' to the gray pickup with the dented fenders, now, would you, Mrs. Cooper?"

"The one and the same."

"Aye, that it is," Cooper replied proudly. "Of course, like its owner it doesn't always start on cold mornings and tends to cough and sputter in the heat." He burst into self-deprecating laughter, then added, "We're both about ready for the junk heap, I'm afraid."

"Oh, I don't know about that . . ." Grace said with a seductive smile. She caressed his face, looked lovingly into his eyes and kissed him, deeply. As their lips parted, she whispered, "I've a feeling we'll find a way to get your motor cranked up and running."

Chapter Eighty-Two

O n landing in Bournemouth, the Coopers took the coastal railway line to the port of Southampton, thirty miles east, from where many ocean-going liners sailed. Concern that Germany would not only bomb but might also invade the mainland was prompting many citizens to seek temporary refuge in Canada, the United States, and even South America. Consequently, bookings were hard to come by; and Cooper was forced to pay a hefty premium to secure immediate passage to Boston for himself and Grace on the *Georgic* which, like its sister ship, the *Britannic,* sailed under the White Star Line flag.

Approximately a month had passed since Cooper had left Boston. In that time, France had fallen, and the German war machine was gearing up to defeat Great Britain, making transatlantic crossings all the more perilous.

After departing the Southampton harbour, the *Georgic* joined a convoy of freighters and passenger liners off the Isle of Wight.

The ensuing nine-day voyage proved uneventful, thanks to an escort of British warships that kept the German U-boats at bay. Despite the ever-present tension, the time at sea allowed

Cooper and Grace to get reacquainted and turned out to be the kind of honeymoon they never had.

As Cooper had hoped, they arrived in Boston and returned to Newbury in time to renew their vows on their wedding anniversary. Indeed, they had more than a week to spare, and used it to get settled in the cottage, allow Grace to become familiar with her neighbors and community, and prepare for the upcoming ceremony.

Like their first wedding, twenty-two years ago, this one took place on a sunny afternoon in mid-July. An offshore breeze was blowing through Town Square and across the grounds as the guests assembled in Newbury Community Church, joining the bride and groom, who had arrived in Cooper's gray pickup truck.

Everyone who had wished Cooper bon voyage when he had departed had been invited: Joe and Alicia Clements and their six-month-old baby, Joseph, Joe's employees and their families, Dr. Cheever and his wife, Boston book distributor Arthur Hastings. In addition, gallery owner Peter Van Dusen—whose gallery had brought Cooper and Grace together and who, Cooper knew, would especially enjoy seeing her—was in attendance. They were joined by other townsfolk and church members who had turned out to welcome Grace home and back into the community.

Beams of sunlight streamed through the church's modest stained glass windows as the happy couple stood at the foot of the altar with Pastor Martin, staring into each other's eyes the way newlyweds do.

Grace looked absolutely radiant in an off-white eyelet dress and a broad-brimmed sun hat, beneath which her tresses tumbled in waves of gray-streaked amber. Her wedding bouquet was an arrangement of wildflowers that she had picked from the grounds of their cottage.

Cooper, in perfect character and contrast, looked absolutely uncomfortable in a beige linen suit that, along with his starched white shirt, black bowtie and two-tone shoes, had been purchased for the occasion at Grace's insistence. His unruly white mane glowed in the light as they exchanged vows and wedding bands at Pastor Martin's direction.

After pronouncing them husband and wife, the pastor dispatched them to the first pew, and stepped to his pulpit to address the guests. "Thank you all for being here on this truly glorious and special day," he began, his voice trembling with emotion. "Having been privileged to perform their wedding ceremony—twenty-two years ago to the day, I might add—it is especially gratifying for me to renew their vows, because, as strange as this may sound, Dylan and Grace wouldn't be with us now, had they not been married." He paused, giving the guests a moment to ponder the mystery.

"That's right," he resumed, pleased at their puzzled expressions. "Despite being kept apart, and denied the truth, by life's cruel vicissitudes, they somehow remained husband and wife, in their hearts, minds and souls, for more than two decades. Indeed, the fact that their commitment to each other survived such tragic adversity is what enabled them to escape the horrors of war and the evils of Nazi domination that are threatening to destroy our world and very way of life." The pastor paused again, as a murmur of acknowledgment and understanding rippled through the church.

When all was quiet, he raised his eyes and, in fervent supplication, prayed, "Dear Lord, we ask for Your help in prevailing over this unconscionable aggression, and that You guide and protect our sons and daughters who are so bravely serving our nation at home and abroad. Furthermore, we wish to thank You for this gift that You have bestowed upon Dylan and Grace, and upon all of us. For it was their faith in

You, and their commitment to the enduring sanctity of marriage, which is of Your making, that are responsible for their being here today." He paused briefly, then, addressing the congregation, said, "Now, please join me in a moment of silent tribute to those who have already made the ultimate sacrifice in the cause of freedom." He bowed his head, as did all those in attendance.

A few seconds had passed when the hush was broken by a baby's cry. Alicia, who had Joseph cradled in her arms, stroked his cheek and began swaying to and fro, which quieted him.

"Thank you for that reminder, Joseph," the pastor quipped good-naturedly. Then, in a more serious tone, he added, "Indeed, it is also fitting that we pray for their child in Heaven who is surely partaking of his parents' joy and happiness today; and now, I'd like to invite anyone who wishes to take Christ into his heart and embrace eternal life in the Kingdom of Heaven to come forward."

A number of those in attendance slipped out of the pews and began walking down the aisle toward the altar where Pastor Martin waited.

Cooper watched with ambivalence, then leaned close to Grace and whispered, "I suppose if he's right—I mean about Heaven—then, one day, the three of us could be . . . be reunited there, couldn't we?"

Grace broke into a hopeful smile and nodded. "He's right, Dylan. I know in my heart he is."

Cooper looked at her, wrestling with it. "Aye, I'm afraid, I'm not sure if I'm up to it today, lass."

"It's all right," Grace said with an affectionate smile that absolved him. "Why don't you just live with it for a while?"

"Bless you, Grace," Cooper said, relieved. Then, lest there be any doubt that, in the future, he would seriously consider undergoing what the pastor would call "a conversion," added, "I will. You have my word."

* * *

After the ceremony everyone gathered outside for the reception. A long table and folding chairs had been set up on the church lawn, and a sumptuous feast—of locally caught lobster and crab, along with fresh vegetables, homemade salads, several wines, pitchers of iced tea and of Cooper's favorite ale—was spread out across it. A tiered wedding cake topped with luscious strawberries was at its center.

"Grace, what a lovely dress," the pastor's wife said as everyone took their seats.

"Thank you, Mrs. Martin," Grace said, dismissing the compliment humbly. "It's an old friend. I found it years ago in a thrift shop in Glasgow."

"Well, you still look as if you stepped out of a fashion magazine," Alicia said.

"Those days are gone forever," Grace cracked, with a wink to Cooper, who needed no reminder of the fashion photographs he'd taken of her all those years ago.

"I'll be the judge of that, lass," Cooper said with a jaunty smile.

"Well," Dr. Cheever said, matching it, "the missus and I went to the pictures last week, and Grace looks just like Scarlet O'Hara to me."

"I felt like her, too, when the Germans bombed the long wharf in St. Peter Port, believe me," Grace said with a laugh, though she was only half-joking.

"Aye, it may not have compared with the burnin' of Atlanta, but you could've fooled me," Cooper added. He was squirming in his finery and undid his bowtie, slipping it from his collar with a dramatic flourish. Then, sweeping his eyes across everyone at the table, he warned, "God help the poor soul who's foolish enough to liken me to that Rhett Butler character."

"Oh, I suspect there's little danger of anyone doing that, Dylan," Alicia teased, eliciting hearty laughter from the group.

"Well, truth be told, my husband was quite manly and courageous when it came to standing up to the Nazis," Grace said proudly.

"Aye, I had them shakin' in their jackboots," Cooper said with a self-deprecating cackle.

"Well," Joe chimed in. "I think Mark Twain without the moustache would be more like it, anyway."

"I thought he was a sarcastic old coot with a cantankerous disposition," Arthur Hastings said, eliciting another round of laughter from the group.

Cooper took it all good-naturedly

Later, after appetites had been satisfied and thirsts quenched, Grace leaned to her husband and whispered, "Come, I've something to show you." She took her bouquet from the table with one hand, and took Cooper's hand in the other, and walked a short distance to a gnarled crab apple tree that was off by itself in the churchyard. Grace circled its trunk as if trying to get her bearings; then she stopped and, dropping to one knee, gently brushed aside some leaves and grass cuttings, revealing a small stone marker set flush with the earth. Neatly engraved in the dark gray granite were the words:

Baby Boy Cooper
19 February 1919

Grace placed the bouquet of wildflowers atop the marker and knelt in prayer for a moment, then stood and looked at Cooper with a courageous smile. His eyes were brimming, and he was biting a lip to keep from sobbing. "A long time ago," Grace said softly, "I came here with Colin, hoping and praying you were safe, and . . . and that you'd soon come home from the war to be here with me; and then, when I . . . when I was notified you'd been killed . . ." She trailed off and took a moment to collect herself. "Well," she said, the words still catching in her throat, "I can't . . . I can't believe we're finally here, together; but . . . but we are, Dylan, aren't we?"

Cooper was stunned and moved beyond words. Tears ran down his cheeks as if a floodgate had been breeched. He exhaled in a long, heartbroken sigh and, like Grace, took a moment to compose himself. "I . . . I mean . . . all these years . . ." he whispered, his voice breaking. "I . . . I never knew. Colin never . . . never told me. No one ever said anything. I . . ."

Grace brushed a tear from his cheek, then, with a sweet smile said, "Yes, as we know all too well, my brother has his faults; but every now and then"—she gestured to the marker—"he finds a way to make up for them."

"This was Colin's doing . . ." Cooper said in an amazed whisper.

"Yes," Grace replied softly. "He . . . He arranged for it just before I returned to Scotland." She gave Cooper a moment to comprehend it all, then added, "You know, I was going to . . . to give our baby your name; but, then, well . . . the thought of . . . of losing two Dylan Coopers was more than I could bear, so . . ." She shrugged, then looked up at him with watery eyes.

There were no words now. A poignant sigh and the undying love in his eyes were all Cooper could manage. They stood together beneath the tree's arching canopy, the years melting away, as they had in the seaside pavilion on Guernsey when they stood face-to-face for the first time in decades, and now here, on their second wedding day, in wistful joy and bittersweet silence.

The moment was broken by a child's giggle. They turned to see little Joseph crawling across the grass in their direction, with Alicia, Joe and others hurrying after him. Grace bent down as he approached and scooped him up into her arms, hugging him to her bosom as she had the infant she had lost so many years ago.

Cooper couldn't help but reflect on the photograph of the

young immigrant mother cradling her infant that he had taken at Boston North Station decades earlier.

"I'd say he's won his Aunt Grace's heart," Joe said as he and the others gathered around, sharing the heartwarming moment.

"And she, his," Alicia added, misty-eyed as the baby touched Grace's face with his tiny fingers and continued to giggle.

After the ceremony, Cooper and Grace hurried to the gray pickup truck in a hailstorm of rice and a cascade of good wishes. Someone had written: JUST MARRIED AGAIN! on the back window with a bar of soap and had tied a bunch of tin cans to the rear bumper, which made a jangling racket as they drove off.

A short time later, they had driven up the winding coastal road and climbed the hill to the rambling cottage above the sea. Dusk was falling and the sun was dappling its choppy surface with splashes of orange and pink as waves went crashing against the rocks below. In awe of nature's power and beauty, over-whelmed by their good fortune and consumed with their love for each other, they watched as the fireball slipped slowly below the horizon, sending shafts of light streaking across the sky.

"I'll wait a lifetime for you, Grace," Cooper whispered softly as they embraced.

"And I for you, Dylan," Grace replied with a tender smile.

"Aye," Cooper sighed. "Good things *do* come to those who wait, don't they?"